His Name Was Nigel

Portrait of a Killer Zombie

David O. Zeus

This Edition 1.1 Published by DOZ
ISBN: 978-0-9955917-5-2

Cover illustration (and on inside page) by Michael Hensley, reproduced
here with his kind permission.
Illustration Copyright © Michael Hensley. All Rights Reserved.
See Acknowledgements for further details.
Cover design by Liliana Resende.

Disclaimer: This is a work of fiction. Names, characters, places and
incidents either are the product of the author's imagination or are used
fictitiously. Any resemblance to actual persons, living or dead, events or
locales is entirely coincidental.

In infirmitas, claritas; in morte, vita.

Trigger Warning:

More Death

For Art

and all who came before

CONTENTS

Foreword & Introductions

Hello. My name is Josh. If you are reading this, I am most probably dead (or is it 'enlightened'? I don't know anymore). It is late in the battle for London (or rather the whole country) and I think all will be lost soon. I had started compiling these notes and diary entries many, many months ago and intended to use them for my doctoral thesis, or a book – an insider's guide to the events of the 21st Century plague. I have to say I have been inspired by Nigel and it is because of his writings that I decided to commit the events of the last eight months or so to paper. Once upon a time I felt sure any publisher would jump at the chance to publish the inside story of the plague once this had all blown over, but now, as I write this Foreword, the publishers' office buildings all stand empty and any printing presses have fallen silent, never to turn again, I suspect. Nigel has reached into the very heart of this society and ripped it out. In less than a year the authorities ran the gamut of reactions – laughed, mocked, fretted, procrastinated, panicked and finally failed. Now they're all dead (and walking the streets), I suspect.

From early on I had been convinced that Nigel's memoirs, his blog, was not a hoax. I tried hard to convince the powers-that-be that it was authentic and was a genuine insight into the threat we were facing, but it was well nigh impossible – even now, so late in the game, there are detractors. It is too late now. I confess there have been times when I haven't believed enough too. Not so long ago the theories of Ben Garfunkel were too far-fetched for me, but now, as London – the 'metropolis dump' – burns, I suspect that Ben was right. It had all been foreseen, foretold. And that is a very scary thing indeed.

It is ironic that it was the most advanced civilisation that was the undoing of *Homo sapiens*. It was destiny. Pride comes before the apocalypse. Pride is a sickness. But in sickness there is clarity. And in clarity there is death.

I don't have time for sadness. The last eight months or so have been increasingly hectic and bizarre – brilliant and wonderfully stimulating, ghastly and utterly horrifying. Even when things took a turn for the worse I was always totally committed to our mission and had confidence things would turn out for the better (like everybody, I suppose), but I hadn't banked on Nigel – his brilliance, his insight and his abilities. Complacency dies at death and not before.

I am unsure Nigel's own words, his reflections, do him justice. I have seen him in the, er, 'flesh' and seen him operate. If he personifies the next stage of the human story, I cannot complain. He is a remarkable creature.

I will reference some of Nigel's chapters here. The documents I forwarded to the various government agencies included most of Nigel's chapters as an appendix – to give the authorities an idea of what we were dealing with. But I did not include all. I also forwarded some of Nigel's writings to the Whistleblower, so, should further passages appear, I will vouch for them from the grave.

Who am I? What is my claim to fame? I was the first person who identified Nigel as, how shall I say, the source of our problems. That is not to say I was there from the beginning. I wasn't. I came onboard the 'MDP'-monitoring project at least three months after Nigel's death, but I only properly identified him as a 'Muter' of interest, probably three months after that. I had to fight hard over the subsequent three months to allow policing and military resources to focus on Nigel – build up a picture of him and his colleagues, by which point there was not enough time to stem the tide of death. The Great Change came a month or so later and the rest you probably know. In fact, by now you know more than me.

Even in these last light-darks I try to find a way to prove myself wrong, but my hollow bones echo with the knowledge of the truth of our shared deathstiny. I suppose that is the same with everyone in the end. It is the nature of the human condition – a desperate wish for an arrival point when all the while the journey, painful as it is, leads to some nondescript dark, soily place that holds you for eternity. (Or until Plot comes knocking.)

I didn't know whether to write this as a report, an academic thesis, a memoir, a non-fiction historical piece or even a novel based on real events. I won't have time to complete it, so it might be a bit of a hotch-potch of styles. I doubt I will live long enough to polish it up into its final form, so forgive me. The ending will have to be written by someone else.

Of course, this is all about Nigel, but I cannot exclude myself from these pages – my experiences, my world view, my interactions. You will notice from the above text that I have used some of Nigel's vocabulary. Please be patient and accommodating. I have been poring over Nigel's words for so many 'lunar cycles' now, light-dark in, light-dark out, it comes easy to me. In some instances, I preferred his vocabulary – Beans, Has-Beans, Cloth-Heads (cloth-capped police officers) and Rubber Beans (rubber-suited police) – to the common English terms. So it is that as I compile these notes and writings, I feel it would be remiss of me to not echo Nigel. I have developed a fondness for his nomenclature and a curiosity about his world view. In truth, he has won me over in many ways, so imitate him I shall – after all, soon we all will (you included) – and we'll be brothers all.

With that said, I shall start my story on my forever home – the Black Road.

Thank you.

The author, Josh.

1. The Black Road and Mia

For the few solar cycles leading up to present times, I lived on the Black Road – London's River Thames. I had always been drawn to water and wanted to spend more time on the ocean, but carving out a career (and, yes, being 'responsible' and paying into a pension) meant I had to cut my teeth in a metropolis. I needed education, contacts and opportunities, so the largest metropolis in the UK was the dump of my choice. If the end of the world were to come, there's no better place for it to start than in the dump built on the Black Road. For many years I had shared flats and houses, it was expensive and there was always someone disagreeable in the bathroom. On the verge of quitting the metropolis, I was offered an opportunity to house-sit a partially-refurbished houseboat near Tower Bridge. I was doing the owner a favour and, long story short, it turned into a longer-term arrangement. I took it as a sign to stick around in the city. The houseboat was a pleasant place to live – soothing, quiet, cool and a step away from the land. It was a metaphorical and literal compromise. I wasn't quite alone; there were a few other houseboats dotted on the south bank, including Mia's.

I was in a reasonably happy place in my existence and had endured thirty-three summers. My undergraduate degree was in anthropology and my Masters in Urban Development. After my Masters I was working as a civil servant in London's City Hall tasked with improving infrastructure (mostly related to transport). I was focused on how a population interacts with its surroundings in an urban setting. By understanding the behaviours of an urban populace, one could learn how best to design and manage the supporting infrastructure. It was a subject that combined a number of loves – the study of people in their environment and the best way to design a city. It was not all about the present either. I studied past peoples and civilizations and their cities and worked with engineers and futurologists who were paid to think about how technologically-advanced cities of the future might work. I spent time in libraries, in museums, in labs and at science fairs. It was all about the future. I was going to design the city and life we were all destined to have. Or so I thought.

I was toying with the idea of returning to education to complete a doctoral thesis to take this all further and become a guiding light on the subject, which was ironic really because all I ever wanted to do was live by (and be at one with) the water. But, as I have said, pension contributions have to be made, so I settled for a simple existence in my houseboat. Maybe, just maybe, I could get involved in developing cities based on a shoreline. I would have the best of both worlds and I would be lord of my dominion – the sea.

I have pondered long and hard about how I should describe my relationship with Mia. Normally I would be coy about such things but, assuming that I'm dead, it doesn't really matter now, I suppose. So, here it goes: there was no relationship. That's right. There was no relationship. But I wish there had been. I fancied her not because she was my type, because she was warm, because she had a great smile (from a distance), because she was in great physical shape and because she seemed to be talented in a sporty way, no, it was because she was eminently fanciable. What was there not to like? Besides, she was Brazilian. (More of that later.)

I would say she was between two to five summers younger than me. Not only was she fanciable, she seemed calm, well-measured, at peace. But, in truth, there was a little bit of intensity about her, but it didn't scare me because she channelled that through her love of existence on the Black Road. I suspect you would never see her on the Underground train network. Usually casually dressed in Lycra or some sporty gear, I probably saw her more in a wetsuit and hoodie than anything else as she paddled her way to her next appointment.

She had both the mountain bike and the road bike. She ran. She did everything that the gym pretended to do – gym machines were based on her everyday activities. She wouldn't visit climbing walls, she would hike in the hills and climb in the mountains. She didn't do aerobics class, she went to boxing and martial arts classes. She had done it for years. As far as I could gather she was a freelance personal trainer of sorts.

Mia's presence was also playing on another weakness of mine. She was Brazilian. I knew because I had heard her speaking on the mobile phone. I knew the language (sort of) and the accent. I felt life was teasing me. I had once had some, er, business in Brazil and spent a year there. I had become attached to a local Brazilian girl and I had given serious consideration to spending my life there, but had returned to the UK for educational reasons (my Master's degree) and for men's reasons – panic and plans. So, here I was again being drawn to another Brazilian woman. Was I being drawn into the future? Or being drawn into the past? If something is unfinished, how does it resolve itself – by addressing the past? Or addressing the future? Her presence had reawakened something in me.

I would see Mia most days; she was living on the adjacent houseboat (albeit a far more rundown version), but we rarely spoke. Ours was more of a nodding relationship. In fact, I probably nodded to her more than anybody else in my life. But there was a bonding of sorts, we were kindred spirits. She would either paddle away before I was up or I was too tired to start a conversation on a

3

weekend morning. All I needed was a little time – the plan was: an opportunity would present itself.

Therefore, it was all the more shocking when I learned she was dead.

Or rather, missing, presumed dead.

I was first alerted to her absence when I returned home from the office one Thursday evening and I saw a few men nosing about her boat. Initially concerned, I relaxed when I saw a uniformed police officer among them. They were knocking on the door, looking through the window. I wrote it off as the police making enquiries or a crime had taken place in the area and she might have been a witness. Her boat was all locked up from the outside so she was probably off on one of her activities, perhaps hiking up north. I made a mental note to rise early on Saturday morning and casually mention the police visit to her. My opportunity had come.

Indeed up early at the weekend I noticed she was still not to be seen. She had probably gone away for a week, I concluded, but when a group of two men and one woman walked down the plank to her boat and started hunting around again I grabbed my coffee and walked out casually onto the deck.

'Haven't seen her for a few days. She's often out. Can I help?' I called out – more as a challenge than an offer of assistance. They could be police officers or detectives, but I couldn't see ID badges from my distance.

One male and one female officer nodded, waved and walked back up the plank and down to my own, leaving the third officer to nosy around Mia's boat. After cursory introductions, the officers informed me that Mia was indeed missing, presumed dead. My shock obviously told on my face.

'How?' I asked, now shaken.

'We believe she headed out with a few friends to Bermondsey. Hasn't been seen since.'

'Who was she with?'

'Two acquaintances from her martial arts club. Michael Muick and Jonny Sandy,' the officer replied. I recognised neither name.

'What were they doing?' I muttered, beginning to feel a little sick.

'Apparently Michael and Jonny had heard there had been some trouble around the railway yards and they fancied practising their martial art skills fighting some criminal cause.'

I pulled a face and shook my head. I didn't know Michael and Jonny but I could picture their type – those who had been introduced to martial arts through YouTube and broadcast MMA and had classes for 12 months thinking they were becoming effective street-fighters. I shouldn't be too ungrateful, such stupidity had been utilised to fight wars and build businesses, but to have it impact my love-life was disheartening.

'Stupid, I know,' said the female officer with a sigh (without mentioning the word 'men' out of courtesy for her police colleague), 'Mia, tried to talk them out of it apparently, but went along as back-stop. They were her students, after all.'

'Why do you think she is dead?'

'We've found the body of Jonny hidden in the undergrowth near some railway yards near Deptford.'

'Murdered?'

They nodded.

'Gangland?'

They shook their heads. 'No, we don't think so.'

'Drugs? Random?'

They half-heartedly nodded, snatching glances at each other.

'You sure Mia was with them?' I asked, half-hoping she might still be alive.

'Text messages sent between them suggest they asked her along and asked her to bring her "chuks". Both her phone and her deceased friend's phone were found in the area. Extensive blood loss of the friend and a….dismembered leg.'

'My god. Whose?'

'It's being tested now, but Michael's, we think. Both Mia and Michael have disappeared.'

'Can't dogs track them?' I offered, desperately trying to fight through the fog in my head.

Again the detectives shook their heads trying in vain to hide the fact that they were withholding information.

'Do you know what the "chuks" might be?' the woman detective asked.

I paused. An image of Mia perched on the edge of the boat came to mind.

'Nunchucks?' I suggested. 'One of her martial art weapons? Two short sticks connected by a short chain. She was pretty accomplished at that kind of thing.'

The detective scribbled it down.

'Did you know her well?'

'No. I saw a lot of her. Very active, sporty. But…' I poised. 'Quite intense, at times, I think.'

'What do you mean?' said the officer, suddenly curious.

'Focused. You wouldn't want to mess with her. I had the feeling she could unleash hell on you if you got on the wrong side of her. But fiercely on the side of…good.'

'Took no shit?'

'No, absolutely not, she would eat you for breakfast if you tried anything.'

'Thanks. Here are my details. I'm Detective Baker,' said the woman detective handing over her card. We may be back in touch, but if you have anything else or she returns and you hear any news, let us know.'

'Absolutely,' I said. 'I hope you catch the gang.'

Detective Baker nodded.

'You could try talking to Ron Cha too,' I added nodding westwards along the river. 'He's an old South Korean merchant seaman who runs the Anchor River Taxi Service. Ron and Mia were close.'

With that, the officers turned and walked back up the plank and waved at their own colleague to join them. Halfway up the gangplank, the female detective turned and shouted back to me.

'If you *do* see her, call us immediately. Don't approach her, don't say anything to anybody. Call us any time, day or night.'

'What do you mean? She might be alive?' I shouted back. Hadn't the police detective made it clear Mia was probably dead? 'Is she in danger?'

The police detective paused, looking as if she might want to reply, but she didn't.

'She's mixed up with a bad crowd?' I called out.

'It's important,' the detective said, ignoring my question. 'Call us straightaway. And keep your distance from her.'

'Okay,' I muttered, and watched them disappear.

And that was the first time that the plague touched my existence. Though I didn't know it at the time that was my first introduction to the horrors that would eventually devour London, the metropolis. Nigel would have been proud.

Of course, I never saw Mia 'alive' again. Over the next few weeks, other people visited Mia's boat, including other officers, but it was roped off and secured. I had snippets of conversation with some of those attending, but they shared little. I was saddened. Mia was in the prime of her own life and an option in mine. That appealing prospect was now over. At times I had little glimmers of hope she would reappear, whereupon I could inform the police that there had been a misunderstanding and all was well. But it was not to be.

Not quite.

2. Boat Life

Living on a boat you get used to the sounds of quietness – the water gently lapping against the side of the hull, the distant chug of vessels on the river, the hum of voices as people wander past on the quayside above. The ear and mind acclimatise to everything. It generates a sensation to what one might associate with the peace of, um, death.

Perhaps a month (lunar cycle) after Mia's disappearance, and over a series of nights, I would wake in the middle of the night. I didn't know why, at first, but then I realised there was another, new peculiar sound to the night's musical score. A new musical instrument. Or rather, an old one. Once I realised that the anomaly-in-the-night was a sound, I knew its cause. It was the sound of a paddleboard.

The sound of a paddleboard was not strictly new. But to hear the sound of a paddleboard moving across the water towards my houseboat in the middle of the night was new. Nobody goes out on a paddleboard during the night hours. Not even Mia did that. Well, rarely.

During these nights I would jump out of bed and peak through the blinds. On a couple of occasions I saw a figure forty yards away silhouetted against the lights on the other side of the river paddling slowly on a board. Hooded and clad in black, it could have been Mia, I was unsure. The figure would loiter for a while then depart. It was when I rose from my bed at three o'clock in the morning having heard the paddleboard again, to look through the blinds to see the figure standing on the launch deck of

Mia's houseboat that I became unnerved. It was, as far as I could tell, Mia. It was her shape and presence. The figure did nothing, just stand and gaze at the Black Road and the surroundings before slipping away without me noticing.

Why didn't I approach her at the time? I can tell you. Something was not quite right. I waited until the morning and phoned Detective Constable Baker. Thinking I would be met with thanks, I was somewhat surprised and irritated that I was met with some anger – *'why didn't you phone us straightaway?'*

To be on the receiving end of such gruffness, ingratitude, when I was trying to be of assistance first threw me, then irritated me. I politely explained it had been the middle of the night and I was thinking of them, as exhausted police detectives, tucked up in bed resting from an honest day's work. Besides, I said, it was good news, Mia was apparently safe. Perhaps she was keeping a low profile, avoiding some gangland people, I argued. Alas, my supposition was met by a huff at the end of the telephone line.

The woman detective met me in my office later that day and took a statement. She had calmed down and I was more inquisitive.

'So, Mia is safe, she is alive, I'm sure it was her,' I said, surprised that it didn't close the matter.

'Did she appear different? Did she appear to know her surroundings?' asked Detective Constable Baker.

'Yes, why wouldn't she? Is she in trouble? Is someone after her? Is there a warrant out for her arrest? What is going on?' I asked, masking my own perturbation with irritation.

The detective said nothing.

'I'll speak to her next time,'

'No, don't,' DC Baker said, sharply.

I didn't reply, inviting the detective to fill the silence. She did after a few moments.

'It's dangerous.'

I remained quiet and fixed my gaze on her.

'Do you have a camera phone?' she said, calmly.

I nodded.

'Of course.'

'Does it work in low light?'

I nodded again.

'No worse than any other, I suppose.'

'Having phoned us and alerted us to Mia's presence. Please video record her.'

'I could do better than that,' I interrupted.

'No. Remain behind a locked door. In fact, I suggest you reinforce all entrances to your houseboat.'

'Why?' I protested, becoming exasperated.

The detective now fixed me with a glare.

It dawned on me.

'Mia *is*...dead?' I whispered. 'She is now one of the infected with this new plague-thing?'

The detective blinked before dipping her head in a discreet nod of acknowledgement.

I paused, took a breath and exhaled. I had heard about the virus, but there had been so many viruses and mini-scares that I was as philosophical as the next person about the coming apocalypse. (With 'philosophical' read 'tired and indifferent'.)

'I thought you knocked them off as soon as they appeared? They are hardly difficult to catch,' I whispered.

'That used to be the case, but they are becoming more...elusive.'

'Does the public know?'

'No. No cause for alarm. We have it under control.'

An idea suddenly flashed into my mind. Another opportunity. Perhaps Mia had a role in my life after all.

'Who is studying them?' I asked.

'Studying them?

'You are doing some research? Surely?' I said, trying to sound as indignant as possible.

The detective shook her head.

'Of course,' I thought. They are just the police. It might fall between stools – police officers policed and the medical profession didn't...monitor the dead. The undertaker industry was hardly equipped. The infected were just an anomaly bounced between departments.

'Someone must be *watching* them, surely?' I asked.

I was rapidly warming to the idea. Perhaps the best way to learn about Mia's fate was to get involved myself. I felt I owed her something and, in a curious sort of way, it would provide some sort of closure to my infatuation and sadness. Who knows, maybe I would get to approach her and have that face-to-face after all.

'And I might know just the man who could help,' I said to the detective, adopting as authoritative a tone as I could for such a self-interested statement.

3. Secondment

I took the detective's advice and beefed up my houseboat security. I added locks to anything that could be opened and placed furniture in such a way that it could be moved quickly in front of doors and across windows. I upgraded my fire extinguishers – not only to 'fire' (i.e. unload) on an attacker but also as a type of club I could swing with relative ease. I picked up a few other possible weapons – a police-like baton, a high-intensity strobe light, a loud aerosol-based sound alarm and anything that might disorientate a corpse. Finally, I plotted a number of escape routes from my houseboat. It was all slightly surreal. I wasn't so much motivated by genuine concern or panic, but by feeling good about being prepared. (A subtle, but real, difference.)

If this were another book, I would talk at length about my elaborate ploy to insert myself in the investigations. I had initially thought the best way to get involved was to just barge in, but over a few days I began to formulate a plan and fortuitously the opportunity presented itself. I shall keep it brief, but it is important because it gives an idea of how my role was conceived...and then how it developed.

In my role in the office of City Planning and Logistics I had a frazzled but competent supervisor, Robbie Andrews. An Irishman by birth still wielding a soft Irish lilt to charm or harague you, Robbie's role was to manage the various planning applications for building and infrastructure projects around London – changes to roadways, roundabouts, traffic lights, scaffolding and building projects (from café refurbishments to skyscrapers) that would impact the efficient running of roadways, access and traffic flow. Everything had to go across his desk for a review for efficiency and cost-saving purposes. This involved coordination with private contractors, utility companies and other bodies such as the Environment Agency. Some of the matters that arose included: did the proposed work increase carbon emissions i.e. by time spent in stationary vehicles? Did the proposed work impact traffic arrangements to such a degree that congestion resulted further down the road? Would, for example, the roadworks and any road closures (by gas and other utilities companies) mean that commuters were more likely to move onto the other forms of transport including the Underground train network? What were the estimated costs to business, to London and what measures could be put in place to mitigate these short, medium and long-term financial costs. In simple terms, Robbie's department reviewed traffic and 'people-flow' both above ground and on London's Underground transport system. Everything was about 'synergy' when it came to review and approval.

I assisted him in all respects, but with my Master's degree in Urban Development, I had quietly pushed for my role to take a slightly longer-term view – particularly the monitoring and predicting of human behaviour in the capital. I would review all projects, give my input and was charged with compiling longer term plans and practices and developing institutional, city-wide awareness. This might involve considering the ways technology would change how people worked and moved about the capital (for both work and recreational reasons). The recent pandemic and subsequent lockdowns had really brought all this to the fore because many people and companies were adjusting their work practices in expectation, even fear, of something similar happening again. More recently I had been monitoring how home-based working was encouraged by different companies and technology sectors, while being discouraged by others. All this impacted traffic flow (Underground trains, over-ground buses, cars, taxis, bicycles) in and around London.

With improved technology allowing for many tasks and services (the delivery of goods) to move online, I was tasked (two days a week) with looking forward, developing quick-response plans to sudden events – all based on human behaviour.

So, when – this is the fortuitous moment – a report came across my desk from the Metropolitan ('Met') Police about rules of engagement for the occasional 'Mobile Deceased Person' (MDP) roaming the streets, I saw my chance. When Robbie sighed and swore at the sight of the report – just another nuisance to respond to – I volunteered to take the lead.

The report detailed how there had been eighty instances in the previous month of solo MDPs found wandering the streets. The police had therefore closed a few roads, mobilised a few armed police personnel and addressed the matter – usually by bumbling them into the van and whizzing them away to a secure medical facility. Occasionally the MDPs had been fired upon by the police marksmen, which meant the surrounding streets were closed for longer as the area became a crime scene and/or a police-shooting incident requiring a report to be compiled. This was more paperwork, more of a headache for Robbie and the Met police. You might think that a police marksman discharging his or her weapon was entirely justified because the MDP had been stumbling towards a group of innocent bystanders. And, yes, you would be right, but this was all complicated by the early rumblings of disquiet from a few legal groups voicing their concerns about excessive police force on the 'unarmed deceased'.

Consequently, the Met had drawn up a Rules of Engagement document that included the policy and procedures of closing streets, sometimes for hours at a time to contain an infectant and process the scene afterwards if there was indeed a shooting 'dead' of a deceased person. If it was a confirmed shooting then the scene had to be not only closed for forensics but also for medical clean-up because it was unclear how dangerous (that is, 'infectious') body parts, bodily fluid and tissue-matter might be. It was all just another headache for Robbie.

'I'll look at it,' I said, taking the report from Robbie's hands after our initial discussion.

'You sure?' Robbbie replied, looking a little surprised and confused.

'Yep. I'll nip it in the bud. Take a lead. They probably want to cover their arses and need another department to insist on a speedy turnaround.'

'Okay,' mumbled Robbie, squinting. I could see that he was wracking his brains to find an ulterior motive for my volunteering to take on additional work.

'I'll need to liaise with the Met and get some inside info.,' I said, nodding sagely. 'I suspect they'll want to keep it quiet.'

I flicked through the report and saw a couple of useful sentences.

'Yep, looks like they expect cases to double next month, possibly quadruple the following month and they want to move quickly.'

'Liaise away,' said Robbie, relieved and leaning back in his chair.

And so it was that I was able to legitimately wangle my way into meeting the police.

I responded to the report writer (a Chief Inspector) and initiated a meeting. I let him present the report. I nodded sagely (again), stroked my chin and dropped in a few meaningful sentences such as: *I agree we should be clear on what the police should do, in part to protect you. City Hall is committed to protecting London's citizens ensuring that they can safely go about their business.*

Having softened up the Chief Inspector, I made two specific requests. Firstly, I needed more data that would help me draft a supportive response to the report – data such as the specifics of incidents, past cases and missing persons who were suspected as being victims. Secondly, I suggested that it would also be advantageous to talk to some frontline officers so that I could get a handle of the situation on the ground.

After a bit more furrowing of my brow and nodding of my head, I secured a letter from the Chief Inspector authorising (in fact, *requiring*) all officers city-wide to cooperate with me as I fast-tracked a response to the Met's request. With that formally logged in my office records and on their police systems I picked up an office phone and called Detective Constable Baker saying I needed to meet with her on behalf of City Hall and directing her to check my validation with the Met.

I walked into her office the following day.

'Oh, wow, fancy meeting you,' I said, my eyes wide and with a suitably quizzical look. 'What are the odds? I should have put two and two together.'

DC Baker appeared confused.

I helped her out.

'You are the detective I met on the houseboat of my neighbour, Mia, down Tower Bridge way?'

The penny dropped.

'Yes, you're Josh?'

'The very same.'

'Here to talk policy, strategy and rules of engagement?' she said slowly.

'Your detective skills are impressive.'

'What a coincidence,' she murmured, her eyes squinting mimicking Robbie's. 'For a moment there, I thought you might be pulling a fast one to get information on your girlfriend.'

I did my best to appear shocked, then hurt, then fraught with suppressed irritation.

'As much as I would like to think I can manipulate City Hall and Chief Inspector Biggins into giving me clearance to insist all police officers cooperate, without question, I am going to have to disappoint you.....'

'Are you here to make my life difficult?' she asked, still suspicious.

'Quite the opposite, in fact, I would like to think I am even more motivated to help you guys out.'

We settled down to coffee and sunk deep into a three hour discussion. It was a pivotal moment in the scheme of things. If Nigel's pivotal moment was being bitten in the first place, my morning with DC Baker was possibly the second most important (second only to actually identifying Nigel as the author of his blog) in my learning of the crisis about to engulf the metropolis.

We talked about what was happening around London.

'Why don't we talk about specific examples,' I said forty-five minutes into our discussion.

'Okaaay,' came the reply.

'Let's talk about Mia,' I said.

'Well, sorry to disappoint you, but I cannot go into detail with you.'

'Why not? I have authority.'

'Firstly, you don't.'

'I have been given authority,' I protested.

'No, we've been instructed to cooperate. I am cooperating. Individual cases are classified. All the directive is making me do is answer the phone, chat with you and share ideas. Until you hold 'classified status' you're a civilian. Besides, you're a possible witness.'

'So, what can you tell me about Mia's case?'

Detective Constable Baker smiled, shrugged. 'Nothing.'

I did think of playing hardball, but I thought it best to bank goodwill rather than spend brownie points. Apparently, my recommendation that she talk to Ron Cha, the local taxi ferryman, had been of some use, but then he had asked for some coins for his troubles and then clammed up when money was not forthcoming. You could tell Ron's mood by his eyes; 'grumpy' was the best I had seen, flashing angry eyes weren't uncommon. I switched subjects and, in the final hour or so, we talked about the people and agencies I would need to talk to. In that last hour of conversation I began to formulate a plan.

As I walked back to my office I developed my plan yet further and by the time I reached my office floor and my supervisor's Robbie's office, it was fully formulated.

'Robbie?' I said, knocking on his door. He looked up, tired, his despondent eyes sitting plumped up on the pillow bags under his eyes. 'This is getting bigger than I thought. Can we meet tomorrow?' I said, with a sigh and a despondent shake of my head.

'A headache?' Robbie asked despondently.

'Yes, but I think there might be a way to insulate the department from its consequences.'

'Oh yes?'

With a seed of encouragement planted, I nodded and retreated.

'You rest,' I said, closing the door.

The meeting the following day went well. I had sketched out a plan in the afternoon and written up a simple proposal overnight. By the end of the hour, Robbie was on board. I say onboard, I knew he was onboard, but an independent observer might say otherwise. I think he probably clocked what I was doing, but it still worked in his interest. (His own, as well as the department's.) Besides, there was a very real prospect I could secure extra funds covering both my secondment and even a little additional help for him and me.

In most virus-outbreak situations there was a track-and-trace system that could be activated at relatively short notice – a system that could identify those who had contracted the virus, then track their movements and trace to see who had been in contact with them. However, with this virus there was a problem. The Government was reluctant to formally institute (and announce) a track-and-trace system. In earlier pandemics governments had been judged very harshly on the efficacy of their track-and-trace and other monitoring systems. It had led to governments to implode then fall. Why introduce a stick with which to beat yourself? Better to have a carrot. If the carrot is used against you, it does not hurt as much as a stick. So in those early days a track-and-trace was never announced, but after a while there were some measures being undertaken behind the scenes. (Largely at my behest, I have to say.)

4. Fieldwork and MDPs

Conducting fieldwork was important for many reasons. Firstly, it was crucial to get a real sense of what was happening on the streets. No surprise there. Secondly, it helped keep me away from the office desk. In order to establish myself (and my new liaison role), I needed to be busy and unreachable, otherwise I might get sucked backwards into my old work. In those early days, any sighting of a Mobile Deceased Person was handled by the police. If a call was received it was directed to the nearest patrol car, the officers would cordon off the area, assess the mobility, capabilities and intent of the MDP and follow a course of action approved at the time. Wearing standard issue face masks, the officers would approach and detain the MDP and 'it' would be transferred to a local facility for treatment (usually meaning disposal). In the early days the police would try to keep the incident low-key in the hope it did not raise too much ire from, for instance, 'human rights' groups. It was for this reason that MDPs were not taken to police stations (and placed in custody in police cells) because it would provide ammunition for the human rights groups' causes. Nobody in authority wanted to give even the slightest suggestion that the detained MDP should be processed under human rights law and be given access to a solicitor.

Similarly, MDPs would not be taken to hospitals because, it could be argued, that they might be entitled to medical treatment. After all, how could you medically treat a deceased person (mobile or not)? The police were ably supported in this interpretation by many hospital administrators and senior clinicians not wanting another headache. Treating the dead in hospital would draw more sources away from the living, surely? If you listened carefully, you would hear people muttering: how can a clinician treat death? Anyone afflicted with death should not be under the purview of hospital trusts, surely? Besides, the police did not want to bring any unknown virus into a hospital environment when there was a limited understanding of the mechanics of transmission of the virus. It was reasonable to assume that death was very catching.

In summary, it was left to the police to devise and administer these 'health and safety' procedures for the welfare of the general public and to maintain law and order. For this reason, MDPs were transported to hastily erected facilities (often housed in temporary buildings, or tents), adjacent to morgues and crematoria. They could be processed quickly and efficiently and the bodies cremated without much ado. The MDPs fell into two groups – those who were known to be dead and were already in receipt of death certificates, and, secondly, those not previously known to be dead (and were found wandering the streets). The latter group prompted a rapid and discrete change in the law allowing for physicians to issue a certificate in the field.

The first type of Mobile Deceased Person had risen from morgues or hospitals and had been identified as deceased at crime scenes or accidents. To date no MDP had risen from a grave, but authorities were nervous of such a case happening and, I was surprised to learn, already had in place a plan and procedure for dealing with it. Should it happen, families were not to be informed of an MDP rising to limit protests and legal complications. Nobody wanted the public to learn that the dead were rising from the grave. After all, this wasn't the apocalypse.

The second type were those who were not previously reported as deceased. Perhaps they had fallen ill, collapsed or had been assaulted, passed away by natural causes and risen as an MDP. On these occasions the police patrol would make an initial assessment and recommend the deceased be directed to an MDP disposal facility instead of a hospital. It was not called an 'MDP disposal facility', but a mobile emergency room. It just happened to be next to an MDP facility, which itself was, usually, an annex of a crematorium.

Along with all of this, the arrangements surrounding the issuance of a DSMA-Notice (Defence and Security Media Advisory Notice) were simplified. A DSMA-Notice was, in effect, a media blackout on the reporting of an incident. All this was in place because it was after all a minor outbreak of a bizarre virus. No government wanted to blow it up into something unnecessary. It was still too scarred from the rolling, variant-laden pandemics of recent years. The economic fall-out of the previous pandemic still haunted the country.

My life 'in the field' began with me receiving police radio dispatches as soon as an MDP-relevant call came in, then jumping in a taxi and racing the incident. In the early days I would often arrive a little late at the incident therefore I made efforts to embed myself in a patrol team, which had been designated as the first unit to respond if an MDP was identified in the area.

This was all well and good, but I soon gleaned that the police were becoming nervous. My 'cooperation-directive' from the Chief Inspector meant some of the police officers relaxed and I learned of 'response and control' measures that had not been included in the Met report (that had largely focussed on the impact of traffic and movement of people around the capital). At first I was shocked at some of the police's operational procedures, then fascinated. I realised my fascination was touching on the deeper interest of human behaviour – not the behaviour of the dead, but the behaviour of the *living* and how they (the living) were treating the dead. I was beginning to see panic in the living, not about the dead, but about how to control information about the dead. I suspected many of the police's measures were being undertaken without the full knowledge of the politicians and the government. Or, perhaps I was being cynical and there was a tacit understanding, a blind eye being turned. What happens on the streets, stays on the streets.

But as the number of cases rose, things became more complicated. There were a number of incidents where deceased people had risen in front of the crematorium staff. There were cases of staff walking out of the crematorium because the MDP had to be restrained or there were indications that relatively docile MDPs might assault staff. In time, undertakers or crematorium staff would not accept MDPs in their establishments at all. Restraining a corpse was a very disconcerting experience for all concerned. This was compounded by the fear of infection. As a result of a few particular incidents and the fear of an escalation, 'specialists' were brought in who had a particular set of skills. These specialists would perform procedures demobilising any MDP – usually involving the dismemberment of the infectant on arrival at the facility – before disposal by crematorium staff.

All this information began to overwhelm me. I really could not see how I could address the issue, let alone compile recommendations for Robbie and his superiors. This was not about traffic and people movement. This was far bigger. Why it was not already regarded as a massive problem was because, in part, nobody wanted to take responsibility for it. The government would tell the police to just get on with it, the police wanted to involve the medical professionals, but the medical professionals said any medical responsibility ended at death, therefore it was over to the police. The undertakers and crematoria staff were just wholly unqualified. It takes a particular type of person to spend their waking days working with corpses. It is a wholly different kind of person to spend their days in refrigerated conditions with mobile, often aggressive, cadavers. The police suggested involving the army, but that was blocked by Downing Street. No politician wanted to see the military on the streets suggesting that things were getting dangerous. Furthermore, many police officers did not look as if they were psychologically equipped to deal with the problem judging by the reaction and behaviour of many officers on the front line. Not only was nobody prepared to take responsibility, nobody was looking at the bigger picture. And that's where I came in.

There are too many incidents to recount in these pages and besides, being largely similar, they would make for tedious reading. However, there were three incidents that would prove to be significant lines of investigation – the first being the visit to the flat of Felicity Goodban. The second incident of note was the robbery of a Camberwell jewellers, and finally, the third centred on the tragic, fiery death of a street juggler. But before I share those stories, I need to introduce you to the plague and 'the help' – two interns (Fiona and Tom) – without whom I would not have been able to find a way to articulate (and escalate to my superiors) the threat the MDP challenge posed to London.

5. The Plague; The Help

One of the best ways to secure funding was to undertake work and provide impressive results (in the form of a report, predictions and recommendations), then walk away and let the boss come running back for more.

Provide a valuable service.

Prove to be of use to someone…

Then withdraw if funding or support is not given.

It is a far more effective strategy to engage the attention from higher-powers than just proposing a hypothetical thesis along with a proposed budget.

With this in mind I decided I needed to acquire hard evidence if I were to take my project further. But in order to achieve solid results, I needed one other thing – help. Acquiring help would be more likely to lead to results.

Having attended a reasonable number of call-outs by the police, I had a rough idea of how to proceed, but I needed help compiling case studies and data. Furthermore, a series of off-the-cuff remarks by a few officers suggested there was a pattern behind some of the attacks by MDPs, possibly even *learned* behaviour. This worried some officers, but only in respect to their own safety rather than for the wider public concern. The implications troubled me.

But I didn't have funding to expand yet.

My ability to provide a 'valuable service' that I could then 'withdraw' was limited because I was on my own. I couldn't build an empire and claim territory by myself. In the (privately-owned) business world I would take out a loan, seek venture capital and buy in help. But I didn't work in such a business world, I was a civil servant. What do public servants do? Well, arrange secondments. But secondments cost money. What costs less money? Internships. There wasn't time to arrange an internship programme myself, but perhaps I could acquire a few interns from another programme. So it was that I hung around my supervisor Robbie in a few meetings, chatted in corridors and loitered in doorways. I knew that he was obliged to host a handful of interns as part of getting regional participation from other parts of the UK. Perhaps I could pinch one, or two. My loitering paid off. Just as we had shared a few words in a doorway, his secretary came up to him, tapped him on the elbow and said – 'They're waiting for you'.

Robbie sighed and his head dropped to his chest.

I jumped at the sigh-and-head-drop.

'Interns? I can take a couple off your hands if you want? Keep them busy,' I said, turning on my heel and walking off. I couldn't be sure if his eyes darted towards me as I walked off, but I felt something (a gaze, perhaps?) hitting my back as I retreated.

An hour later his head appeared around the door.

'You sure?'

'What?'

'You want a couple of interns? Take them off my hands?'

I wasn't born yesterday. I played the part: I let my head fall onto my chest as I let out a sigh. I threw in a rub of the chin, a regretful shake of the head and another sigh.

'Sure, why not. I owe you,…but you'll owe me.'

'Great, thanks, Josh. I'll send you a Scottish chap and a Welsh lady. Both nice. You'll like them.'

'No more than six months though,' I called after him as he disappeared down the sight.

'I'll do my best,' echoed the reply.

And that is how I began to build my empire and provide an invaluable service.

I interviewed the two interns the following day. They were both twenty-four year old recent Master's graduates who were relatively new to London, but by no means simple and starry-eyed. That said, interns can be more trouble than they are worth. They need more hand-holding and they have the evil triumvirate of being keen, thinking they have something to offer while having no real-world experience. This is compounded by the fact that they had no knowledge of the *whys* and *wherefores* of a hierarchical bureaucracy. Robbie had been required to accept the interns as part of a government programme to offer civil service experience to young people from the regions. So, Tom and Fiona, being from different parts of the UK (Scotland and Wales respectively), their enthusiasm did not sit so comfortably beside the brooding cynicism of the London-based (albeit Irish), eternally grumpy Robbie.

Although I had offered to take the interns for six months, I suspected Robbie wouldn't want them back and they would serve out their twelve-month internship with me in the MDP-monitoring squad. Later I also intimated to Robbie that if I was unable to cope with all the Met police liaison and rising cases, then responsibility for all the work would come back to the department. He acquiesced. As for Tom and Fiona, they were excited and delighted to be considered for roles in a 'cutting edge departmental task force' as both Robbie and I described it to them. I was pleased.

I didn't have time (or the patience) to interview them separately, so I invited them both to my newly-appointed attic office (a desk amidst filing cabinets and storage boxes) for a meeting. What the hell? I answered to no one. There was no HR department, so I asked them both to come in.

'So, you're the first two?' I said as they walked in and settled down on two chairs. 'I hope you don't mind me interviewing in groups of two, I have to be in the field shortly.'

'Of course, of course, no, no, no,' they both said, excitedly and bushy-tailed.

My instinctive reaction was that they were both pleasant and I would be sighing and stroking my chin and giving them the job within the hour. I asked themselves to introduce themselves:

'Hello, I'm Tom. As you can tell I'm from Scotland. The Isle of Skye. I graduated with a Master's in Local Government from Durham University .

'Hello, I'm Fiona. As you can probably tell, I'm from Dyfed in Wales,' she giggled. 'Never heard of this Scotland place, I'm sorry,' she said, glancing at Tom beside her. 'I've done a Master's in Urban Spaces and I graduated last summer from Cardiff University.'

It was an easy forty seconds and I thought it would be nice to have a few different soft accents around the place. I thought I ought to give them twenty minutes to look as if I was making an effort.

'What has Robbie told you?' I said, frowning.

'That you are watching the MDPs and engaged in civic planning around them?'

'Yes, I'm monitoring behaviour and helping with response-planning by the police and interested parties. That said, I am becoming more interested in learning about MDP behaviour and gathering evidence.'

I paused for dramatic effect.

'So, what do you know about the virus? Its origins? Government policy et cetera,' I asked, furrowing my brow.

Both looked a little bashful. They exchanged looks.

'What do you mean?' asked Fiona.

I nodded. At least they passed the first test – diplomacy in a bureaucracy.

'Well, firstly tell me the official government line. Then tell me what social media has been telling you and finally, tell me what you actually believe.'

'Okay,' Fiona said, with uncertainty.

'Look, I said, trying to reassure her. 'Think of this unit as a start-up. We are not here to satisfy people, but to dig deep in this new challenge. Although I answer to Robbie, I am not on the books anywhere in City Hall or the Government's Whitehall set-up, but I do need clear thinking from those I work with and an awareness of the competing interests and demands in and around Whitehall surrounding the plague, the virus, call it what you will.'

Fiona took a deep breath.

'Okay, well, in terms of the official government line, there is none – no official line,' she began. 'As far as the Government is concerned this is a mild infection that generates a form of mobility (or physical 'life') after death. The infected are called "Mobile Deceased Persons". They are generally regarded as harmless, but can be dangerous if cornered or provoked. They should not be approached by members of the public and the police's rules of engagement are, how should I say, "evolving", which is presumably where you come in?'

I nodded.

Tom chipped in: 'The Government certainly isn't going to describe it as 'a virus to worry about'. It is certainly not something that will lead to a pandemic. Its transmission is not airborne, like a conventional respiratory virus. Transmission is through the digestion of fluid or from bites. The virus ideally has to be absorbed directly into the bloodstream and/or ingested in relatively significant quantities (perhaps a teaspoon) or absorbed through the mouth, nose, eyes. It did not kill you either, so not all bad. It only becomes 'effective' after death. So, if you didn't die by it alone, no problem. If you had underlying medical conditions then it could be problematic. Victims of bites *can* die, but those who ingest fluids through mouth, nose or eyes usually just become ill – death does not follow in the vast, vast majority of cases. As the government is politically motivated, it does not want to go to the place of other pandemics. It has learned its lesson – the lessons still being raw, economically and socially.'

'So, you would say this 'plague' is of just mild public interest?' I asked, my eyes narrowing.

'Yes,' they both said, nodding.

'Oh, but that is not to say it diminishes the importance of your work,' said Fiona, suddenly alarmed.

'No, no, no. Fiona's completely right – it is of mild public concern right now, but it has to be managed in the longer term…behind the scenes,' said Tom, hastily agreeing.

'Okay, thank you,' I said, doodling my initials on the pad on my knee for the tenth time. 'What about the origins of the virus itself?' I asked.

'Okaaay,' Fiona said, thinking carefully. 'It's messy. There is talk that the virus came from China.'

'Don't all viruses?' muttered Tom, rolling his eyes.

'But not *directly* from a lab this time. I've read that it might have its origins in the Siberian permafrost then found its way via various animals to a lab. I've also heard that complications from past vaccines might have harmed the immune response in humans…?' said Fiona, with her intonation rising at the end of the sentence. She obviously didn't want to commit herself to a theory, but wanted to show she had done some research.

Not to be outdone, Tom chipped in – 'I am unsure about that, although mugging around with the human immune system might not have helped. I have more time for the main cause coming from viruses emerging from the permafrost.'

'Emerging into conditions ripe for it to flourish?' I added.

Tom and Fiona nodded eagerly.

I was largely of the same opinion. The trouble was that everything had become so politicised. Climate change, pandemics and vaccines, big tech, big pharma, big business. It was difficult to separate government interests from corporate interests. It was all some soggy mess. They called themselves 'elites' as if that gave themselves some entitlement to take societies down the path that suited them. Once upon a time the government might have held corporate bodies and multinationals at arms length for the benefit of the average citizen. Not now.

Digging deep into the soggy mess, I was inclined to agree that rising temperatures across the planet (leading to a greater frequency of storms, flooding, melting glaciers, rising sea levels, retreating coastline) in turn led to unforeseen consequences. When it was cited in literature and media, it was often in the context of billions of tons of methane (a greenhouse gas one hundred times more potent than carbon dioxide) being released into the atmosphere resulting in a non-containable irreversible acceleration of the global rise in temperature. A point of no return.

One such consequence was quite possibly the release of viruses that had been trapped in the Siberian permafrost. The region, known as Western Siberia, was a huge, sparsely populated expanse with the local population engaged only in the simple farming of animals. Ironically, one account in my background reading referred to the etymology of the word 'Siberia'. It meant 'sleeping land'. In the circumstances, it was rather prophetic and ominous, for what was 'sleeping' there? Some peat bogs in Western Siberia had been frozen for millions of years. But the bogs did not contain methane. The bogs contained the remains and evidence of previous life forms. Not only the large fauna – mammoths, sabre-tooth tigers and other mighty beasts, but also the small, even invisible and 'insignificant' life forms. Fears over the re-emergence of these new life forms were realised when Russian scientists confirmed that the melting permafrost was exposing bacteria and viruses that had lain frozen and dormant in the permafrost for many thousands (if not millions) of years. Scientists had known in the early part of the twenty-first century that they could bring back to life some of these viruses, but the number of re-emergent threats was unknown. Concerns escalated when a number of giant viruses were discovered emerging like demons from the frozen landscape – some possibly never before seen by man...ever. Now the thing with Giant viruses is that they are so big they can be larger than bacteria – the first giant virus was identified in France in 2003 and was mistakenly identified to be a bacterium. They were so unknown that it was like finding a virus from the moon or another planet. A handful of decades later the qualities of the giant virus (commonly known as a 'Girus') were still not fully understood. What was concerning to the scientific community was that these Giruses often contained many genes not found in any other lifeforms on earth.

I dug deeper with Tom to see how much he knew.

'So, what virus from the permafrost?' I asked.

Tom gulped and knew he was being tested.

'Well,' he began, uncertainly, 'I think it was a virus called something like "Megavirus chilensis"? It emerged from the permafrost, found its way in the guts of antelopes, killing them. In fact wiping out the whole species in a few years? The carcasses were sold and ground up for feed for cattle. Eventually it found its way to China and the animal markets? Then there were a bunch of cover-ups by Russia and China.'

I half-nodded in a non-committal approving way.

'It wasn't Megavirus chilensis, but a distant cousin, sort of. But a megavirus, yes.' I said. 'Yes, it was related to the Saiga antelope die-off in Central Asia. The cover-up blamed another virus and, believe it or not, the weather. Hundreds of thousands of antelope died within days. Most were buried, but, as you say, a very great many carcasses were sold and ground up for cattle feed in markets further east.'

I turned to Fiona.

'Do you know how the virus reached Europe?' I asked.

Now it was Fiona's turn to gulp. She paused and looked at Tom.

'Well,' interrupted Tom, 'didn't it first arrive via merchant shipping?'

It was true, the plague had landed rather innocuously in Southern Europe, brought by a crew member of a container ship sailing from Asia that docked in Athens. The virus was eventually caught by a Greek mink farmer who, having returned to the island of Alonissos after a business trip, passed it on to his mink. On instruction, he destroyed the sick animals and buried them in a mass grave. The trouble was, the dead mink rose from the earthy confines a few weeks later and he was bitten again. He died, was buried, then rose again a week later. The virus was evolving – moving between human to animal and back to human. There had been minor outbreaks about Europe, but the virus had a firmer foothold in the UK's capital.

My feelings about the origins of the virus itself were mixed; it was a confluence of factors, a perfect storm. So perfect, in fact, that at times I instinctively felt that it had an eerie 'by-design' quality. I don't mean 'by design' by humans (although there was an element of that), but 'by nature's design', even….fate. I was beginning to ask myself if there was something 'anthropic' about the emergence of the plague.

'Okay, finally, what are the problems we are facing with this "plague"? And what can you do to help?' I asked my two fresh-faced interviewees.

I turned to the Welsh intern.

'Fiona?'

Fiona paused, looked down at her lap and thought. I liked that. A thinking young person. Someone who would not fire back-chat.

She looked up.

'Humankind is relatively new to living in metropolises – small areas housing millions, perhaps tens of millions of people living on top of one another. We have to be alert to threats that can disrupt that. The Black Death in the 1600s killed an estimated third to a half of the population of Europe. The 1918 Spanish flu pandemic killed an estimated fifty million people within a two year period – at a time when the world's population was 1.2 billion people and they rarely travelled by air, land or sea. Our own pandemic killed hundreds of thousands to a handful of million depending on how you count the causes of death. However, if things go awry, the last pandemic could be a pale precursor to what could happen – the next pandemic could involve hundreds of millions, even billions, of deaths.'

I turned and looked at Tom.

'And our hands are tied by other factors,' he said, scrambling for input.

'Such as?'

'Managing any outbreak. The concerns over experimental vaccines rushed out to meet demand – just look at the other health scares. Also, recent epidemics and pandemics have lessened the public's patience, let alone interest, in possible medical emergencies. It was just another one to be managed. Throw in the many shortsighted vested interests – politicians, big pharma, big tech. It is all complicated by social media companies and their agendas. People are getting wise or polarised – take your pick. Anyway, a significant proportion of people would be far more reluctant to take emergency vaccines, as it would undoubtedly be the case, to combat a new virus threat. And of course, there is the emergence of antibiotics resistance, which doesn't help.'

It was true: a nasty paradox of medical progress – antibiotics. Modern antibiotics had an ability to reduce or mask symptoms allowing the average person the ability to continue to live normally rather than succumbing to infections. This increased use led to the dramatic rise of antibiotic resistance, which meant antibiotics were ultimately rendered useless.

'For all the brilliance of modern science, we are painting ourselves into a corner,' Tom said, hoping he was doing enough to stay in the game.

I had been giving a lot of thought to the conundrum and envied the Middle Ages – a time when there was no high-speed travel or a heaving metropolis an hour away. The development of the virus was a perfect storm of modern scientific 'improvements'. A few decades ago people started talking about the 'anthropocene' – a new geopolitical epoch based on the assumption that humans' impact on the earth and its ecosystems was significant enough to merit its own 'epoch' in the planet's history.

Tom interrupted my musing.

'This is all aided and abetted by modern society,' he said. 'The enclosed, busy metropolises, crowded transport networks, central heating. Throw in a few other modern inventions – political media, social media – and you have the ideal ingredients for catastrophic results for human civilisation.'

'The world's population is now approaching eight billion,' Fiona added. 'And with estimates of between one and six million people being in the air at any one time, bad things on a global scale can happen very swiftly. In a world like this we have to be alert to dangers on the macro and micro scale. The next pandemic will take root in a place like London and could, within hours, seed the world….'

'With death,' muttered Tom, nodding.

'It could start with one person. And that one person could be wandering the streets of London as we speak,' said Fiona, ominously.

'The harbinger of the apocalypse?' I said with a nod and a smile.

'Yep,' they both said, nodding excitedly.

'So?' I said. 'You want to meet this harbinger of death? Do you want to watch, study and catch this ghoul before he brings an end to the world as we know it?'

'Sure. Why not?' they both said, breaking into wide smiles. 'Sound great. Does that mean we get the job?'

6. Fiona, Tom and...Felicity

Tom and Fiona soon became acclimated to the attic and set up their own desks in an open-plan 'space' outside my own office. I was still developing my relationships with police officers and didn't want bright-eyed and bushy-tailed interns souring relations, so I start Tom and Fiona slowly, but life was moving quickly and I soon realised that they should join me in the field. Their help gathering evidence would be invaluable.

This brings me to the first incident of note. It was the second fieldwork assignment on which I took along my two new interns to the flat of a young woman, Felicity. (To those readers familiar with Nigel's own writings, this was the flat of CatNaps. Of course, at this stage I was unaware of Nigel and his work, but months later I shuddered at the thought I had actually been at the place where he had acquired one of his most devoted and accomplished colleagues.)

A phone call came in from the public relating to a missing woman by the name of Felicity Goodban. Rather than the local police patrol being called, the police dispatcher had put in a request for an MDP-squad to attend the flat in Balham, south of the Black Road, just in case an MDP had to be handled. It was reported that Felicity had not been seen in her flat for over two weeks (perhaps more).

At the time of her disappearance, Felicity had been working from home as a freelance graphic designer. When she had failed to deliver design work to her clients and had not answered follow-ups, the clients had just moved on. She had no family in the city and there was a coolness between some family members. After two weeks of her silence (and no activity visible on her few social media channels), an uncle had travelled to London and knocked on her flat's front door. A pale, somewhat haggard-looking Felicity appeared. The uncle was relieved and asked a few questions, but received no reply, just a morose stare. Felicity's rectitude was not entirely unexpected, the uncle had had an affair and a broken marriage ten years earlier that had hit Felicity quite hard as a much younger woman. She never really forgave her uncle and the frostiness had never really disappeared. So far, so (relatively) normal. Nevertheless, the uncle had reported that he had been aware of (but not seen) at least two other people in the flat. Consequently, he assumed his niece had some company so he was not worried in the short term. But, after a further few weeks of inactivity, and growing concerns from other family members, calls were made to the police requesting that they check on Felicity's flat. This was when I (with Tom and Fiona) tagged along.

Arriving at Felicity's flat, I tasked my interns with video-recording everything, making notes of any witness statements being given to the police (which we should also have access to, I hoped), and start to think about what CCTV might be in the area (attached to the other residences themselves or to traffic cameras at the end of the road or in local shops). Receiving no response to a knock on the door, a locksmith broke open the lock and we entered the flat. It was a small, neat-ish space, but it had a feel of not being well-maintained. A mouldiness hung in the air. There were no bloodstains, severed body parts, no signs of a struggle. It was almost as if it had not been 'lived in' for six weeks. Sensing there were no real clues and not wanting to interfere with the police as they made an inspection, I thought more progress would be made consulting with possible witnesses.

Consequently, once the police had interviewed the owners of the flats above and below, I invited Fiona to join me by my side (thinking a young, smiley, attractive woman would help solicit information from both men and women) and approached the neighbours.

The occupiers of the flat below Felicity (a young, unmarried, professional couple) were more helpful than those in the flat above. Warming up as I probed and requesting they rack their brains for memories and clues, I learned that Felicity had indeed not been seen for over four weeks. The couple had not worried because footsteps were often heard in the flat above. The footsteps belonged to more than one person, suggesting there was company.

'Male or female?' I asked.

'I'm sorry, what?' the young woman replied.

'The footsteps – male or female? Stilettos, heels? Heavier shoes, boots?' I asked.

The couple paused and thought.

'Well, female. But possibly male too?'

I gave a quizzical look waiting for them to fill the silence.

'Female, certainly. Several females, perhaps more,' said the woman looking at her partner for help. 'But there was a heavier – yet softer – footstep too.'

I furrowed my brow and pursed my lips in true police fashion suggesting they weren't being altogether helpful.

'Heavier – male, but not wearing shoes,' the female resident said.

'No, certainly no shoes. A slower pace, heavier,' her partner added. 'Yes, very probably male.'

'Okay, thank you. That is helpful.'

'And a child,' the woman said, almost as an afterthought.

'What? A child?'

'Yes, certainly a child,' said the man, nodding in agreement.

'Possibly between six and nine years old?' the woman continued. 'A light, quicker step.'

'Did you hear a child's voice?' I asked, suddenly bemused and a touch disappointed. Perhaps these weren't MDPs at all.

'No, nothing.'

'But maybe some giggling. Squeals of delight. That kind of thing,' the lady resident said.

'What voices did you hear?' asked Fiona. 'Men, women? Any arguing, laughter between the adults? People on the telephone? Communicating to anyone?'

The couple paused and adopted a look of contemplation.

'No, nothing.'

'No, nothing what?' asked Fiona.

'No voices, no laughter, no phones,' the woman replied, with the man nodding. 'Not even music, the radio or television.'

'Which is something you would normally hear?' I asked, now curious again.

'Yes,' they both replied. 'Up until six weeks weeks ago.'

'Not even a meow to be honest,' said the man turning to his girlfriend.

'Absolutely, yes, you're right!' she replied, suddenly alarmed. 'Not even a meow!'

With startled and shocked looks, the pair both turned to me and Fiona. Realising we were obviously missing something, the woman said: 'She had a cat. Felicity had a cat. We would hear it meow all the time.'

'But nothing for six weeks?' I asked.

'No,' they said, both shaking their heads. 'I'm sure we have seen it around since, but certainly not seen or heard it in the upstairs flat for ages.'

'Ok, thank you. Intriguing. Do you remember anything occurring around the time of Felicity's disappearance? Anything usual?'

'No,' they replied. 'Oh...'

'What?' I said, quietly thinking we might be close to something useful.

'Unless...what did Lucy and Nick say? That night?'

'Your birthday?'

'They said it was from the street?'

'They said "outside", not the street specifically,' the man replied.

'What?' I asked, again.

'The meow and scream.'

'The scream?' both Fiona and I said in unison, startled.

Fiona and I learned that on the occasion of the woman's birthday, a small dinner party had taken place in their flat. All had gone well until one point late in the evening when two of the guests, Lucy and Nick who were sitting near the open window, heard what they thought was cat meow (or rather squeal) then a brief scream before a whoosh, then a slight, squelchy thud. The guests were adamant it was not from above (otherwise everybody would have heard it) and it was from 'outside' rather than on street (which would have produced a brief echo). At the time a quick glance out of the window had confirmed that the dark street was empty and it was concluded that it was a bird, perhaps an owl, flying into a building or lamppost, had been responsible.

This was very intriguing information. Fiona and I nodded, made notes and gathered a few more details. Having thought Felicity's disappearance would be a dead-end, I was suddenly beginning to think that the disappearance of Felicity was a matter for investigation and could result in the identification of an MDP. What was especially intriguing was the report of different types of footsteps being heard in the flat above for weeks afterwards.

'Make sure we get as much of our own video footage of Felicity's flat before the police lock it all up,' I instructed Fiona. The police's videographer might not capture everything. They can be slapdash because it is not officially a crime scene just yet.'

Fiona nodded.

'Also, we must make sure that we get a list of anything the police seize from the flat and the results of any forensics,' I added. 'If we can learn as much about Felicity's life before her death, it might help us put together how she met her end. Phone records, Internet activity, social media all help. So, sweet-talk the forensics team and officers so that we have a better chance of them disclosing any information and results further down the line.'

I was thanking my lucky stars for my acquisition of a good-looking pair of interns. Of course, in modern times one should never reflect on one's colleagues' looks nor seek to employ their charms to further an agenda, but, holy hell, this was turning into a matter of life and death.

'This sounds odd,' Fiona muttered as we made our way out of the residence. I could sense her excitement. Forget traffic logistics, murder detective was much more exciting.

Of course, I did not disclose my clandestine interest in MDPs to Tom and Fiona right away. I had to be careful, because they had been seconded to my team largely to help with logistic implications of police (crime) investigations and how it might impact road closures, but I could not deny the impact that both Tom's and Fiona's excitement had on me.

Later that day, at drinks after work, I made sure they understood that we were not conducting our own investigations into such occurrences, but we could frame our 'investigation' as a form of studying the efficiency and effectiveness of police work within the confines of road closures. In order to understand the effectiveness of the police's work, there was no harm in us carrying out complementary investigations of our own. Our results could then form the basis of our reports to Robbie, perhaps with a view of expanding operations. That said, we were a new team, a new task force, and we might make a few missteps as we followed and shadowed police when trying to get a better grasp of MDP activity.

'One thing we must do is start building a database of suspected MDP activity to look for patterns and even behaviour. But let's be discreet. If all goes well, we might reach a point where we can predict MDP behaviour and therefore the impact on police resources and thereby disruption to traffic management et cetera,' I said with a cheesy wink. 'And if we are successful in that endeavour, then we can budget for it.'

7. Z-Squads

Felicity's disappearance was the first real MDP lead that I could get stuck into. It had so many variables that suggested the undead might be becoming socially-organised and exhibiting a social behaviour (living together), to date not credited to mobile corpses. If Felicity had indeed been taken and was now wandering the metropolis as a Mobile Deceased Person, she somehow was successfully avoiding detection.

While we waited for the police forensics reports the avenues for investigation open to us were limited to those outside Felicity's flat. We had no time to waste, Tom, Fiona and I needed to do some legwork. We quickly identified two lines of investigation – CCTV from the surrounding area and the whereabouts (or fate) of Felicity's pet cat.

Tom took it upon himself to find out what the 'whoosh-squelchy-thud' had been. According to our best guess at timelines, that 'sound' was the critical point – the moment when things changed – the last time Felicity was seen, possibly the last time the cat was heard. Within a few days Tom had hunted down footage from closed circuit cameras from either end of the street (from a corner shop and a residential driveway) that had recorded any persons who had entered (or exited) the street. Nothing unusual leapt out, but to identify everybody who left the street would take many man-hours. Man-hours I could not afford. Besides, knocking on too many neighbours' doors might get us into trouble.

Tom also managed to secure footage of a CCTV attached to the front of a property almost opposite Felicity's residence.

Although of poor quality, the ground and first floor of the building could be seen. The first floor flat belonged to the neighbours Fiona and I had interviewed. Felicity's second floor flat was just out of frame, unfortunately.

Tom and I scoured the footage and did see a pixelated, blocky shadow descend rapidly downwards and perhaps stop on the railing. Then another blocky shadow followed it in a more controlled fashion. The blocky shadows merged then ascended back upwards and out of frame. Could they be a bird, an owl bumping into the building and falling, then recovering and flying away? It seemed pretty large to be a bird, but perhaps the blocky pixelated footage was not giving a clear representation of the objects in motion? We wondered if it was the cat. Had the cat fallen out of the window, landed on the railing or wall perhaps dragging a blanket with it that floated down in a more controlled fashion? Having recovered it had scampered back up the building.

We could see the front door of the flat and watched to see if Felicity had panicked on seeing the feline fall out of the window and had raced downstairs to investigate. When outside of the flat looking for her pet, perhaps Felicity had been attacked and abducted (or at least bitten)? We ran the footage over and over but could not see anybody leaving the flat. Desperate for clues we both studied the CCTV available from both ends of the street but could not find any figures entering the street at the appropriate time and/or an image of what could be Felicity leaving, escorted by another figure or not.

Deflated, Tom committed to return to the scene to see if he could work out what might have happened. Meanwhile Fiona had visited other residences on the street and, borrowing a little dog from her friend, she walked up and down the street and, as if I should doubt it, she successfully made friends with a few old ladies. Conversations turned to cats and dogs and the disappearance of the young woman at number thirty-four. Such was Fiona's Welsh charm, she almost had a profile of Felicity's cat and its movements over the last year. Some of the neighbours knew Felicity and had their own theories of her disappearance, none related to her being an MDP. One thing that did become clear from the conversations was that Felicity was not the type of person to abandon her cat.

Reports of the cat's whereabouts after the 'whoosh-squelchy-thud' abounded, although we couldn't be sure that the reports from the old ladies were accurate. What Fiona did learn was that the cat had exhibited unusual behaviour after Felicity's disappearance. In particular, the cat had refused to go nearer its former home. It looked increasingly emaciated as the weeks went on. Occasionally fed by a few neighbours, it had lost the strut of a confident cat and seemed very edgy. Eventually it disappeared altogether.

Although the behaviour of Felicity's cat was useful information, it did not lead to any conclusions that could be included in any official report. Nevertheless, taken with other information yet to come in, it might help paint a picture. Fortunately, Tom's expedition had come up with a possible clue that could indeed find itself in a report to superiors. When examining the railings below Felicity's second floor flat he thought he could discern an unusual residue on the railing spikes themselves. Thinking it might be blood, he had taken a sample and we had sent it off for the forensic examination. Although many weeks old and no doubt washed repeatedly by rain, this little bit of flakey residue might be crucial.

In summary, I was pleased that I had Fiona and Tom onboard – two motivated, curious individuals. They worked well together too and if we started making progress, life was going to get busy. We were the only ones who were doing this kind of work in the capital, so we had to deliver. I was also thanking my lucky stars that I hadn't been required to go through any formal route of recruitment – no advertising and interviewing. I just got lucky.

Secondments and internships were the way to go as there was no formal budget to be submitted, debated and approved by Human Resources (HR). Nevertheless, as a matter of courtesy, I submitted a simple note on the estimated 'task-force expenses' to HR as a back-up and confirmed their 'secondments' of twelve months each for Tom and Fiona. HR wouldn't want anything less, because it just complicated their life and budget sheets if it was anything shorter. (Of course, in time, my efforts and foresight were both sad and ironic. The budget note was not necessary in the end – neither intern lasted more than four months. Both were claimed by Nigel – one in body, the other in spirit.)

While all this was going on I heard whisperings of a new policing body being set up to manage the evolving MDP challenge. Known unofficially as the 'z-squad', it would consist of the tougher police officers carrying firearms. They had to be, of course, comfortable with weapons, but also prepared to get up close and physical with the MDPs. The authorities had to insist on the requirement that pulling a weapon was not the first port of call. It wasn't shoot first, then ask questions (or cover up), later. Too many governments had fallen and politicians' careers and legacies had been compromised by such practices. No, if every MDP ended up as a shooting, it would create more turmoil, more attention, more politics.

The political leaders were also aware that attending to incidents was having its toll on the police officers. There had been trouble with crematoria and undertakers and the last thing the authorities wanted was for the morale of police personnel to take a dive. So it was that the z-squad was piloted. If successful, it would be rolled out across the capital.

I would like to think that some of my reports supporting the introduction of such specialist units helped in securing approval from the authorities. After all, I had made sure that I not only copied my reports and recommendations to the appropriate officials in the policing and security ranks, but also to influential colleagues in the civil service. I saw no harm in banking good will wherever I could. I spoke to the police commander reminding him that he was benefitting from my support. My charm would never win him over, but the hard-nosed commander was politically astute enough to know that having a supportive, report-writing civilian could have its benefits. In this context my requests for me (or anybody in my team) to be embedded in a z-squad were first met with a smirk, sigh, but eventually a nod.

'Describe me, or my team member, as a specialist advisor,' I said to Commander Rhodes. 'Government agencies are stuffed full of advisors. It's a term they recognise.'

'To be frank, as long as you keep the positive reports coming, I'm not worried,' Commander Rhodes replied. 'But be under no illusion, if this relationship is going to benefit you, it benefits us first.'

'Understood,' I said.

I had never thought of myself as one with machiavellian leanings, thinking it was beneath me, but I had not counted on the advantages it brought.

'Perhaps, you can help draft our rules of engagement?' Commander Rhodes said.

'They're changing?' I asked. 'First I've heard of it.'

'What do *you* think?' he replied. 'These squads are not to be messed with. If you give a weapon to these officers and ask them to go up against these MDP things, the officers are not going to sit around and debate ethics when the time comes. They will just open fire. So, we need you to write up the rules of engagement to ensure they are not shafted further down the line.'

I nodded. I confess I had a slightly different agenda in mind. There might come a time when I wanted the police to hold fire because I wanted to study the behaviour of the MDPs and not have them blasted them to kingdom come. But that was a discussion for another day. I needed to get embedded first.

'Again, understood,' I said.

'And we'll be needing your support for a few of our initiatives.'

'Go on.'

'We know that someone is infected with the plague when brain matter, bodily fluids are ingested through the nose, mouth, eyes.'

'Yes?'

'They need protection from exposure to this virus. It needs a different kind of uniform.'

I nodded and racked my brains for what he was after.

'The kit has to look the part…, if you know what I mean. In order to attract the best and keep the best in our ranks…'

'Look the part? Got it,' I whispered, nodding.

I did not hesitate getting to work on the report and rammed it full of data, warnings, threats, but built in slivers of hope, smart recommendations and concluded the report with a reassuring wave of remarks that could only be appreciated by brilliant readers. Should that reader be a politician or ambitious civil servant, he or she would reap the benefits a hundredfold.

It was a tricky needle to thread – appealing to the insatiable vanity of the politician while simultaneously planting seeds of fear if the report's contents were not heeded. It was a document that could never be written by a Cloth-Head.

Within a lunar cycle, the kit had been designed, issued and was in the field. And, boy, did it look the part. Black, rubberised, sleek, air-tight masks. Cool. Very cool. I did wonder how many design iterations the uniform had gone through – there was the danger this new squad might be mistaken for a sexual fetish group, but that had been avoided. All credit to the designer.

And the result of my initiative? My own interns could be safely embedded in the z-squads. Job done.

Now all I had to do was to try and establish why and how the MDPs were becoming socially organised. Was it a gene, another variant of the virus, something in the environment? Or was I seeing patterns in the clouds?

Little did I know at the time that responsibility lay with one, single, lone MDP itself.

8. Unknown Target A

Of course, I didn't know Nigel from the beginning. Nobody did. Although we didn't know his name, his presence was felt in those early days. He was everywhere. And nowhere. So, yes, there was a time before Nigel became known to us, but there wasn't really a time *before* Nigel. In hindsight, it seems so obvious. I don't know if it was down to our ineptitude, or Nigel's skill. Whichever, I don't think it would have made much difference….however much I might hope it would.

That said, in terms of our investigations – before Nigel became known to us – he was known as 'Unknown Target A'.

One of my early successes in z-squad deployment was being able to secure the funds for some additional observational or monitoring teams. I say 'teams', each team was really one person who acted as videographer, photographer, interviewer and record-taker. These additional interns would accompany police officers attending scenes where an MDP might be present. It was an improvement on the early days when we were relying solely on the reports of police officers (er, Cloth-Heads) working in the field. In those days the officers would write up their interactions with the MDPs. The reports were only useful to a point because, almost without fail, each interaction resulted in the obliteration of the deceased. However, fortunately for us, this practice of 'obliteration by firearm' slowed after a series of incidents were filmed by members of the public on their mobile phones as each 'deceased' met a (second) grisly end.

As the number of these incidents rose and the evidence was circulated on social media, protests and 'human rights' groups got involved, followed by the mainstream media. Within a relatively short period of time the police were obliged to rein in their aggressive use of force in 'making safe' any situation involving the undead.

Their body-cam footage, crime scene notes were mostly useless. How many times can one read this in a report?:

"The deceased approached the vehicle at a slow, albeit constant, pace. My colleague shouted at the mobile deceased individual instructing it to stop. The deceased failed to halt and proceeded to try and gain ingress into said vehicle with a blatant disregard for the living woman and her similarly alive child situated within the vehicular confines. After a second warning from my colleague (which went unheeded), we opened fire. The deceased was hit in the head multiple times and collapsed, holy [sic] deceased and immobile."

After weeks of reading reports like this we failed to learn anything about the MDP behaviour.

And so, after yet more weeks of protestations, I secured eight (one-man) teams to accompany the z-squads when responding to calls of events involving MDPs. (I kept calling them 'teams' thinking it would be easier should I try to expand the programme.) Initially, there seemed little to learn from my teams attending these incidents, but one evening as I was poring over reports and scrolling through images captured by my colleagues, I swear I started to see a few of the same MDPs appear at different incidents. They were captured not only on mobile phone cameras, the teams' cameras, but also on CCTV and other private security cameras. One of the first break-throughs came with the repeated sightings of two particular individuals breaking into premises and stealing high-end goods. They were known to the police in their 'previous life' so they were easy to identify – they were John

Reuel and Clive Staples, small-time crooks who robbed jewellery stores, stealing also electronic designer items to trade on the black market.

With this knowledge I frantically pressed my contacts for disclosure of police reports on seemingly innocuous crimes in the hope of catching Reuel and Staples in other 'less high-value' robbery settings. I managed to acquire CCTV of half-a-dozen shop burglaries by the now-deceased John Reuel and Clive Staples. Watching their behaviour in the premises, they seemed coherent, organised and intentional in their actions. They were not the rambling dead of yore.

I concluded that what I needed was CCTV of their earlier raids as MDPs. Had they shown a coherence in behaviour from the very first moment? It was when I was considering this, that a wave of horror and excitement washed over me. If Reuel and Staples were indeed regular thieves and johnny-no-goods, as the police had said, was it possible that they were even claimed by death *during* such a raid? If they were killed and converted by an MDP (or MDPs) while in progress of robbing a shop, might it be argued that the activity in which they were engaging in at the moment of their death had a direct influence on their behaviour as MDPs themselves? In other words, they were lost in a purgatory of their last moments? Locked in stasis, damned for eternity to repeat their last moments like a stuck needle on a spinning vinyl record? In death, at death.

Or were the habits of a lifetime to blame? A career of criminality that influenced their subsequent behaviour? Like muscle memory – but after death?

Truth be told, I was more excited at the prospect of the former theory – that the moment of death was crucial in predicting MDP behaviour. It would be a massive discovery. The moment of death could literally define the MDP. Therefore, what I needed was evidence of what Reuel and Staples were doing at the moment of death. Dare I, *dare I*, consider that there was CCTV evidence of the burglary in which they were first claimed?

I put both Tom and Fiona onto searching for evidence to support my theory as a matter of priority. We were, after all, trying to establish the behaviour of the MDPs, their organising capabilities. If I could take any evidence supporting the theory to Robbie and the authorities it might be the way to suggest new ways to manage the plague, predict the behaviour of the infected, and, in so doing, secure funding for further expansion of my activities.

Thus, I pressed Tom and Fiona to dig harder and deeper. They should closely coordinate with videographer teams to monitor any burglaries and respond to as many incidents as possible. It would be enormously challenging in a large metropolis such as London, but we had to try. If they were unable to attend an incident, then they must immediately try to obtain footage (CCTV, bodycam or other) from the police.

Even though we had some success, it was difficult to track-and-trace MDPs like Reuel and Staples. It was ironic that in recent times the authorities had set up systems to monitor the living on the supposition that it would save them (the living) from sickness and death. Yet all these same high-tech systems could not track-and-trace the dead, who had, ironically, reached a state beyond sickness.

Unfortunately, the deceased did not carry smartphones...yet (this was, of course, before Nigel took advantage of the Bean habit of carrying 'telephonic communication devices'). Compliance with these track-and-trace systems was not one of the habits that carried over into death. The authorities did have access to primitive face recognition technologies, but the degrading of the facial features of the dead made it largely redundant. DNA samples were acquired from crime scenes, but this was costly, slow and the samples were often degraded. Z-DNA technology was an entirely different challenge to 'normal' DNA.

Reuel and Staples were not our only leads, of course. The numbers of MDPs were rising across the metropolis and my teams were acquiring much useful footage of other activities. It created more work, of course, as we tried to determine if their behaviour, as MDPs, differed from their behaviour before their demise as Beans.

Of course, the matter was very sensitive and we were soon prevented from approaching the families of the deceased because of the complications arising from the rising profile of the humanitarian case for MDPs in the mainstream media. Some MDPs were identified by family members who then campaigned for their deceased family members to, at the very least, be treated with respect, even with full human rights. In time, the police were prevented from shooting dead (again) MDPs walking the streets even if they were attacking the living.

It was in this context that we were thwarted in being able to build up a picture of the deceased's life – their habits, behaviour, vices etc. – to see if behaviour really did carry over into death. It was a fateful, even cowardly, policy and instrumental in us losing ground in the fight against Nigel and his colleagues. It meant the plague established a foothold in the metropolis.

With my hands tied, I had to cover all options and try to keep all sorts of balls in the air. The trouble was, some of those balls were being juggled by my partners in crime – the police – and I was under no illusion that the police would drop many of them. There were moments when I had distinctly irritating reminders that the police could be a dead end. One crucial example was a report of a burglary in Camberwell that had most probably involved Reuel and Staples at about the time they went missing from the land of the living. The police report and other documentation of crime scene evidence referred to the existence of the shop's CCTV footage recorded during the robbery. The footage had been handed over to the police. And lost. Or deleted. Whichever, it was not available.

'Fucking typical' became my catchphrase answering the phone on more occasions than I care to mention. Such video footage could be evidence of the largest breakthrough in the study of death, the biggest story for 100,000 years, and a Cloth-Head had lost it.

The jewellery shop and electronic store in question was to be found in a fairly uninspiring part of town and the shop itself was on a regular street that, given the choice, you were more likely to avoid travelling along at night. The shop had a simple alarm that had been disabled. The thieves had gained access through the back of the shop having cut through the glass of the first floor window. The police photos and the police crime scene footage were giving off conflicting signals about the nature of the robbery. A number of the glass cabinets holding jewellery, electronic items (including smartphones and more) had been prised open with a degree of care. ('Care' in a standard-jewellery-thief sort of way.) This was at odds with many cabinets being completely smashed, which suggested less of a robbery and more of a struggle in the shop. But between whom?

The police had believed Reuel and Staples were the two thieves, but it was thought very unlikely that they would turn on one another. They had grown up two streets away from each other and had become long-term criminal partners who had been in and out of prison. Furthermore, both had gone missing immediately after the robbery. Police officers had followed up with the criminals' family and contacts, but, as expected, no information was forthcoming. Interestingly, the officers had noted the family members had seemed particularly pensive and sincere in their denials of having knowledge of the robbers' whereabouts.

I checked the dates. The timing worked – John Reuel and Clive Staples started appearing at similar heists a month or so later. The police assumed that the families had initially reported them missing to put the police off the scent. It was only when one of my police constable colleagues speculated in passing that perhaps that the two criminals were now possibly MDPs did they first appear on my radar.

But, unfortunately, still no CCTV.

Nevertheless, I put the word out among my police contacts that should they (or even any of their own contacts in the community) come across any information relating to the break-in, they must get in touch with me without delay.

All was not despair, however, there were a number of other deceased individuals who had enough of a police record to build up a picture that might just support my theory of behaviour carried over from life to death. One such line of enquiry was centred around a young woman called Ashli Eco.

Half-Filipina, Ashli had been in a mentally unhappy place for a number of years and had attempted suicide on a few occasions. The police had a record of her and had picked her up at a number of suicide spots around the country – bridges, parks, cliffs and beside train tracks. What we learned was that a number of people who had visited these suicide spots had not actually died by suicide. They had been attacked by an MDP. Using CCTV, the police had managed to piece together the movements of people around some of these incidents and Ashli had been identified. Initially, being known as someone with a suicidal ideation, it was thought coincidental that she was lingering in these places at the time of the incidents, but having been unable to identify an MDP responsible, it looked increasingly likely that Ashli was the culprit. We added her to our list of MDPs to look out for. We knew her past behaviour and it was looking as if she was retracing steps to her usual hang-outs.

So it was that we had two (almost) confirmed cases of MDPs 'acting out' on behaviour relating to their previous life. But another question arose: how had Ashli met her own demise?

It was very exciting. In death Reuel and Staples indulged in criminal work and Ashli, er, haunted her past stomping grounds. I pleaded to all police tiers of influence that all efforts be focused on these two to see if they could be tracked and understood. Then, when we were ready, I would work with Tom and Fiona and draw up a list of predictions of their behaviour. If I could present my findings (and thereby predict events), everything might change in terms of how we addressed the plague. But I was not naive enough to realise that everything could be lost in a flash of gunfire.

At this time I made every effort to pull strings, write emails, speak to police z-squad commanders and mutter veiled threats – Reuel, Staples and Ashli must not be 'taken out' under any circumstances. We needed to observe them, study them. Only then could we understand the best way to move forward, which was to everybody's benefit.

In hindsight was this the right decision? Who knows. Much later, as I pondered on events in the last light-darks of the apocalypse in a portakabin surrounded by fire and the panicking, crying American military personnel, I did wonder if I had made a mistake. But, no, I told myself. It would have made no difference. After all, by keeping Reuel, Staples and Ashli as functioning MDPs, it led us eventually to their leader – which gave us a fighting chance.

We began to acquire evidence of Reuel, Staples and Ashli operating in the same group, or rather, network. We caught them at a number of gatherings. Were they learning from each other? Were they sharing skills? As MDPs they could act in groups or independently. Sometimes they switched roles. It was almost as if they were players on the sports park being swapped on and off the field of play. Although, by this stage I was not conscious of the obvious question – who or what was managing them? Switching them back and forth? Adjusting partnerships? Identifying targets? Managing skills development? Coaching? Dealing with strategy?

If I had been a little less busy, I might have become more conscious of this question, but with so much going on and so much at stake, I remained focused on what I could do and what I could learn about how the MDPs were evolving.

There was a turning point for me. With my teams tracking these three individuals (I told them to video record anything and everything), we acquired masses of footage. Using long telephoto lenses (often in poor light) meant many of the images we acquired were poor, so we struggled to identify the acquaintances of Ashli, Reuel and Staples. I was not prepared for the next development.

Fiona would regularly bring me other footage. In time, we began to see on a regular basis others in the company of our three targets. Some were obviously MDPs (visible body damage, facial injuries), others less so. There was a young woman in a white blouse covered in splashes of dried blood who would often be in the company of a male with a broken neck (that soon acquired a type of neck brace). We were beginning to see glimpses of a tall, dread-locked man very poorly disfigured, perhaps by fire. To date, the MDPs had not used fire as a means of inducing death, so it was an interesting development. I asked Tom to look into the origins of 'Fireman'. There were other MDPs, of course, but these seemed the most skilled and organised. Finally, there was a character that might have been around for a while but had been missed, or rather 'dismissed', as a threat. It was a blond, blue-eyed, angelic-looking, young child who was often seen loitering in the vicinity of the MDP group. At first we thought she was a lost child and in danger of being snatched by the MDPs, but there were anecdotal reports that she was also proving to be dangerous. On one occasion it was alleged that two police officers tried to snatch her away to safety, but the child turned on the two officers so swiftly and viciously that the whole police team had to retreat to safety leaving the two Cloth-Heads to their fate. It was certainly a disconcerting report and whether it was indeed a young child, I could not be sure; but this was not the shock I am talking about.

The shock was the repeated sightings of a slim, hooded figure moving quietly on the fringes.

'It's a female,' said Tom, confidently.

'Why do you say that?' asked Fiona.

'The way it moves,' replied Tom. 'Fast, agile. Not too much body mass.'

'Maybe muscle mass has rotted away?' said Fiona with a touch of indignation. 'Decomposition before it rose.'

Normally I would add my two cents to discussions, but I remained quiet. I was managing my stomach – it had just fallen through the floor. The cause? A realisation. A fear. I knew Tom was not being disrespectful to the MDP. It was clear the MDP was very effective. It was a shame the MDP's hood prevented any clear identification as to its gender, but there was a part of me that was thankful. The revelation was something I could do without, I was finding to my surprise. I was inclined to agree with Tom. It looked like a woman. An athletic, sporty woman. Aggressive and effective.

'Perhaps a martial artist,' said Tom, studying the figure on the screen.

I'm surprised neither Tom nor Fiona picked up on my reticence as I licked my lips to counter the dryness of my mouth.

Although the hunt for Mia had been the trigger for my interest in MDPs, I had not seen a sign of her for months, so I presumed either I was mistaken and she had never visited the houseboat at night, or she had been lost to a fight and succumbed to her injuries. Or perhaps she had been obliterated in police gunfire before there had been a moratorium on destroying MDPs.

I felt sick and weak. I was seeing shapes and patterns in the plague clouds gathering over my life and the metropolis. I couldn't get sentimental about my work. London had a population of ten million people. The odds this martial artist was Mia were tiny.

Nevertheless, I needed to change the subject and my eye fell upon another figure on the edge of the video frame.

'Who's this guy?' I asked Fiona, pointing at the tall, slim figure with a zen-like manner. I had just realised that this figure was often in the centre of the group before an incident then he would hang back and observe, only joining in at the end.

'No idea,' she replied. 'But he does seem to crop up in other places too.'

'He seems to be acquainted with all of these MDPs,' I said, determined not to let the conversation slip back to Mia.

'He's been around for a while,' said Tom.

'Yes, it is true,' said Fiona, warming to the idea. 'I've seen him with Staples, Reuel, Ashli Eco and even with the Fireman guy.'

'And the baby girl kid,' said Tom, warming to the idea.

'So, why don't we know him?' I asked, playing the grumpy boss.

'He's always been on the outskirts. More like a hanger-on. So we thought he was not that important.'

I raised my eyebrows in a familiar sign of questioning annoyance.

'We think he is one of the old ones,' Tom protested, 'so not so relevant.'

'Or, could he, in fact, be more of a mentor then?' I asked. 'If he is indeed an "old one".'

'Maybe.' Tom replied, eyes wide in a questioning manner as if it was the first time he had considered it.

'Do we have a name for him in his previous life?' I asked.

Both Tom and Fiona shook their heads, seemingly embarrassed.

'I thought we had identified all the old ones?' I continued.

'Yes. I mean, no. In the early days they were all incinerated pretty quickly and the records were pretty good. However, we have heard rumours that when the crematoria staff went on strike and before the other facilities were put in place, there were a few that escaped one crematorium's premises in particular. So, there might be a handful of old MDPs out there that have never been accounted for. The records would list them as incinerated so we ignored them, but they might be MDPs.'

I studied the pictures again including those of the robbers, John Reuel and Clive Staples.

'We still have no idea which MDP acquired Reuel and Staples? Maybe in the Camberwell jewellers burglary?' I asked.

'No,' replied Fiona. 'Still no CCTV from the police yet. Still missing.'

'Lost, you mean,' said Tom.

'Chase that CCTV,' I said, sensing we were missing a piece of the jigsaw. 'And we need to know who he is,' I said, pointing to the tall, slim, aloof MDP in the picture with an ever so slight premonition coming over me. 'Let's see if his Z-DNA leads us anywhere.'

'Z-DNA?'

'Do we have his Z-DNA profile?' I asked.

'No,' said Fiona, shaking her head. 'But we do have a couple dozen unidentified Z-DNA profiles.'

'Might these be new variants?' asked Tom. 'How do we know if these new variants are not mixing?'

We were getting results back from the lab. The science of Z-DNA was in its infancy, but the scientists were catching up. The z-virus was destroying normal DNA so a lot of the techniques for comparing DNA samples had to be completely re-worked. The DNA strands of an infected person would break, distort, and it was almost impossible to use the sample to trace back to a living person. *However*, there was hope this new science could trace the infection i.e. it could trace death, but not life. It might be possible to identify the MDP (and its ancestral line) from the DNA sample. Perhaps, in time, we could establish which MDPs were successfully operating in London and recruiting the most followers. If we could discern a pattern of infection around the capital (and the MDPs responsible) we could come up with a plan.

'Should we get one of the teams to keep an eye out for him?' asked Fiona, turning to me.

'Yes. And for now, let's call him "Unknown Target, er...A".'

9. Felicity's Laptop

Felicity Goodban was a graduate of the University of Kent with a degree in History. She was thirty-four years old at the time of her death. She was (or had been) a reasonably attractive young woman, but had had a patchy love life. She had dated Dr Richard Hughes for three years after her stint as a student, but it had fizzled out.

So it was that I learned about the background to the (presumed) late-Felicity Goodban. Fiona had done excellent work at putting together a profile of the young woman – often by surreptitious means. I had turned a blind eye to Fiona's violation of all our procedures to investigate the best lead we had. As a result, Fiona had approached family and friends and had used her Welsh charm to good effect. By now Fiona, Tom and I had a strong hunch Felicity was indeed 'dead and well' in the metropolis. If we could find her, watch her and compare her to how she lived her life before death with that of her death-life as an MDP, it would provide absolutely crucial evidence on the behaviour of the dead and how they carried over behaviour (or not) from their previous existence.

Having graduated, Felicity had moved into graphic design and had a mix of working with small agencies and as a freelancer. She had exhibited an interest in other creative endeavours. There were references to her wanting to write her first novel – about, quelle surprise, a young single woman making her way through life in the capital.

At the age of thirty-two and with the help of a small inheritance from her beloved grandmother, Felicity bought the smallest of one bedroom flats in Balham. The inheritance paid for the deposit of the flat. It squeezed her finances and she lived frugally while continuing to do freelance graphic design work. Hit hard by the loss of her beloved grandmother, and generally unhappy, she split up with her then-boyfriend Rupert. She spent more time in her flat and to keep her company she had acquired a cat that she named Grace, after her grandmother. She was at a low-ish point in her life in the metropolis and obviously became very attached to the cat.

I had made a point of treating her disappearance as a possible MDP attack. I mobilised colleagues to work on this assumption. If we were correct, then it would be the first time we had been 'there at the beginning' of the birth or conception (whatever the word) of an undead. It was also an opportunity to explore all sorts of avenues and exploit any piece of technology to monitor the development of the plague and the behaviour of the infected. As part of this track-and-trace exercise, her flat had been thoroughly examined just in case it led to some interesting developments. Her laptop had been seized and interrogated by the police. The unofficial word was that it contained nothing of interest. Nothing other than some non-contentious social media activity, a fictional blog of life in modern day London and various design work.

I had my own list of things I too wanted to review. I was not expecting much, but we hoped to glean something from her social media accounts. Perhaps the blog or diary might describe her state of mind. Of course, I fully expected any entries to stop at her disappearance, so the laptop was of limited value, but as the weeks went on its existence niggled me. It could give us a base-line of behaviour and, if she did turn up as an MDP, we might be able to predict her behaviour, even her attacks rather than join the dots afterwards as we had done with Ashli, Reuel and Staples.

So, I was pleased when the laptop did indeed find its way to me. Its arrival had been delayed, not so much as a result of police indifference, but because of complications arising from administrative matters.

To be generous, there had been a typo – someone had written the phrase 'the infested' and referred to 'infested persons' and the 'infested collective' rather than using the word 'infection' or derivations of the word thereof. To be less generous it was a poor choice of word, to put it mildly. Anyway, the document in which the terms had been used had found its way into the public domain and somebody somewhere had objected. References to an 'infestation' in the capital (often concentrated in particular boroughs) were especially objectionable, apparently. As a result, there was a clamp-down on nomenclature in all government documentation. Even internal reports had to go through a word-audit committee to check wording and phrases, not only for those words or descriptions perceived to be objectionable on *that* particular day, but also to anticipate what might be objected to in the future. Regardless, protest groups continued to spring up. Individuals on social media took it as their solemn duty to complain to the Press and to government agencies. Often the government caved, fearing litigation – bad Press and damaged election appeal. Not only that, court cases spurred on by families and pressure groups became more regular.

Why am I telling you this? Because it had an impact on how information was shared between the departments. If there is ever an authoritative history of these times, it should not only blame the downfall of civilisation on a virus, but also mankind's folly. Human existence had turned in on itself and viewed the planet only as a collection of Bean systems. It was this insularity that impeded the containment of the plague and what it brought about – namely the rise of the MDPs. Arguably the MDPs were the physical manifestation (a living death and an all-powerful devourer) of what had happened to Beankind's systems.

It was in this context that Felicity's computer was delayed in arriving at my office. When I did receive it – hand-delivered by a grumpy Cloth-Head – it was dumped on my desk with a shrug and the words 'there's nothing on there. Enjoy.'

My mistake was that I took the Cloth-Head at his word, at least initially. The police forensics had broken through the device's passwords, so everything was accessible. The police forensics teams also supplied a handful of other passwords (including to back-up Cloud accounts) – any remaining passwords were provided by the various tech companies on receipt of court orders. Reports from Internet streaming companies suggested Felicity had not watched any films, drama and anything online from the date of her disappearance and had in fact ceased on the evening of the 'thud-squish' event. I scanned the forensics report noting lists of images, word-processing documents, bank statements, email correspondence. It looked as if everything on the hard drive had stopped on the date of the birthday celebration of the couple living in the flat below.

So far, so interesting, but also, so useless. It confirmed she was indeed missing, presumed dead. If she was now an MDP we would have to confirm that too before we spent too much time picking through her past life. We did not have the time to conduct a deep-dive into all leads.

Consequently all teams were on the lookout for an MDP matching Felicity's description. Of course, there was no knowing how much decomposition had taken place. It was possible that she would not be identified by facial recognition technology embedded in some of the CCTV camera systems around the capital. Nevertheless I was hopeful.

For this reason I did not interrogate Felicity's laptop as a matter of urgency....until, that is, I did, a few weeks later.

It was a slow day. I was fed up with sending emails, chasing down leads, hunting for new cases that might be relevant and everybody was out of the office working on business I had decided as a priority. 'Leave it to the teams to come to me, for once,' I reassured myself. It was going to be a slow, late afternoon in the office with just me.

Not feeling too guilty, I nipped out, picked up a coffee and a couple of pastries – I'll just serve out the last few hours then mooch on home to my houseboat.

With my feet up on the table tucking into my cinnamon whirl and sipping a cafe latte, my eyes drifted out to the skyline of London out of the window, then moved slowly inside my office to the piles of paper reports from the police, stacks of hard-drives containing videos of possible sightings. Finally, my eyes alighted on the laptop on a side-table. Damn, I haven't looked at it, I thought. But maybe I can spend the last hour or so 'working' by reviewing its contents. Maybe that rumoured blog or diary of Felicity's might throw up some useful ideas, I pondered. Perhaps she mentioned her favourite places I could get Tom to visit. Or perhaps it referred to a network of friends I could get Fiona to interrogate, just in case it led to a mobile, deceased Felicity.

With that, I retrieved the laptop from its pile. Flipped it open and, with a coffee in one hand and pastry in the other, navigated my way with my little finger on the touchpad, moved between files and scrolled through images, documents.

I was conscious that files of interest might not only be confined to the computer's harddrive; there might be more on the Cloud service backups. But an early attempt to log on to our Wifi was thwarted by our own departmental WiFi firewall security. Reviewing any additional files saved in the Cloud would have to wait – and only done with careful supervision to ensure nothing was inadvertently lost in an ever so common 'IT failure'.

Nevertheless there seemed to be ample files to review that formed part of the 'blog'...if that is what it was.

There were numerous MSWord files in no particular order. Some files were only half a page, others, many pages long. They were oddly named (if named at all). Dipping in and out of the documents, my confusion slowly turned to curiosity.

The files formed a loose narrative – was this what the police report had referred to as Felicity's blog? There were entries that read more dark and novelistic in nature than a factual account. At times it read as violent fiction. Darker than anything I had ever read, even in my youth – a time when I experimented with all the usual rebellious stuff. I was struggling to comprehend what Felicity must have been thinking when she was typing out these passages.

She was writing (in the first person) in the character of an MDP who was wandering around London murdering people with, what I can only describe as, a muted glee. She was questioning their existence and pitying their lives before dispatching them – to become an MDP. She even described a learned desire to nurture their development.

It all started with a passage of the narrator (a male, it seemed) 'rising' from a waste-dump south of the 'Black Road' (as 'he' called it), which I took to be the River Thames. He had other words for the living – 'Beans' – and the MDPs he called 'Muters'. There was a passage on his 'first feed' – an attack of a group of 'Beanteens' in a park late at night. He described his delight at the delicious devouring of the youths. This was followed by a passage of him stalking a pair of lovers before violently attacking the female (of twenty-five 'summers') and, once again, delighting at the 'pale, smooth vistas of [the] unblemished flesh' of her abdomen, before gorging on the 'Lover-Bean'.

Then, after a few 'light-darks' ('days', I presumed), the narrator spoke of the first acquisition of his first follower (or 'colleague'). I wondered at the power of Felicity's imagination or whether she was projecting her fantasies through the character. In this scene set on a rooftop of, presumably a London residence, the narrator was in discussion with a man who was complaining about his lot in life – an important relationship had apparently broken down and the Bean was claiming to be a victim of life. It seemed a fairly typical description of a thirty- or forty-something man in mid-life and career throes. The narrator – Felicity's hero – was listening attentively and pitying him, not in the way a normal person would pity someone experiencing strife, but pitying the very existence of the (suicidal) man. After a while the narrator said he grew bored at the complaining man – 'self-pity is not a spectator sport' – and threw the complaining man off the roof, granting the Bean his final wish.

I scrolled through other documents and passages and managed to piece together a rough timeline of events. The passages that followed described the narrator waiting for his friend, his colleague, to rise. As he waited for a few days (light-darks) he killed another 'Lady Bean' dog owner and stored her in a safe place before she too was expected to rise. At the end of this particular passage the narrator described the rising of his first colleague who he christened 'RooftopSuicide' or 'Rooftop' for short. What was curious was that the narrator was naming his new friends by the manner of their death or something related to their death. The dog owner was named 'DogSmells'. I didn't pay not much attention to it at the time, but it was an interesting notion that a person could be named at the point of death that began to haunt me much later as the narrator acquired more 'colleagues'.

The final passages available on the laptop described the narrator following RooftopSuicide to a London residence that I (and the narrator himself) deduced was the home of Rooftop's former partner. On opening the front door the partner recognised Rooftop and initially tried to engage in conversation before she realised Rooftop was now a Mobile Deceased Person. She did not last long. In a brutal few moments both Rooftop and the narrator attacked the young lady Bean in the hallway splashing her white coloured blouse in 'juice' while also dispatching her partner who tried to come to the rescue. The narrator and Rooftop then dragged their new 'colleague'-to-be to the rooftop and stuffed her in between the chimneys where she would remain until she would no doubtedly rise a few light-darks later. Not only this, but horror of horrors, the narrator also left a young child to die on the rooftops, trapped in the same hiding place as the yet-to-rise 'ColourSplash'.

All of these episodes were interspersed with passages on the narrator reflecting on life. It threw me initially as it was a little odd. We always assume reflection and rumination on existence ends at the moment of death, but here was a creature (albeit fictional) engaged in reflections on life *after* death.

I was getting very tired and I gave up on the idea of returning home for a good night's sleep and my mind was a whirl of information. Was I learning anything useful about Felicity's state of mind? Were these passages in fact more informative about her state-of-mind than any discussion with her friends and family? They were perhaps far more useful than a 'deep-dive' on her social media?

Was Felicity in fact unwell? Suffering from mental health issues? In the middle of a psychological episode? Had she sunk into a depression, then had a mental breakdown? Was this evidence of her being in a suicidal frame of mind – living vicariously through death and using MDPs as a means to do it? And where did this cannibalistic impulse come from?

She was writing as if she were a male. Was this evidence of a split personality? A conscious or unconscious way of expressing an unholy rage? Or was this evidence of a creative soul at work? Was she exploring a dark side of herself? Subverting her image as a regular woman trying to make her way in London?

Whichever, it was both compelling and unnerving.

In the very early hours I settled down on the campbed in the corner of the office to snatch a few hours of sleep. Before I dozed off I made a mental note to check in with our IT services team to see if we could log on to any Cloud account service to see if there were any other files of use that might have been deleted. We might at least be able to see when the files in my possession had been backed up (if at all). It might give an indication of Felicity's movements and intentions. It had to be done with care. Not only because I did not want it to get out that I was looking into the authenticity of a blog, but, right now, it was the only lead that might lead to a breakthrough.

His Name Was Nigel

10. The Juggler

Like any new line-manager, I soon fell into the habit of offering tips to my team. "Tips are the tipping point," I would say to Tom and Fiona. "You never know when the tipping point will come and what the gold nugget, a silver bullet, will look like."

It was my attempt to be an encouraging line-manager. Mixing, nay, crushing metaphors was something I hadn't intended to do, but I was new to line-managing after all and rarely planned motivational speeches. Unfortunately, the words would come back to haunt me. Clues, tips, theories, tidbits of information would come our way day in, day out, from interactions with the police, civil servants and administrators, the general public. Gold nuggets, diamonds were rarely presented on a platter. It was a matter of patiently sifting through the rubbish hoping that something might glint in the murkiness begging to be saved. Once retrieved and placed on the scales of investigation, they would change the story and the pile-on of mixed metaphors would not matter a jot.

In a similar fashion, I would encourage Tom and Fiona to both question and log everything before bringing them to me to consider. My reasoning was, in part, selfish – they would have the mundane business of filtering the rubbish before I saw it. The trouble was, this meant that whenever Tom and Fiona *did* bring something to me I had to give them the time of day. There's no point in saying "look at and question everything" if I didn't look at everything they brought to me.

I had largely forgotten this arrangement in the days following my perusal of the files on Felicity's computer. The morning after my first interrogation of the laptop I had contacted the IT team and pressed for an urgent task to be undertaken by their best, most reliable technician. I learned, somewhat indignantly, that in my role I was not able to request an 'urgent' review. I swallowed my pride and indignation, wishing for the day when the apocalypse made it up their list of priorities. In the meantime, I would have to wait – for wait, I must, because I did not trust anybody else to handle it. I did not even alert Tom and Fiona to my discovery, nor hint at my emerging theory. I did not want to contradict my own standards. I needed a solid body of evidence to back up my theory about Felicity's state of mind. Therefore I fought to remain patient and wait for the moment when I could personally hand over the laptop to the best technician I could find.

I had a clear set of requirements for the laptop that I felt obliged to share with the IT technician. I wanted him or her to configure secure access to any Cloud service and files without there being any possibility of corrupting files or permissions on the computer harddrive or in the Cloud. I also wanted security installed on the device that meant I could only access its contents in 'read-only' mode. I didn't want to screw up any files or settings; I certainly did not want to change anything – including 'date modified' on any documents. I did not want to trigger any auto-correct nor inadvertently wipe over previous versions. My final request to IT was that I wanted to access the Cloud files from off-site i.e. from my houseboat without compromising the files in any way. Long hours in the office were resulting in fatigue and I wanted to take time to study the laptop from my houseboat.

While I was waiting patiently for the return of the laptop, my mixed-metaphor-gold-nugget-in-the-rubbish-strategy bore fruit. Tom and Fiona's efforts in questioning everything did turn up a diamond. I was reminded that my own lead – Felicity's laptop – was not the only game in town. No one thing would crack the case – it would be a fruit salad of clues, stronger and tastier if cooked up and served together. When Tom and Fiona brought their lead to me I was grateful that I bit my tongue and let them brief me in full, without interruption.

Normally we would only ever investigate theories and leads if there was something credible to go on – DNA, clear CCTV, decent quality mobile phone footage, a home that had been raided, good reliable witnesses, whatever. But they brought no new footage of a previously unknown MDP behaviour, nor anything concrete that changed the current understanding of Mobile Deceased Persons. On the face of it, there was nothing new, but it had the whiff of 'the everything' about it.

Arriving excited in my office, they shared the news of what they thought might be gold. I nodded and said nothing.

They thrust a laptop in front of me and pointed at the video clip while giving me a commentary as it played. The image on the laptop screen was nothing but a shaky brief clip of mobile phone footage; their commentary was about a reported death in the capital that was being ignored by the police.

The case was a late-thirty-something male who had been set alight and burned to death, according to witnesses, by a handful of youths. What was unusual was that, reportedly, the victim had been carried away by an MDP. Evidence was scant. There was no CCTV, no formal police statements, no dead body, no individual reported missing (or family clamouring for their missing loved one) and no confirmed involvement of MDPs from any emergency service. The alleged victim didn't have a name – or at least a name known by any person or government agency – nor did he have an address. Not that I have anything against loners or homeless people, I know how difficult it can be to hold down a living if you fall below the breadline, but at least those with a regular life can be tracked and traced. We never found his name, so he (ironically, I noted) was given the name of something related to his moment of death.

The 'juggler' had been seen around in the vicinity of Notting Hill on and off for years. He would turn up on street corners and on the edge of markets juggling his skittles during the day. At night he would use flammable sticks, by day he would juggle and sword-swallow. A big man, perhaps of Jamaican heritage, he was an imposing figure, but by all accounts he was a gentle soul. Always polite and grateful when passers-by threw coins into his cap laid out on the pavement in front of him. It must have been a difficult job sword-swallowing and juggling, oftentimes with hazardous burning sticks, for hours at a time.

Fiona said she had done some preliminary investigation and it was a case worth following up. The shaky camera phone footage had been pulled from a very short excerpt from a video shared on social media, but it was of poor quality. In short, it did not pass any of my tests in its current state. Not only was there no evidence (physical or otherwise) of MDP involvement, but there was no track-and-traceable behaviour of the victim or of any MDP. It was just a tragic death, a (presumed) murder in the capital city, possibly involving teenage boys. Hardly big news.

I think my expression said it all.

'We think we can pull a few usable frames from the footage,' said Fiona, hopefully, '...and there are a few witnesses on the video who said that the person who carried the juggler away was an MDP.'

'You say the person who took the footage was drunk?' I asked with a hint of indifference. 'Hardly reliable.'

'We can track the witnesses down. There are reports that the four teenage boys involved in the attack went missing in the area that night,' said Fiona, her hope morphing into a plea. 'Maybe they were victims of the MDP too?'

'Sounds more like gangland shenanigans? Not our business,' I said, purposefully challenging her to fight her corner. 'Do we have confirmation the missing boys were in the vicinity immediately prior to the attack?'

'No.'

'Do we have any footage of the boys being attacked or abducted?'

'No, but we are almost certain the boys were the ones who set the juggler alight,' said Tom, jumping in.

'I think this could be the origin of the Fireman we have seen with Ashli, John Reuel and Clive Staples and the Unknown Target A,' said Fiona excitedly, now rallying.

I sighed. I wanted to keep Fiona onside, but I was learning it could be an effort. That's the trouble with line-management, you have to expend energy on keeping youth motivated. Don't get me wrong, it is important, because I know full well that a motivated young person is not only more productive, but less draining for the supervisor. That said, I have to confess that there was something in their presentation that warranted further investigation. It had potential. There was a whiff of something.

'Do we have any footage or reports of where the juggler victim was carried off to?' I asked.

'No,' Fiona replied. 'We've checked hospitals already.'

'But it could be a good samaritan?'

'Yes, but no. The person who filmed it said it was a tall, slim dead guy – his face partially torn off. Possibly the Unknown Target A.'

'Well, there are two questions you need to address: firstly, is the deceased juggler the same as the Fireman MDP? Cross-reference timelines, compare heights and bodily proportions with the images we have of the Fireman. Secondly, a fireball in the street must have attracted a lot of attention. There should be other phone footage available. Keep an eye on social media to see if any images or footage has been uploaded while being aware that not everybody wishes to upload stuff to the Internet. It may come from a different route.'

'Great, I will,' said Fiona, sighing with relief.

'But bear in mind, the details in any other footage will be similarly burnt out by the flames.'

'Can I send the footage we have for analysis?'

'Yes, but be selective what you send – it costs money and it means they will probably turn any enhancement around quicker.'

'Great. Will do, thanks Josh.'

It was a tiring business dealing with crimes and violence.

'It is a shocking business,' I muttered, despairing at the images of the juggler's grisly end allegedly at the hands of teenagers. 'Dare I say it, but if those boys did meet a messy end at the hands of an MDP, maybe there is justice in this life.'

'Justice in death, I like it,' muttered Fiona, with a smile and wink.

'Justice for an unknown man who spent his days quietly getting by. Shame he didn't have a chance to use his sword on the teenagers.'

'You think this juggler is the Fireman-guy Tom is looking into?' I said, nodding at Fiona's colleague standing beside her.

'Looks very possible,' said Fiona, a smidge pleased.

'Well, then, why don't you two both liaise and do your jobs?'

I didn't have to wait long.

Three days later I received an urgent phone call from Fiona. She was on the other side of town.

'Can you get to Pimlico Police Station now?'

'Er, why? Why can't you? I'm a …'

'Now,' she interrupted, 'I'm miles away. We have a witness at the Pimlico station wanting to share something with the police about the juggler incident, but the police receptionist thinks the witness might not stay.'

'So?' I asked bemused. 'It's not my job to run around for you.'

'One of my police reception leads has phoned me saying someone has walked into the police station.'

'Again, I feel I have to repeat myself. "So…?" '

'They have video, Josh,' she shouted down the phone, almost drowned out by traffic. 'A witness. With video. Of both the Juggler and the MDP that carried him away.'

'Have they uploaded it to social media?'

'No, it's an old guy with a simple smartphone. He doesn't have social media accounts or email on his phone and doesn't know how to do it even if he did.'

And with that, I was gone. I headed down to Pimlico and met the witness. It was a man, Arthur, in his late-seventies who had been given the phone by his daughter as a means of communicating with his grandchildren living on the other side of the country using a live video-chat app. His skills were limited to switching on the camera and recording, that was it. Apparently.

Arthur and I chatted in the station reception as we both sized up the other. Sensing I needed to impress and reassure him, I waved my ID at the receptionist, dropped the name of the local DCI Inspector and requested access to a quiet interview room. Moving into the room the old gent and I chatted some more and I learned that, when taking a late evening stroll, he had witnessed a sudden ball of fire explode on the street ahead of him. To his horror, he could see a man flailing about in the flames. He instantly thought of the juggler who he had often seen at that same spot. Arthur couldn't be sure why the juggler had burst into flames, but the old man suspected mischief knowing the lawlessness in the area. Furthermore, he saw what could have been youths running away from the scene.

Arthur had raced to the scene with a handful of others – some of whom had stumbled out of the pub. A few of them had tried to

David O. Zeus

put out the burning man, but the fire was too intense. He pulled out his phone to call the police, but others were quicker than him. Seeing others filming the incident on the phone he was at first disgusted, then realised that if he did the same it might provide some evidence for the police investigation. So, with his phone already in his hand, he filmed some footage as best he could.

Although technically a smartphone, Arthur's device was a primitive model with a small screen. He showed me the video and it looked promising – a ball of fire almost burning out the image, figures moving about trying to help, then about sixty seconds into the ghastly episode a figure walks up slowly to the now-unmoving juggler (with sword still strapped to his back) curled up on the ground. Interestingly, Arthur's footage also caught the reaction of others crowded over the dying (and still burning) juggler. Rather than remaining close to the injured man, the crowd moved away as this figure joined them. It was a strange sight. The new arrival bent over the juggler, slung him over his shoulder, sword and all, and walked away into the darkness.

'Why didn't you hand this over to the police,' I asked Arthur as calmly as possible, desperately trying to suppress my, dare I say, excitement. Although the phone's screen was too small to really determine how much useful information was there, it looked far better than the footage Fiona had pulled from social media.

'I hung around for a while,' replied Arthur with a mix of hurt and indignation, 'but I didn't see the point as so many others were there. Besides, I didn't get any footage of the attackers. A bunch of young lads, I was told by others who were there before me. It's criminal, I tell you. The little bastards. Anyway, I left the scene as I was getting cold and thinking the other witnesses would share the story. I intended to bring the footage to the police station. Not that it will help catch the bastards.'

'Right..,' I muttered. Arthur was unaware that I had no real interest in the teenage bastards, just the good Samaritan.

'This is my second attempt to bring it in. They keep me waiting as if it's not important.'

'What happened the first time you came in?' I asked.

'I gave it to the police officer, he looked at it, said there was not much to see, but he asked if he could take my phone. But I can't give him my phone. This is how I communicate with my grandchildren.'

I nodded.

In the circumstances, I explained to Arthur that if he and I jumped into a cab together, we could go to my building, download the footage and then put him in a cab home with his phone intact. Arthur agreed. Within an hour, I had downloaded the footage and put the kind, helpful gentleman in the cab home never to see him again.

I had a hunch it was as golden as gold could be in the circumstances.

I was buzzing. Maybe Fiona's instinct had been right. Maybe there was something in the incident. If this was 'Unknown Target A' saving a 'Bean' (in what I thought, at the time, was Felicity's word), that would be extraordinary. I checked with authorities and asked if any unidentified charred corpse had been found in the ten days following the incident. The answer came back negative. So, before Fiona and Tom arrived back at base, I set up the office ready for us to spend a few hours studying Arthur's footage on a large screen, taking screenshots and comparing it with CCTV and other reports to establish if the Fireman MDP was indeed the juggler. Nobody would describe him as a 'juggler' of course, but, assuming the fire had severely disfigured him, the report of a tall, scary MDP would rise to the top of reports. If we could place the Fireman-Juggler alongside his rescuer and back it up with video footage of both the rescue and their subsequent working relationship, that would indeed be…a gold nugget salad. A real coup d'or.

11. The Break-in

Fiona and Tom were as equally excited as me when they arrived breathless at the office and we headed to a mini-conference room in which we had now set up a large television screen operated from a laptop. Arthur's footage did not disappoint. As Fiona and I examined every frame, Tom pored over the reports and images of the Fireman seen at incidents he had been working on for weeks. It was a double bingo – we managed to pull clean images of the Unknown Target A crouching over and tending to the 'deceased' juggler. Tom managed to get clean images from incidents caught on CCTV that gave us comparisons of the juggler's long trench coat, with black leather patches and trims, that matched the coat that was visible in Arthur's footage as the Unknown Target A lifted the juggler over his shoulder and carried him away. Facial comparison of the juggler with the Fireman was more tricky, but Fireman's features were clearly consistent with burn injuries. The fire was fierce enough to melt the features and skin with the trench coat giving the MDP's appearance as one red, brown and black, melted alien organism.

All in all, I was satisfied Arthur's footage coupled with Tom's research was convincing evidence of primitive forms of intelligent coordination, even community cohesion in the MDP community. We could prove, visually, that the Unknown Target A had rescued the juggler and within a few weeks they were both working together. Tom and Fiona were wholly convinced, but I felt obliged to be the cynic in the room. After all, we would certainly encounter cynicism from Robbie and others.

'No, we need more,' I muttered.

'Why?' both interns protested. 'It's a slam-dunk, surely?'

'It could be a coincidence.'

'Coincidence?!' the interns spat in unison.

'Prove it's not a coincidence,' I said calmly.

'Surely, that's, that's…a non-falsifiable theory. It's not valid,' they protested.

'My supervisory colleagues and their betters (government ministers) are not as well-informed as you. That will mean nothing to them,' I said, nodding at the television screen.

I surprised myself – it silenced them both. They were turning into a proper double-act.

Then, as chance would have it, there was a breakthrough in the Reuel and Staples case. My own careful nurturing of relationships with the police was paying off.

What always surprised me at this time in the 'apocalypse', if I can call it that, was that I still found myself falling into episodes of complacency. I suppose it is the human condition. I almost dismissed the telephone caller that brought things together.

Inevitably a lot of calls were coming into the office and, of course, I would have to bat many of them away. Sometimes they were from other government departments, a few stray journalists (who I directed elsewhere – I wasn't going to enter that minefield) and then a few international calls from government bodies, law enforcement personnel, academics who all wanted to pick my brains and develop relationships. I didn't know how they had found my details as my work (and indeed my role) was off all official listings. Besides, I didn't have the inclination or energy to start conversations with friends or foes overseas – it would only complicate my life. Of course, the virus had popped up in other places across the world, but the MDPs were isolated and contained effectively. London had been a different story, partly because of its size but also because the government had purposefully adopted a low-key approach (i.e. no hint of a health scare, let alone a lockdown) to minimise media and public fall-out. Recent pandemics had re-written rules and drawn lines on government overreach. Democratic administrations across the world had learned similar things – the lessons from (and fears of) 'panpanics' were very much at the forefront of politicians' minds. So, it was in this context that, early one morning, I received a call from a rather timid-sounding woman. She asked after me by name and explained she was from Camberwell police station.

'Are you a dispatcher?' I asked, after she had introduced herself.

'No, I am a community support officer doing some desk work while on reduced service. (As a 'Community Support Officer', she wasn't even a proper police officer. She was a cheap part-timer, for Christ's sake.)

'But I'm also a Fraud Investigation clerk in an insurance firm in Camberwell.'

(What does a Fraud Investigation clerk do and how could it possibly be relevant to me and my day, I wanted to ask.)

'Okay. How can I help? Is there an incident involving an MDP?' I asked politely.

'No.'

'Has an individual gone missing?'

'No.'

'An attack by an unknown assailant?'

'No.'

'Has an MDP submitted a fraudulent insurance claim?' I muttered, with artfully concealed sarcasm.

'No.'

I sighed quietly, almost wishing it had been an overseas journalist that I could shut down completely, but as a matter of courtesy I paused and was about to utter words of thanks and suggest she consult with her colleagues when I gave her one last opportunity to explain how she could be of any use to me. Being gracious is difficult when one's whole bodily instinct is to sigh.

'So, no deaths – reported or expected? No missing people? No insurance fraud?'

'No,' she replied falteringly. 'I'm from the robbery team of the insurance fraud department. Shoplifting to be exact.'

'Shoplifting? So no one is hurt?' I asked, almost incredulous at the waste of my time.

I took in a deep, frustrated breath (why would I be interested in shoplifting, I was shouting in my head). Before I was about to expel the contents of my lungs in a final sigh, she interrupted my thought process.

'We have large teams of your MDPs shoplifting.'

'What? Say again.'

'I'm watching CCTV of what looks like (or in fact I know that some of them are) Mobile Deceased Persons.'

I was silent, trying to process the information and a tsunami of implications came crashing in if I was hearing her correctly.

'Are you interested? she asked, uncertain. 'It is an unusual activity, isn't it?'

I was suddenly aware that I was being offered information about something I had not come across.

'Yes, I whispered. 'It certainly is. What's your name again?'

Within forty-five minutes I was round at her workplace squinting at her computer screen studying the CCTV from a high street department store. The community support officer was, on the face of it, correct. My eyes were drawn to John Reuel and Clive Staples. I had seen enough CCTV, but my interest was piqued when we even secured footage of them leading other MDPs (many of whom were female) on their thieving (and sometimes murderous) escapades.

Perhaps a dozen figures, male and female, were walking around the store aisles helping themselves to items hanging on display (purses, handbags) and, tracked by other cameras, other items in the store's electrical section including mobile phones, expensive watches. Scrolling through the footage we watched as they moved from section to section filling black bin liners with goods. The MDPs seemed coherent, organised and intentional in their actions. They weren't mindlessly following Staples and John Reuel's lead, this 'crew' were selecting high-end goods, and ignoring clothing, other low-end accessories. How could they discern this and had they been coached? And why would they do it? For 'organisation' implies a purpose. What was the purpose?

'Some of the silent alarms were tripped,' said the Community Support Officer. 'Security guards visited the premises but, having identified a number of MDPs loitering at the entrances, the security guards did not progress further.'

'The guards called for backup?'

'Yes, but just regular…'

'Cloth-Heads turned up,' I added, using the term I had seen Felicity use in her blog.

She gave me a quizzical should-I-be-offended look.

'It's code. Rather than hardhats (the military),' I muttered.

'The military is now on standby?' she asked, suddenly worried.

I shrugged and rolled my eyes.

'I'm saying nothing,' I whispered.

'Do you know any of them?' she asked, pointing at the computer screen.

'I suspect some of them are known to my team,' I sighed. 'Send over all the footage you have and we'll take a look.'

I was certain John Reuel and Clive Staples were among the dozen of shoplifters, but I would leave it to Fiona and Tom to study. I didn't see Unknown Target A among them, but I was soon coming to the conclusion that if there was any thought or coordination involved, then Unknown Target A might not be too far away. He had his bony fingers in all sorts of pies.

'What does this mean, do you think?' the community support officer asked, breaking my ponderings.

'Consumerism runs deep. Materialism survives death.'

I thanked her and left, but, as with most revelations nowadays, it both excited and worried me. What did it mean? Was it just a habit that rolled over into death? Did capitalism and the consumerism instinct survive an individual's passing? Or was it as innocent as a crow picking up sparkly things? Were the Muters simple creatures after all? Easily drawn to sparkly things? Was this evidence of their shallow nature living on? But again, the same question returned and kept nagging at me – *organisation implies a purpose*. What was the purpose?

Perhaps those MDPs in the footage were yet to evolve? Nevertheless, it was an interesting development and posed yet another challenge. Any theory I might have would need to be supported by evidence. But how do I acquire evidence for a 'purpose'? A purpose, a motivation, exists in the mind. As I raced back to the office my own mind was consumed with how to resolve the conundrum. I had a partially formed answer – evidence for a purpose could be found in the resulting action. That was the only logical result. But what was the 'resulting action' for shoplifted goods? What was the resulting action for *any* shoplifted goods? Either for use of the stolen items themselves, or for trade. But trade the items for what? What could an MDP seek to trade?

When back at the office I emailed the Community Support Officer and asked her to send over a list and any images of the items stolen by the Muters. If the shoplifted items turned up somewhere, our questions might be answered. I also asked for any exterior CCTV cameras that might have caught those Muters loitering (or was it guarding?) the entrances.

I briefed Tom and Fiona shortly afterwards. They were similarly intrigued. What did it mean?

I was tired and was about to leave the office, but I found that the IT department had returned Felicity's laptop to me. Almost as an inconsequential afterthought I booted it up to ensure it was running okay. Without any intervention from me the laptop immediately connected to the departmental WiFi whereupon something truly horrible happened. As the computer connected to the Cloud (through the department's WiFi) and, as I was about to continue reading, a sudden flood of other documents appeared on the computer. The folder had been set to sort the documents by 'Date Modified'. Suddenly a dozen more files appeared. 'Syncing files' was the dialogue box message.

How could the Cloud files be 'syncing'?

At first I was super irritated. I had handed over the laptop to the IT expert with the explicit instruction to prevent me from mistakenly making changes. I had not thought to check the settings to automatically sync to the Cloud. I had told the IT expert that I wanted it to connect to the Cloud to see what was saved up there and how it compared to the files on the laptop, but it had not occurred to me that additional files would be downloaded onto (and synced with) Felicity's laptop, possibly over-writing other files. But, in the midst of my resentment, I checked myself. Perhaps this was a good thing. Perhaps it will show something.

Frustrations with IT colleagues aside, it still flummoxed me. How could there be more files uploading to the Cloud, then downloaded onto *this* device? I had not touched the device for four, five days. Where was it syncing from? Where were the files coming from? Was Felicity still active? Still alive? Was she trapped somewhere? Had she been abducted? Was this her way to send a message for help? Or was she sitting in a cottage in Wales working on her dark fictional memoir on another device?

I sat down and made myself comfortable for a long night of reading.

12. Memoirs

Holy shit. Holy f*cking shit. F*ck me.

I had not moved from my chair. I had started reading the documents at five o'clock in the afternoon thinking I would slip away from the office at six o'clock, but, no, I did not move (except for a few comfort breaks) until 12.30 a.m.. What was odd was that I found myself running to the lavatory then running back. The second time, I walked but carried the laptop with me with a sense of panic in case I inadvertently splashed water onto the device, frying its electronics. I could not let the device out of my sight. I had some food delivered and cracked straight on through to the early hours.

I could, of course, have worked through to the 'later early hours' of the morning, but I was conscious I had to be functioning the next day. I was already working long hours and my body had been sending me messages to slow down for weeks.

The reason I took so long was not because there were huge numbers of blog entries. I just kept re-reading each one then checking my own records to see if it tallied with my MDP log of attacks over recent months.

There are too many passages to include here. Perhaps I will compile them in a separate edition or get someone else to compile the blog entries, but there were three passages in particular that sent shivers down my spine that night for different reasons. The three passages were to be found in chapters titled 'House Parties', 'Making Friends' and 'Spread the Love'. In each chapter the narrator took the reader through his escapades moving about London (the 'metropolis') and hunting down 'Beans' and either feasting on them or converting them, inducting them to 'Muterdom'. There were encounters in wastelands bordering railway tracks, in the streets and in residential properties. If there was a hint of truth about these new uploads it could possibly be an absolute goldmine. But how could it be? This must surely be Felicity's creative mind hard at work? Yet everything seemed to have the ring of truth about it.

One passage that gave me heart palpitations was from a chapter entitled 'House Parties'; the narrator described how, while roaming over rooftops, he had come across a dinner party in a residential property only to be distracted by the sight of a lone woman (who the narrator later christened 'CatNaps') asleep on her window seat in the flat above. The description of the scene and acquisition of the CatNaps character had the echoes of Felicity's flat and her disappearance. The 'Lady Bean' in the passage was sleeping with her cat snuggled in her arms until the narrator's presence disturbed the feline, which opened its eyes and, in terror, bolted out the window. Startled awake herself by the cat's sudden violent move (and, no doubt, the presence of an MDP looking down upon her) the Lady Bean lunged after the cat only to fall out of the window and be impaled on the property's railings at street level below. The narrator then descended to the street, removed the character 'CatNaps' (as a now 'Has-Bean') from the railings and placed her on a nearby roof to rise later as an MDP or 'Muter' herself.

The narrator then described how CatNaps' apartment was used as a base for a few weeks by the narrator and his MDP crew. The narrator even referred to family members of CatNaps and 'Cloth-Heads' paying visits to the flat looking for the flat-owner-now-Muter and being met by a mute, uncooperative Felicity.

Was it a fictional account by Felicity as part of a creative exercise? She was indeed undergoing a kind of creative nervous breakdown? Perhaps she wrote it then used it as a cover to fake her disappearance? A very possible explanation. Yet, the passage had an eerily credible feel to it. I also considered that it could be inspired by events that actually took place in Felicity's flat – an accurate record of Felicity being attacked and acquired by an MDP – but she had somehow survived and was now writing up the story as part of an autobiography, of sorts, with the narrator being an out-of-body expression of her life in London at that time.

Alternatively, Felicity was hallucinating having been bitten by an MDP and the account was her way of dealing with it? Had she retreated back to the flat and over the following few weeks fallen into sickness and written the passages in a hazy blur? Was this evidence of what the virus infection did to the brain? Although it was possible to construct a theory that Felicity was the author and narrator of the blog, there was something that I could not quite put my finger on.

I did consider a third theory, but struggled to admit it to myself that I was ever entertaining the idea. I was torn and berated myself. In fact I almost felt obliged to dismiss the theory because it was the most disturbing of the three. This third theory was that the passages were *real* and actually written by a real-life MDP. I found myself shaking my head almost in an attempt to shake the theory free from my head – it was just too incredible a proposition, a Mobile Deceased Person writing up his 'life' experiences in the metropolis, Surely not? The implications were too terrible.

Of course, the urge to share these theories with colleagues was strong, but I could only imagine the ridicule and pushback. After all, what would be the answer from someone like Robbie to my third theory?:

"You have found a story that has no corroboration. It is just words on the computer of a creative person, a graphic designer,

who might be writing a book and was depressed about her life. And yet you're saying it was written by a Mobile Deceased Person? A deceased person with no name and has not been accounted for anywhere?"

No. I would lose all credibility. I needed to dig deeper. I knew reputations that took time to build could be lost in a flash. I had to be careful. I had been careful to build influence. One careless word, allusion, and my world would come crashing down.

So, as I read on, I was looking for reasons to validate the first two theories – a completely fictional story written by Felicity to mask her disappearance or an embellished account written up by Felicity afterwards (perhaps nursing wounds somewhere safe). I could not accept she was writing it up as a fully-fledged MDP. Perhaps a sick, infected and hallucinating Bean, but nothing more.

The trouble was, these first two theories were soon dashed – not because they appeared less convincing as I read on, but because 'she' (or 'he' or whoever the author was) was writing about episodes that mirrored two events that Tom, Fiona and I had been investigating out in the real world. The accounts reeked of authenticity. The accounts were about Fireman Juggler and John Reuel and Clive Staples no less.

In the chapter titled 'Spread the Love' the narrator described an event that succinctly described what could only be the acquisition of the Juggler-Fireman. The narrator spoke of watching a street juggler being approached by four teenagers who had then dosed the street entertainer in a flammable liquid. The narrator watched the juggler flail around in a ball of fire before he collapsed in a heap. The four 'Beanteens' subsequently escaped into an alley, but unwittingly ran into the arms of the writer. The youngsters were dispatched and feasted upon 'beyond recognition or function' by the two of the narrator's followers ('Chubby' and 'Tracks'). The narrator described approaching the dying juggler (prompting the retreat by a small crowd of onlookers), picking up the juggler and transporting him away to the rooftops to 'rest and recover'. I realised that the fearsome MDP-Muter, Fireman-Juggler, that Tom, Fiona and I had been tracking, had been given the name 'Diesel' by the writer.

By the time I had finished reading this passage my mouth was completely dry. I struggled to comprehend it and had to re-read it several times. I then, of course, watched the available footage of the incident in question. As I studied the street CCTV and the footage provided by Arthur that I had watched dozens of times before, it dawned on me that there was *no way* that Felicity could have known about these events. Not only was the passage so detailed and matched the video footage, but Diesel's acquisition, death, birth, rising, whatever, had occurred *after* her own disappearance. Arthur had reported that a number of youths, who Arthur assumed had been responsible for creating the fireball, had run away from the scene moments before. Furthermore, Arthur's footage had matched the description of the 'known unknown' MDP (Unknown Target A) that had apparently rescued the Fireman-Juggler not Felicity. There was nothing in the description of the incident that contradicted the testimony of witnesses or video evidence.

But the night was still young. I read on.

My stomach continued to turn over – I was unsure whether it was because the food I had delivered was disagreeing with me or the dawning realisation of the importance and veracity of these new passages.

I skipped through a chapter on Cloth-Heads and Rubber Beans (the narrator's terms for the police; terms now familiar to me) and a 'Second Bean Paradox' explaining the Beans' obsession with ownership and control – not because it was uninteresting and might provide an insight into the author's thinking, but because it did not give a clue to the identity of the writer-narrator.

The author then devoted a whole chapter on an incident in a chapter called 'Stolen Kisses: GlassCutter and DoorStop'. It was becoming clear that he was indeed naming his acquisitions, his followers, with an aspect of or something related to their death. As I started reading the chapter I almost willed it to refer to something that was directly contradicted by the evidence I already had in my possession; something I could hang my hat on and say – that's false. However, I was to be disappointed. As it turned out the account of the incident might well, on its own, crack the case of the writer's identity.

In the passage, the narrator was again watching Bean activity from the rooftops and saw a man break into a shop in the middle of the night. The narrator referenced 'glittery' things being taken, which I took to be jewellery. He also referenced swinging the DoorStop-elect character into glass cabinets smashing them to pieces. This matched police crime scene photos of the scene – the glass cabinets having indeed been smashed up. It had been everyone's view that the destruction was a result of a big fight on the shop's premises rather than a robber just trying to gain access to the precious goods inside.

The mode of entrance described by the writer (cutting the glass) also matched the police report. What I hadn't previously fully appreciated was that an MDP was involved in the struggle. As I read on I was of the opinion that I was reading an accurate account of the incident.

But what also struck me at this time was that there were elements in the story that both intrigued and alarmed me. Firstly, the narrator reported the interaction between the two robbers (named GlassCutter and DoorStop). There was no confusion (in the writer's account) about the verbal exchanges between the robbers. It not only showed that the narrator understood what was being said but also the context in which it was said. In other words, the MDP was able to read between the lines. The MDP, as narrator, understood that he was being insulted by the two robbers. Not only that, but the MDP then chose *not* to retaliate. The narrator was rising above the loutish behaviour of the two robbers. It showed a whole different level of comprehension and strategy that nobody, not even me, had anticipated (and I was the greatest advocate for a cognisant, self-conscious MDP). If this written account were true then the extent of their cognisance was revelatory. Here was an MDP carefully deliberating the actions of the men in front of him and making an assessment about their behaviour and weighing up ways to respond.

It also became clear that the narrator, as an MDP (or 'Muter'), was exhibiting an 'unholy strength'. A strength that surprised the attacker, DoorStop apparently. If DoorStop was indeed Staples then that would suggest considerable physical prowess, because Staples was, according to his police records, six foot three and a pretty solidly-built man.

So here we had an account that matched not only the police crime report (GlassCutter and DoorStop), but also the video testimony and witness testimony (Arthur's report of the Fireman-Juggler's demise). As I finished re-reading the chapter it was my sincere belief that GlassCutter and DoorStop were in fact John Reuel and Clive Staples.

In those midnight hours, and as darkness and quietness hung over the capital, I sat and pondered all the implications. But it was all too difficult. I needed to rest for a while. Tomorrow would be a long day. My brain was too fried and I was too tired to consider how to move forward.

As my eyelids hung heavy I did consider whether I should include Tom and Fiona in my discovery, but I instinctively knew they had enough on their plate and I had to be absolutely sure of my case, such was the remarkable nature of the new passages. I also felt obliged to consider all the possible alternatives in the brightness of the day. Literal sunlight was a good disinfectant.

Perhaps, when I was feeling as fresh as a daisy, I could link it to Felicity – her efforts at fiction, her disappearance as a way to escape her life. Or perhaps I could build my own narrative that a police officer was playing games with me. But police officers in my experience didn't have an ounce of creativity in them. Besides, there were many reflective passages in the blog that I had yet to truly digest – similarly, far beyond the capability of a Cloth-Head.

Or perhaps the author was a random blogger who was somehow connected to the same Cloud account? Someone known to Felicity. Even though I was exhausted I found such an explanation easy to discount. How would the blogger know about scenes that mirrored incidents we were actively investigating? I had a sudden panic that maybe someone within my own team was involved, either innocently or mischievously. But, no, nobody had the time to bring it together so elaborately. And I knew they were overworked. Besides, nobody had all such information in one place.

The passages were saved as different documents and they were jumbled up, so I needed to examine the timelines and timeframes. Although the documents were, in themselves, all coherent, it was not in a format for a publisher. It still needed work. Editing.

I scanned back through past passages for the name of the narrator. I came across a name 'Nigel', but it was a conventional name and a little out of place. Why didn't the narrator reference his own death? Why didn't he give himself a death-name? If Nigel was indeed his name, how did he know it?

It niggled me, so I made a conscious note to make time to read more. Whoever was writing it was obviously connected from another device to the Cloud. Hopefully further passages would be uploaded in due course. This realisation encouraged me to keep it to myself. On the present evidence what would I be proposing? An MDP was so self-aware, it was not only writing accounts of its own existence but, presumably, so cognisant that it had the presence of mind to manage its files and backups in the Cloud? Impossible.

By 12.30 a.m., I was exhausted. My head was well and truly scrambled, but in my blurred racing mind there was one possible gap. A gap that could yet be filled by our work. If it did, then that would be mind-blowing. That gap was the missing CCTV video of the Camberwell jewellery break-in. It had apparently been lost by the police. I had a glimmer of hope though. Sometimes police evidence is not lost forever. Don't get me wrong, the police do lose evidence, but it is only truly lost if it is advantageous to the police to lose it. In this case there was no real need for the police to lose the CCTV footage, so perhaps it might turn up. And if it did turn up and it showed John Reuel and Clive Staples (GlassCutter and DoorStop) interacting with an MDP that matched the written account, then that would surely seal the deal? Case closed. Taken together (CatNaps, Diesel and the robbery) all other possible alternative explanations simply melted away. There was no way a creative-writing Felicity, a random blogger, a bored police officer or a mischievous member of my own team could have covered all the bases.

As I wandered home to catch a few hours of sleep I shook my head and let out a groan in the hope my thoughts, ridiculous ideas, would shake themselves free from my head and dissolve on hitting the cold night air.

I couldn't go to anybody else just yet. Certainly not my supervisor, Robbie. But I concluded that I shouldn't yet mention my discoveries and theories even to my trusted confidants, Fiona and Tom. There was the danger it would scramble their thinking just as it had mine. No, I wanted them to have clear heads. They needed to remain objective so that when I did reveal my findings they could meet it head on with barrels of scepticism. If there was merit in my understanding of the origins of this blog (and therefore the whole plague issue) then it had to at least withstand the examination from allies. If I satisfied them at that point, I could take it further and approach Robbie.

All this is not to say I could not involve Tom and Fiona in my plan. I had to artfully involve them in confirming my theories without them thinking something was afoot. I needed to direct them towards incidents involving specific MDPs (Unknown Target A himself or his colleagues) that could validate my theory. We had to correlate all the written passages with real-world events and have corroborating evidence by CCTV, police reports and witnesses. After all, there could be something I was missing. We would need to get to a point of corroborating evidence that would also show that *I*, me, Josh, was not the author of the blog. That might even be the bigger challenge. The evidence taken together had to be beyond my means of creating and falsifying it.

Thought needed to be given to the strategy of revealing the blog to the world. For this reason and for the time being it would just be me and the blogger himself (or herself) sharing a secret.

As I reached my bed at two o'clock that morning I did not want to admit it, but I had a strong feeling I knew who the blogger was – Unknown Target A...the MDP who called himself 'Nigel'.

13. His Name Was...

From the disappearance of Mia to the time when I was barricaded in a Portakabin in the middle of the burning metropolis (on the eve of the Great Handover), there occurred a handful of 'momentous moments' that will stay with me forever. Arguably the most defining momentous moment was when two ideas came together into one realisation – a realisation that would have implications for the whole of *Homo sapiens* – past, present and future.

Forty-eight hours after the idea first popped into my head I was convinced that 'Unknown Target A' was indeed the blog's author ('Nigel') and was one of the leaders, if not *the* leader of the MDPs – a self-aware creature who had a wholly different experience of existence and time from the rest of us. We had not yet been able to determine if the Z-DNA we had acquired from a number of crime scenes led back to Nigel, but it was becoming increasingly likely. It was both scary and 'monumentally, scientifically and significantly significant' (as I wrote in my notes). I needed more data before I formally pushed it up the chain of command. I could be laughed out of the room (by men in white coats). Why do people trust people in white lab coats? I simultaneously made a mental note to acquire my own lab coat. It might buy me a few minutes in any given meeting.

That said, although my whole being was convinced I was correct in identifying the author of the blog, I tried with all my might to try and keep my gut apart and separate from my head. I should not announce it prematurely. Data, data, data.

I endeavoured to monitor the blog and hoped that the author kept uploading his thoughts, methodology and writing up those incidents in which he or his followers ('colleagues') were involved. I was anxious that there would be no hiccups with the author's Cloud connection and/or the devices he was using. I also thought about involving IT experts and the police to identify the device the blogger was using (and when and where it was being updated), but I was hesitant to involve others just yet in case they blundered in and we lost updates to the blog or Nigel himself.

The priority now was being able to prove my theory by providing valuable insight into the details of reported incidents before they were fully investigated by the police. If I could even predict events it would help my case.

There were still some questions lingering. I now had footage of the Muters apparently shoplifting in teams. I understood that to be learned behaviour from the likes of GlassCutter and DoorStop, but what happened to the stolen goods? Was it dumped somewhere? Did it form part of a trade? One might argue the attraction to sparkly things was a primitive response and might suggest that the Muters were not 'evolving' as I had thought. It was assumed that the average MDP had the average bird-brain, but Nigel's writings suggested otherwise. Surely he could not just be an anomaly? A one-off?

I tried to anticipate every question that I might be asked. I did not want to be asked something only to um, er, stutter and stumble through a reply. I might get only one chance to make an impression with senior civil servants. I realised that my strategy had to be based around corroborating the blog entries. That also included chasing the lab results (via Tom) of the blood retrieved from the railings below Felicity's flat. The lab had been struggling to read the DNA.

It was then that the Camberwell 'break-in' became the Camberwell 'breakthrough'.

I was working in the office when the phone rang.

'Hey, are you Josh?' said the voice.

'Yes.' I mumbled.

'I've got your stuff, your footage.'

'I'm sorry?' I replied.

'The jewellery shop break-in? In Camberwell?'

My heart jumped. Holy cow.

'Er, yeah, great. How did you find it?' I said, trying to remain calm.

'It was backed-up by a brother of the owner for insurance purposes as soon as it happened. He wasn't going to hand over the only copy to the police,' the voice said. 'We got it from the insurance company when they asked for verification of the robbery.'

'That is great. Um, who are you?'

'I'm the disclosure officer at Camberwell police station.'

'Okay,' I muttered, still in disbelief at my luck. 'Thanks.'

What was it with the insurance business? It was delivering far more impressive results than the police. Perhaps I should set up a formal liaison with insurance agents rather than police officers.

'I've watched it. There is a third person in the shop. There is a fight. Don't know if it is your dead guy though.'

'Okay, great,' I said. 'As a matter of interest, why.... '

'I lost an ex-girlfriend to one of the bastards.'

'Oh, I'm sorry'

'Forget it mate. But she was my first love at school. Hadn't seen her for years, but, you know, how you always think that maybe one day you'll bump into them and realise you were meant to be together forever?'

I nodded. I was reminded and humbled that my project had real world consequences. Even though I was fascinated with the

Muters, at the end of day they were in the business of death. A business of extinguishing the dreams, the hopes, of any man or woman walking the streets.

I thanked the caller profusely and he sent me a secure link to the footage. I almost wet myself with anticipation as the file downloaded.

I called Tom and Fiona into the office. It was only fair that we watched it all together. What would the quality be like? CCTV tended to be of variable quality.

Or so we thought.

Rather than play it on my average-sized screen, we set up the CCTV footage to stream to a large television in a conference room down the hall at 8.30 p.m. that evening.

The video was several hours long, but we had been given a list of the time-codes of the sequences of interest. The footage was captured from two cameras in the main shop showroom and displayed side-by-side and synced. The first camera angle was from a camera placed high in the corner of the shop pointing down capturing the shopfloor (with the floor area comparable in size to typical medium-sized van) surrounded by waist-high display cabinets. The front door was just off-screen to the left of the frame.

The second camera was placed at the back of the shop, not at as high an angle as the first camera, but it was fortunately facing towards the front entrance. All the (van-sized) floor area was clearly in view. The resolution quality was excellent.

There had apparently been other cameras in the back room and an outside view of the main entrance, but they had been disabled ahead of the break-in. It would appear that the thieves had not been aware that these two cameras were powered off an independent electrical source and were recording their footage on hidden drives separate to all computer networks that had also been disabled by the robber.

There was no sound.

According to the timestamp, at 2.40 a.m. a balaclava-clad figure appeared from the back room and moved quietly around the shop floor. Confident the area was clear, he moved to the front entrance, broke open the door, and rolled up the shop's external metal security-grill to knee level. He then moved back into the shop and started cutting the glass on the display cabinets. Once a cabinet was breached he made quick work of transferring the treasure within (jewellery and high-end goods) to a series of black sacks. Having emptied a number of cabinets he disappeared back into the back room of the shop and out of view. The shop floor was quiet and empty for a minute at least.

I was watching this with Fiona and Tom. They were glued to the screens desperate to know what happened next. I was also glued to the screen, but I *did* know what was going to happen next. Or at least I thought I did – I had read Nigel's description of events numerous times. So far, so good.

'Maybe it is all happening off screen?' said Fiona with a hint of disappointment. 'He's being attacked in the back room?'

'We don't have footage from the back room?' asked Tom, looking at me like an unhappy eight year old.

'No, it was disabled. These cameras were on a different network for this very reason,' I said quietly suppressing a little smile, not quite believing that I was watching the blog come to life.

'Damn,' said Tom, his head dropping to his chest in disappointment.

'Be patient,' I muttered quietly without removing my eyes from the television screen. 'Have faith. I think we might be in luck today.'

Tom and Fiona both turned to me pulling a face. With their eyes on me, I nodded at the television screen. Three seconds later another tall, slim, athletic figure moved slowly into frame and stopped in the middle of frame right in the middle of the shop floor with the robber's black bags of treasure at his feet.

'Holy shit,' gasped Tom. 'That's Unknown Target A. I'm sure of it.'

I nodded and smiled.

Fiona turned towards me, almost breathless herself. 'You've seen this already?' she spat.

'Nope, first time.' I replied with a smile. 'Now shssh. Let's watch. I think it is going to get interesting.'

The figure remained still, exquisitely framed, slowly looking around in the commanding, zen-like fashion as he had done so on so many other CCTV videos. Then we spotted movement just outside the shop entrance. The roll-grill appeared to rise a few feet before a figure of another large man appeared at the shop entrance. He stopped. The first intruder appeared again at the door leading to the back room. The three figures stood still with only their heads moving.

'They're talking.'

'Damn. Why can't security systems record sound?'

'Do you think they know he's an MDP?'

'Maybe they're unsure what to do?'

Of course, I knew exactly what was being said. Nigel had written it all up.

The first intruder disappeared and started to collect the bags from the back room.

'Why doesn't Unknown Target A attack the second intruder?' asked Fiona.

I remained silent. I had to remind myself that neither of them had any knowledge of the blog and Nigel's detailed account of events and his thinking.

The first intruder ('GlassCutter-elect') reappeared and cautiously started to collect the bags around Nigel's feet and move them to the front entrance. Unknown Target A stepped towards

GlassCutter who immediately grabbed a weapon from his backpack.

'A baseball bat?' gasped Fiona.

After a movement, GlassCutter-elect swung the bat violently at the head of the MDP who caught it without blinking and appeared to hold it fast. GlassCutter-elect tried to shake it free, but the MDP's grip was firm.

The following tussle happened very quickly and was accompanied by swearing and exclamations of shock from Tom and Fiona. The MDP, Nigel, still holding the baseball bat firmly, thrust out his other hand towards the throat of the GlassCutter-elect and, although it was difficult to see on the video, caused a massive neck injury that sent the robber convulsing in shock and pain. I knew that Nigel had ripped out GlassCutter's windpipe. After more cries of horror and disbelief from my colleagues, the MDP bit his attacker and threw him head over heels into the glass cabinets. The other intruder whom I knew to be 'DoorStop-elect' was similarly bitten and dispatched and thrown away. There were a few pathetic attempts by both intruders to push past the MDP and escape, but after a few more throws and broken cabinets, they succumbed to their injuries.

The video matched the blog. Tom and Fiona were buzzing and incredulous at what they had just seen. I was buzzing too, but not at what I had just seen, but what I had been reading. This corroborated the blog and its author, surely. How could Felicity have known it? Of course, she couldn't and didn't. It happened *before* she had disappeared. The blog had indeed been written by Nigel.

The important parts of the video were less than five minutes long, but we watched it a dozen times. Initially it was excitement, then wonder, then curiosity, then sombre realisation. I was more sombre than them. They didn't know the implications just yet.

'You had seen this hadn't you?' asked Fiona, with a hint of frustration.

I shook my head.

'Well, then someone told you.'

I shook my head again.

She didn't believe me. 'How can you remain so calm? This is absolutely incredible,' she said, waving at the screen with the frozen image of the MDP and two robbers, John Reuel and Clive Staples, just before the attack.

It was a Friday and by ten o'clock we were all exhausted and I sent Tom and Fiona home explaining that they could not count on me being available to them over the weekend. I needed to recharge my batteries and had to start drafting a report. Too many late nights were taking their toll and I was conscious work was going to get busier in the coming weeks.

Strangely enough I slept very soundly that night. The water also had a knack of rocking me to sleep. I half thought I heard a paddleboard in the middle of the night, but I was too tired to care. Besides, I might have been dreaming. The world of the wake and the world of the death wake were merging into one.

The following mid-morning I stood on my boat with my morning coffee watching the river traffic pass by. It was one of those cold sharp mornings that sharpens the brain. My breath formed clouds of moisture that hung in the air before dissolving to nought. In truth, it echoed the nature of *Homo sapiens*. My exhalation, literally the breath of life, hung momentarily in its own firmament before dissolving to nothingness. Humanity was just as fleeting and no more significant. I looked up to the quayside and watched the people wander past on their Saturday morning activities oblivious to the way the world was changing. It was good they were ignorant. My new-found understanding of the world would be too much for them. Let them have hope.

Who could I share my secret with? Who would understand? I saw Ron Cha ferrying his river taxi passengers back to his jetty. Perhaps he would understand. He was old and wise enough to have seen the curious ways of the world. He might appreciate my thoughts.

In the stillness of the morning, I felt there was a clarity descending on my work. I tried to play devil's advocate and make the case for the opposition. But there was nothing. The case for a sentient MDP was sound and solid. I had three incidents that, taken together, *proved* it could *not* be Felicity, could *not* be a hoax by a police officer or someone close to the investigation. CatNaps was real; Diesel was real; GlassCutter and DoorStop were real. The case was closed.

I felt that, as a representative of *Homo sapiens*, 'modern' humans were now behind the curve. Standing on the stern of my boat, in my long shorts and hoodie, sipping a coffee and looking at a world going about its business, I realised that only I knew evolution had taken a quiet step towards a new future. A future that possibly did not include *Homo sapiens* at all. I defy anyone to think that was not a momentous moment. Death was not now the absence of action or life. Death was not cold, hard, still. It was now mobile, with intent. On a new path. It had a personality. Death now had both a face and a name. Yes, it was an unshakeable truth – Unknown Target A was the blogger. He was real.

His name, indeed, was Nigel.

14. Legal

I felt completely refreshed in mind (though still a little tired in body) on the Monday following. At last I had something (I say 'something', I mean 'everything') to go on. I almost felt that I had reinvented everything and come up with a new 'Theory of Everything'. I was almost child-like with excitement, but I knew I had to fight the instinct. I had to remain (or act as) the adult in the room. That said, the way forward was becoming clearer. But it was still clear to me that I should keep my discovery to myself for the time being.

What could I do now? I could discreetly establish who his (the narrator's, 'Nigel') followers really were. If I could prove there were followers of a particular MDP then that would suggest the 'Muters' were organising into some sort of 'society'. It could be explosive in so many ways. Firstly, it would be an incredible finding in anthropological terms, but, secondly, it had legal complications. If it could be shown that 'the dead' were organising, it would perhaps strengthen the case for imbuing them, or rather assigning them, with human rights. The implications would cascade down to law enforcement, which could ultimately impact me and our study of the MDPs. If the Muters were assigned legal rights then what would be the rules of engagement for the police? (Could it get even more complicated than things already were?) There had already been a few cases that had ended up in the courts.

Thankfully, those legal cases never came across my desk. If I had a hint of a case that could become legal (and thereby political),

I side-stepped it. But for how much longer? The MDPs were growing in number. Everybody was trying to head them off – the police, the civil servants, the government officials, even a large proportion of the legal community, but the tide could not be stopped. I was acutely aware that my discovery (and any further research) could make things enormously difficult for everybody.

As an example: the previous month, Roger Thistle had been arrested and charged with the rape and murder of a young woman, Mary Smith. Although the evidence was overwhelming (not least the video evidence and mobile phone evidence), Mary Smith's body had never been recovered. The police suspected her dead (or dying) body had been dumped in a canal. A week before the trial, it emerged that Mary Smith was now a Mobile Deceased Person. She had been caught on CCTV at various MDP incidents including on one occasion when she had attacked a local publican who had recognised her. Roger Thistle's defence team had therefore requested an emergency court hearing and petitioned the judge to throw out the case against their defendant. The defence team argued that the accused should not be on trial for murder because the 'victim' was walking the streets of London. It had thrown up all manner of legal problems and the trial was, of course, delayed. There were discussions about what constituted death. In medical terms, death meant brain-death. In legal terms, death meant medical death, unless it could be challenged by some legal philosophy (or whatever the next of kin 'felt' death was). Ethics described death in whatever terms you wanted. Then there was death as defined by other groups. Ask a priest or religious person and you would find some reference to the sanctity and soul. Death could only be pronounced when God or 'a god' claimed the person. (And it wasn't as if Nigel was a god.) And on and on it went.

In another case, almost the mirroring of the first, a Bean by the name of 'Jemima King' had brutally murdered her own mother. This alleged murderer, Jemima, had suddenly disappeared when a warrant was out for her arrest. She was picked up by the police a few weeks later – not as a Bean, but as a freshly-risen (and relatively docile) MDP. Her appointed defence team was claiming that now, as an MDP, Jemima could not be held responsible for the violent attack visited upon her mother. The Muter Jemima was in secure custody and, as court regulations required, had appeared in court in the glass-enclosed dock flanked by nervous, armed guards. The mother had been cremated quickly because there were fears she might have become infected, but she had been cremated without consulting the family who were suing the authorities for violating the mother's rights to a burial. In a bizarre legal twist, if Jemima was prosecuted formally, the authorities could defer responsibility to Jemima and be immune from the civil case.

Both cases ended up in the High Court at the same time and the Press had a mini-field day. Jemima was not the only MDP to end up in court, although the rules were shortly changed when an MDP suddenly attacked the armed guard in the court dock. Word had it that the horror of the actual attack was masked from the jury's eyes by the blood running down the inside of the glass walls of the reinforced dock.

So it was that the authorities were sinking into pickles of their own making. If I were to come up with yet more information that suggested that the average MDP was sentient, cognizant of its surroundings and even the consequences of its actions, then everything would kick off. Lawyers, politicians, police, even judges would all come for my throat. I might even be shut down.

After a brief discussion with my supervisor, Robbie, where I only very slightly hinted that I *might* have some evidence that the MDPs *might* be exhibiting 'normal' human behaviour, he shut me down straight away and informed me that I was not to commit anything to paper that complicated matters (in other words, his life). It occurred to me that if the plague were to take over the world and drive everything into the abyss the one thing that would survive (or, at the least, be the last to disappear) would be politics. So, in summary, honesty and transparency about my findings were not things I was in favour of. It could get too complicated too quickly. However, this position was about to be challenged.

My efforts were focused upstream of these legal cases, yet some matters did travel upstream to muddy the waters. If I sought legal guidance on whether we could do this or that (talk to family members, request DNA), the legal teams came back citing precedence from cases like those described above. Even the lawyers were nervous about the public reaction. If news got out on social media or in the mainstream news that certain legal manoeuvres were afoot then they felt their reputation (and therefore business) could suffer. So, we had to be cautious about whose feathers we ruffled. There were rumours that some of these cases would be resolved ahead of a court appearance and outside a public legal setting. Due process does not apply to the dead, apparently.

Not all the negative media attention was a bad thing. With attacks and court cases getting a bigger profile, it proved to be an opportune moment for some. There was talk of upgrading an MDP-specific force to deal with increased 'workload'. This force could include ex-military. The police were not equipped – not only literally, but also emotionally – to deal with the challenge. A not-insignificant number of police had been lost to suspected infections from attacks, so morale was low. But I was wary – legal niceties would soon give way to search-and-destroy policies.

In this context many of our lines of investigation (such as interviewing family members of recently-risen MDPs) were thwarted, much to Tom and Fiona's frustration. In order to keep them motivated, I decided to get them busy with building a picture of Nigel and his team of colleagues. After all, some of Nigel's followers (or 'colleagues') had been around for a fair few months, so their families had come to terms with their loss and were unlikely to ask difficult questions.

15. Colleagues All

I had been skimming Nigel's blog for passages that I could compare with evidence we already had (video, police reports, witness statements). With luck and hard work, the three of us (helped by our growing number of interns) hoped to build a picture of Nigel's past existence (in life and death) and learn the backstories of the early team members (and the events surrounding their acquisition by Nigel). There was one small snag. We didn't actually know who Nigel had been in life.

It was in this context that I was monitoring the blogs for updates. It was an anxious time, I could not expect him to upload regularly, he answered to no one. Besides, who knows, he might stop writing altogether. I was also devoting hours re-reading his blog looking for clues to his past Bean life or his current operations, even plans. Yet I was fearful that I might get sucked down a rabbit hole. Should I be spending time investigating and verifying details that Nigel only obliquely referred to? Was that a constructive use of my time? I was conscious I must not be so distracted by Nigel and his blog that I missed other evidence or clues popping up in police reports or in my interns' other work.

Like the best of us, he would not always make it easy. Writing that he was heading to a 'run down part of town' was not terribly informative. Besides, what did 'run-down' mean to a deceased person? It might mean something completely different to a Bean.

With this in mind, I concluded that what I could do was study every passage and get Tom and Fiona (and the other interns) to build up full profiles of Nigel's closest colleagues whom we had largely ignored for a variety of reasons. Who was 'RooftopSuicide'? Was Rooftop an ex-boyfriend or husband of 'ColourSplash'? Who was this 'ChubbyCheeks' MDP-child (or 'Muterling') who Nigel was so enamoured with? What was the Muterling's relationship to ColourSplash? Why had the child been in the same house? There must be reports of the disappearance of a child in an MDP attack on a private residence, surely? Nigel described the child as a most accomplished killer. Did we have CCTV evidence of an MDP-child being involved in attacks? Or had we overlooked it? What did this mean for the plague and how it affected children?

Who was Chain-and-Stiks and BeanPole?

Who was DogSmells?

Did the police have a record of Nigel's attack on the two illicit lovers as described in his passage entitled 'House Parties'?

And many more.

There was a danger that we would be overwhelmed with information. We had limited resources. Central to our plan must be acquiring corroborating evidence. And because people are lazy, the best corroborating evidence was video evidence. Give a seventy-page report to a civil servant and it will be placed on a pile of other reports. Sit him (or her) down for ten minutes and tell a story with CCTV and mobile phone footage, you will have their attention.

I sat Fiona and Tom in our little conference room surrounded by computers and television monitors on which to view promising video footage. They were both still in the dark about Nigel's blog, so were not thinking the way I was.

'We can't respond to all the new stuff coming in,' I said. 'There are too many legal complications especially with the freshly-risen. I want to focus on some of the long-standing Muters.'

'Er, what?' said Tom, pulling a face.

'I mean 'MDPs',' I said, suddenly correcting (and cursing) myself.

'Focusing on their individual back-stories and how they organise?' Fiona asked, trying to gain an edge on Tom.

'Exactly,' I replied. 'Freshly-risen, er, MDPs, are relatively simple. But they evolve. The longer they exist, the more developed their behaviour becomes. We have seen John Reuel and Clive Staples and the Fireman. Let's go further back. We won't have trouble with families of the long-dead. Let's select a handful of the oldest and find out who they are. If Reuel and Staples are engaged in shoplifting, what about those MDPs who pre-date them? What were they doing, what skills did they possess and how advanced are their skills development now?'

'MDPs like Unknown Target A?' said Fiona, helpfully and unknowingly falling in line with my plan.

'Yes, exactly. And his team. Who knows, we might be able to identify someone, an MDP, who could be of use.'

Both Fiona and Tom furrowed their brows. I was not making sense.

'Perhaps there is an MDP who is the off-spring of a politician. Maybe the politician doesn't know their son or daughter had *not* died in a car crash and been burned beyond recognition as they had been told by the police. Perhaps the politician's daughter is now one of the long-standing MDPs we're watching day in, day out without knowing who they are. Perhaps there is the business tycoon with influence in political circles who lost a loved one – ignorant of the fact his love is walking the streets of London. Rather than compiling reports to send up to Robbie and Whitehall, let's make it personal for someone – a politician, a businessman, a lawyer – so we can use it for leverage.'

Tom and Fiona started to nod. It had been a struggle to find a way to dupe them into investigating the MDPs I had in mind, but I got there in the end.

'While simultaneously learning the behavioural extent of their development,' I continued, capitalising on my success. 'And are the older Mu..., I mean, MDPs mentoring the younger, fresher ones?'

Both my interns looked eager-eyed at my talk, but it was not quite sinking in. I had to get into specifics.

'For instance,' I continued, 'who is the female Muter with the white blouse that appears to be splashed with colour – perhaps dried blood.'

'Target N-39?' said Fiona.

'Yes, but why don't we call her...., oh, I don't know, "ColourSplash"? I lose track of all these codenames.'

The two interns nodded.

'And the child who we see loitering around sometimes. Who is she?'

'Target K-07? She seems like a little hanger-on,' said Tom, shrugging. 'Not important.'

'But *is* she? Do we have any reference to her attacking people?'

'This is the little girl in the long white nightie and the flowing blond locks?' asked Tom.

'Yes, with the chubby cheeks,' I replied, artfully.

Again my two interns nodded.

'Hey, why don't we call her "ChubbyCheeks"?' I said.

Again, nothing from the interns. I didn't dally and cracked on:

'Where does ChubbyCheeks go? Where does she hang out? If John Reuel and Clive Staples are robbing and shoplifting, what is ChubbyCheeks doing? She has been around far longer than Reuel and Staples.'

'What names should we give to Reuel and Staples?' asked Fiona.

'Oooo, let me think,' I said.

'Shoplifter?' said Tom. 'Robber One, Robber Two?'

'But which one is which? How does it relate to the CCTV footage?' I said, cueing up my proposal.

'Well, one was standing by the door blocking the exit,' said Fiona.

'DoorBlocker?' said Tom.

'Sounds like a diarrhoea treatment,' Fiona said, with a wince and a smirk. 'Why not "Colostomy Bag"?' she added, sarcastically.

'How about "DoorStop"?' I interrupted. 'And the other?'

Tom was now subdued.

'Well,' I continued, 'how did he break into the jewellers?'

'He cut through the glass at the back of the shop,' mumbled Tom.

'Okay, that's settled. Let's call him GlassCutter,' I said quickly.

'The tall, skinny, lanky one? How about Lanky Man?' offered Fiona warming to the task.

'You mean the bean-pole one?' I said, surprising myself at my ingenuity.

'Yeah, I prefer "BeanPole", ' said Tom, looking Fiona straight in the eye.

'Done,' I said.

'Well, in terms of learning more about the background to these MDPs,' huffed Fiona, changing the subject, 'John Reuel's and Clive Staples' families will be pretty difficult to pry open, but we don't know much about the man who hangs out with ColourSplash and the young, athletic woman who you never see her face – she always wears a hoodie.'

' "Hoodie" ?,' said Tom.

'Good, get to work. Bring me everything about the early ones.'

'And Unknown Target A? He's been difficult to track down.'

'Don't worry about him for now. Focus on his team.'

'No, I mean, what do we call Unknown Target A?' asked Tom. 'I do find it a mouthful.'

Dare I say 'Nigel', I thought? No, I daren't.

'He's always in the background. A shady character who lurks in the shadows,' whispered Fiona playfully. 'He's the scary one.'

' "The Shadow"?' said Tom, hopefully, desperately trying to christen his second MDP.

'He's not a cartoon comic character,' replied Fiona with a roll of the eyes, crushing Tom's efforts.

' "Shade",' I said, wanting to end the conversation. 'Now get to work.'

Within a week I had results. Tom and Fiona excitedly invited me into the conference room.

'We have found two great incidents that might give us some leverage and it involves some of the old ones – including Hoodie and Shade,' said Fiona. 'We have some great video footage of both incidents at different points in the evening. In one incident the victims were city bankers who are bound to have influential contacts we could use to call in some favours.'

'Great,' I said. 'Show me everything.'

The incident sounded new and it had not yet written up by Nigel.

The incident was intriguing. CCTV had been pulled from a pub, a street CCTV camera and some external cameras attached to shops and local residences. The three thirty-something bankers had started their evening in a pub and ended their evening getting into a taxi not far away. There was some footage suggesting they were followed from the pub to the taxi. Were they being watched in the pub? The three bankers were pulled from the taxi and dragged away (and disappeared). I was almost certain Nigel was visible in the footage, but there were indeed others involved. It looked like GlassCutter and DoorStop. The fourth MDP was indeed the athletic, female MDP always wearing a hoodie. I suspected this was the MDP Nigel had christened "Chain-and-Sticks".

Tom and Fiona showed me another incident.

'This one is with Hoodie alone,' said Fiona

'We had wondered why we haven't come across much footage of Hoodie,' said Tom, 'even though she is one of the early MDPs and, when seen, it is usually in the company of Shade.'

'We now think her elusiveness is owing to two contributory factors. One, she likes to work alone, a bit like Shade, and secondly, she moves about London via the Thames, or waterways – the Regent's canal, the Hertford Union canal among others – and not by the streets.'

Okay, I nodded. 'Play the tape.'

Tom tapped on the keyboard. 'It is not so much one incident, but a series of incidents following a very similar pattern.'

The video popped up on the screen. It showed a regular twenty-something female Bean alternating between talking to and pouting to her camera phone, no doubt in readiness for uploading to social media. Thankfully the video had no sound – her words would carry no weight in life. Fortunately, the footage captured her setting – along the embankment with the Houses of Parliament's lights twinkling in the background on the other side of the river. There was no one in the immediate area until a shadowy figure seemed to climb up over the river wall and then loiter a dozen yards away. The social media user was oblivious to what was going on behind her – consumed with what was in front of her (namely her reflected image on the phone's screen). Suddenly the figure, now seen to be clearly hooded, moved quickly towards the filming Bean and the camera phone soon did a series of whirls showing sky, concrete, twinkling street lights before falling onto the ground.

The next clip played. It was a similar scenario where a walker was video-streaming a conversation while walking along alongside the River Thames. Suddenly a hooded figure appeared then the camera took a similar tumble. Then Tom showed me a clip from street CCTV showing a towpath running alongside a small canal. From left of frame a woman appeared walking along minding her own business when a hooded figure pounced from the shadows. Then Tom showed me more clips. It was obvious the MDP was the same individual – Hoodie – and it was true that all the clips were beside a waterway, large or small. Not only that, those few clips (like street CCTV) that showed the aftermath, saw the Hoodie disappear back over the river wall or, seemingly, down towards the water itself and out of view.

'We have some flashes of close-ups of Hoodie, just a frame or two,' said Fiona excitedly.

'How does she move around on the water?' I asked, slowly, my stomach beginning to turn.

'We don't think she swims, otherwise we would see that she is wet. We think a canoe or a paddleboard? Do you know what a paddleboard is, Josh?'

I nodded. My stomach was turning more.

The meeting finished, I thanked them and asked to see the enhanced images from the Hoodie attacks. I left and returned to my office. I knew of no passages that described attacks like this by the water, but that made sense because Hoodie was working alone, however there might be other passages in which Hoodie was referred to. Of course, Nigel didn't call her Hoodie, he called her Chain-and-Stiks. I still needed to be sure that Hoodie and Stiks were one and the same. But that was not what had been making my stomach turn.

Opening the laptop, I scoured Nigel's blog. I was in luck. Nigel had uploaded a passage about the bankers. I was not so much interested in what the bankers (the 'Three Stooges') were in death (Nigel had been dismissive), but what Nigel had alluded to – the bankers had been assigned to Stiks for early stage mentoring.

I trawled our database of unexamined, pending cases looking for CCTV of any incident involving staff members of the banks associated with the Three Stooges. I also looked for incidents in and around the pubs in the vicinity of the deceased bankers' former workplaces. Maybe, just maybe, like GlassCutter, DoorStop and TrainTracks, the bankers might return to old haunts or, like RooftopSuicide, visit individuals they had known in life. Lo and behold, I tracked down two incidents. One in the home of a banker – the doorbell security camera caught sight of Moe arriving and attacking the silver-haired home-owner and right there in the background, a hooded figure – slight in build but undoubtedly with an imposing presence – was visible waiting and watching.

Second, an incident late at night near a pub. An inebriated banker was walking home when one of the Stooges, Curly, appeared in front of him on the pavement blocking his way. Laughing at and mocking the new MDP, the Banker-Bean pulled out his phone and started filming Curly who appeared to be slow to act. Then Stiks appeared. The mocking stopped. The camera phone flew in circles in the struggle. Fortunately, we had the camera phone. I sent the footage off requesting enhanced image analysis and used all my credibility to get an urgent response. Within thirty hours an email popped up on my screen. I opened it and reviewed the dozen or so enhanced images of the doorbell footage and phone footage. They were clear. My heart and stomach did a merry jig. I was unsure how to read my own body's reaction. Excitement? Horror? Disappointment? Sadness? Hope? Or a whirring mixture of all of them? I don't know. Whatever it was. I could not articulate it.

16. Chain-and-Stiks

Hoodie, Chain-and-Stiks, was, of course, Mia.

Surely there could be no doubt?

Revisiting Nigel's early writings, I found the 'TrainTracks' incident in which Stiks had been originally claimed by Nigel. It roughly tallied with what the detective had told me all those months before – Mia had gone off with a few 'martial artists' from one of her clubs to sort out a few baddies. No doubt they had heard there was an MDP in the area of the train tracks and were intending to 'legally' try out their fighting skills on a mobile deceased person. (By this stage I was almost certain that Ashli Eco was TrainTracks.)

Even hours after opening the email and reviewing the enhanced images I did not really know how to feel about the revelation. Perhaps I should have been more alert to the possibility that Mia was among the MDPs I was following, but her disappearance had been months ago, before I knew any MDPs at all.

The inkling I had had weeks earlier had been well-founded. My former neighbour, the object of my idle affection, had survived and was part of this community of MDPs. As far as I knew, Mia had no family, so there wasn't anybody who could provide us with information on her former life and habits. No family at all who could fill in the gaps of her life. Nobody at all...just a neighbour.

I could not rush both my emotional and psychological response. That said, I knew it was going to be fairly depressing, so I left work early and headed home to my houseboat. I picked up a bottle of whiskey and a few bottles of ginger ale. Whiskey and ginger had been a tipple of choice in my teens, but as a student I realised I liked it too much and made a point of not having a bottle lying around at home. I would only entertain the idea of purchasing a bottle if I was on weekends away with friends. I knew that if I had a bottle on the houseboat and started with a tipple early in the evening, I'd have another, then another. The alcohol would slip down too easily. In recent years I had allowed myself to buy a toy-sized bottle as a treat, which I would make last for as long as possible; but heading home on this particular night, I felt it was an important moment and I needed some 'assistance' with my reflection. Single-malt stepped up and answered the call.

I sat on my houseboat deck and watched the darkness sweep across the heavens, leaving a twinkling metropolis skyline under a nondescript black-orange haze. I couldn't help thinking that man's technology was itself wholly transitory and would one day disappear only for the majesty of the firmament to appear above us once again. Taking in the view, I caught sight of Mia's boat still locked up in darkness.

Was I right to call her Mia now? Did that name still apply? A Bean is given a name at birth, Nigel gives another name inspired by the moment of death. Was that a more accurate description of one's (eternal) existence? Nigel's choice of name would last far longer than the Bean name – it could even last for eternity. But what was eternity? A thousand years? Ten thousand years? A hundred thousand years? Or really a million years? So, with some reluctance, I had to admit that Chain-and-Stiks was therefore the more appropriate name for my old neighbour. Should I therefore bury the name 'Mia' even though she was still walking the streets at night? Was 'Mia' now dead to me? Should I now refer only to the creature known as 'Chain-and-Sticks'? 'Stiks'?

On reflection I understood Nigel's naming policy – at least it reflected *something* about one's existence. A name at birth is completely arbitrary. Why was I called 'Josh'? It's not as if a Bean name is preordained, predicted or predestined. How does one's experience inform one's identity? Was my own name "Josh" temporary? Would I be given another name within twelve months? Six months? Was the name at death our real name, our real identity? I was not allowed to be master of my own name? If I could not at least be master of my own name, what could I be master of?

I looked at the surface of the Black Road shimmering and swirling before me.

My eyes swimming, my head swimming. I needed another whiskey.

Yet, what of 'Nigel'? It was the one anomaly. Nigel called himself by his Bean name. Why? Because he knew of no other? He didn't know or have any memory of how he had died? What memory did he have of his own life? As far as I was concerned I wanted to know his 'real' Bean name. Perhaps 'Shade' was indeed an appropriate name for him. It suited him. Just as he handed out names, so I would hand a name to him. A name he could hold for eternity. A variation, perhaps of 'Shade'.

I mulled these thoughts over as I gazed across the Black Road. The silhouette of boats (occasionally framed by their onboard lights) would glide past a hundred yards away, the gentle putt-putt sound bounced over the surface of the water. The boats' wake would rock me gently until I felt I was floating on a pool of reflection. For years I had plans built on (and within) a fabric of the existence that I thought I understood. Now, through Nigel's writings, I was being shown a different way of looking at everything – the physical, biological, philosophical, ethical, moral worlds. And it was not an academic, theoretical, fictional perspective. It was *real* – my former houseboat neighbour was very much part of it and would remain so, most probably far longer than I would exist in my own world. Had I been misled?

Had I been 'had', duped into a way of thinking about the world by my small-minded Beankindedness?

With the whiskey and the undulation of the houseboat, I sunk deeper into introspection. I was thinking, was the whiskey getting to me? Or was it the day-job (and Nigel) getting beneath my skin? Why was I thinking like this? It dawned on me that it was now personal. The revelation of the last twenty-four hours had moved things on. The death of Mia and the arrival of 'Stiks' had shaken me, rocked me, but it was not a sudden, single event. No, I concluded, it was one event of many; like the repeated rocking motion of my houseboat, I realised the foundations on which I had built my life were shifting over time – and getting faster. It was detectable. That evening I realised (even feared) that Nigel's writings were becoming the foundation on which I was beginning to base my own existence. Conventional Bean-thinking was slowly losing its grip on me. It was as if the waters were shaking me free of Bean-thought and revealing something entirely new.

On my previous foundation of 'land' I had planted and nurtured values on which I had formulated plans. In the vaguest of ways, I had included Mia as part of those plans. I hadn't realised my subconscious reliance on her presence until her removal as an option in my future. Strangely, because she was now an MDP, she was a constant reminder of both what had been my heart's desires and the harsh reality of the present. The reality of the present is a very different place to the hopes of the past.

How should I adjust? For adjust I must. I suppose I had to take the lead from Nigel. I needed to study him more, watch him harder. It was my duty to encourage the authorities to do so, because we had some learning to do. So, while ethics were discussed in courtrooms, the media columns, on social media and in political circles, it was all the more important to learn directly from Nigel and his disciples.

The darkness of the night grew deeper and my thoughts grew weaker. I would have to retire soon. Would Stiks appear tonight? Would she paddle up and appear at her former place of Bean? Was she a threat to me? Would she seek to gain entrance to my houseboat? Would there be a part of her that would resist attacking me on meeting her former neighbour? I had never been a threat to her. In fact, had I ever been on her radar? Would I be of any interest to her now? And, if not, should I be disappointed?

I poured myself another drink and gazed across the water – a place that I would forever call home. I had one thought as the night concluded – that I must retire to the interior of my houseboat and lock myself safely within.

I returned to the office the following day and greeted Fiona and Tom as normal. I felt a little worse for wear and drank litres of water to rehydrate, but even in this sober state I knew I had turned a corner. I thought we might be in for a battle for our very civilisation against a mighty enemy whose philosophy was becoming, dare I say, more coherent to me than western civilisation's.

I said nothing to Fiona and Tom because I did not want to worry them. Or rather worry them further – I sometimes saw traces of anxiety in their features. Initially it had all been about excitement, drama and career-building, but having spent hundreds of hours reviewing the increasing number of Muters, their social cohesion, I could see my intern colleagues were becoming pensive.

My ruminations from the previous night held firm – I had to learn more about Nigel and how he evolved. I needed to know more about who he had been in his Bean-life. We still had not identified who he was exactly. Tom had established that there might be many dozens of corpses that official records suggested had been incinerated but might have actually 'walked' out of crematoria. It would take a lot of work to track-and-trace each one.

My resources were limited and such information had not been seen as a priority. But now it was most certainly a priority. I knew that. I also knew that the time was soon coming when I needed to share my little secret with Tom and Fiona. They had already been wondering how I was getting all this inside information. It was dawning on me that they not only had to know about the existence of Nigel's blog, they needed to see the blog in action. They needed to see how it worked. How it might allow us to predict behaviour, predict events. We needed to be ahead of the police, not following them to MDP incidents or chasing CCTV and writing up mobile footage from witnesses for reports for civil servants in Whitehall. We needed to find a way to send the police to places where they weren't looking.

I scoured Nigel's blog patiently and waited and watched for an upload. When it came there was no doubt in my mind. A plan just slipped beautifully into my mind.

Jumping up from my desk I ran out of my office looking for them.

'Do either of you have any experience with brothels?' I asked them both, catching them alone in a corridor talking together quietly.

'Er, what?' Tom replied, blushing.

'Ever spent time in one?' I asked again, looking him hard in the eye and surprised I wasn't making myself clear.

'Err, I dunno…., I mean,' Tom mumbled.

I turned to Fiona. 'How about you?'

'Me? *Why* are you asking such a thing? *Who* are you asking?' she said, also blushing.

'*Both* of you,' I said, incredulous that I had to spell it out. '*Either* of you? Jeez.'

17. Brothels

Apparently I hadn't quite been aware of the effect my brothel question had had on Tom and Fiona. After a few more shocked looks I proposed a change of scene to discuss something of importance. It was better to be away from the office and the information should be digested on a full stomach. Within an hour we were sitting in comfort in a dark corner booth of an old pub and with a scampi and chips, a lasagne and a chicken salad on order. After the first round of drinks had been sunk and the small talk exhausted, I explained that not only would what I was about to share with them would change their understanding of the work we were doing, but it would possibly shake the very foundations of the lives they were leading.

They leaned forward, sipping their shandies and white wine and looked as eager as any intern could.

I took a deep breath and broke the news about Nigel's blog.

I spent about an hour explaining the background, my journey with the blog and its authenticity (or not). I explained CatNaps, GlassCutter, DoorStop, Stiks, ChubbyCheeks and others. (I did not allude to my acquaintanceship with Stiks in her previous life, that was still too raw, besides, it could be argued that it clouded my judgement if I had known an MDP in a previous life.) I gave them printouts of selected scenes from Nigel's blog and asked them to read the passages then to destroy the paper copies. I was not going to give them electronic versions. Electronic versions are a security risk. Although I trusted my two colleagues, accidents happen. USB sticks are lost, laptops are stolen, computers hacked.

Confused, dismissive frowns of the interns soon evolved into shock and concern. This transmogrified into pensive curiosity, which in turn evolved into bewilderment, excitement and horror. If you took a still image of their faces at thirty-second intervals during that hour, you would have had examples of every facial emotion listed in the Mullins' *Encyclopaedia of Human Facial Expressions*.

Of course, we could have talked about the blog all night, so after an hour and a half, I moved on to my plan of action. I explained I was sharing the existence of Nigel's blog for one reason only – I needed their assistance with the execution of a plan that could seal the deal in terms of proving the authenticity of Nigel's blog. Nobody but the three of us around that table knew about my theory, but there would come a time when I needed to share it with Robbie, my supervisor, and others in Whitehall if I was going to address the challenge of averting the, er, zombie apocalypse.

If my plan was executed properly and the anticipated results and every element were exceptionally well documented, it would be the greatest breakthrough in our mission and change the landscape of MDP understanding entirely.

'Remember,' I said, 'it has to be watertight. It will come up against a lot of incredulity and resistance. We have to be sure we have all the evidence and documents in place.'

They both nodded.

'So, we need to get ahead of the game,' I continued. 'Up to this point we have been tracking past events or investigating incidents reported to us by the police or through other (official) sources. We have then been cross-referencing those reported incidents with passages in Nigel's blog. What we have to do now is use Nigel's blog, and his descriptions of incidents, to *lead* the police authorities to incidents that have yet to come to light.'

'Sure,' said Tom, nodding. 'Take information to the police that could only have come from someone who was directly involved in the MDP activity.'

'Exactly.' I said.

'And maybe, even predict events *before* they happen?' added Fiona.

'That too,' I replied, nodding. 'Depending on when and what Nigel uploads, he might refer to the planning events.'

'Wow,' said Tom, slumping back in his seat, his stomach full of lasagne and chips and no doubt feeling a little inebriated. He looked up and around him at the pub walls covered in pictures of past generations of Londoners long dead. Once upon the time the dead could be confined to the past, now they were very much actors in the present, possibly even the future.

'So, what's the plan?' said Fiona leaning forward, her chicken salad and white wine having a slightly different effect on her being.

'This afternoon, just before I approached you two whispering in the corridors, I was reading a new passage uploaded by Nigel earlier today.'

'And?'

'And, I saw an opening, an opportunity – a reference to a new MDP involved in a new ('Muter') practice that no one person, no police or investigating authority, has yet come across.'

With that, they were both hooked. Tom struggled forward from his slumped position to join Fiona leaning towards me, elbows on the pub table, necks craning forward as I spoke in low, conspiratorial tones.

For the reader, a little bit about the background of this new Muter:

I had seen references to her in other passages by Nigel, but she was a relatively new Muter and still in the learning (or self-discovery) phase. As Nigel described, she had been acquired by him on a patch of urban wasteland of grass, broken tarmac and soil that was no doubt owned by some developer yet to acquire permissions to re-develop the land. A black vehicle full of unsavoury individuals had spotted a group of MDPs on the wasteland, driven up to them and thrown out the broken, beaten body of a young woman, no doubt as some sort of sacrifice or punishment. In terms of MDPs to study, I had put her to one side as we were committing our very limited resources to investigate the background of the very early Muters. What was interesting about this new passage however, was the activity this new Muter was engaged in – it was completely novel. Not only that, Nigel was mentoring this new MDP himself in part because he was exploring the concept of 'unfinished business' of the recently deceased.

I explained to Tom and Fiona that we needed to try and pull together as much information on this new Muter as possible. We had a lot of useful leads from Nigel in his writings, but it would take some ingenuity in identifying the Muter's identity in her previous life. Establishing what the Muter did and her background and movements were important for two reasons. Firstly, if Nigel's 'unfinished business' impulse of the recently deceased was true (and, my instincts were that it was a very credible hypothesis), then it might not only allow us to both 'guesstimate' incidents that had occurred (but were not known to police), but it would provide us with enough details around which we could involve the police in a plan – a 'great reveal', if you like. If it worked, we would play the role of the annoying little brother trailing around after the police, yet simultaneously playing the role of a commander laying down the strategy for the police to follow.

We wrapped up the evening and started to plot out the grand plan and the great reveal.

'Don't get ahead of yourself,' I said to an exhaustedly excited Fiona at the end of the evening. 'We have one chance to get this right. We need to identify the Muter that Nigel acquired on the wasteland and know her haunts and habits in her previous Beanlife. Then we need to finalise the plan to take to the police. Like anything we do, it has to be...'

'Watertight, we know,' interrupted Tom and Fiona in unison, nodding tiredly.

'Good,' I replied, squinting at them. 'Glad to see my interns are paying attention.'

The next few days, in fact week, were quiet. Both Tom and Fiona knew what had to be done and I left them to it. I let them read the blog on the seized laptop, which excited and motivated them more.

Within ten days Fiona had done some excellent work and we had identified the MDP in question (early twenties in Bean terms) and learned a little about her background. Her name had been Erika. She had been trafficked into the UK three years earlier from Romania. Slight in build, she had had a tough ride in life. She had thought she was coming to the UK to work in a fruit-picking capacity in the summer, hoping to stay in the country and then get work as a barista in London during the winter months. Soon after arriving she had been forced into prostitution and her spirit, quite simply, had been broken over two years. Her Romanian handlers had given up on her. She wasn't getting the custom that she had when she was first brought over. She wanted to return to Romania, but the gangsters made her work for her return fare. She resisted and the handlers were inclined to dispense with her altogether, perhaps as an example to others. But how do you do that without drawing attention to her disappearance? Fortunately, there was a plague outbreak in London and apparently a boozy discussion prompted the idea. So, after a final confrontation (and, no doubt, some abuse) the three Romanian handlers bundled Erika into their large black SUV, drove her to a piece of wasteland in east London looking for a rumoured group of MDPs loitering on the land. They had driven around in circles until, having identified the dead, turned the vehicle onto the wasteland, approached the MDPs at some speed, threw open the door and pushed Erika out onto the broken asphalt in front of a few rough and scary-looking MDPs.

Of course, we learned all this after much cross-referencing of Nigel's blog with witnesses and gossip from Erika's former friends. Fiona (with some input from Tom) had done some quite remarkable work identifying Erika and her friends. Working on the assumption that Erika was a victim of human sex-trafficking (largely based on Nigel's writings), Tom had used social media to pose as a client looking for his favourite Romanian squeeze. Once Fiona had a shortlist of names, she then posed as a friend of Erika's to confirm her identity – a young Romanian prostitute who had gone missing, now presumed dead. With that Fiona had tracked down a couple of other young women in a similar position to Erika's who could give us the background to the gang and their treatment of Erika and her demise. The young women were all too ready to talk – very possibly as a result of feeling safe after the break-up of the Romanian gang – a result of a very gruesome murder of its three leaders, in which, as you may know from his blog entries, Nigel had been instrumental.

Erika was, of course, TarmacTired.

There was a degree of satisfaction to learn that the Romanian handlers had met their match in the new (and 'enlightened') TarmacTired, but the police had no idea who the perpetrators of the gruesome murders were. Reports from the police suggested that they had 'mostly' dismissed the idea of an MDP attack because the storming of the gang's headquarters had all the hallmarks of being highly organised, so it was assumed to be a hit by a rival gang. Fiona, Tom and I, of course, did nothing to disabuse the police of their assumption, but, looking at the crime scene photos of the butchery visited upon the gang members, I was reminded of the dark and dangerous nature of Nigel and his team.

What was of help was Nigel's descriptions of TarmacTired's subsequent death skill. Put simply – luring men into brothels. Tarmac would take over a brothel, 'enlighten' the working girls and bring them over to her side and....wait. For clients....to run into their arms. The trouble for the police investigators (which was advantageous to us) was that the clients would not inform their friends, family or work colleagues of where they were going. Men (of all ages) were just disappearing. The urge to share our inside knowledge (Nigel's blog) with the police was overwhelming, because we learned that the police were scouring wasteland, cemeteries, derelict buildings and other places for missing persons. The Cloth-Heads were stumped, but we remained resolute in withholding our 'intelligence'.

With the identity of Erika confirmed and, with a shortlist of places where Erika had worked (provided by Erika's friends), we cross-referenced it with the police reports of missing persons (males) and picked up the phone to the most senior Met police officers who would meet with me. They both respected me as far as any police officer respected a civil servant running after the mobile dead. I explained it would be in their interest.

Within days we were meeting with Chief Superintendent Ian Davie and DCI Luciana Vaccarelli. I took both Fiona and Tom along as observers to the meeting at the Metropolitan Police's Scotland Yard HQ. My interns had done most of the heavy lifting in terms of investigation of TarmacTired's origins, so it was only fair they should witness the fruits of their labour. Besides, I thought it would be a good learning experience for them and the presence of others might help apply pressure to the police officers. It was going to get quite uncomfortable for the Cloth-Heads.

'Just scowl and frown,' I told Tom and Fiona as we climbed the stairs to the conference room. 'This is all about pressure.'

'And the great reveal,' murmured Fiona.

'Not yet. Patience,' I replied under my breath.

We sat waiting in the conference room for twenty minutes before a harried Chief and stone-faced DCI walked in.

'I don't have much time and I might need to leave,' said Chief Davie, pulling up a chair and sitting down.

'Then I'll get straight to the point,' I said, waving a brown paper folder in my hand that held a report forwarded to me by Chief Davie's team forty-eight hours earlier. 'Any sign of PC Hills, DC Markham, DCI Micklethwaite yet?'

'No,' he sighed. 'You think they might have been acquired by MDPs?'

I decided to go in for the kill (for dramatic effect).

'Do any of your men frequent hookers?'

'What?!' Chief Davie asked, stunned, before suddenly rising from his chair, tutting and huffing as if he was about to leave the room. Had DCI Vaccarelli not been present I doubt he would have been so indignant and expressive.

'You need to ask their friends and colleagues,' I said.

'Why?' Chief Davie huffed with a manufactured puff of disgust.

'You might find them on the roof of a brothel.'

'What?' Chief Davie now spat, incredulously.

'How do you know this?' asked DCI Vaccarelli.

'I have my sources.'

'Who?'

'I'll let you know once we have made a few visits to these brothels,' I said, pushing a list across the table.

'Your regular haunts?' he muttered, pleased to make a point in front of his junior colleague.

'Just recommended establishments from the confidential newsletter circular of the Men's Police Officer Association – the one for which you are co-chair,' I replied, dead-pan.

Chief Davie went a little pale. I almost thought I had struck lucky by mistake. I didn't let him suffer, I needed him on my side. I wanted to be on those raids.

'Just kidding,' I said with a smile and wink.

I was surprised the meeting went so well. I had obviously rattled the Chief. I was unsure why – was it the thought of his team members being lost to MDPs or officers under his command who had been caught in a brothel? And so it was that the day after next, Fiona, Tom and I were accompanying a team of 'Rubber Beans' (police in their fancy rubberised suits) to the four establishments that my splendid interns had identified. Fiona had longlisted a dozen brothels then Tom had phoned each of them. There was no answer from four establishments, so it was game on. I thought it was reasonable to assume that TarmacTired and any accomplices had yet to acquire the skill of answering the phone. That is not to say clients might not have been visiting the premises – regular clients may well have been visiting not knowing of the dangers lurking within.

At the Chief's requests it would be a 'low-key' approach and ingress to the premises. The MDPs were not terrorists and did not carry weapons, nevertheless, the sight of a dozen men in black rubber suits creeping towards a bland residential door looked odd. I was stationed on the road outside with the Chief and DCI who both wanted to see what was going on. I suspected the Chief wanted to be on the ground so that he could take rapid control if his officers were indeed located inside. He could manage (or rather, muzzle) the story at source.

At ten o'clock on a bright, sunny morning we visited 27 Belle Vue Place.

Can you hit a jackpot of death? I'm not sure, but I was hopeful.

The Rubber Beans breached the door and moved slowly through the premises. It was given the all clear and we were invited inside. There was no sign of TarmacTired, but we found.... thirty-two bodies on the rooftop – including the three police officers, one Rubber Bean, an accountant, blue collar and white collar, a variety of ages.

'How did you know this?' asked Chief Davie, somewhat shell-shocked.

'I have an inside source. I am trying to verify it,' I replied, barely unable to contain my glee.

'Consider it verified,' muttered Chief Davie in reply.

'When you say "inside", do you mean someone working within the infected group?' DCI Vaccarelli asked, incredulously. 'Someone posing as an MDP?'

It was an interesting idea and actually tickled me. I suppressed a chuckle. As if a Bean could outwit the likes of Nigel and his team. I would love to see an undercover Cloth-Head try.

'Um,' I sighed, and huffed myself and paused for dramatic effect. 'Not quite. It's classified.'

I didn't really know what "classified" meant in that context. Nothing was classified. I was working on my own in the attic space of a civil department with a handful of interns to help me. But it worked. The police officers just nodded and shut up. I was surprised they took it at face value, but I was fast learning how lying and posturing worked. That said, I made a note to speak to my supervisor, Robbie, to get something on paper so I could use the phrase again. It could prove useful if I wanted to muscle my way into the hierarchies of decision-making.

Over the course of the next seven hours we visited the other three brothel establishments – 10 Eboracum Road, 195 Hedly Way and 87 Mill Street. Jackpots all.

In total one hundred and eleven bodies were recovered. Fourteen were showing signs of beginning to rise.

In summary, the 'great reveal' had delivered. I had credibility and, I am ashamed to say, I had tasted power. I knew something the Cloth-Heads didn't. Power (and a bit of mystery) garners respect, which in turn garners more power.

18. I'm Classified!

Chief Superintendent Davie's reaction to my brothel success had intrigued me. Within forty-eight hours it became clear to me that I needed to capitalise on my success. News went whizzing around the police networks. Of course, 'no Press' was the order. Not that it mattered, news flies faster when it is embargoed. So, within a few days I had started dropping the phrase 'classified' more and more. But it could only last for so long, I needed to get it official. On second thoughts I realised I shouldn't try to involve Robbie in case it slowed things down, so I went to Chief Superintendent Davie's boss – the Deputy Chief Constable – on the assumption that news of my success had both risen up the chain of command as well as filtered down to the rank and file. After all, why wouldn't it? Such news would rattle any employer – not least those who claimed to have a moral authority in all things.

I met Deputy Chief Constable Corbould in his office. No conference room setting here. It was a plush space in the Met's Scotland Yard with a pleasant window view and comfy chairs around a coffee table. I kept the conversation short and I remained standing. I was not here to converse and bargain over the goods, I was here to deliver the goods.

I adopted a frown and a sigh. I threw the latest report on his desk.

'Here is the report listing fourteen police officers who were frequenting prostitutes,' I said with a sigh, before adding, 'Seven of them while on duty.'

He said nothing.

I raised an eyebrow and fixed my gaze on him.

'I wish I could keep this classified, but I don't have the authority,' I said. 'I am getting blocked at every turn. I am going to have to share this with anyone who asks.'

'We should be grateful if we all could keep this confidential until we have ascertained the true nature of the situation,' the Deputy Chief Constable said, quietly.

I squinted.

'You mean, your police officers were visiting brothels undercover?'

The pause.

The Deputy Chief Constable knew what I had been referring to. Recently police officers had been exposed infiltrating environmental and anti-war groups and forming relationships with the women. It had been reported in the Press and had become ugly and costly. Careers (even of 'senior' commanders) had ended because of it. It would look very shoddy if something similar was happening all over again.

Like many of the Cloth-Heads I had been meeting recently, he looked a bit ashen. I decided to give him a way out.

'Look, I have bigger fish to fry, namely these MDPs themselves, but I don't want to have to piss around trying to protect the police if they're dipping their wicks into waxed professionals.'

He nodded and breathed out. I had planted the seed, now I went in for the kill.

'I am assuming it is not a case of the Metropolitan police force being infiltrated by necrophiliacs?'

'Necrophiliacs?' he gasped. 'You think these men wanted to have sex with MDPs?'

'It doesn't matter what *I* think. It matters what the Daily Gazette thinks…. And by "thinks", I mean "thinks will sell newspapers or click-bait banner advertising".'

More silence. At times like this I wished I had an audience.

'I wish I could help,' I said, cueing up the answer that I hoped would pop into his head. I know what you guys do and what you are up against, but I answer to mandarins, civil servants, the Press.'

At last – he spun around. 'I will arrange for you to have discretionary Top Secret status. Citing "it's classified", it means you can refuse to speak to anybody right up to the Chief Constable and the Police Commissioner himself. Even junior ministers. In fact, even me.'

I sighed a serious sigh and nodded.

'That might just work,' I murmured, now nodding pensively.

'But if you get this discretionary Top Secret – everything's classified – status, that still means you talk to people like me and Chief Superintendent Davie.'

'Sure,'

'It just means you don't *have* to talk to anybody else.'

And with that, I was classified. It actually came through the following day. I was given an ID card with different logos, a reference number and a barcode for scanning. I could wave it around and refuse to speak to anybody. If stopped or questioned, I could flash the card and the police officer or civil servant would scan the barcode number that dialled a number. The caller would be informed that the card-holder (me) could refuse to answer any questions about anything.

Realising the advantage of printed stationery to wave in front of people's faces as I tried to gain the upper hand, I took the opportunity to print up some business cards with my contact details and the contact details of my intern team. I could hand them out to police officers and others who might be able to feed us some useful information. I included the department's logo and slipped in a phrase 'Special Ops' that was sufficiently vague. I made the point of artfully slipping the term into the conversation with Robbie in case the phrase came back to bite me.

Successes like Chief Superintendent Davie and the Deputy Chief Constable Corbould helped. It buoyed me up. Gave me options. But it did not alleviate the worries. Now that Tom and Fiona were in the loop about Nigel's blog, we began discussing its implications in detail and searching for passages we could corroborate. Furthermore, CCTV footage was always coming in so we had to stay alert of opportunities to repeat the success of the brothels exercise. You would think sharing with colleagues would alleviate the worries. It did, for some things, but for other things it compounded the anxiety. There is no point rising to great heights only to fail to make progress understanding Nigel. The danger was, the higher the height, the harder the fall. We understood some things, but were at a loss about what to do with others.

One major, nagging concern was Nigel's talk about "unfinished business". What did he mean? We had behaviour that had been carried over from Beanlife, that was fine. We understood that. It had a logic to it and was predictable. But Nigel was referencing this 'unfinished business' of Muters. Did it mean that not only were habits transferring from life to death, but a form of motivation too?

I needed to sit down with Tom and Fiona and discuss it – to now look for patterns. Habits were known before death and would come up in background checks of Muters' past lives. But 'unfinished business' would not come up in a background check and, arguably, this unfinished business might tend towards violence like TarmacTired and her former gang leaders. There was the danger we would attract the spotlight only to spectacularly crash in full view by failing to predict other events.

For this reason I decided to hint about it in the reports that I was sending up to Robbie and into Whitehall, but not enough that I would be questioned or challenged about it. I didn't want to put myself under any undue pressure. After all, I was still fairly junior. I might have the business cards and the classified status, but they were tools. I needed to confirm my status by delivering results. I needed to be able to flash a card around and, with a wave of the hand, be known as the man who is authorised to say nothing. Not only should I become unaccountable, I needed to be seen to be unaccountable. Even a little bit. It might save my skin one day. The deference that Chief Superintendent Davie and DCI Vaccarelli showed me at the great reveal had been eye-opening.

I checked in with Robbie who was still my protector. I walked into his office unannounced and was, I have to say, flattered that he was thumbing through some of my reports. I decided to come clean about the classified-status thing. I could see his mind turning as he studied the "I'm classified" card. He said nothing and handed it back to me, but I read his reaction that the development might prove useful for him too. He could dodge questions because the police had classified the work and even he, as supervisor, was in the dark. He moved on to other matters.

'Can we give them another name?' he asked.

'Like what?'

'People upstairs, mostly politicians, don't like the word zombie, MDP and anything that refers to a plague, infection or anything related to medical disease and death. We don't want anything negative to become too entrenched that could be embarrassing.'

'How about "Muter"?'

'Where does that come from?'

'Er, it's the term that a blogger uses.'

'A blogger?'

'Known as, er, Nigel…. He's writing up all sorts of stuff. He's a sort of intern who feeds information to our team from the outside…of our team.'

'You mean, from the "inside"?'

'Er, well, you know, I think, maybe, how can I say…..'

'He's working undercover as an MDP? You have a mole?'

My mouth opened, but it was a false alarm. Nothing came out.

'I have contacts too, you know Josh, and I've heard rumours you might indeed have someone on the inside? Is this true? Your reports have been making waves,' Robbie said, tapping my handiwork on the desk in front of him.

I just went for it.

'I'm sorry, Robbie. It's classified.'

Robbie squinted, said nothing. It was a standoff.

I decided to surrender (and give my supervisor a pyrrhic victory).

'Nigel has his ear to the ground in the Muter realm,' I said. 'He gives us a perspective of what is happening beyond these four walls. Some of it is quite useful, in fact.'

'What does this "Muter" term stand for?' said Robbie, moving on.

'I'm not sure,' I lied. (I had a theory for the word's origin that was based on an obscure passage by Nigel.) 'Sometimes his words have origins in the English language or use a logic that can be deduced.'

Robbie returned his attention to my confidential reports on his desk.

'I've been reading about this "Unknown Target A" you've been referring to...,' said Robbie, helpfully moving on to a completely different subject. 'Now known as "Shade"?'

'Yes.'

'Have you identified him yet? Does he have a name?' asked Robbie looking inquisitively over his glasses.

'Noooo, but we think we are close. He was an early Muter – those very early crematorium records were either unreliable or destroyed, so it's proving tricky.'

'Does Nigel know about Shade?'

By now I was struggling to manage the conversation in my head.

'Yes. Er, Nigel likes him; thinks Shade is an important player.'

'Okay, make sure you use the word "Muter" in your reports from now on.'

'And if anyone asks where it comes from?'

'Pull a face and say "it's classified" of course,' Robbie said, shaking his head. I took it as my cue to leave the room. (I knew Robbie had a lot on his plate and probably didn't want to talk. Not only was he supervising the road closure teams, but work on a high-speed rail-link project was scheduled to start next year keeping him enormously busy.) Sometimes I left his office feeling edgy, deflated, this time I was tickled. I was gaining some traction, some credibility, and it was all down to Nigel. At the very least, I needed to invest time and effort into Unknown Target A – Shade, Nigel – he was my ticket to progress.

That said, there were times when I had to remind myself not to be complacent. I knew I had to keep people on side, but I had thought that the patrolling Cloth-Heads were the way to go. After all, they were the people I was meeting on the streets and developing personal relationships with, but I feared I was neglecting others, including the dispatchers, so when possible I would drop by a police station or a police dispatcher centre (some now with teams dedicated to MDP activity) and introduce myself, flash my fabulous new ID and hand out a few business cards.

There was one other job to do with my new-found status. I requested the full police report on Mia's disappearance. It arrived promptly. No questions asked. The police file was filled with 'crime scene' photos, the description of the evidence and the location matched the description in Nigel's blog. Nigel's reference to being attacked by a woman who used a 'chain-and-sticks' implement as a weapon matched my own memory of Mia doing her nunchucks practice on her houseboat. The file also contained pictures of a smiling Mia from her time in Brazil. There were also pictures of Mia engaging in martial arts. I had known for a while that Mia was Chain-and-Stiks. I say 'known', but it was suspected as strongly as one could, but comparing the police file to Nigel's account and reviewing the images of the same 'humanoid' before and after death was sobering. It made it personal. All doubt was removed.

I sighed and placed the police file in my box of incontrovertible evidence. Even though Mia and I were nodding neighbours, the pictures of Brazilian beaches and laughter reminded me not only of my past Brazilian life but also a life of what was yet supposed to be. If my London-based Brazilian neighbour could be taken from me, so could my original Brazilian love be removed from the land of the living. Perhaps I should reconnect with my sweetheart before I lost her altogether too.

19. Chubby at Play

The brothel exercise was still buying me credit with everybody. Tom and Fiona were now onboard. They trusted me. My nurturing of relationships with Cloth-Heads was also paying off. I was getting phone calls and text messages from officers being called to scenes of 'carnage'. Life was good.

But soon, unfortunately, there was too much information coming in and I felt there was a danger I was going to end up poring over reports in the office and fielding phone calls. I wanted to be in the actual field – meeting people, going to scenes of incidents. But as my intern team was growing in number I had to be selective. So, again, I turned to Nigel. I was becoming distracted by Nigel's regular references to ChubbyCheeks and her effectiveness at targeting anybody and everybody. The trouble was, it was not really showing up in formal police reports. There had been occasional references to a small child – blond and cherubic – in the vicinity to some disappearances or attacks and anecdotal reports of aggression, but nothing verifiable. So, although an MDP of interest, she (a 'Muterling') was largely dismissed as a threat. After all, no one in their right mind would assume that a small child could be a killer.

We knew the destructive power of TarmacTired, DoorStop, Diesel and others, but nothing really about a Muterling like Chubby. What was she doing? Was she a look-out? Bait? An observer? It had come up in conversation with Tom and Fiona, but the three of us, having seen the violence and destruction inflicted on the human body by Muters, struggled to believe it had been

149

inflicted by a child (albeit a deceased one). Not only did we think it was *physically* impossible, but I suspect the thought that a six or seven year old girl was capable of it, was too terrifying. That was our mistake.

So, when there was a report that a possible MDP attack had taken place in a children's playground (resulting in the death of both a mother and child, with a young, blond girl being seen in the vicinity), I jumped at the chance to do some fieldwork. Sensing it could be an important lead, I took Tom and Fiona along. Eye-witness reports were often confused and conflicting and I needed my most experienced interns onsite to sift through the rubbish.

The three of us arrived at a grassy park (the size of a football pitch) that looked like any other park in a fairly run-down residential area. In one corner of the park there was the typical fenced off area for the young children with rubber mats around climbing frames, brightly coloured roundabouts, see-saws, swings and fibreglass animals secured to the ground on springs. This corner of the park had now been cordoned off behind police tape; a couple of Cloth-Heads were mulling about chatting to worried parents who were clutching their children close. Police forensic white tents had been erected over two parts of the playground.

With Tom and Fiona, I strode across the grass to the rubber-matted play area and flashed my badge at any officer who even so much as glanced in my direction. It felt good and a little part of me thanked Nigel for bringing me to this part of my life. I felt the eyes of the local mothers on us as we headed into the dead-zone.

I entered the first white tent to see a forensics team poring over a blood-stained rocking rabbit. There was no body or entrails. The second tent was partially covering a point halfway between the rocking rabbit and a park bench. It was covering a large blood stain and what looked like some intestines. There were no bodies. I asked for the police officer who had been first on the scene and another who had received the preliminary witness statements. This is what we learnt.

One witness said that a small, blond, female child was attacking another small toddler-boy who had been riding the rocking rabbit after which a woman, presumed to be the mother, rose from the park bench and tried to intervene. Another report contradicted it saying that, no, a tall, mean, fearsome-looking MDP had attacked two children playing around the rocking rabbit and then the 'mother' came to a rescue. The tall mature MDP then disappeared with the two children and the mother.

It was a perfectly understandable conclusion to reach – that a male, adult MDP was responsible for all the violence and mayhem. After all, the alternative was too terrible a thought – that the plague virus was transforming primary school children into maniacal killers. But I instinctively thought the first account was correct – Chubby had been 'working the park', but with an adult Muter as backup. I was encouraged. This incident might be the break we were waiting for and lead us to a better understanding of Chubby herself and Muterlings' development in general. Nevertheless, it was not lost on me that it could be politically explosive, so when conversing with the Cloth-Head I made a conscious effort to ensure my reaction suggested that the male MDP-as-lead-attacker was probably the more likely of the two stories and the Muterling-killer was a misreading of events. The Cloth-Head didn't question it (but then he was a Cloth-Head).

That said, I had to remain cynical. We needed more information than the Cloth-Heads had gathered. Why did the MDP choose this place? Or *did* the MDP choose this place? Perhaps it just stumbled across the playground? It sounded like it could be Nigel. If so, then Nigel wasn't quite so random. Perhaps I would just have to wait until he updated his blog.

As I mulled over my options I surveyed the surrounding area. I was looking for inspiration. The two sides of the main park were bordered by a metal fence with a double-gate in the middle large enough for a lorry to enter that led onto the main road. The park was the sort of place that would host a small travelling fair in the summer, or a council-organised fireworks on bonfire night. But the other two sides of the rectangular park were bordered by trees (which no doubt provided shade for sunbathers and picnickers on warmer summer days) and beyond that, just discernible, a path for walkers and joggers. I had a quick look at my smartphone and surveyed the satellite images of the surrounding area. Beyond the path were the rear gardens and garages of local residences. The path, running between the park boundary and the gardens, connected with other walkways that ran in between yet more gardens. Rather than have rear gardens backing on to other rear gardens, this path snaked around the residential neighbourhood and later connected up with cycle paths and towpaths running alongside canals.

I was familiar with this type of urban design and I knew these walk and cycle paths were maintained by the local boroughs. The town hall encouraged the further development of these pathways to encourage people to cycle and walk rather than adding to congestion to the area by jumping in the car. The paths would be frequently used by cyclists taking the back ways to work or by pedestrians heading to the underground tube station or by parents walking their children to school.

Comprising sandy and pebble paths, it would be a pleasant running and cycle route to get around the neighbourhood especially during the day and summer months. During the night, it could prove a tricky route to take for the safety conscious. The enclosed rubber-matted playground was on the side nearer the walker-bicycle path. Although the play area was itself enclosed behind wire fencing, it was far enough away from the road that, should a toddler escape from its confines, a parent would have nearly one hundred yards before the toddler reached the road and traffic. Surveying the scene it was reasonable to assume any 'cognisant' MDP would approach and enter the park and playground from the tree-bordered footpath.

I checked with the Cloth-Head who had been first on the scene and asked him if an MDP had been reported loitering in the neighbourhood or near the road in the days or hours running up to the attack. The reply came back negative. This was quite unusual. The average freshly-risen MDPs were usually slow meandering walkers. They would drift around the roads, but there were now a handful of cases where attacks on people seemed to come from nowhere.

I was puzzled. I nodded to Tom and Fiona in the direction of the local mothers watching us from behind the police tape. We needed more witness statements to compare with each other. There was unlikely to be any CCTV or mobile phone footage of the event or from the nearby area.

I decided to join my interns and spotted a young boy (perhaps twelve years old) being dragged away from the group as Fiona approached. The mother and son were arguing about something. As the young mother was trying to drag him away, he seemed intent on staying and waiting for Fiona to reach him. There were a few moments when, at a distance of twenty yards, the boy and I 'locked eyes'. Believing the boy might have something to share, I sauntered over with a smile, more for the benefit of the mother. Getting the perspective on the incident from someone who actually used playgrounds might prove illuminating.

'Hi, there,' I called out, 'how are you?'

'We're just leaving,' snapped the mother.

'Any idea what happened here?' I said, trying to rescue the situation.

'Yes,' said the boy, much to the annoyance of his mother.

'Okay, great,' I said, nodding, 'we'd love to hear it.'

'We have little to add to what we've already told the police,' the mother said.

'I'm not the police,' I said.

'You're not?' said the boy. I could sense his disappointment.

'Special Ops,' I said quietly, washing his disappointment away.

I flashed my new business card as casually as I could muster. (It was the first time I had flashed it to a civilian and was glad that my stationery was being put to good use.)

'My team and I,' I said, nodding towards Tom and Fiona, 'assist and advise the police on management of new threats.'

'You mean the zombies?' the boy said.

His mother flinched with irritation.

'Those who might have caught the virus and threaten the safety of...playgrounds and more,' I replied. 'We wouldn't want places like this to become dangerous for young children.'

'I'm not a child, I'm nearly thirteen,' the boy almost spat with disgust, as if I would make such a routine mistake as mistaking his age.

'I wasn't talking about you,' I said, mirroring his shocked confusion, 'but if young men, like you, can help us develop our... 'intelligence' on such incidents, it would be much appreciated by all at Special Ops.'

I had him. His face fell in wonder morphing into a silent, desperate plea to be fast-tracked for admission into the Special Ops programme himself.

'No, we must go,' said the mother, turning and ignoring the offered business card and pulling her son away. Fortunately, out of his mother's view, the boy snatched the card from my hand and slipped it expertly into his coat and away from the gaze of his mother. I looked him hard in the eye.

'Email me,' I mouthed, tapping my fingers on an invisible keyboard.

The boy nodded solemnly before turning away and jogging off with his mother.

I turned back to the scene. I would await information from the forensics and see what Tom and Fiona's reports would come back with, but I had hopes for the boy's eye-witness account. He might even prove to be the best witness to Nigel and Chubby we had ever had. If it matched with anything Nigel might later write, then that would be yet another jigsaw piece in my gold-plated fruit salad bowl of evidence.

20. Lite-Bites

It was coming. We always knew that knee-knackering problems would come our way and hobble our progress by the sheer amount of time they took up. Problems that would turn our rising progress curve into a flat plateau of bureaucracy. The problems took the form of reports produced by other government departments that needed a written response, or individual cases that had caught the attention of an ambitious politician or meddling civil servant.... and also needed a response. When possible, I would sit on the problem (a report or a specific case) until somebody higher up was moaning. Robbie would start asking questions, so I would have to pull interns off our own investigations to investigate, gather data and draft responses.

In this particular instance, it was both a 'report' *and* a 'case' merged into one unholy time-consuming mess.

First, the report:

We had received a report from a police committee that noted that larger numbers of random members of the public were just disappearing – at an alarming rate, much higher than the usual background rate. Many of these people did not match the typical profile of 'disappeared persons' i.e. teenagers or young adults running away from home or criminals lying low. From our perspective, we couldn't all ascribe them to TarmacTired and brothel visitors. I suspected some might be run-of-the-mill MDP victims, but what could we do? It was a matter for the police. What was unusual was that an increasing number of these 'disappeared' were often well-to-do middle-aged (and older) people just disappearing from the face of the earth. They either left the house one day and didn't come back. Or they were (allegedly) at home, then just disappeared, often without a sign of a struggle, no blood stains and no reports of an attack.

My success at making friends in the police meant that dispatchers and police detectives were contacting us and suggesting that the MDPs were developing a new kind of activity and were asking us to help. 'Did any of our contacts (even our undercover MDP operatives) know what was going on?' they would ask. Fortunately, the "*It's classified*" reply was helping, but there were only so many times I could use it.

I had not been officially briefed on the disappearances because there was no *formal* evidence of MDPs' involvement. On the face of it, the numbers disappearing were not (initially, at least) reflected in the rising number of MDPs reported (or corpses found). In this context the report had found its way to me to investigate and compare with our own data. I had heard murmurings that Whitehall wanted my team to get involved, but I was wary. I knew that as soon as it became public knowledge my unit was involved, it would not be long before I would have hysterical relatives phoning in and asking what was going on.

Trying to pre-empt us getting more formally involved, I instituted a watch-list of missing persons and briefed Tom and Fiona on the coming storm. We needed to stay alert to Nigel's uploads and see if there was any reference to a new kind of activity that might explain the disappearances. What troubled me was that Nigel usually wrote about activities that he was personally involved in, but if he wasn't present, then the incident might not be recorded. I hoped, beyond hope, that he would reference it in some form.

Secondly, the individual case:

This did not come from a document, a report, an email, a phone call. It came from somewhere much worse – Robbie, my supervisor.

Hunched over my desk in the office, I sensed the door fly open, but nobody had knocked. Interns always knocked. Robbie plonked himself down in the chair opposite.

'We need to talk,' he said, sighing and with a pained look on his face.

'I'm listening,' I replied.

'I hear that you are doing some monitoring of missing persons?'

'Yes, just in case they turn up on CCTV in some Muter activity,' I replied, more slowly.

'And have they?'

'Not directly from the missing person list, but we have only just started. We are not officially in the loop.'

'Well, you are now,' Robbie said, rising from his chair.

That was a quick (and useful) talk, I thought.

'Somebody important has gone missing,' he said, pacing about the room and studying the charts, maps and images of MDPs on the walls.

'Everybody's important. Death does that. Equality – better than any government programme.'

'We move in different circles,' he muttered.

'Dr Caroline Godall and her husband, Dr John Godall, have gone missing from their townhouse in Pimlico.'

'Friends of yours, or…?'

'Family and friends of *theirs* are concerned.'

'Understood,' I muttered. The Godalls were friends or acquaintances of someone higher up the food chain.

'Police broke into their home when they had not been heard from for a few days. No sign of them, nothing obviously disturbed. No blood. No struggle.'

'Send over their details and I'll keep an eye out.'

'But the family said the woman, Dr Caroline Godall, reported to them that she had had a brief interaction with an MDP, Muterthing, in her garden a few evenings before. She thinks it might have nipped her in the calf before being scared off.'

'Okay.'

'You think it might be your friend, Shade, or one of his gang?'

I shrugged.

'Your reports suggest they are becoming more sophisticated. Perhaps they are lifting people from their homes?'

I nodded in a non-committal way.

I was partly disappointed that it had come to this. Who was someone to denote that someone was more important than another someone, requiring preferential treatment in death? I could guess that there was either money or politics involved. My mind turned to one tragic story that no one was asking about. It only became an interesting story because it was gruesomely reported in the Daily Gazette after which everybody went on their merry way and moved on with their lives. It involved a loving, late-twenty-something couple who were married in a beautiful church in Richmond, South London, on a Friday afternoon. They were staying in a luxury hotel for Saturday and Sunday and were expected to fly out from Heathrow airport for a honeymoon on Monday.

The newspaper ran a photo of them in a loving pose to camera after their wedding. Beside the happy wedding photo the paper ran another photo taken by a family member who had snapped them (as a surprise) as they were coming out of their wedding suite on Monday morning en route to the airport. The loving couple was caught in almost an identical pose, but with less flesh on their bones and an altogether different look.

David O. Zeus

Fortunately or unfortunately, the family member managed to snatch a series of other images of the bride and groom as they attacked him.

The newly-weds (or "Newly-Deads" as the paper's headline screamed) were blasted with shotguns and beaten to a pulp by shovels wielded by tearful wedding guests who had turned up to wish them well on their new life together. It transpired that nobody had disturbed them since the Friday night wedding reception and 'something had happened' resulting in their putrid-looking appearance on Monday morning.

Apparently, the newspaper had reported, all of this Monday morning drama had been wildly disconcerting to an engaged couple arriving at the wedding venue to view the premises for their own wedding booked for a few months later.

The newspaper story was not without its dark humour. Apparently a blood-spattered hotel receptionist and manager were reported to have been expressing enthusiasm for the visiting couple's impending nuptials as the bloodied corpses (still dressed in morning suit and wedding dress) were repeatedly run over by a Landrover on the gravel drive outside the venue's main entrance.

So, was this young married couple important to someone enough to want answers in death? No, I thought not.

With my head back in the conversation with Robbie, I realised that an opportunity was presenting itself.

'If Dr Godall and Dr Godall are so important, perhaps their friends and families can do something for me?' I said to Robbie, fixing him with a steely glare.

'Um, go ahead.'

'You know I have a small team largely made up of enthusiastic interns, but who have limited specialist tech skills to offer?'

Robbie nodded.

'All the video footage we receive,' I continued, 'whether it be CCTV or mobile phone has to be scanned visually and logged. There is some face-recognition software, but it is primitive and unreliable. It also becomes increasingly difficult as MDPs' faces decay to some degree before reaching a point of stasis. The work is very labour intensive.'

'Go on.'

'Perhaps your friends...'

'They're not *my* friends,' Robbie interrupted, 'but go on'.

'Perhaps "the" friends and families can arrange for GCHQ, MI5 or some other secret spy agency to use their super computers and super software to run city-wide face-recognition on Muters and missing people, family members, deceased citizens that we pass to them. We could send the secret spy agencies images and information on the Muters and the 'missing' people we want to track allowing us to speedily locate people and/or track their movements.'

'Sound like a plan,' Robbie said.

'It won't be cheap and it will need fast-track authorisation,' I said, 'by which I mean authorisation from "the" friends and families.'

'Sounds like a plan,' Robbie replied without batting an eyelid.

'Agreed. I'll be waiting patiently.'

Robbie nodded, turned and headed to the door. He turned and now fixed me with a steely glare.

'Of course, you'll need to start identifying a few Muters or missing people to run tests and calibrate the face-recognition systems?'

'Ooo, let me think,' I said, stroking my chin. 'Perhaps we could start with Dr Godall and Dr Godall?'

'I'll send over the details I have and start making a few calls,' Robbie replied before disappearing out the door.

'Sounds like a plan,' I muttered.

It is amazing what a few phone calls can do. Within a week we were all set up and we had a link set-up with GCHQ and access to high-definition face-recognition systems. We could send selected MDPs and selected missing persons over to the super-spy agency and they would run it through their systems. Before long we were receiving daily reports on missing people and MDPs. I had, of course, sent Nigel's images over, but we weren't getting too many hits and feedback was poor. Apparently, his face was too degraded. Having set up the service and had a few helpful phone calls with technicians in GCHQ, I raised the possibility of extending some of the functionality to tracking social media accounts and even web-connected devices and phones. I thought if Nigel was engaging in cloud-based technologies, perhaps some of the other Muters (or missing persons) might use devices too.

A week later I was marvelling at what "friends and families" will do for their loved ones. Now all I needed was Nigel to upload a passage that could show that I was justified in making such a request and, what would you know, he did. It was fast becoming the case that, of all the people I could trust in this MDP-monitoring enterprise, Nigel was the man.

Fiona was the person to see the upload first.

'Eureka!' I heard her squeal from next door.

She came running into the office holding the laptop. Tom followed soon after.

'Lite-Bites,' she said breathlessly. 'A new activity. A new way of working.'

'A new threat,' mumbled Tom.

'A new challenge,' I mumbled in return.

21. Coming Clean, Getting Dirty

This was the emergence of the 'Lite-Bite'. Muters were not only *feasting* on their targets, but now selecting them to develop skills and nipping them lightly, infecting them with just enough juice to kill them. Consequently, the Lite-Bites remained largely intact and indistinguishable from a regular Bean. Horrifyingly, we realised, they could move about the metropolis largely undetected. How many Muters-in-disguise were now walking about the metropolis? We did not know. The numbers of infected might be vastly under-estimated and that was a very disconcerting thought.

Fortunately, Nigel's first lite-bite was indeed Dr Godall – the wife. She had been christened 'PlumpCalf' and was fast becoming a most competent and accomplished MDP according to Nigel's blogs. Her husband became ChimneyBlack.

This was all excellent news for Robbie and further improved our cooperation with the security services and spy agencies. I even managed to get a few more interns added to my team. We were approaching twenty-strong in number. In the face of death, things were looking good. All interns had short-term contracts, of course. The plague would be over in a few months now that we seemed to be getting on top of things, Robbie begrudgingly admitted, though I was more cautious. If we had Lite-Bites running around the capital, the numbers could be rising exponentially and we would never know it, I reminded him. But that didn't worry everyone because we were getting excellent data. What could go wrong?

With things going well and the increasing challenge of dancing around the identity of Nigel and Shade, I started to entertain the idea of widening the circle of knowledge. The main question was *how* to come clean to my supervisor, Robbie. Of course, I had dropped hints that I was monitoring police intelligence and that I had a few moles within the police force feeding me tidbits of information. When asked if a mole could be trusted, I shrugged.

'As long as we're not paying them,' he said, 'I don't care.'

I just shrugged again.

'But keep the information coming, he said. 'Whatever you're doing.'

With more reports landing on his desk charting our successes and overall progress, he was asking more questions. He was impressed. He would now even volunteer his compliments. It was then that I felt I was almost on safe ground. Not totally safe, but close. However, I needed to deliver the killer blow. It was do or die.

So my strategy was to make it official. I compiled a detailed report on everything I had learned and wrote an extensive report on its implications going forward. I was half-minded to even go over Robbie's head and send it to a selection of civil servants in Whitehall, even the Prime Minister in Downing Street. There was the danger that if I went in half-cocked, I might get shut down and the opportunity would be lost. There were two other elements, I concluded, that needed to be in place before I could share my findings. The first was timing. Dare I say it, but there might be a time of crisis when he was desperate for progress. If things were looking too good the report on the existence of a sentient, self-aware Muter, could be dismissed out of hand. As I had learnt, a 'great reveal' has as much to do with timing as anything else. Finally, I sensed there was a third element, but to be honest, I didn't know what it was, but I felt I would know it when I saw it.

And I did – at approximately eleven o'clock on a Tuesday morning. That third and final element was, quite simply, a compliment. Not directly from Robbie. It was a reported compliment. Robbie was reporting back to me the good news coming from Downing Street itself, of all places.

My previous report had found its way to the Prime Minister. Robbie had been called into Downing Street earlier that very morning along with a bunch of Whitehall figures. Fearing the worst, he had braced himself for a dressing down, but was pleasantly surprised by the welcome sounds of encouragement. The Prime Minister wanted to hear more and requested all future reports be copied to Downing Street.

I said there were three elements that were needed for me to come clean to Robbie. The first, timing, was primed and ready – my reports had given me credibility. The second, crisis, grew out of the first and landed along with the third 'mystery' element that turned out to be 'involving children', which dialled up the opportunity burger to eleven.

When Robbie had been with the Prime Minister, the mid-morning meeting had been cut short. Or rather, the PM had to step out of the room. He came back later, ashen and vexed. Robbie learned that there had been an attack by MDPs at a primary school. Not by adult MDPs, but by (allegedly) child MDPs.

I heard about it first from my police contacts and I knew immediately who (or what) it was – Chubby. I was unaware of other child MDPs unless..., unless Chubby (assuming it had indeed been Chubby) had trained up the child she was responsible for snatching during the playground incident. But it was too early to jump to such conclusions, I still hadn't received any email from the boy who had witnessed the playground attack.

So it was that Robbie returned to the office and stormed up to us. I could see he felt cornered. I spoke in code to one of the nearby junior interns to go and fetch Tom and Fiona. Even though

Robbie was vulnerable, I needed numbers on my side. Moreover, they needed to see what kind of vexed supervisor I was dealing with.

When the four of us were gathered in my office, I closed the door. Nobody sat, we were all too jittery. We all had something at stake, but we couldn't show it, hence the tableau visible from outside the room was of colleagues casually leaning against desks and 'chatting'.

Robbie started by passing on the compliments from Downing Street then reported on the news of the school and the reaction in Downing Street. Robbie made it clear he wanted answers. As news of the attack on the school was unfolding in the media he would come under extreme pressure in the next forty-eight hours. What had started as a good day, with glowing comments from the PM himself, had suddenly descended into the beginnings of the worst thing that could happen to him and his department. Had he somehow let this happen? Nobody was asking yet, he was (and so were we) expecting the worst.

'I have no more time for obfuscation. I want to know who you are getting your tips from and how they could have missed this attack on the school.'

I paused, weighing up carefully what I should say next. Was this the moment? Had the time arrived to come clean?

'Don't fuck with me, Josh,' he said quietly, fixing me with a stone cold glare. 'If you fuck with me, I will fuck you so hard they'll have to redefine the word "fuck" for the common man.'

Robbie wasn't normally one to speak so colourfully. I took him at his word.

I started by explaining our efforts of scouring CCTV for robberies and how we managed to identify John Reuel and Clive Staples (and a few of their accomplices) as MDPs in numerous burglaries. I described how it demonstrated not only learned (or re-acquired) behaviour in death, it showed an evolving degree of organisation. The MDPs looked as if they were becoming more efficient. They were not rambling around premises and department stores, they were reviewing the items, selecting them and managing their MDP teams.

To those that knew him, Robbie was gob-smacked, but to those who didn't (and I'll include Tom and Fiona among them) he looked slightly incredulous and angry. Still stoney-faced, he listened. I could see his brain whirring. Was a deceased person inevitably going to return to their learned habits by way of being deceased? Was it a natural element of death? Or was the deceased individual somehow nurtured *after* death and encouraged to engage in such activities? If so, by whom, by what? Or was it a combination of both? Nature and/or nurture?

Just before he was about to question the origins of the behaviour, the cooperation, the team-working and planning, I moved on to the blog – Nigel's blog and how it corroborated everything and more. I explained that the blog showed that the MDPs (and one in particular) was totally sentient. Self-conscious. Thinking...er, individuals. Once I finished my spiel, I fell silent. I glanced at both Tom and Fiona and shook my head intimating that, no, they should not fill the silence. Robbie had the floor. It was his turn to speak.

We had to wait a few moments.

'You're saying an MDP has been writing a blog?'

I nodded.

'And this MDP's blog is where you are getting all this information on activities, behaviour? And this blog alerts you to incidents before anybody else, including the police and MI5, has come across it?'

I nodded.

As he stared at the floor, Robbie took a deep slow breath. In fact, he looked as if he was having difficulty breathing.

'How can an MDP, a zombie, write a blog?' he said quietly. 'They are brain-dead.'

'Well, we don't know that for sure.'

He looked at me as if I had just defecated on his front lawn (on a Sunday morning).

'Yes, we do,' he replied in an unnervingly calm manner that, in polite company, would not invite an answer.

So I paused as I considered my next words carefully. What I didn't anticipate was that I was shaking my head unknowingly.

'Well, then find out,' he hissed. 'Prove it.'

Before I could say 'how?', my twitching brow had said it all.

'Put one of your fucking zombies in a Magnetic Resonance Scanner and scan its shitty brain. If what you say is true, then we can get some specialist to show there is recognisable brain activity – suggesting...whatever you want to call it, consciousness.'

I looked at him unsure of what to say.

'Unless someone has done that already?' he whispered. 'In fact, no, I take that back. Surely someone has *already* done that?'

'No,' I sighed. 'We haven't. We've tried. Or rather, we've explored the possibility of it.'

'It's with the High Court,' chipped in Fiona. 'Any person has to give consent to undergo a medical procedure like a brain scan.'

Robbie sighed almost like it was his last, and his head fell onto his chest. We all knew the previous pandemic had raised all sorts of ugly issues about individual rights, body autonomy and government mandates that had 'readjusted the understanding around' or 'plain violated' human rights (depending on to whom you spoke).

'Jesus, well, get their family to approve it.'

'Tried that,' said Tom, stepping up in support. 'No family will because if it is found that there is brain death, then technically, the MDP can be disposed of. No family is willing to take that risk.'

'A cadaver has rights?'

'Well, in this day and age, an earthworm in a nature reserve has rights.'

'Jesus, Josh. Get it done. Get an MDP on a MRI and scan its fucking head.'

And with that, Robbie stormed out.

'I'll talk to legal,' I said to Fiona and Tom.

'And go and check out that primary school,' Robbie's voice echoed from the corridor outside.

I realised that the stakes were getting higher. I needed to scale up my efforts and start getting hard data, solid indisputable results. I didn't have time to get answers. I had to get results. And in doing so, I had to get dirty.

But what is dirty? Playing fast and loose with rules? Issuing mild threats? Withholding information here? Letting a crisis develop there? People might die, but they would die anyway. If MDPs could shake up the government, then let it be. Maybe Nigel and his colleagues could work with me.

Within minutes of the meeting ending I had a call from Robbie to join him in his office before I left for the primary school 'incident'. He was a little calmer. He looked tired. Beaten. I know it wasn't me. Pressure was coming from above – junior ministers, civil servants in Whitehall (who in turn were under pressure from senior ministers and the Press). Robbie didn't reference the conversation a few minutes earlier. He had moved on.

'Okay, two other things,' he said. 'Firstly, we're moving. They want us based in Whitehall. They have some attic space that can accommodate your team. I am coming with you, but will be looking after other things.'

I nodded. I guessed that Robbie's continued involvement was the result of a senior Whitehall mandarin not wanting to supervise me; besides, the move would suit Robbie because being closer to the seat of power would help his transport infrastructure projects.

'Secondly, I am fed up with going to these briefings. I cannot stand them.'

'The people or the meetings?'

'Anything and all of them. The self-important, gutless junior politicians and the smug civil servants who don't have the guts to be politicians themselves yet think they run the country.'

'Okay,' I muttered and shrugged, thinking that was the end of the conversation and wondering if it occurred to Robbie that both he and I were arguably civil servants ourselves. (But not Whitehall mandarins, I suppose.)

'So, I'm sending you.'

'Me? Why?''

'Somebody has to do it. So it is time for you to crawl out of your shell and make the case for your research and funding. You convince them. Better than me stumbling through your reports and enduring the eye-rolling from across the table.'

'So they'll hate me?'

'Sure. Most of them, but there are a few allies.'

'Like who?'

'I will put you in touch with Bob Beaumont. He is a director of communications for one of the junior ministers. Very good. He attends all the meetings and committees you will be called to. Listen to him and keep him in the loop. He knows his stuff and how to work the politicians and civil servants.'

'Right, okay,' I said, my heart sinking.

'In normal circumstances I would wish you good luck on this promotion, but I suspect that before long you will wish you were dead and walking the streets yourself.'

22. Chubby at School; Sobbing Cloth-Heads

With my secret now shared with Robbie and my new responsibilities, I knew things had taken a turn. But the morning was not over. It was just getting started. I now had to get a grip on what had happened in the school. Whatever it was, I had to make it work for me. I was now front and centre in all this business.

Tom, Fiona and I undertook a quick review of the known facts as we were driven to the school. My hunch was that Chubby had been involved. Chubby had been busy indeed. I had mixed feelings about the Muterling. Living seven year olds are rarely held to account for their actions, but a *dead* seven year old? How could I hold Chubby responsible for the horrors she was inflicting upon others?

My team and I arrived at the school and were waved through the tight security – armed Cloth-Heads and crime scene investigators dressed in white paper suits and masks. We rapidly identified the officer in charge – Chief Dixon – fortunately someone known to us. He looked ashen. Catching his eye I nodded towards a quiet area of the school playground. The four of us stood in a huddle and let him speak. It was brutal.

We learned that there were at least twenty dead children aged between five years and nine years of age. There were perhaps forty lite-bites and half-a-dozen children missing altogether. Six teachers were dead. Two were injured (lite-bites) and another two were left unscathed (except for psychological trauma). There might be other injuries, but that was the best Dixon could do. By all accounts, two Muterlings were the perpetrators. A boy and girl. The boy might have been a former pupil at the school Dixon had heard from one of the traumatised teachers. The blond girl was unknown. Such was the confusion Dixon said he couldn't be sure there weren't other Muterlings involved.

'Were there any adult MDPs present?' I asked Dixon.

He shook his head. He had been on the premises ninety minutes and he was already exhausted. 'It's carnage in there. I can't believe two kids did that.'

'We're taking the CCTV,' I said to Dixon. It wasn't a request, it was a command. 'My team is probably far better placed to identify the MDPs involved. If asked, you can say you've handed it on to specialist authorities.'

Dixon nodded.

'We'll also interrogate the surviving teachers and those children that can string a sentence together. Speed is of the essence. Leave that to us.'

'Thank you,' muttered Dixon.

I turned to Fiona:

'Secure that CCTV footage from the school and any other footage from mobile phones although I doubt in a school there will be much, if any, available. Do not let *any* footage fall into other people's hands. After that, try and get an idea about what happened from any of the kids, or lite-bites.'

'Won't they be headed to the hospital?'

'Once any child leaves these premises, we will have lost them forever. Don't let a parent near them. Tell the parents anything – even that their kid is dead. The parent will be pleased to later learn their child has survived. It might buy us time.'

I turned to Tom (who, it has to be said, looked a little shocked at my businesslike tone):

'Find those two teachers and get everything you can from them. Descriptions of the Muterlings, how they got access, what they did before they attacked, any hint there were adult Muters in the vicinity, how they left the premises and details on all exit routes. Don't let the teachers go to the hospital. Say they are being held in quarantine until we give the all clear.'

Tom and Fiona, both flushed and breathless, nodded.

'I'll debrief the first Cloth-Heads on the scene and make some calls to ensure our work isn't interrupted.'

My interns both dashed off. I turned back to Chief Dixon. He looked distracted at something over my shoulder. I turned around and saw some other civilians being waved through security. I did not recognise them, but I guessed they weren't police. I suspected they were damage-limitation handlers from Whitehall. The name of that primary school would go down in infamy. I guessed that newspaper headline writers were already tossing around pun-laden, click-baity headlines. The government would need to get ahead of the story. Perhaps a smokescreen would be put out, which would be no bad thing – it might buy me some time.

As I was walking over to the new arrivals, my phone rang. I glanced at the screen intending to reject the call, but recognised it was coming from Robbie's office. I answered.

'Hello, Josh? I just wanted to introduce myself. I'm Bob. Bob Beaumont. Robbie has just put my call through to you. Just to say, we need to manage how this is presented to the media. Robbie suspects you might know who the attacker is and it might possibly be a child? We don't want that getting out there. There are a couple of Whitehall chaps and chapesses arriving. They'll handle the Press.'

'Okay, thanks,' I replied. 'Do one thing for me.'

'Sure. If I can.'

'Keep your friends and anybody else away from interfering with my team here. If you want answers, leave us alone. Get the message out.'

'Consider it done. Looking forward to meeting you in Whitehall. I'll keep an eye out for you. Events of this morning will change things.'

With that, the call finished.

I waved at the civilians arriving and shouted: 'Just spoken to Bob. Bob Beaumont. He needs to speak to you. No need to trouble me and my team. We're fine.'

I saw them stop and check their phones. Job done.

Having put on white forensics suit and shoe covers, I walked through the school corridors and classrooms. It was indeed carnage. A few lone bodies of children were found in the corridors. Other bodies were piled up in corners of classrooms. There were severe injuries to necks, legs and abdomens. Some children even had their half-eaten intestines in a pile next to their body. Often eyes had been removed. It was brutal. I had seen something similar before on a number of occasions, but seeing the bodies of children in such a state was shocking.

'Chubby,' I muttered to myself. 'What have you been doing?'

One other observation that surprised me was seeing the crime scene investigators use wrist-ties to tie the wrists of the deceased children to radiators and other wall-fittings in the school. I knew why. It was because the investigators were fearful that the children might rise. They didn't know it was normally a few days before a Muter would rise. Walking into a small school gym I came across the forty suspected lite-bites similarly being tied by their wrists to gym bars and radiators for the same reason. I could have intervened, I suppose, and reassured the crime scene investigators there was no need, but my priorities lay elsewhere.

The rest of the school was quiet except for the sobbing, not from the surviving children huddled together in the assembly hall, but from a number of Cloth-Heads. I sympathised but also resented it. It dawned on me that the standard Cloth-Heads – even those recruited into the z-squads – couldn't cut it. We needed Cloth-

174

Heads who could remain focused on the job in hand in very stressful and bloody situations. It was likely that there would be equally gruesome scenes to deal with in the future and, not only that, there might be times when we would have to engage with aggressive, attacking Muters. (Not to mention, Muterlings.)

I had submitted a request for better equipped officers for dealing with MDPs – including upgraded rubber-based uniforms, anti-biting armour and, of course, more powerful firearms. The government had been resistant to create such a different-looking law-enforcement group. It would raise tensions further in the metropolis. It would suggest the government was either overplaying its hand in order to exert more control (something the previous pandemic had seen and ultimately back-fired) or that matters were indeed getting out of control. A little local trouble was becoming a crisis. Neither appealed to sensitive politicians.

Fiona, clad in a white forensics suit herself and clutching a canvas bag, suddenly appeared at my side.

'I have all the CCTV. I have had the briefest of looks in the control room. It does look like Chubby and another child – perhaps the child from the playground, but I also think TrainTracks and ColourSplash might be involved.'

'Perhaps mistaken for parents?' I replied.

'Probably didn't get too involved, leaving it to Chubby.'

I nodded.

'Has Nigel given Chubby's playground friend a name yet?' Fiona asked.

I shook my head. 'No, but his blog is due for an update.'

'Do you think Nigel will describe this?' asked Fiona looking around her.

'Um, no,' I said, thinking. 'If he wasn't here, then probably not. He doesn't really refer much to the work of his colleagues.'

Fiona nodded.

'You okay?' I asked.

She nodded again.

'This is important work. We need to stay focused. Go and get some witness statements from the kids, they are tied up in the assembly hall.'

I returned to my thoughts on playing dirty – making the most of the situation. I could formally re-submit the request for the recruitment of harder, tougher individuals and the delivery of upgraded uniforms and weaponry as standard. We would still have to recruit from the ranks of the police, but we should not have too much problem finding those up for the challenge. I could also request direct access to such teams. I could argue that, should I come across intelligence of an impending attack, I could deploy a squad of enhanced rubber-suited Beans myself. A fast-response squad. Perhaps it was a tall order, but there was no harm in asking.

If what Bob had said on the phone was right ('This changes things') then I might need to move quickly. I suspected the government would play the incident down. Perhaps there would be stories in the media of a school shooter? Or perhaps the government would invoke a media blackout – DSMA-Notice (Defence and Security Media Advisory Notice)? But the truth would slip out though eventually. Yes, to be able to deploy my own squad, without questions, would be a useful development for me. But why not raise the possibility of involving the army? While we militarised the Cloth-Heads, we could start thinking about training up some actual military, perhaps? Plant a seed while the iron was hot? Perhaps a halfway house would help – get some retired military into the police? I had already heard that there was government resistance to having green camouflage military uniforms on the streets, but, in the meantime, getting some military personnel into upgraded black uniforms would be a manageable compromise. Something must be done. I would have to put a case together.

So, returning to the office I let Tom and Fiona draft the report on the events of the St Mary's School massacre while I drafted further recommendations for an improved Rubber Bean force. This would indeed change things if I played my cards right.

As with all things, events, revelations, worries don't come along in a linear fashion. They come along in threes (at least). Two of the worries were pressing on my mind and were known to all – the emergence of 'Lite-Bites' and the attack on the primary school. The third was my own.

I checked Nigel's blog and reviewed passages on his 'Lite-Bites' and a subsequent passage on him 'down at the pub' listening to a couple of Beans he called Beardy and Tubby whining about their love lives. What pricked my attention was Beardy's reference to his own Brazilian love, Chiara, and the possibility of visiting her again to confess his feelings. Nigel had opted to make Beardy a Lite-Bite in the hope Beardy would kiss his former love and send her (and no doubt all of Brazil) down the path to enlightenment). The reference to the Brazilian girlfriend obviously reminded me once again of the love that I had left in the South American country. My fears of the plague breaking out over the Brazil filled me with despair – not at the thought of hundreds of millions of South Americans meeting their deaths, but the thought of one in particular meeting hers.

There had already been some plague outbreaks in South America, but nothing like what London was experiencing. Part of my commitment to trying to understand Nigel and his ilk had been my way of containing Nigel (and his plague variant) within these shores. But here was Nigel plotting to extend his reach to the beaches of Brazil…and into my past. I could not have that.

I ploughed through past emails from overseas government agencies each requesting insight into London's MDP containment strategy. After dozens of seconds of consideration, I violated all Foreign Office protocols and got in touch with my equivalent in

San Paulo and asked him to check and screen (and pull all strings possible to quarantine) all thirty-something male Londoners flying from London to Brazil in the last two weeks. No sooner had I sent the email to an address ending in the extension '.br', I typed out another email to the one other person in my contacts book with the same email extension. I would procrastinate no more. I asked Maria-Amphi to be careful, apologised for my neglectfulness and committed myself to meeting her soon.

23. The Boy Who Saw

The following day, as I was putting the finishing touches to the report, an email landed in my inbox. I didn't recognise the sender. I quickly scanned the email's subject header looking for clues to the sender's identity and the content, but it looked as if it was from one of those MDP-groupies that had somehow acquired my personal email address. I was about to forward it to the general email account (that was getting all sorts of rubbish) for the interns to deal with, when it dawned on me. The email was from the boy who saw the attack on the child on the rocking rabbit in the playground – the attack in which Chubby was possibly involved. If Chubby *had* been involved, maybe, just maybe, Nigel had been involved too. I had been monitoring Nigel's blog, but had yet to see any mention of it.

The email read as follows:

Dear Director of Special Ops (MDP Division)

We met at the South Park playground when the young boy was attacked and was killed in a bloody mess. I witnessed the zombie attack and you gave me your card. This is my email. I have taken a lot of time to write it. I wrote it down first on paper secretly because my mum didn't want me to have anything to do with you. It is partly because she has had problems with the police in the past. I explained that you are not the police, but Special Ops. But she doesn't believe me. She thinks you are 'plain-clothed police scum'. I'm not so sure. I am willing to give you the benefit of the doubt. Anyway, I wrote it down on paper. Then I rewrote it down on paper again because I realised I had left a few details out of my first version. Then there was a weekend when I was too busy because I was playing in a football tournament. Eventually, after a few more versions, I had to find a computer to send the email from. I could not use my mum's computer because she would ask me what I was doing. So I had to think hard. Then I thought of other places. I could list the places I thought about, but it would take me too long to type up. So I won't. I also thought about secrecy too. Therefore I am sending this from a library so you cannot trace it just in case you really are plain-clothed police scum. (I don't think so myself. You looked clever and too soft.)

I had gone to the park to practise football. Anyway, I was practising my dribbling. The park was pretty empty but there is an area closed off for the young kids. I could see there was a little boy playing on the roundabout and rocking on the rabbit. His mother was sitting off to the side on a bench looking at her phone. (I left my mum at home, but she insisted that I take my mobile phone. I don't have a smartphone, like with a screen, it is an old one. (I think my mum doesn't want me to have a smart phone because of the sex. She thinks I will become addicted to porn, but I don't think so, I love football too much. (I've played football with girls and its rubbish, so why would sex with girls be any different?) I just live a few minutes away from the house, so my mum thought it was safe.

After a while I could see another little girl hanging around in the playground. She was about seven years old. I didn't see anybody with her. She looked pretty harmless. The mother was ignoring her. Then just as I was about to practise my penalties, I heard a scream. I looked up. It was the little boy on the rocking rabbit. He was screaming. The little girl was bent over him. I thought she was helping him, but when the mother got up from the bench the little blond girl turned and her face was covered in blood. I thought she had a bloody nose because the boy had hit her in her face with his knee. His thigh was covered in blood too. Then the little girl bit into the boy's thigh and tore out a chunk of meat.

The boy was really screaming now. I swear I saw a chunk of flesh in her mouth. It was gross.

The mother then started to run to her son, but suddenly a tall man appeared out of nowhere and approached the mother. I thought he was there to help, but then he grabbed the mother and, you know, did his biting thing. That was gross too. He was starting to eat her. Then there was loads of blood. But he was really calm. It was like the weirdest family outing. (Believe me, I'm glad I have a dysfunctional family.) The boy stopped screaming because the little blond girl had control of him. Then really quickly they all trotted off. The tall man was carrying the mother over his shoulder and carrying the little boy in his other arm.

I didn't know what to do, so I did what always calms me – I practised keepy-uppy, then did some corner-kicking practice.

If you need to recruit smaller, fitter, more agile agents to your team, I would be willing to consider it. I think you need special agents who know how children-zombies operate. They would think differently. I do not need a uniform as I will be in disguise, but I think a baseball cap with a secret code or sign on it would be useful. Then others in the Special Ops (the grown-ups) would know what I was doing.

Anyway, send a reply to this email address. I will check it once a week from the library on the way back from football.

I will not use my real name here in case the proper scum police are monitoring your email. This is my code name.

From,
The Boy Who Saw.

I felt my heart beating a little faster as I realised the email could prove useful. It was independent corroboration of the incident and there was the high possibility that the tall man was Nigel. I forwarded the email to Tom and Fiona. The boy raised an interesting point. Should we think of other ways to monitor

Muterlings? Was a different approach needed? How does the threat posed from Muterlings differ from fully-grown Muters? Does a Muterling's motivation differ? What do dead children think about? Lots of food for thought.

I regret to say that pushback from the government offices in Whitehall was becoming a thing. That said, it was a welcome change from earlier in the 'z-demic' when to describe anything as a 'thing' would have been a result. In the early days it was just indifference or being ignored, but now I could sense irritation when I picked up the phone asking for favours or when I petitioned other departments for more information. My *"I'm Classified"* status was wearing thin with some self-important tosspots. If I were being more gracious, I might attribute the pushback to jealousy of our success – namely the involvement of the security services in tracking Muters (and missing people) around the metropolis. Nevertheless, I sensed a corner had been turned and technology would resolve it in the end.

On another matter, it was encouraging to meet the Communications Director of a government department that Robbie had told me about. His name was Bob Beaumont and he worked for one of the junior ministers, but I soon learned that Bob was very highly regarded, well-connected and well-liked by ministerial and civil servant colleagues alike. He had his hand in pretty much everything and I suspected he had been assigned to a junior minister not because Bob was junior himself, but because senior leadership wanted the junior minister 'managed'. Bob was always courteous and pleasant and would often pull me to one side after meetings, large and small, and ask me thoughtful questions and offer advice. He would leap to my defence in meetings and head off bumps in the road outside of meetings. I usually had a bit-part in the meetings that were usually convened to manage the PR (by which I mean – play the plague down) and devise a plan for 'winning the peace' once it was all over. Rarely were those people present curious about the evolving nature of MDPs, but Bob was a man of the world and it was his job to think hard and fast of stuff going on beyond the horizon. All storms start in a teacup.

As for Bob-the-man, he was the type of person any politician would trust to keep things running in the background. A senior figure in the civil service and in his fifties, his interest and genuine concern for a man nearly twenty years his junior was not lost on me. For these reasons I always had time for him, so when he sidled up to me and tugged my sleeve after one forgettable meeting, I stepped to the side and joined him in the corner of the room as the group was breaking up around us.

'Look, Josh,' he said, 'I have a hell of a lot of time for what you are doing. The trouble is, as you know by now, the junior government ministers and secretaries of state don't want to play things up because of the roasting and hardships from the previous pandemic. It knackered politicians' credibility, the country's finances, everything. So there is almost no interest in ramping up government action and locking everything down again for who knows how long.'

'But Bob, this plague is escalating, albeit quietly, and it could be really serious.'

I knew Bob had seen some of my early reports identifying Nigel as an MDP of interest and the implications of what a cognisant MDP meant for the metropolis, but we had not discussed it in detail. My reports about the true nature of Nigel were kept to a very tight circle and Bob had let slip a few details that meant he was aware of my belief that Nigel was the author of the blog. Every indication suggested Bob was open to the idea of a self-aware, learning, even erudite, Mobile Deceased Person.

'I know, I know, I get it and, trust me, I have tried,' Bob said, 'but politicians only focus on what is in the news today or tomorrow.'

'So, what do you suggest?'

'Well, as I said, they focus on what is in the news. I have a contact who used to work in civil service quite high up, but has quit because of how the government is responding to the virus. I will share no names, for your sake, but he lost someone very close to him to an MDP early in the z-demic. It broke him and he is committed to using all his expertise to apply pressure in ways I cannot do.'

'How?'

'He writes. The pen is his weapon. He can write thunderous prose and often writes columns under a pseudonym for a variety of newspapers. He intends to bring pressure to bear via the newspaper and television media, social media influencers and overseas media outlets. He is very well-connected in media circles. I am going to feed him some information anyway, but I want you to consider feeding information to him directly too. Something that will keep the newspaper editors happy. My contact, let's call him "the Whistleblower", a brother-in-arms if you like, will also disseminate bits of information to podcasters and activist groups to have a rounded approach.'

'Right, I see,' I replied, unsure about how I felt about it. 'Anyone else you want to involve in our discussions?'

Bob paused and thought. It had not been a genuine question. I didn't want to suddenly find myself in an anti-government conspiracy and violating a dozen clauses of the Official Secrets Act.

'Funny you should say that,' replied Bob. 'There is an old university friend of mine who I am meeting soon who is very keen to meet you. He thinks he might be able to help you and I suspect he would indeed be helpful. I'll get back to you on that.'

'You know I was kidding.'

'I do. But these are serious times, Josh. You have convinced me of that.'

'The pen is the weapon?' I muttered. 'Cue thunderous prose.'

'The Whistleblower will strike fear into the hearts of mortal men,' said Bob with a smile and wink, 'and will shake things up in our favour.'

I nodded.

'Thanks for all you are doing, Josh. If you see a few little tidbits appear in the newspapers and reported on news that only came from your work, don't panic. I have it under control. It's how business is done around here. I'll protect you.'

I nodded again.

'Oh, I hear you and your team are moving into Whitehall?' Bob said chirpily. 'Welcome to the lion's den.'

'I'll look forward to it,' I replied, forcing a smile.

Bob winked, patted me on the arm and walked out.

24. PearlLavaliere and 'Tinned Meet'

When you are doing the things you enjoy and are immersed in its daily business, you have good days and bad days. The days' successes and failures (or, in our case, horrors) are felt more keenly. The common theme in both was, of course, Nigel himself. Reader, do you want the good news first or the bad news?

I shall report in chronological order i.e. the good news. (It made the subsequent crash down to earth all the harder.)

The team was working well and, we thought, the winds were blowing in our favour. We managed a swift move of my team to new premises – a converted attic space in one of the grand Whitehall buildings in the City of Westminster where all government business took place. Robbie too moved and was allocated an office a few floors below us. Technically he would still be my line manager, which, all things considered, was a good thing; he was a reluctant ally.

Although our move to Whitehall was a significant physical change, there was no change in our thinking. In fact, Tom, Fiona and I were all the more convinced that Nigel was indeed the key to dealing with the MDP threat. The numbers of Muters were rising in the capital, but they were a pretty disparate lot. There were minor pockets of organisation, then there was Nigel and his colleagues. They were by far the most organised MDP group in the capital. There were too many Muters to track-and-trace and study, so we decided to focus on the main players, the greatest threat, that is, Nigel.

We needed to understand his motivation, his thinking and also learn about his life as a Bean. No sooner had this been established as an absolute priority, Nigel updated his blog. It appears he and I were thinking along the same lines. He was beginning to see the pattern of 'unfinished business' in the awakening of his Muter colleagues. A fine and clearly documented example was the TarmacTired revenge on the human-traffickers who had handled her during her life. RooftopSuicide had been instinctively drawn to visit his ex (thereby recruiting ColourSplash to the metropolis's ranks of mass-killers). There was GlassCutter and DoorStop. But what was not clear (and Nigel himself was self-aware himself to acknowledge) was Nigel's own unfinished business. That was until the picture became clearer when a piece of the jigsaw (a blog entry) was written up about his meeting with (and recruitment of) PearlLavaliere.

It was a touching description. Nigel was trying to fathom why he was drawn to rooftops. It must not only be because it was easier to move around the city, but there was something else. Finally, in his passage about his kiss with an old acquaintance, presumably his own former love, on that rooftop, it became clear. In death, Nigel had christened her 'PearlLavaliere' after the engagement gift he had given her in Beanlife.

I gave Fiona the opportunity to read Nigel's entry first. She looked up from the computer screen, with fire in her eyes.

'I'll do it,' she said.

We both knew what the plan was.

'Drop everything and work on his ex. Find her.'

'....and we find *him*,' Fiona said, breathing heavily.

Within a week Fiona and Tom had compiled the basics. PearlLavaliere (formerly known as Emily) was the break we had been waiting for. Emily, as described in Nigel's blog, was easy to identify from reports of recent missing women living in rooftop flats with a greenhouse – there was only one. It provided a direct line back to Nigel. From there, it was just a matter of compiling a report on both Emily and Nigel-Bean. It was almost odd to think of Nigel as a Bean. A man who smiled, laughed, loved and wept.

Of course, I was itching for news and juicy details, but when she said she was keen to deliver a comprehensive report, my brow furrowed.

'Okay, I can do a preliminary report with the basics,' she said, thinking I might pull rank on her, 'but I need time to go down a few rabbit holes.'

'Okay, understood. Give me something by the end of the week though,' I said. 'You're not the only one that is excited by this. Keep it tight and accurate. Try and corroborate what we already know. See if any of his behaviours are carrying over from life. No talking to anyone else about it. Including the other interns.'

Fiona agreed. But she couldn't wait a week. She came to me with the basic summary after three days. It was humbling to read.

Nigel and Emily had been partners for seven years. She became pregnant and they had a child. Nigel had proposed (the pearl necklace had been an engagement gift). They were living happily together in a rooftop apartment. The child had been sick. The child had died. This put a strain on the relationship and they had a trial separation that went on for a year or so. Then Nigel had ingested bodily matter (brain matter, in fact) of an MDP as it had been shot in the head as he tried to leave his London office block early to avoid being trapped in a locked down building (as a result of a rambling MDP in the area). He was treated in a medical facility, then walking home that night he had been attacked again by another MDP and had not survived. His remains had been due to be incinerated at Pentonville Crematorium, but a perfect storm of mismanagement, work disruption and dodgy paperwork meant there were delays and there was 'confirmed speculation' that a few MDPs had risen and escaped the premises even though the crematorium staff had completed the paperwork stating that all cadavers had been cremated. (Of course, there was no evidence to suggest otherwise.) This had prevented us from identifying Nigel earlier.

Even though Emily and Nigel had been broken up for a year before his death, she had been distraught at his loss. After the loss of her child, Emily had been attending therapy and self-help groups, but had struggled and early reports suggested that she had resented some of the experience. She had been encouraged by friends to start dating again and get her life together. She had become friendly with one individual (later christened Crackleneck) who Nigel had met (and dispatched) on the night he enlightened Emily and welcomed Pearl.

I felt sorry for Pearl. Fiona was obviously affected too. To lose a child and then have a relationship disintegrate, then lose that partner to a plague was a lot for anyone to cope with.

'How did the child die?' I asked Fiona, when we met with Tom to review findings.

'Don't know. Medical records are sealed for some reason. Cannot get hold of them. Some rare illness or something. She was being treated at St Bart's Hospital and never made it. But I am digging further.'

'How old?'

'Nearly three.'

'You should talk to the doctors who treated her. They might have a memory of Nigel and Emily.'

'You think it might have something to do with Nigel's unfinished business?' Fiona asked, now a little reflective.

'Or maybe reuniting with Emily was Nigel's unfinished business?' said Tom. 'Just that.'

'Could be,' said Fiona, nodding, but even I could see she wasn't totally convinced. I was similarly cautious. Surely it couldn't be that simple?

'Maybe reuniting the whole family in death?' said Tom trying to sell his theory. 'Nigel has been hanging around cemeteries, we've seen that. I thought he was recruiting colleagues, but maybe the child was buried and he was searching for her, albeit unknowingly.'

'Hang on,' interrupted Fiona. 'Let me check. I think I read somewhere that the child was cremated.'

'Check it all out,' I said, deciding to move the discussion to a close. 'This could be an important piece of the puzzle. We could talk and theorise all day and night. In the meantime, well done.'

My most accomplished interns nodded, grabbed their papers and laptops from the table and exited the office.

Over the following week Tom, despite his Scottish charm, was unable to get much background information from Nigel's or Emily's families. Inevitably frustrated with his failure, I encouraged him to play the long game. Information would be forthcoming. Tom reluctantly agreed and then focused on trying to gain access to the medical records of the deceased child, but again privacy laws and the completion of consent forms thwarted his efforts. This immediate lack of progress didn't worry me. I saw value in Tom learning of the struggle against bureaucratic organisations. Results would come. I encouraged him to be patient and keep at it. The good times would be all the sweeter for it.

Fortunately, Fiona was making progress in building up a picture of Nigel's and Emily's relationship from Emily's perspective. Through both a deep dive into social media and establishing a relationship with Emily's circle of friends, Fiona acquired pictures of Emily regularly wearing her pearl necklace after the relationship break-up. What was interesting was that Emily wore it regularly *after* the death of Nigel, which added a touch of pathos to our investigation. As Nigel described in his blog, she was wearing the necklace on the night Nigel claimed her.

As for Nigel himself, the facts suggested that, by virtue of his Bean-life being conducted in rooftop flats, his instinct for moving on the rooftops as an MDP was almost certainly informed by his life with Emily. What was intriguing was that if he and Emily had lived in ground-floor flats, then he might not have been drawn to the rooftops and ended his early days as an MDP in an extermination-by-Cloth-Head at street level. I didn't know whether to feel grateful or cursed.

Overall, I was pleased. Progress was good.

Now the bad news.

Another recently recruited intern charged with responsibility for monitoring social media and news outlets for anything of use came running into the office a few days later.

'Something's happening at Bond Street station,' she panted.

'What? Shoppers attacked on Oxford Street?' asked Tom.

'No, the Underground. Details are sketchy, but I think MDPs have attacked a Tube train.'

My stomach sank. I immediately understood the implications.

'Random or…organised?' I muttered.

'Difficult to say, but judging by the original postings on social media casualties could run into the hundreds.'

'Are there people trapped down in the Tube trains?' asked Tom.

Just then another intern came running in.

'Reports from police – get to Oxford Circus now.'

'Oxford Circus?' asked Tom.

The reality dawned on me. In all likelihood the attack on the Underground trains might span several stations and the tunnels between them. It could be gargantuan.

'Are they sending the Rubber Beans?'

'They're sending everybody it sounds like,' said the second intern.

Arriving at Bond Street station Tom and I (with a few interns with cameras) were waved through the controls and entered the Underground train station. (Fiona was out on fieldwork elsewhere in the capital. I sent her a message to get back to the office to manage the incoming hullabaloo and start barking down the phone for CCTV, seized mobile phone footage, anything.)

As we arrived at the entrance to the Tube station, blacked-out vans were pulling in and a new type of creature was disembarking the vehicles. Dozens of heavily armed men dressed in a type of black rubber armour and ant-head-like face masks. These upgraded 'Black Rubber Beans' were the result of my successful campaign for a more professional MDP-response team, drawn ideally from those with some military experience. They were hardcore and looked the part.

My team was stopped at the top of the escalators leading down to platforms. Apparently the route down to the platform was not secure, so we had to wait until there was an 'agreed plan'. Eventually, the Rubber Beans started to make their way very slowly down the escalators to the pedestrian tunnels leading to the platforms. Pausing at each corner and curve (apparently to 'secure' all bends and crevices by announcing "clear" at every opportunity), we followed behind making deathly slow progress. To tell you the truth I shook my head knowing that leaving it any longer was not going to help the people down on the platforms. Perhaps the Rubber Beans were fearful of a wave of MDPs surging upward from the train platforms to the surface. As far as I could see, it all seemed relatively calm.

'Okay, time to move it along,' I uttered at intervals, trying to be encouraging.

It didn't work. A couple of the rubber-clad Beans turned to face me with their weapons pointing at me. I couldn't see their faces sealed behind the rubber masks, but knew they wanted to scare me. It wouldn't work, a weapon held by a man in a gimp suit would never scare me, I thought to myself, not when you know what I was dealing with every day.

No bodies were to be found on the route down, but that did not give me comfort. My fears mounted as we headed deeper underground. I was expecting a bloodbath. I wasn't disappointed.

Just as we reached the platform level I motioned to Tom and my other interns to wait in place until we had determined the coast was clear. Thirty paces later, as the lead Rubber Beans and I reached the platform, the scale of the drama hit home.

The platform was two-sided – a platform for travelling east, a platform for travelling west. The westbound platform was empty; the eastbound platform had a train stopped at the platform with the carriage doors all open. There were no intact bodies to be seen on the platforms. It was silent, but for the sounds of gentle splashes from careful footsteps of the leading Rubber Beans stepping through pools of blood.

We approached the middle carriage. The torso and head of a male was lying half on the platform, half in the carriage. The doors were trying to close, but were bumping up against his body. There was a scattering of dismembered limbs on the platform. Nobody said a word.

With some Rubber Beans patrolling down the outside of the other carriages, rifles trained on their insides, and other Rubber Beans taking aim at the ominously dark tunnel entrances at the ends of the platforms, a couple of Rubber Beans entered the central carriage. After a moment we were waved forward. There appeared to be no Muters present in any of the carriages, no threat. Behind three Rubber Beans I entered the carriage with my team. The insides were also bereft of intact bodies (but dismembered limbs were plentiful), what was striking was the sight of the train carriage walls and ceiling dripping with red juice. It was not as if an explosion had gone off, it was as if the fire brigade had professionally hosed down the interiors...with blood. Maybe eighty jugular veins had been breached. Thinking like Nigel in a cynical moment I thought of the inefficiencies of the mass killing because so much juice had been wasted and had missed the lips of the dozen or so Muters who had feasted there.

Suddenly there was a growling, deep wailing behind me. Alarmed, I span round to see a Rubber Bean, with headgear removed, being sick in the corner of the carriage. His digested yellow and green lunch now swirling in pretty patterns in the red juice pooling on the carriage floor. I stepped out of the carriage onto the platform to see other Rubber Beans emerging from carriages up and down the platform, removing their headgear and throwing up into waste bins or on the floor. Other than the retching of Bean stomachs, the only other sounds I could discern in that underground cavern was the gentle sobbing of other Cloth-Heads in attendance. They had seen nothing like it. I had seen more similar scenes than anybody else in the metropolis and even I was impressed. I pulled out my phone and messaged my team to come on down and record the carnage. The Muters were long-gone from this particular station. God knows how many Has-Beans they took with them. I approached the lead Rubber-Bean who was wiping his mouth as if he too had been sick.

'The train is clear, but there may be MDPs further down the line in between stations. There may be other trains stuck between stations. You need to get the tunnel entrances secure.'

'They'll be back?' he spluttered, eyes wide, all bravado gone.

'No, almost certainly not, they've had their fill as you can see, but it will be reassuring for those working here.'

He nodded and moved away. I was joined by my team members, including Tom.

'Take a breath and get to work,' I said.

They nodded and moved off to video record the incident. A little bit of pride surged through me as they got straight to work walking through the crowds of Rubber Beans still hunched over waste-baskets vomiting or leaning, dazed and pale against the support columns.

It became clear that this story could not be controlled in the way the attack on St Mary's primary school had been 'media-managed'. As I reached the surface again, I pulled out my mobile phone and reacquired a signal. I dialled Bob Beaumont to both give him an update on the scale of the assault and seek advice on next steps. It would be a nightmare for the government. He picked up pretty swiftly.

'Yes?' he panted down the phone.

'Look, Bob, it's Josh here. No doubt you are being updated, but I am down at the scene. It is brutal. My man might be involved, but I suspect there are other groups involved. Too many dead.'

'How many?' he asked.

I detected a shallowness in his breathing, which was odd. Normally he was very calm; a true unruffled professional.

'Hundreds dead, maybe very many dozens snatched.'

'What line?'

'The Central Line'

'Time of attack?'

'Probably started less than an hour ago. It might have gone on undetected for thirty minutes.'

'Look, Josh, I've got to go. Some family business. I'll be in touch.'

And with that, he was gone.

I headed back to the office. There was nothing I could do at the Underground station. The formal request for any footage recorded in the trains had been made by Fiona and I was sufficiently confident that it would be granted. There would be hell to pay if it was not – that was something I could arrange with my recently-found status and support from the likes of Bob. However, I hoped that the events of the day would help, and not hinder, my attempts at incident-control. Whichever, the day had reminded me of the horrors that could be visited upon the unsuspecting Beans of the metropolis.

In those next few days, I turned a corner even though I didn't quite know it myself. Deep down I knew that things were not going to end well. Of course, Nigel also wrote up this episode (in a passage called 'Hunting Grounds: Going Underground') and spoke of the attack as being important enough to be recognised annually in some sort of anniversary. The trouble was, an anniversary requires twelve lunar cycles to pass before it is celebrated. In twelve months what kind of world would we be living in?

25. The Bean-Counters Paradox

To be honest, for the next twenty-four hours I was in a state of shock. The attack on the Underground did not go unnoticed, of course. It was all over the news – 'yet another MDP attack'. There was no royal baby to announce, no leaking of a political sex scandal nor a celebrity hair-cut drama, but I could see the machinations of the government trying to stop the attack on the Underground dominating the news – the news media referenced a 'fire' and a 'possible terrorist attack'.

Fortunately (if I can say that), nobody survived the actual underground train carriage attack and the handful of people on the platform that had seen the train stop, then take on more unsuspecting passengers, had all been forcibly removed to quarantine. I suspect that words were whispered in their ears that it was not in their interest to speak of what they saw; otherwise, who knows, perhaps they would be shunned as possible infectants.

I hoped that after such a momentous event for Nigel (how could he not be involved in some way?) he would update his blog relatively swiftly. I hoped beyond hope, that my hope would not be in vain.

After returning to the office I was notified that I was required to attend a confidential meeting in nearby Whitehall government offices the following day and I should expect to be grilled. It was such an important meeting that a number of government ministers (responsible for police, security, healthcare, logistics, transport, social services and more) were expected. I was not too alarmed initially. The few meetings with senior politicians that I had already attended had a pattern – the bigger the cheese, the more it waffled and whiffed to others around the table. Such was their importance, the politicians would most likely do all the talking themselves. The experts (of which I included myself) would probably not be called upon to speak.

Arriving in the grand lobby of No. 27 Whitehall, I looked out for Bob Beamont, but he was not to be found in the lobby, room foyer or the corridors. Ministers and civil servants huddled in corners and on stairways talking animatedly. They had gone into this line of business to make a name for themselves. Now they were in the position of being named by the Press for all the wrong reasons. How easily death can upset the ambitions of the ambitious. Every few minutes I scoured every entrance for signs of Bob, but nothing. I had a sinking feeling that his rushed, distracted manner on the phone less than two days earlier suggested that maybe a family member had been pulled into the attack. I hoped not, but the lack of communication from him and his absence from the building so far, implied bad news.

Strangely, for an emergency meeting, we were kept waiting in corridors for a couple of hours. Meetings in Downing Street and senior security meetings were delaying the arrival of a few key personnel – the big, whiffy cheeses. An hour before the meeting my phone pinged with an irregular notification. I checked – there had been an upload to the blog on the Cloud. Opening the laptop, I logged on – Nigel had indeed uploaded passages on the Underground Attack and a new passage on the 'First Bean Paradox – The Destiny Impulse' (which followed on from his earlier reference to the 'Second Bean Paradox – Ownership and Control'). With my head spinning and while being jostled by the waiting crowds, I scanned the blog to see if anything leapt out in case it proved useful for me to report in the meeting. There was a lot to digest from this new upload and, as much as I tried to calm myself, I was too nervous to study it in depth as I loitered in the corridor.

Suddenly a man appeared in the foyer and announced to the many suited and business-suit-skirted individuals present that the meeting was due to start and invited us into one of the largest meeting rooms in the Whitehall building. There was not enough room around the large horseshoe table (seating about forty people), so the rest stood, or sat on the overflow chairs lining the walls. All in all there were nearly one hundred people in the room. I managed to grab a seat at the corner of the table furthest from the chairman. I nudged the chair back until I was out of his eyeline and lost in a wall of dark pinstripe tailoring. With my laptop perched on my lap I did my best to read what Nigel had written as the meeting got started. At times I glanced up looking for friendly faces (ideally Bob's), but there was still no sign of him or anyone else I trusted, so I felt a little exposed should I be called upon to speak. If asked, I could report that the CCTV had not been released to me, so I could not offer much insight to the meeting's attendees.

As the meeting dragged on I surreptitiously spent more time gazing at Nigel's latest blog upload on my laptop. He had indeed been fully involved in the Underground attack, but he also suggested there were other groups now operating somewhat independently. They too had acquired skills, awareness and learning, albeit not to the extent of Nigel's team, I suspected. Many of the attackers had been mentored by Nigel or mentored by his own colleagues. The attack, as described by Nigel, had been coordinated. I shuddered as I read the brutality of the incident. I didn't really want to see any video footage secured from inside the train carriages, but I knew that if I could compare it with the blog entry and compile a report, it would make a compelling piece of evidence for the authenticity of Nigel's blog. I would need to involve Bob on how best to release the footage and my findings to government departments and agencies.

Nigel described how some of the police activities on the surface had led to more Muters seeking refuge in the Underground tunnels consequently encouraging more organisation between individual MDPs. Apparently a train had stopped between stations and became a sitting duck for an attack by Nigel and his colleagues, including one of DoorStop's own acquisitions – 'CentralLine'. Nigel had gained access to one of the stationary trains, swiftly dealt with the guard or driver, then moved into the carriage itself. The other carriage doors were either prised open by other Muters in the tunnel or were opened by the passengers inside thinking they were helping regular Beans. The bloody Bean 'feast' that followed impressed even Nigel.

As I read I could feel my whole being instinctively adapting my future behaviour; my body would never allow me to step onto the London Underground train network again. Why volunteer my body to be packed like sardines in a tubular can ready to be consumed by the merchants of death?

I read on.

Nigel reflected on the incident, but he also reflected on the impulse for Beans to spend time underground, to commit themselves to moving across the metropolis in a daily ritual of self-abuse. He speculated that it was the Beans' unconscious desire to exist in an underworld; it was their destiny calling. Destiny-as-death was fast becoming a theme in Nigel's work.

Suddenly, I was shaken to my senses when someone up the other end of the table utter the immortal words:

'Is the zombie guy here?'

I looked up to see nearly one hundred pairs of eyes turn towards me.

I raised a hand.

'What can you tell us?' asked the chairman.

'I should have more information soon. I was hoping Bob Beaumont might be here and assist me in acquiring the CCTV footage from the train carriages.'

'I'm afraid Bob's daughter is missing. We believe she was on the Central Line train.'

A hushed murmur rolled around the room. Many of those present knew Bob and liked him. No doubt they would be shaken at the news that the plague had affected one of their own.

All the more reason for me to get the footage, I thought. And all the more reason for Bob to help me get the footage.

'If you have any trouble getting what you need, come straight to me,' said the chair. 'We need to know exactly what happened.'

'Thank you, chairman,' I replied, nodding and hoping that would be my only contribution to the meeting. Little did everyone in the room know that I knew exactly what had happened and, if I wasn't disturbed, I would soon know more than any camera footage would show – I had a first-hand account in, er, 'exquisite' detail, written within hours by the lead MDP.

I returned to my laptop, but not before I decided to drop Bob an SMS text. Surely, it was inconvenient, even tasteless, but time was of the essence and he would be, I hoped, understanding and extremely motivated to help me. In the text message I expressed my sorrow at the news of his missing daughter and said I would do everything in my power to help. Speaking of which (and as tactfully as I could), I asked if he could assist me in getting the CCTV footage and, if he wanted to, provide a few images of his daughter and a description of what she might have been wearing. I would get our video forensics teams to review and cross-reference as a priority. I left it at that.

As the meeting trundled on, I took the opportunity to review the other passage included in the upload – the 'First Bean Paradox' – in which Nigel described how he had been accompanying PearlLavaliere (formerly known as Emily) on a light-touch mentoring excursion. They had ended up at an 'affliction group' – presumably some sort of 'self-help' group, a place where Beans gathered to find meaning in their lives (or find out why there wasn't any 'meaning' to their lives). This tallied with some early research Fiona had done on Emily's life. Nigel suggested that the visit was possibly prompted by Pearl's unfinished business – Pearl was familiar with the venue. Of course, Nigel's and Pearl's visit to the affliction group didn't end happily for the afflicted (self-help groups and therapists should take note), but along the way, the gathering did give Nigel further valuable insight into the minds of afflicted Beans.

As I sat and listened to the discussion going on around me I could see Nigel's Second Bean Paradox (ownership and control) and the First Bean Paradox being played out before me by the suited wannabe power-brokers – the politicians pursuing power and glory, the civil servants and mandarins pursuing, well, just power. As Nigel knew – all ambitions turn to dust. Even the records of these power-brokers' discussions, their contributions to the law-making of their country, would either be burnt to a crisp (if paper) or melted (if recorded on computer hard drives) in Nigel's apocalypse. In case you didn't know it, committee meetings are a form of living death. As the committee members argued around me, I read Nigel's words. I saw the irony. Discussion, all discussion, is about improving and extending life – that is, the attempt to delay death. Therefore, both the concept and the very act of 'discussing things' only exist because there is an awareness of a destiny – death. Nigel didn't have this problem. I had never heard him reference any 'meetings' or discussions with his colleagues. It would be anathema to them because Muters were not burdened with the destiny impulse. For them, their destiny had been realised.

Paradoxes belonged to Bean alone; they had no place in death.

Burying my head in Nigel's world continued to open my mind. I was questioning everything. More and more, as I watched the Bean world around me, I would think – what would be Nigel's take on this?

Sitting in that deathly committee I pondered the reasoning of such an activity – the deliberation and establishment of 'laws'. Why was so much time and energy invested into a process of creating laws and holding other people, other Beans, to account? Arguably, Bean laws existed to protect Beans from their own failures. How crazy was that? One of the founding tenets of a civilization – its laws – were founded on managing its creators' inherent failures? Not only that, societies took *pride* in their laws. Law-abiding citizens were a hallmark of a successful, civilised society. Beans endeavoured to raise Beanlings to be law-abiding citizens. In other words – Beans celebrated and honoured failure.

Bean laws – a way to codify failure. As Nigel would have it, Muters didn't have such failures therefore did not require not only laws but also the very concept of legality. Where on earth or in the heavens was there the notion of laws? Beans talk about Nature's laws, but that is just projection. Nowhere in the physical world do laws exist. Behaviour and patterns exist, for sure, in fractals, geometry, physics, biology, but arguably not 'laws'. No, I was beginning to think, law is a fiction created by the failing Bean mind.

And so it was that I started to think like Nigel.

Beans were so arrogant, presumptuous, that they thought everything should be communicated and shared through language, which brought me nicely back to what was going on around me, the committee. How do starlings flock? Fish school? They do it through an unspoken understanding, not through language or laws but through a common, shared behaviour. That was the better understanding of Nature.

As the hours rolled by, I would need a break from analysing Nigel's words and looked up and listened to what was being discussed.

'We need to lockdown,' an individual, unknown to me, said. Seated halfway down the table he must have held a position of some importance.

'It is not like the last pandemic,' replied another. 'We just cannot lock people in their homes. They will not stand for it this time.'

More seated individuals chipped in with their observations.

'But death is literally walking the streets,'

'But you said that last time. How did that end?'

'There are other cases springing up in Birmingham and Liverpool and Manchester. We can't let this get out of control.'

'How about the army?'

There was a pause. Glances were either exchanged or directed downwards at notepads; sighs of nervousness were quietly disguised.

'The Americans are asking what is going on.'

'Is that a bad thing? In fact, a handful of Americans have died. Perhaps we can use that?'

'What do you mean?

'Well, it means they're invested.'

'Some political figures are calling for all American citizens to return to the States. If you're not careful, and before you know it, they will close the borders. How much will that cost the country?'

Then, one calmer vice seated towards the head of the table chipped in:

'Minister, can you tell us if there is any truth to the rumour that the Americans have offered to help?'

If a hushed quietness could tingle, the tingling in the room at that moment would have been dialled up to eleven.

The Minister seated at the head of the table beside the chair sighed, which to all intents and purposes looked like an affirmative response.

The original questioner filled the silence.

'If American military personnel are seen on the streets of London, that would signal the government has lost control of the situation.'

'And the Europeans would love that – there is talk of Brussels wanting to quarantine the UK,' a lone voice added.

The Minister sighed and nodded. He looked as if he was searching for the right words.

'There are discussions,' the Minister said, 'about having some American observers on the ground, perhaps some embedded in our own police MDP units.'

I heard someone further down the table make a whispered aside that carried further than the speaker intended – 'have you ever known an American to just observe?'

'How many are we talking?' a voice piped up from somewhere around the table.

In a previous life I might have been engrossed in the conversation, but I was fast thinking all this discussion was hot air. All I could think about was Nigel. He was really running the show. He would manage anything that was thrown at him. He would soon weary of a committee gathering of Beans. What were they doing? Just filling the days. Counting the days down to their destiny. These Beans were making laws, counting laws, counting deaths, counting observers, counting Americans. All in an attempt to control. But as Nigel's Second Bean Paradox had taught me, there was no such thing as control. Any attempt to assert control disrupts that which is being targeted for control. Like the 'observer effect', the very act of observation (and measurement) of things disrupts the 'things' themselves. And if that was the case, then why attempt to control?

By the time the deathly meeting was drawing to a close I almost had Nigel whispering in my ear. Like a veil falling away from my eyes, I realised that there was only destiny.

As I was heading home I had a call from an unknown number. I answered.

'Is this Josh?'

'Yes.'

'Your Bond street CCTV footage can be downloaded from a secure site being emailed to you now....'

'I need the train carriage footage too.'

'You'll have everything.'

I assumed the call had been organised by Bob. I took a punt.

'Thank Bob for me.'

There was a pause.

'I shall.'

Then the voice was gone.

Later that evening I received half-a-dozen images on my phone of a young smiling, blond woman in her early twenties; two of which showed a woman in a Lycra-like leotard sports kit.

I spent the night poring over Nigel's description of the attack and comparing it with the images and footage we had available. Nigel had mentioned a young woman in Lycra. I put Tom onto it first thing the following morning asking him to carry out a search for Nigel and the woman. Tom soon pulled a few stills from the footage of a young woman in a Lycra outfit before she fell into the clutches of Nigel. I sent them to Bob.

The phone rang immediately.

'It's her,' he said panting. 'Is she alive?'

'We're working on it right now. Should know within 24 hours,' I lied.

I felt guilty as Bob thanked me and signed off with the plea 'keep me informed'.

I knew from Nigel's passage and the footage that Bob's daughter was now an MDP and Nigel had given her a name – LycraStew. I did not know what would be better – to know your darling daughter was an MDP and probably wandering the streets of the metropolis, or that she had been feasted upon to a point that she was incapable of mobility, but was now 'at peace'.

I would figure out a way to tell Bob before I saw him next.

It had been a very long few days. The last act of the day was to open a brown envelope left on my desk. I opened it and removed a thirty-page, double-line-spaced report. Attached to the front of the report was a handwritten note from Fiona:

Josh, I know you must be exhausted. Here's a short summary on Nigel and Emily. I do have more, but before I hand it over I need to verify a few things and follow up a few leads. It could be interesting. Thought you might want to see this in the meantime. Best, Fiona.

26. Summers of Existence

I needed to get back to my houseboat. My head was a jumble of anything and everything. I was exhausted – physically, emotionally, psychologically – and I was beginning to question myself, my abilities and the decisions I was making as I was now seeing the impact of the plague on ordinary people's lives. I knew Bob's life would forever change after the death of his daughter. I thought about Emily's (Pearl's) life being turned upside down by death. I thought of Nigel as a Bean – the loving partner, the proud father. Death had a lot to answer for.

I started to thumb through Fiona's simple report on Nigel and PearlLavaliere. It was easier to find background information on Pearl first – records were up to date and people were willing to talk. We now had a family name, background, details.

Nigel had been brought up in Oxford. He had a brother and a sister. His parents were alive but in poor health. He had been sporty and also a fan of CS Lewis and Tolkien. He worked in an office in central London, but Fiona had purposely avoided diving too deep into Nigel's early life in case it became too much of a distraction. We were interested in Nigel's existence in the immediate (few years) run up to his death – the loss of his child, the disintegration of his relationship with one 'Emily Purse'. Their child, Melinoë, had been diagnosed with an undisclosed disease and was undergoing new specialist treatment, but unfortunately, she had gone downhill very rapidly and had died. The report noted that Fiona was still having trouble getting more details about the illness and the circumstances around the death. Access to the medical records required careful negotiation and the hospital staff were being obstructive or incompetent (or both). Fiona had thought she had identified the doctor – Dr Chayan Founti – responsible for treating the child, but had yet to successfully make contact with him.

Fiona and Tom had then tried to build a picture of Nigel's and Emily's relationship. Sympathetic friends had been helpful, but attempts to gather information from the grieving family had proved more difficult. However, what they had learned was that during the six months of the child's illness Nigel had become more distant. The worry had been hitting him hard. Apparently he had spent many long nights sitting in his rooftop garden looking across the capital. If he wasn't in his rooftop garden, he was hanging around the hospital and spending long nights on its roof while his daughter was being treated in the paediatric ward below.

After the child's death, Nigel's and Emily's relationship had been strained and they had taken time away from each other to work through their grief and reflect on their future together (or not). Tom managed to acquire yet more photographs of Emily wearing the pearl necklace after the relationship break-up. (Apparently, Fiona had learned, the necklace symbolised a daisy chain inspired by the moment Nigel had first met Emily – she had been flower-picking in a park.) Fiona speculated that the break-up had been solely the result of the heartache of loss of the child rather than loss of affection between the two parents. It was probable that the separation was a coping mechanism, not a failure.

Fiona's reports ran through more chronology of the now-deceased couple's relationship and provided details of their living arrangements, work arrangements, their families, Emily's therapy sessions after the loss of her child (and, following that, the loss of Nigel). It all seemed to knit together – there was evidence of behaviour being carried over from life to death from both Nigel and Emily. The unfinished business was manifesting itself in the attack on the self-help group and Nigel's search for Emily. But was there more? The hospital and child's death was an interesting angle and Fiona was digging deeper. It would take time and care.

The more I read, the less of a killer zombie I saw and more of an average man (and woman) shaken to their core(s) by everyday experiences accumulated over a few dozen summers.

Fiona's report was sobering reading and I reflected on my own writings. When I started making these notes I intended them to be a record of the events – in part to run alongside the reports I had been writing for others (for Robbie and any interested Whitehall department). I hadn't been writing for myself. I had tried to be objective in my reporting of events, but reading the back-stories of PearlLavaliere and Nigel, I realised that their existence-stories would now undoubtedly have an impact on my work. And *should* have an impact on my work.

Not only would these revelations have an impact on my day job, but they were making me reflect deeply on my own existence. Nigel had walked upon the earth for three-dozen-plus summers. What would my thirty-three summers lead me to in death? What life experiences had imprinted themselves so firmly in my own psyche that they might later emerge in my behaviour for an eternity? Are we just a walking bundle of memories and injuries? People talk about living in the present, but isn't the present all about the past? And then there is the question: what actually carries over in death? Beanlife can be gone in a heartbeat, so any individual's future is pure fiction. Perhaps Death is the guardian and ressurector of the past; a guardian whose role is also lord destroyer of fiction.

So it was that, back on my houseboat, my ruminations moved away from Nigel to my own nearly three-dozen summers. What would last for me? The choices I had made during those summers? What injuries would endure – injuries both received and self-inflicted? My thoughts moved, of course, to a Brazilian beauty. Why was I thinking like this? Was this the onset of a slow form of death – my life slowly flashing before my eyes?

That life-defining affair was not my former neighbour. Of course, Mia had made an impression on me, but I now realised she had been assigned a specific role in my journey. She was more of a 'reminder of' or a 'signpost to' rather than the 'manifestation of' my chosen one. Mia was a reminder that the chosen one existed. I recalled that, when gazing at her from afar, I was looking at the representation of the person I should be with. Mia was a guide, a gatekeeper, a ghost of beaches past. I would often see Mia sitting out on the edge of her houseboat, her feet dangling over the side, looking across the river, watching the boats and barges trundle by. If she had a coin for every passing boat, she would have enough to live in a high-rise flat somewhere smart, away from the river. But no, she was destined to be forever at one with the Black Road. She had led me to Nigel – a destiny of mine, of sorts. That was her role. And Nigel's role was to remind me of my destiny – other than death, that honour went to my first Brazilian love.

I had met Maria-Amphi when I was twenty-seven and she was twenty-six. I had been warned that the late twenties were a vulnerable period for a man. Still in the UK at the time, I had been wondering about what I should do in life (the remaining sixty summers). I was interested in urban design, urban living but I was missing a focus. Furthermore, at twenty-seven, I felt I ought to be settled by thirty years of age, or at least know what I was going to do by thirty. It was a puzzle and preoccupied me deeply. While I reflected, I decided to take some time off from my work in a dead-end London-based, civil service role in order to travel. I thought that clearing the clutter from my life and my head (after all that's where all life's clutter is to be found) would allow me to just settle on priorities and objectives. So where do you go to clear your head? There were three options as I saw it: the desert, the mountains, the sea. In another life I might have chosen the desert or the mountains, but I knew water had to be part of the equation. The mountains were indeed a possibility – a distant second – but when I thought of mountains (and valleys) I always pictured waterfalls and rivers…all of which led to the sea. 'Water' was the necessary ingredient and was lord over me.

So, I walked into a travel agent, looked around at the images adorning the walls, looking for one that was blue with water. My eye came immediately to a battered poster of a blue sea, a yellow sandy beach and a city. Rio.

I booked a flight on the spot, handed in my resignation at work and spent the next four weeks reading up on Brazil, Rio itself and learning Brazilian Portuguese. I scoured the Internet for simple jobs – bartending, hotel work by the sea, English language teaching – and jumped on a plane.

Brazil was great. It was the most formative time of my life to date. Any doubts I had about my destiny, my needs, my very being were extinguished when I walked onto the beach and up to the water's edge. I fell in love with the idea of a city right on the water and it soon morphed into a mission, my mission, to help design and facilitate living by the ocean. It is where I fell in love with paddleboarding and fell in love with Maria-Amphi.

Having fortunately secured work at both a tourist agency and in a language school near the beach, I soon cultivated the habit of both starting and ending the day by the water. The wind, the spray, the wide open space set me up for the day and brought peace. I would swim, paddleboard, or just walk. Maria-Amphi was one of those figures I would see riding a horse on the beach back and forth. Sometimes during the day I would see her giving tourist horse rides on the beach. Other times I would see her gallop through the breaking waves. We would smile at each other, then one day we met and talked. In my broken Brazilian Portuguese and her reasonable English, we chatted. Learning of her role, I promised to send tourists her way from my work at the tourist agency. We swapped details and she apologised for her English. Not missing an opportunity, I offered my skills as a native speaker if she ever needed it.

Just as I was frantically thinking of ways to spend more time with her, the door of my English class swung open and I saw Maria-Amphi walking down the corridor towards my class. She entered. It was as if fate had taken human form and walked into my class, my domain.

Those months in Rio were the most enraptured of my life. We spent a long, long summer together. Apparently I was a natural on the horse. If there were ever to be a painting of my life I would want it to capture those moments – riding up and down a beach with Maria-Amphi by my side, trying to spear fish in the shallows. You only really know what highlights your life, when it is thrown into shadow.

As the tourist season wound down, she decided to return home to Santa Catarina for a few months to save money and work on her father's farm. With money saved, she could earn enough to travel to the UK and we could think about a life together. I stayed in Rio, but, with her gone, I began thinking longer term myself. I realised if I was going to provide for a life with Maria-Amphi, I needed a proper income, a career – something that I might need to return to the UK to pursue in the first instance.

As I pondered, the decision was made for me. My father was admitted to hospital. He was alone (my mother having died when I was a teenager). I returned to the UK. I needed to get serious with a plan and the plan consisted of getting vocational qualifications. This was only emphasised with the death of my father. I needed to be the provider. I enrolled on my Master's degree on Urban Development, all the while thinking of how I could then get to a place by the sea and build, with Maria-Amphi by my side. Taking the houseboat was a way of reminding myself of Rio and these ambitions. It was comfortable in many ways yet challenging enough to keep me restless, on my toes.

And now here I was a few years further down the line. Although I had visited her in Rio, plans to bring Maria-Amphi to the UK had stalled, paused. But I hadn't worried – because there was always time, right? Always still the 'future'.

How much of life was about running away from something and how much was about heading towards something? The irony was not lost on me – to run away from something, you run towards something else. Nigel had taught me that. And that something else was called destiny.

Was I on a similar path to Nigel? Had Nigel been running away from Emily and those summers he had shared with her? Had he been 'on pause'? Was I running away from Maria-Amphi? Was I 'on pause' too? Nigel had met Emily again in death. Was it in death that I was destined to meet Maria-Amphi again?

I was reflecting on my own mortality now and it was depressing me. I was becoming more aware of the time available to me. How many summers should I spend chasing death – Nigel? Or should I do something more creative with the summers left to me? Should I jump on a plane to Brazil now? Before it was too late?

If a horse, a beach and the sea were the meaning of life, why was I rocking myself to sleep on a cold houseboat on a river trapped in a metropolis of misery? Perhaps death was a release forced upon us, because left to our own devices, we would never break free from our foolishness.

And my own unfinished business? Would I know at the point of my death? Or would it reveal itself in the afterlife? The only sense I had was that it could be one of two things (or even both) – water and/or Maria-Amphi.

It was a shame. I couldn't put some of these reflections in my reports for Whitehall, nevertheless it was cathartic for me to write them down. My journal was becoming something that I needed. I was surrounded by death. I studied it, I followed it, I could even see it in the faces of people in the office and in the coffee shops. The fear in people's eyes sprung from the knowledge that there was a limit to their existence. Fear – something that would make no sense to Nigel. Where did the people's nervousness come from? The unknown? The mystery of death? If Nigel was doing anything, he was forcing us to reflect. Was that so bad?

I was almost at a stage where I could write a book about death myself, but it was beyond me. Perhaps I could leave my reflections, my words to the Whistleblower. He could make sense of them. I knew his circumstances – the loss of someone close to him – but I had no idea of his take on Muterdom or his relationship with Nigel. The last few months had taken their toll on me, but god knows how he must be feeling. Was the Whistleblower ahead of me (more knowledgeable, calm, reflective), or a few months behind (engaged, anxious, motivated)?

As I was rocked into a slumber I suspected that Nigel and I were on similar paths. He was ahead of me. The Black Road divided us. He had died and had found his meaning, his identity. When I died, would I be similarly blessed? We were two travellers on either side of the river of death – two creatures moving away from a fiction towards a certainty, a destiny.

27. The Zombie Guy Meets Ben

After the 'Tube of Terror' episode (or 'Tinned Meat' as Nigel called it), I was becoming a known-Bean in Whitehall – 'the zombie guy' moniker had stuck, but I was fast learning, it was a moniker of both attraction and repulsion (or was it derision?). It was my role to advise various groups on the theory of evolution of the Muters and their level of cognisance. After all, it impacted law and order, housing and security, health and safety, medicine, emergency response, family bereavement, counselling, law and the courts, rules of engagement for law enforcement and security personnel, prisons and now London transport (including the Underground). In the corridors of various Whitehall buildings I would have people come running up to me asking if I was the 'zombie guy' followed by earnest questions or excited chatter followed by nervous nods as I would answer their questions. Or I would be referred to as the 'zombie guy' with a roll of the eyes, a snigger, a snort, a sigh. (Admittedly, this was in the relatively early-to-mid light-darks. As the lunar cycles rolled on, it changed; by the 'Great Change in Bean Behaviour' itself I could pretty much walk into any room and people would shut up.)

It was in this context that I met Ben. Or rather his interest in me was brought to my attention.

It was shortly after the Underground attack and I was walking out of a meeting room when Bob drew me to the side once again with a concerned look on his face.

'Firstly, I apologise, it's classified, I know,' Bob said, 'but what can you tell me?' He looked pale and ashen. 'Do you know where she might be? What part of town?'

(In the previous week I had briefed Bob on his daughter's new-found status as the MDP, LycraStew. It had taken a difficult phone call and an awkward discussion over coffee, but he had now largely accepted her fate though it was still a sensitive topic.)

'I suspect she will be undergoing some training, mentoring as she acclimatises to her new…er, life,' I said, as supportingly as possible. What do you say to the father of a dead daughter who was now mobile, in Nigel's view, for eternity.

'By this Nigel guy?' Bob said haltingly.

'No, most probably by one of his close team members – TrainTracks, ColourSplash. I can't be sure.'

I had to stop myself from saying that his daughter was in very capable hands.

'I would recognise her?' Bob asked, his eyes now turned away from mine.

'Err, yes,' I said, my mind whirring. 'By all accounts and, from the footage we have, she was not disfigured.'

'What do you mean "by all accounts"?'

I paused. I was not used to this kind of thing. I was an urban-planner with experience only in office administration. Shouldn't I be thinking about the grieving father's mental health as I shared such information?

'Nigel did refer to her. He was in the same carriage. In fact, he claimed her himself.'

I paused again – let the information sink in, I thought, in the hope that it was enough to satisfy his curiosity and that would be the end of the conversation. But then another thought occurred to me and gave me cause for concern. I looked at the distraught father. I was worried for him.

'What was your relationship like with your daughter?'

'What do you mean?' replied Bob, his gaze returning to mine.

'Was it good? Were you close?'

Bob shook his head, confused.

'There is a pattern of behaviour emerging. Once an MDP, a Muter, is inducted into, um, eternity, there often emerges a form of motivation,' I said.

'Motivation?

'Yes, a motivation to address any unfinished business, as Nigel describes it.'

'Is that a good thing or a bad thing?'

'Well, whichever, it usually ends badly for the living.'

Bob continued to shake his head. I was making no sense to him.

'I'm saying, you should be careful. Lock your doors. Be careful to whom you answer the door. You need to be ruthless with your own feelings. The daughter you knew, has gone.'

Bob nodded. His shoulders and face fell.

'Can you do something for me, Josh?'

'Of course. If I can,' I replied.

'You recall I asked you to meet an old university friend of mine?'

I nodded.

'Well, he is an old and dear, trusted friend, now an ancient history professor at University College London. He would still very much like to meet you.'

'What have you been telling him?' I said, my spirits sinking as I contemplated managing the expectations of another know-all nut-job.

'Just the basics – about Nigel, his followers or "colleagues", whatever you call them.'

'You're right. It is classified.'

'Don't worry, he won't talk to the Press or anyone. All media leaks are going through the Whistleblower. But I think you and

Ben should meet,' said Bob, fixing his eyes on me in a way he had never done so before.

I was puzzled. Bob was looking very troubled. A change had come over him since I had seen him last, not seven light-darks earlier.

'So, what has he got to say?'

'You need to talk to him,' said Bob, still looking hard at me.

'He's got you worried? I thought that was *my* job,' I said, with a forced chuckle. 'I obviously wasn't doing a very good job of it.'

I realise it was probably not the right time for humour. I rearranged my face from a humorous, smiley squint to a look of confused concern.

'We met for dinner the other night and he was saying all sorts of interesting things.'

'Like what?' I replied, now genuinely curious.

'He was talking from a historical perspective. He said that this kind of thing has happened before. It has deep historical, even mythological, roots. You might find something useful in what he has to say.'

I squinted – intentionally giving the impression I was busy and disinclined to follow through.

'Just meet him – here are his details,' he said, thrusting a business card into my hand, before walking away. 'He has an interesting take on what is happening. You might learn something.'

Now, you should know. I was getting lots of requests from friends of friends and family of Bean-colleagues asking me over for tea, a pint in a pub. I entertained a few requests, then got a little bored and frustrated with it all. I wouldn't go into too much detail (classified, you see), but when I did give some tidbits I felt they were not giving Nigel (or Target A, as I referred to him) the respect he deserved. If I wasn't careful those others present would openly mock the idea of a sentient MDP, let alone a reflective and erudite, mobile one. So, I put Ben's business card in a drawer and forgot about it. For a while.

Not two dozen light-darks later I heard that Bob himself had been claimed in an attack. Apparently, he had not heeded my words and he had done out driving around the regular haunts of his daughter, LycraStew.

Reflecting on his untimely departure, I recalled Bob's last words to me and felt duty bound to follow through and meet this professor of ancient history, Ben. Work was extremely busy and I was tempted to drop the matter, but my conscience got the better of me. I picked up the phone and dialled.

A few hours later I was sitting across the table from Ben in a privately-owned, suitably dark corner of a coffee shop. My choice of a coffee-date was intentional. I could keep it short and Ben would have to get to the point straightaway. Ben himself was younger-looking than I expected. Though probably in his early fifties, he looked more like mid-forties. A career in academia and poring over books had been kind to him. That said, he looked earnest. I was unsure if this was a personality trait or due to him being deeply worried about the business in hand.

After shaking hands and exchanging pleasantries, we had sat down.

'I'm here because of Bob,' I said. 'Just so you know.'

'I know, I heard. May he Rest in Peace.'

'Actually, we think he is probably wandering around Stretham right now, along with his daughter, but…that's by the by.'

Ben went pale and twitched.

'Just to say,' I continued, 'I am busy and I have only this cup of coffee to share, so please get to the point. Tell me who you are and what you want.'

'My name is Ben Garfunkel. I am a professor of ancient history and religions relating to perceptions of death and the after-life. My expertise is with Babylonic and Assuryian traditions, I have a general interest in all such matters including ancient world mythology.'

'So....?'

'I want to share with you my research, my knowledge...'

'Your 'theory', you mean?'

This seemed to irritate Ben.

'No,' he replied. 'I believe it is the answer you have been looking for. I think the events of today are not unexpected.'

'And you're going to tell me how I can end it?'

'I'm going to tell you how it is going to end us all,' Ben replied, curtly.

Truth be told, I was a little hooked. I nodded and invited him to continue.

Ben spoke for about twenty minutes straight explaining that the outbreak of the virus was not some irregular, anomalous thing. It was part of a pattern that had been in motion for many thousands of years and was now, quite possibly, finally coming to a close.

'The apocalypse?' I asked.

Ben shuffled in his seat and nodded.

'For want of a better word, yes,' he muttered. 'Or Armageddon.'

Ben obviously read my frown in a non-flattering way.

'Pandemics. Plagues. Death has happened before. The most recent one was...'

'I think I remember the last one,' I said, trying not to be too sarcastic, 'it was only a few...'

'No,' snapped Ben, interrupting. 'That wasn't a plague. The last one was over seven hundred years ago – the Black Death. It wiped out thirty to sixty per cent of the population of Europe. These big ones happen every six to eight hundred years or so.'

'So we're due?'

'Maybe. But it is not that. I believe, and many old civilisations believed, these were not only due, but were part of nature's….plan, for want of a better word.'

'Why now?' I asked.

'In the past the conditions were not right for a global event. Outbreaks might wipe out the villages, mediaeval towns, but were always contained in a valley.'

'And now we're a global village, it will spread?'

Ben nodded.

'What about the one before the Black Death?' I asked.

'The plague of Justinian in the sixth century A.D. that killed twenty per cent of the population of Constantinople and up to sixty per cent of Europe's population over maybe two hundred years.'

'Then the smaller ones,' Ben continued. 'The Antonine Plague of the second century A.D., Plague of Athens 430 B.C., Japanese smallpox epidemic in the eighth century that killed a third of the Japanese population. Then there are the epidemics we do not know about because writings have not survived. What happened in South America to cause such depopulations? The lost civilisations in Central America and the Amazon? Smallpox, for sure, but there are stories of other plagues.'

'So why is this one different? Why not: lots of people die, then we get over it with the wonders of modern medicine?'

'But you know why, Josh. This is not about a virus that ends in death. It is about death that *begins* with a virus then spreads. A virus of Death doesn't die. Death is the new life.'

I suddenly checked myself. I felt Ben was withholding.

'What aren't you telling me?' I said fixing him with a stare.

Ben dropped his head. I could see he was wrestling with something. He was wondering how much he could say.

'I'm doing some research and I'm not there yet. Suffice to say, I think this plague outbreak is different.'

'Go on.'

Ben still wouldn't say anything. I took a punt.

'Bob said you had an interest in ancient cultures and myths?'

It worked. Ben sighed and his shoulders dipped.

'It's more complicated than that. Ancient stories and myths often have a basis in fact or a knowledge or an understanding of the world that we have lost in our modern day complacency. Myth is not just pre-history, it is an understanding far greater; myth captures eternal knowledge beyond the realm of science. Myths speak to the past *and* the future.'

I did wonder if I was talking to a sort of conspiracy theorist.

'You think the answer is in myths?'

Ben ever so slightly nodded then tipped his head in a non-committal way.

'They often contain warnings of what will come to pass,' he muttered, looking very uncomfortable. 'As I said, I am doing research and trying to make sense of it all and we can meet again when I have done some more reading and thinking.'

I realised I would not get much more out of him and was happy to call it day. I had finished my coffee after all. I could wait. I was in no rush. In fact, I held all the cards. He needed me more than I needed him.

'So what has this got to do with me?' I said, changing tack and initiating an end to the conversation. 'How does this pertain to my work? I am just tracking their behaviour.'

'I know about the Whistleblower,' said Ben, now fixing me in the eye. 'You are feeding information to him, via Bob or direct, I don't know.'

'I don't know what you mean,' I replied, suddenly panicking. 'That would be against the Official Secrets Act. Besides, any 'Whistleblower exercise' is about political leverage that Bob has initiated. Not me.'

'Exactly, but I want you to start thinking beyond your four literal and psychological walls. As I say, this is something bigger than a pandemic or plague outbreak. I hope I am planting a seed in you – the idea that this was always going to happen. Don't dismiss little clues. Don't err on the side of disbelief.'

I nodded a 'thank you, let's end it there' and rose to my feet, holding out my hand.

Ben rose to join me.

'Are you familiar with the word and concept of 'Hevel'?' asked Ben.

'Well, no,' I replied.

'I grew up on it. Part of my faith. It means the two things: the vapour of breath – emitted while a man breathes. It also means vanity, futility, meaninglessness. Nothingness.'

'Okay,' I muttered.

'*O Yahweh, what is man, that You take knowledge of him? Or the son of man, that You think of him? Man is like a mere breath; his days are like a passing shadow.* Psalm 144:3-4.'

I nodded. I didn't share with Ben the idea that my houseboat reflections had already led me to that conclusion.

'That is what we are. That is where we are,' said Ben, shaking my hand. 'Thank you. I'd like to meet again.'

28. Result! Regret

Existence is a funny thing. As I reflected on my journey during the previous lunar cycles, there had been both ups and downs, typical of a Bean's existence. But I was fast coming to the conclusion that – over the course of three score summers and ten – with highs, come lows. They are inseparable. Joined at the hip. The ying and yang. One cannot have the ups alone. But, this is the crux: the downs will kill you in the end.

Although a fabulous 'up', a 'result!', is bathed in warmth and sunlight, that same result inevitably casts a shadow. Lurking in that shadow is regret. At this point in my journey, there was one episode that was undeniably the 'result!' I was looking for, but a profound regret and sadness lay hidden, cold and dark, in its shadow. Beans are simple-minded creatures. They live their lives wanting that 'result!', but resent any subsequent regret. Existence certainly is a double-edged sword – either edge can kill you. It is win-win for death, I suppose. Nigel would approve.

The 'result!' I'll deal with later (in the second half of this chapter); firstly, the regret.

You always know what kind of person you are by two things – what you regret and what makes you happy. If you are in any confusion about what makes you happy, it is clarified by what makes you sad. There is one event in this whole z-demic thing that took me to a whole new level of sad. It is related to Fiona and Tom. I will struggle as I write this.

I'm not a leader. Leaders have to be selfish. I am more of a lone freedom kind-a-guy. In an ideal world I don't want to supervise or manage people. My preferred role is that of an adviser. I reflect, I analyse, I plan and I propose. I have no desire to control others. Leaders inevitably make people suffer and are willing to do so. Death always results from leadership. I never wanted to be a leader, but leadership got me in the end.

Fiona and Tom had been a real help over the handful of lunar cycles. As graduate students in their early-to-mid twenties, they were the epitome of enthusiasm and hope. The nine or ten additional summers I had on them, had knocked some sense into me (or hope out of me depending on your point of view). That said, I always presented myself as a 'colleague' to them rather than their boss. They were helping me, not working for me. They had helped establish the unit, acquire data (footage and records) on operational MDPs and had also compiled invaluable information on the MDPs' previous lives and their family backgrounds. They had been crucial in getting on with the hard graft of investigation. They had mentored the other interns and helped me carry the load.

We had been enormously busy for a number of months and, as a result, we were spending a lot of time together, or rather, *they* were spending a lot of time together. I could tell that they were becoming fond of each other. There was a softness in their voices as they spoke to one another in their soft Welsh and Scottish accents and they never harshly challenged each other – a sign of the early days of affection. I sort of noticed it, but did not dwell on it. They made a nice couple, but they never exhibited any inappropriate expressions of affection. They were always professional and I respected that.

It was roundabout this time that Robbie was putting pressure on me to make serious progress. No doubt he was feeling the heat too. I soon gathered it probably stemmed from the procrastination of the political overlords. If they felt any pressure to act, they could turn to their underlings (Robbie in this case) and say 'I need more information. What is the progress? Get me something I can act on.'

I confess, we had indeed plateaued. We were gathering useful information and our database was growing, but my theories on MDP sentience needed fleshing out. I had thought of snatching a simple MDP, one of Nigel's team perhaps, but it was more difficult than you think. The ones most active were the ones most dangerous. DoorStop? GlassCutter? Diesel? Too aggressive. TrainTracks? ColourSplash? Equally vicious. There was, of course, ChubbyCheeks, but she was the one I feared the most. I still hadn't got my head around her capabilities and Nigel spoke so glowingly about her that I thought trying to snatch her could be a bloodbath. If 'Death' himself is impressed with the skills of one of his Muterlings, then it would be a wise man to pay attention. There were others, of course. There was Chain-and-Stiks but I could not quite live with myself if any operation ended in her obliteration. Being the naive boy, I still held out a hope that death would somehow reverse itself and I could save her – Stiks would somehow morph back into my neighbour and 'Mia' would thank me for it. I had heard a rumour the government was trying to get a pharmaceutical company to get a vaccine out, but no company was tempted – it was just too difficult.

When I arrived in the office one day to learn that I had lost two or the junior interns to other administrative positions, I raced downstairs to complain to Robbie. I entered the office with the words – 'you've pulled two of my interns?' I had a speech ready, but the look on his face said it all. He looked bored, indifferent in a fuck-you sort of way.

I walked out knowing that no more funding would come my way and I might even lose more people. Perhaps even Tom and Fiona. I needed to acquire empirical evidence that the Muters were cognisant. It had to be spectacular. I couldn't wait for the police to come through, or legal services to approve brain scans.

As I raced back upstairs to my office my recollection of Robbie's first reaction to my theory of the blog weeks earlier still haunted me. His words had burned into my soul. I think that was his intention. I now realised that I needed to go far beyond the blog. I needed something that would corroborate words saved to a blog in the Cloud. I knew the answer, but denied its existence. It meant Nigel. I had to bring him in. Observing him was not enough. But how do I capture him?

The police had made a few half-hearted attempts, but they were no match for Nigel and their interests quickly moved elsewhere. A fair number of Cloth-Heads had been lost to Nigel as he was often in the company of GlassCutter, Diesel and DoorStop. I had then not pressed for his capture, in part I suppose, because I found him so interesting to study. If Nigel and his writings disappeared, where would I be? I would have no idea what to do and would be completely useless. But the time had come. I realised that we needed to snatch Nigel. But how to lure him in?

I returned to his writing looking for inspiration for what I might do. He needed to come to us. In the past he had referred to different types of Beans including Fighter-Beans and Lover-Beans. When he engaged Fighter-Beans he was often accompanied. But he often spoke of his fondness for Lover-Beans and engaged with them when he was alone. He could detect the Lover-Bean odours in the air and found their taste sweet. Perhaps Lover-Beans were the answer. I needed bait – Lover-Bean bait. But who? Should I audition and select a male and female Cloth-Head to engage in smooching? Some Rubber Beans? No, Nigel would sniff them out (and realise it was a trap). There had to be some genuine heat between the two Beans.

You can see where this is going, I'm sure. Mulling it over the weekend, I made a decision and raised it one Monday morning with Fiona and Tom. The three of us always had a mid-morning coffee break on the first day of the week to touch base. Cramped in a small kitchenette away from desks and computers, files and other interns, it was a useful thirty minutes to shoot the breeze, share things that were bugging us, throw out ideas for lines of investigation, or Muters to study. This particular morning I had my antennae out. I suspected they did not suspect that I suspected something was going on between them. I played along.

'I was thinking,' I said, 'I have a plan. I think we can set a trap, but we need some bait.'

Fiona and Tom turned to me. Their attention energetically engaged, I outlined the plan. We knew some of Nigel's preferred hunting grounds, all we had to do was place a couple of Beans as bait and hope he bit (as it were). We would have a team of Rubber Beans downwind of the trap. As soon as Nigel appeared, we would engage.

'How will you get approval?' asked Fiona.

'If I am not engaging with members of the public I can request a Rubber Bean team of up to twenty strong without jumping through hoops. It will be a closed mission.'

They both nodded and waited for me to continue. I took a breath.

'But finding a Lover-Bean couple will be tricky,' I murmured.

'So?' said Fiona, the idea completely lost on her.

'That's why I was wondering if you two would act as bait?'

'What?' they both said in unison.

'I'm sorry. It would mean you would have to stand at the end of a street and kiss, perhaps for a few hours. Hopefully Nigel will be drawn in.'

'But wouldn't he suspect a trap?' asked Fiona, partially aghast. Tom looked at her as if he didn't know whether her first reaction (not objecting to kissing him) was flattering. He remained silent.

'No, you two know each other. You're comfortable in each other's company. It's better than two strangers kissing. Besides, you know what is expected. I'm just asking. There would be a whole team of twenty Rubber Beans down the street and would move in as soon as we spotted him.'

I was quiet. I could see they were torn. A few hours of kissing the other – all for the greater good. How difficult could that be? It would be on official business.

Anyway, you know the rest. They "reluctantly" agreed and I confirmed the assistance of a team of Rubber Beans. I had twelve hours allotted for the mission, so I put a timeframe of 6.00 p.m. to 6.00 a.m. The Lover-Beans and the twenty Rubber Beans had a one hour's briefing at 4.00 p.m. in the police station nearest the target street (Little Clarendon Street) to run through the basics of 'Operation Kiss'. I explained to them what was happening. As soon as the target appeared he was to be apprehended using non-lethal force as far as possible – pyro-net guns, immobilising foam. Weapons were only to be used in the defence of life. I explained that we had not done this kind of mission before, but I was very hopeful that we could entice a particular MDP into the street allowing us to capture him.

'Why this one?' one of the Rubber Beans asked.

'He's one of their leaders, we think,' I replied,

For the first time I was quite excited.

'Tom and Fiona here have gainfully volunteered to be the bait,' I added.

Tom shrugged and rolled his eyes for the crowd. Nobody was buying it though. Fiona blushed a little.

I had encouraged Fiona and Tom to spend the two previous evenings together practising kissing, so that they looked, sounded and smelled like Lover-Beans. They sighed and agreed, but I noted that they were perfectly eager to leave the office early on the days running up to the snatch operation in order to 'get some training in'.

The incident is described by Nigel himself in his passages. The first few hours of the operation were uneventful. I advised them to talk and touch and kiss and snuggle as best they could a third of the way down the street. In the first hour they were obviously a bit self-conscious. They knew they were being watched by twenty Rubber Beans and filmed. I had given them both an ear-piece and I was updating them over a closed radio channel – just the three of us. It was probably a good thing too. They had no idea of the chatter on the Rubber-Bean radio channel. If they had, I'm sure it would have undermined the whole operation. Rubber Beans tasked with watching a younger man kiss an attractive young woman invites a barrelful of lewd comments.

The operation soon went pear-shaped. Fiona and Tom were in place. I remained at one end of Little Clarendon Street while Tom and Fiona were embracing at the other – perhaps one hundred metres away. By all accounts Tom and Fiona were doing well, but Nigel is no slouch. At eleven o'clock that dark-cycle, he approached Fiona and Tom, but, my goodness, he was quick and engaged both Fiona and Tom before the Rubber Beans could reach them.

I could not see anything 'live' myself. I was tucked away down the street in a makeshift command post with Commander Bathgate in a pop-up tent with a couple of screens and walkie-talkie radios. I did catch Tom on the computer monitor somehow escaping the mêlée and racing away. Calm, indifferent updates over the radios soon turned into tense, short exchanges between the Black Rubber Beans. Then the raised voices followed and the odd bursts of gunfire. This was interspersed with cries of help and panic from the Rubber Beans. Commander Bathgate was flailing around on the radio trying to get someone to listen to him. It was like listening to a mini-apocalypse radio play, worthy of Orson Wells, being broadcast in the 1940s.

The Rubber Beans had been thrown into chaos with the sudden appearance of numerous colleagues of Nigel. We had set up cameras and had a drone flying around, but the drone footage was not much use once one of Nigel's colleagues took out the drone operator stationed on a rooftop and the others started picking off the Rubber Beans and snipers we had in place on the rooftops. By the sounds coming over the radio the Rubber-Beans were being butchered. Nigel's contempt for them as a threat was justified. It was an odd experience listening to screaming confusion over the radios while gunfire echoed up and down the street. As for Nigel, he had disappeared.

In the midst of it, Nigel claimed Fiona. Viewing the video footage much later we saw that, after Nigel's embrace, Fiona was impaled on some nearby railings. Nigel then slipped away into the darkness, which sent everybody into a panic.

So much of my own experience was pretty muted and mundane (until it wasn't).

Commander Bathgate was with me in the makeshift command post. His focus was wholly on the operations and he was barking instructions that he knew went unheard, unactioned amidst the radio carnage. Technically as leader I felt I ought to offer some direction (and even encourage his team to focus) on reacquiring Nigel, but I had a distinct feeling he would pull his pistol and shoot me square between the eyes.

We had chosen the spot to pitch the pop-up tent – in a dark archway beside some shops – as an ideal place to observe, so I could not initially be sure what was happening. Sensing the operation was lost, I took a few steps forward up the street and tried to reach Tom and Fiona on the radio. At least I could try and save them. Suddenly there was a metallic crash sound on the pavement behind me and all electronic chatter ceased (leaving only the distant sounds of the screams and gunfire further up the street). I turned to see a broken walkie-talkie lying on the pavement and Commander Bathgate's feet floating six inches off the ground. Within a second he dropped and collapsed into a heap on the ground revealing a tall, shadowy figure – a silhouette framed by the streetlight and shopfront on the other side of the street. The figure, the creature, the MDP, the blogger, Nigel, stepped towards me.

Nigel's broken features appeared yet more broken in the light from the streetlamps and shop windows. I tried to gather my thoughts and force myself to acknowledge the danger I was in. It was difficult, I was instinctively in a place of wonder. The creature I had been following, by studying hazy images and footage captured on mobile phone and CCTV, was now standing looking at me. It was almost as if I existed. He was acknowledging my presence. I fought the sense of wonder and dragged myself into the present moment knowing that death was a couple of heartbeats away. What should I do? I could not fight him. I had to connect with him.

I was snapped out of my thoughts when I felt myself being physically moved to the precipice of death – in other words, with one hand he grabbed me by the scarf and jacket about my neck, lifted off my feet and carried me deeper into the shadows. In two paces, I found myself pressed up against the wall in the darkest place of the street.

'Stop, Wait. Hang on,' I gasped, struggling to breathe with the tightness around my neck.

'I know who you are. Your name is Nigel. Was Nigel. Whatever. It's Nigel.'

The MDP paused. There was the very slightest relaxation of the grip on the clothing around my neck. It was an invitation to speak. Or if it wasn't, I was going to use it anyway. I knew I only had seconds to make an impression.

'You remember?' I gasped, almost in desperation.

The trouble was, I was struggling to remember stuff myself. My mind was spinning. What tidbit of information could I pull out of my head? It was blank. I had to connect, I had to show him I knew something about him – that I knew who he was.

'I know you have suffered in your life. You have lost people close to you. And then there is Pearl! Pearl! You call her Pearl now. She is one of your colleagues. Pearl? You know?'

I thought for a moment of referring to his deceased daughter, but I didn't know how he would react. Fiona had only just uncovered the basics about his daughter, but Nigel had never referred to her in his writings. Perhaps he didn't even know. It was a gamble, but I refrained from referring to her. Besides, he had stopped and was gazing deeply into me. Perhaps we had connected for a moment. I had his attention, perhaps I could pique his curiosity.

'I know more. I can explain more. Perhaps we can...talk and help each other?'

The flesh and shadow of his rotten features and skull gave nothing away.

Reader, imagine, if you will, standing in front of an angel. Tall, slim, its lean and muscular form embodying a mission beyond your understanding. A bodily form not burdened by the tiredness of a long day, not anxious about the future, reflective of the past. A being that carried no sadness in its gait, nor bore any of life's worries in its brow. A creature at peace with itself and in harmony with a realm that is above and beyond our weak and decaying world. A being in which considerable strength and power reside, yet calmness, care and thoughtfulness inhabit. A physical shape with an unearthly poise as if carved in marble by the Greeks, but as loose and agile as a heroic Olympian athlete in his living prime.

Now imagine its inverse creation.

Not an angel of God and eternal youth, but an angel of Death and eternal damnation. A fallen angel. A demon in all its majesty.

In my foolhardiness, the only thing I could still think of was trying to make a personal connection.

'My name is Josh. Call me Josh,' I said desperately trying to keep my voice from squeaking. 'I can help you.'

Nothing. No reaction. (But I was still alive.)

I could try flattery.

'I need your help too.'

Nothing. (But still alive.)

Now, pleading.

'Perhaps I can help you find what you are looking for,' I said, thinking of his unfinished business. I had to try and get him to see value in keeping me a Bean and not transforming me into a Has-Bean. I could be of use to him as long as I was…alive. How many Beans had given him the time of day? None. I could be the first. I could be that one useful, compliant Bean.

'We could make a good team. Me and you, Nigel. Me? Call me Josh. We can help each other.'

Every sinew of my being wanted to plead, beg, but I was afraid it would fill him with disgust. I had been reading his writings for months. I didn't want to add to his contempt.

The blackness looked deep into me. It took all my strength to refrain from saying anything more. He slowly leaned in towards my face. The darkness of his eye sockets loomed larger. I tried not to breathe out knowing that my 'sweet breath' might set him off in a feasting frenzy. I could do nothing about my general Bean aroma, but my sweet breath I could happily do without for thirty seconds.

There was, of course, a stench of death, but I knew I could not flinch. As the nano-seconds ticked by I did not breathe out and I could not breathe inwards in case the stench made me gag.

I did think of referring to his writings, but I then thought he might realise the extent to which we were monitoring him and might stop uploading his writings to the Cloud. His blog was the only thing that connected us. I could not afford to lose it.

Reflecting later, I realised that I had a real sense of intimacy when faced with death (the concept) and Death (the MDP). I did not think it was just because of Nigel – the MDP I had been pursuing for months – it was because the world melted away and, in that moment, my fear dissolved. I accepted my destiny. I imagined that those people who had similarly had a few moments to reflect before death claimed them might also feel a sense of peace, even homecoming.

I looked deep into Nigel's sockets. What did he see? Could he see? I only saw darkness. A blackness that would make all other blacks pale. It was not an empty blackness. It had meaning, focus. It was not a darkness that was characterised by the absence of light. No, it was a blackness that had intention. Light would never puncture its horizon. It was a darkness that both sucked you in and poured into your soul…until the sense of your very own self was stretched so thin and weak you almost surrendered awareness to all worldly knowledge and understanding. Was I actually being given a glimpse into the nature of death?

'Will you help me? We can help each other. Please,' I heard myself say. 'Please, Nigel.'

Then the blackness came. Nigel leaned inward. I braced myself for the puncture of my skin. I felt something touch and run up the skin of my cheek. Wet, cold, smelling of blood and bile. I realised his face had touched my cheek. (I would say nose, but what nose?) Perhaps it was a tease. Perhaps the touch was to determine if I was tasty enough to feast upon or if he was going to treat me as a Lite-Bite. I waited. Then suddenly the tension around my neck was gone and I dropped six inches to the ground. I fell to my knees and froze. Had I been bitten? Was I now bleeding out? I felt myself breathe again.

Then in a moment I cannot recall, I opened my eyes to see that he was gone.

I slowly rose to my feet and started to discern sounds and movement. The distant gunfire, shouts and screams gradually morphed from a muffled background soundtrack to a more vivid experience. It was as if I had been removed to an entirely different dimension known only to ethereal beings and now I was being returned to a world I knew – sounds became clearer, shapes took on recognisable forms.

Standing with my back pressed against the wall I could not compute the magnitude of what had just happened. It was truly both the most exhilarating and awe-inspiring moment of my life and the most morbidly, ground-shakingly terrifying thirty seconds of my life. I don't know why Nigel had left me alive. Perhaps I had a purpose. Perhaps I was now in his world plan just as he was in mine.

I had looked death in the face. And survived. I had been noticed by the greatest force in the cosmos and it had bequeathed me more time. It was the 'result!' moment of my life – a nod of acknowledgement from oblivion itself.

Once we had regrouped and reinforcements arrived we tried to find Fiona, but she had disappeared. I monitored the blog and in due course Nigel's version of events appeared and his christening of his new acquisition. Her name 'Fiona' would soon fade from the world's memory after no more than twenty-four summers and her new name would last for eternity.

As for Tom, some camera footage had seen him return to the scene, presumably to try and rescue Fiona, but he was shot by a Rubber-Bean in the crossfire confusion and carted away to hospital. Other than the letter I received from him shortly afterwards (of which, more later), I never saw Tom again.

Of course, we had not captured Nigel, he was far too good for that. Much later, when reading his writings, I wondered if he really gave away how much he knew, but I had met him. We had 'spoken' face to face. It confirmed to me without the slightest doubt that he was the author of the blog. He was sentient, cognisant, 'alive' for want of a better word. He had breathed into my face and I had looked into the darkness

29. Debacle! Despair

Operation Kiss hurt everything. It was, literally, the kiss of death. Not only did I lose the opportunity to progress my case with Whitehall departments (let alone satisfy my own curiosity), but the loss of Fiona and Tom hit me hard; not only on a very personal level, but a working professional level too. How could it not?

I couldn't return to the office straight after the incident – my head was too mixed up and there had been blazing arguments with a Black Rubber Bean chief commander who came down to the location after the incident having heard what had happened. I say blazing arguments, I wasn't arguing myself, I was on the receiving end of abuse, much of it went over my head as I was still reeling from my interaction with Nigel. The Bean commander had a point though – of the twenty Rubber Beans involved in the operation, eight had died, four were missing, presumed dead (removed as Has-Beans, I suspected), there were four lite-bites under guard in a medical facility, two had resigned immediately after the operation and two were in a state of shock (probably PTSD and only able to engage in desk work afterwards). Not one Muter had been captured or destroyed.

Returning to work a week later there was a revolving door of people walking into my office, hurling abuse, then leaving. Robbie, my supervisor, was among them somewhere. I didn't share with Robbie my encounter with Nigel. It was not the time, besides, I was overwhelmed with the loss of my own two colleagues.

Arguably, I was the only one mourning their loss. Although nobody said it, there were rumoured comments from the police community – 'well, good job, a bit of karma, the zombie guy lost two of his own'.

Piles of papers were stacked up on Fiona's desk. I had asked her to research as much as possible into Nigel's past and conduct interviews with those who had known him in life. Her assessment was still a work-in-progress. I had been given verbal updates, but she had been working on a detailed report about Nigel's past and, by all accounts, had been making progress. I was unsure how useful Nigel's past life would be; I was more interested in the dead Nigel than the former living one. Just three days previously, before I had prioritised the preparation for Operation Kiss, Fiona was bouncing around the office saying she was formulating a theory on what might be Nigel's unfinished business.

'Wouldn't it be great if we figured out his unfinished business?' she had exclaimed, her eyes wide with the excitement of youth.

Ninety-two hours later she had been impaled on a railing, bleeding out.

And I was responsible.

At the end of the night, when the back-up Rubber Beans had cleared the area, I visited the point where she had been impaled. The blood was still drying. Nigel had taken her away. What I was secretly dreading was perhaps running into her on another operation. What name would Nigel give her?

For days I was refreshing his blog just in case he had updated it, but it was all making me sick. I was even struggling to look at the notes on Fiona's desk and the computer files – some of which were voice files recorded on her phone. Not only notes to herself, but interviews with acquaintances of Nigel and Pearl. I put both her physical and electronic files safely to one side. A couple of interns offered to go through them, but I always made excuses and gave them other jobs. Either I would review them when I had the strength, or I would pass them to a trusted colleague to review. Dare I say it, but my own psychological convalescence was not a sure thing. In fact, the debacle almost broke me. I thought of packing it all in and heading to the coast, hiring a boat and spending my time rocking on the one thing that soothed me, the water. Failing that, I would head to Brazil.

As for Tom, well, we lost him too in the end. He never returned to the office. Having recuperated in hospital for four days he had escaped the metropolis. He would write to me many weeks later, but his story did not end happily.

It wasn't long before I heard that there was a directive that no further attempts were to be made at capturing an MDP without written approval from a Whitehall government minister. I took that as closing the book on any attempted snatches. Once Whitehall had assumed authority for such operations, it meant it would never happen because a minister or faceless bureaucrat would have to authorise it and that was just not worth risking a career over. Coupled with the Cloth-Head rules of engagement forever changing and the law courts being inundated with individual cases, each setting some sort of precedent, it was a time of utter despair to be frank. Nevertheless, I wrote up a report and submitted it to the powers that be.

I was nervous about the come-back. I half-expected a bureaucrat to walk into the office, say thank you very much and show me the door while packing up boxes of all our work (including Fiona's research). I was pondering this one night in bed and started panicking. I knew I had to act, but what should I do? There was only one thing. All the work we had done had to be put to some good use; the intelligence and main findings needed to be shared with the one person who would be interested in reading and protecting it – the Whistleblower. The man with a pen. Let him do what he wants with it. He could write it up and spread the word.

Maybe then someone would take notice. He could embarrass the people in the right places.

I made a special trip to an adjacent Whitehall building the following morning and loitered in the shadows. Spotting George, an assistant to my former friend and ally, Bob Beaumont, I caught his eye at a distance of thirty yards. I nodded to a shadowy space under a grand staircase. I was aware that George might not want to be seen with me – I was toxic news after the debacle and I didn't have Bob to protect me. Seeing George was nervous, I got straight to the point.

'I have something for our brother, I think,' I said, looking him in the eye, willing him to understand.

'You mean *your* brother?' replied George. 'I have nothing to do with him.'

'Sure,' I said. 'How do I get it to him?'

George discreetly opened a hand down by his side, no doubt expecting a USB memory stick.

'It's not only electronic,' I said. 'I have paper files and notebooks by one of my interns.'

George pulled a face, sighed and looked nervously around him.

'Leave it to me,' George said, walking off.

30. Reflections

'Follow your passion' has been a mantra for a generation or two or three. On the face of it, the advice seems wise. If you can do something that you love as a living, then you are on to a certain winner. The mantra had carved out my own aspirations, my dreams, but, like carving clouds, it doesn't really work. Danger lies in those words.

What people don't tell you is that when there are tough times in the dogged and noble pursuit of your 'passion', it can cut you deep. The beauty of being engaged in a profession to which you are indifferent means the hard times do not poison the rest of your life. There is more chance of survival from despair if you don't have a passion that can kill you.

I sat in my houseboat rocking gently back and forth. The lapping of the water against the hull eased me into a reflective reverie. I was mulling over life's purpose, meaning, my career, my aspirations. In the lunar cycles since Mia's disappearance I had tried to keep the houseboat a place away from reflections on the future. My floating home should always be about 'the now'. If I needed to work on a job-related business I would either stay late at the office or head to the library. In an age when technology means you are connected 24/7 to *anything* and everything, it is a wise man who fights for empty space in mind, body and soul. My empty space, my nothingness, was to be found rocking gently on water.

This became more difficult as the plague took a greater hold of the metropolis, but after the Little Clarendon Street debacle I needed that quiet space more than ever. But on one particular day, I failed. I had brought home something from work. An envelope that, when it landed on my desk that morning, had made me feel sick to my stomach. I had recognised the handwriting on the envelope and the postmark. The handwriting was Tom's and the postmark was Isle of Skye – the home of his parents.

Tom had never told me himself that he was staying with his parents because I had never spoken to him after Nigel's embrace of Fiona weeks earlier. I had visited the hospital to be told by a nurse that Tom had checked out of the ward and had 'gone to Scotland'. I put two and two together.

I didn't open the letter straight away. I couldn't face it. I couldn't face learning what he was going through. No doubt he would share his thoughts of Fiona, but I feared that whatever he said, it would be a curt reminder that I was responsible for it all. The letter had sat on my desk all day, haunting me. I knew I couldn't have another day like that, so I decided to take it home and give Tom's words the time and attention they deserved. It was the least I could do.

So, there I was, curled up on my bed propped up by cushions. With a whisky in one hand, I assumed a comfortable position in which I could hold his letter in the other. But for the small, directional spotlight clamped to my bed's headboard I was surrounded by blackness punctuated only by the pins of light rocking slightly in the darkness outside on the other side of the Black Road.

After a sufficient number of swigs of the single malt, I tore open the envelope, unfolded the sheets of closely written lines and took a deep breath.

> *Dear Josh*
>
> *I hope this letter finds you well. I apologise for not getting in touch with you before I left. I needed to get away. Far away. I have returned to my parents in Scotland. It is*

quiet here. Beautiful. The rolling land, the greys and the greens. Harsh but familiar. I grew up here and I can sometimes feel that I never left. London and the last six months never happened.

These lands feel like the right place to come to terms with everything that has happened – not just those few minutes on Little Clarendon Street, but what has happened to the inside of me.

I ran away for self-preservation, but I was running away from the person I now realise I loved. It was the look in her eyes as I stepped away. It felt as if I was witnessing the cleaving of my soul. Watching the creature, Nigel, kiss her was too much – more than I could bear in a lifetime. I ran thirty yards but, with each stride, the greater the tearing of my soul. I ran back towards Fiona and it was then that I was shot by a Rubber Bean. In all the confusion, perhaps a marksman mistook me for an MDP. Whichever, I wish I had been killed. It would have been justice. It would have brought peace, not this raging, searing pain I feel now. How do I vanquish it, Josh?

I loved Fiona. I think. I hadn't really been in love before, but whenever I was with her I was thinking of my future and she was in it – whether it was living with her in different places, travelling to different locations together, enduring difficult times and dancing on beaches with each other or lying together by campfires looking up at a clear night sky. Whatever the scenario, I imagined she would be there by my side. But it never happened, Josh, and it was never meant to be. It was all in my head – I was living the life in my head as if it were a life in the real world – but the real world is one in which Nigel walks. The real world is the place of the dead.

I can only think of Fiona as she was then and how she existed in my dreams and hopes. I regret I never shared those hopes and day-dreams with her. It is my greatest regret among my multitude of regrets. What I fear most is my mind slipping to thoughts of her now. If she was 'dead' in the old sense, I could perhaps navigate a way through my grief, but I know that she is wandering the streets of London now as I write.

Has Nigel given her a name? I have been trying to think of what name he would give her. It would no doubt be related to her death, but she epitomised life, so I cannot imagine what it would be. Please don't tell me, I don't want to know, but I know that Nigel's name for her will far outlast the name that her parents gave to her. In our last month or so together I confess I had thoughts of whether she might take my own name one day. It is such a shame that she will be defined in death and by Death himself. It is not fair, not right. But then life isn't fair, is it? Why is it always those who have seen more of life say such things?

I can hear you saying that by us talking and remembering her as she was, is keeping her alive. But, having seen how the MDPs are evolving in behaviour and exploding in number, I suspect we're all going to meet a grisly end in the not too distant future. Perhaps sooner than you think.

I don't know the future, Josh. I don't know what the future holds for me and what scares me is that I don't care. What can I do? What can anybody do when faced by the likes of Nigel?

I want to thank you for your support and for the handful of months you gave to me and Fiona. I hope you are well and I hope you find your way to peace and contentment on the Black Road and, as far as you can, become master of your own destiny. I think you should leave the country while you still can. I don't think things will end well for these fair and ancient isles.

And there the letter ended. The fact that Tom never criticised me for sending him into danger took me by surprise. It was almost disconcerting. Was it the naivety of youth? Didn't he realise I was responsible for what had happened to him and Fiona? Or was there the slimmest possibility that I wasn't responsible and I was being too tough on myself? Was he mature enough to assume the risk and cruelty of life? Why wasn't he angry? He was obviously in a pretty bad state, physically, emotionally. It was his youth that was killing him. Hope had been brutalised. Or was it that hope itself was brutalising?

I read his letter a few more times; sipping the whiskey and the gentle rocking of the boat helped me absorb its contents. I was looking for clues on how to respond to him. How does one respond to the pain of such personal revelations? Acknowledge it, at least, perhaps?

Inevitably I reflected on Nigel's blog entries too. Was there some truth in the First Bean Paradox? Was despair Death's siren call? Was the story of Raincoat the story of us all? What is it that life does to people? Remove hope and what do you have? Is hope just a veil over inevitability – a veil to be lifted one light-dark by the breeze of deathstiny?

Like the coward I was, I put off reply for a few weeks. I needn't have worried. A few weeks after receiving his letter I heard that Tom had indeed killed himself. He had walked into the sea a few miles away from his parents' home at five-thirty in the morning. His clothes, except for his long coat, were left on the beach. His body was never found. The authorities suspected he had loaded a coat with stones and weights and waded into the water.

I confess I did not shudder at the way he chose to meet his Maker. Water would be my choice, my way to go, so I could not see it as too awful. I suspected Tom was also thinking about the plague. Although Scotland had seen a number of plague cases, it was still pretty safe. But Tom knew the truth. It could all change rapidly.

As for Fiona, she was indeed still roaming the streets of the metropolis acquiring followers. I would still sometimes catch sight of her on CCTV. I dreaded the moment that I might ever see (let alone meet) her 'in the flesh'. Would she recognise me? If she did, would she pause? Or would she attack? Would she ever recall her time with Tom? If Nigel was right, would she be walking the streets of the fallen capital for eternity? To answer Tom's question, yes, Nigel had bequeathed a name to Fiona – 'LoveHurts'.

Tom's and Fiona's story injured me deeply. Such youth – it burned brightly, but it was not to last. The candle flickers in the darkness, but it is the darkness that owns the space. Tom and Fiona had both followed their passion – their passion for their work, then their passion for each other. It had killed them both.

But, as I said, I didn't know Tom's fate that evening on the houseboat. Having mulled over the contents of the letter, I turned off the light and, nicely inebriated, curled up. It didn't help. My mind was racing. So I violated my policy of a no-work space again and turned to Nigel's laptop to see if I could learn anything. It is a sad and difficult day when a thirtysomething man turns to the musings of a corpse for wisdom and insight.

Reading Nigel's passages I was struggling to argue against his logic. When I heard the Cloth-Heads, politicians, Rubber Beans muttering about wiping Nigel and his ilk from the streets of the metropolis I found myself plagued with doubt. How do you beat the darkness? How do you extinguish nothingness?

It made me wonder why I was making the effort. What is the point of fighting inevitability? When I was younger, death was at the end of a long to-do list. Now, it had become a floating item that moved up and down the bucket list. Once upon a time I might have found myself sitting in a pub talking to old people. As the alcohol flowed sometimes they would confess to thinking about death. I found it bizarre. 'You're alive. Why are you thinking about death?' I would think, pitying them (and not necessarily in a gracious way). Now things were different. Was I warming to the idea of death myself? A place, a state, where quite literally all the trials and tribulations of life are shaken off? Was that what death was? Freedom from misery, confusion, stress....life?

Curled up in my houseboat, realising that, whether I liked it or not, death was now not only part of my outlook, but inextricably etched into my life plan.

31. Green Beans & Getting Chubby

I kept a low profile. Nobody had the heart to sack me after the Operation Kiss debacle and loss of Tom and Fiona. Who could replace me? Who would want to replace me? Robbie was having too much of a headache and I was a suitable fall guy. I say fall guy, Robbie never exploited my failure. I think he saw my value by, at the very least, taking some eyes off him (um, in other words, a fall guy, I suppose). So it was that I became more of a liaison guy. People came to me for information. I dared not voice too strong an opinion or, god forbid, develop a theory.

Over time I was slowly getting back into the not so much 'good' books of the Rubber Beans, but rather the 'address' books. The police who remained in the Rubber Beans or z-squad were the toughies. They thought of themselves as the last line of defence, meaning they could do whatever they wanted. Of course, there were still a handful of veterans from the early days, but they were frazzled, haggard and looked as if they had, quite literally, stared death in the face. Those other police officers who had been around at the time of Operation Kiss were either dead, had retired (with PTSD) or had become Muters themselves.

Police numbers were becoming depleted hence the army was quietly being drafted in. The government didn't want soldiers in the streets overtly carrying guns, so rubber-based suits, but in dark green, were commissioned as a compromise. Ironically, as a result of people not knowing who I was, I was ignored when I walked into the briefing rooms; it suited me. An anonymous citizen, I was happy to sit at the back of the briefing room and let the Green

Bean commander brief the new recruits. I carried my white lab coat in the shoulder bag just in case I felt it would be useful to whip it out and slip it on.

On one occasion, I was asked to attend a briefing of two dozen new Black Rubber Beans and a handful of senior army observers. After all, it had been me that had put the idea onto paper after the St Mary's school massacre. I was getting my wish (the involvement of the army), Robbie told me, so I should go along and see what wish-fulfilment looked like.

The main Bean commander (Commander Bream) was giving an update on the MDP threat. Part of the presentation included images of a handful of high value targets – Muters who had been caught on CCTV, other surveillance footage and drones. Those shown didn't quite match my own list of high value targets, but there was some crossover. I was careful to keep the identities and my theories close to my chest. I had already learnt that to share was to risk ridicule and credibility-death.

I sat silently at the back of the room as the commander scrolled through projected images of known MDPs giving a little spiel on each. Nigel was nowhere to be seen. After Operation Kiss I had dropped him from all but the most confidential reports. No Rubber Bean asked questions on his absence – they were either dead or traumatised. However, there were projected images of a few old friends – GlassCutter, Diesel, TarmacTired – but the Commander had his own code-names, not their 'real' names (those death names given by Nigel were a closely guarded secret). GlassCutter and DoorStop were the 'Kray Twins' – most often seen together in each other's company and on account of their a criminal history in the east end of London. They had been in and out of prison numerous times. Diesel (often seen with his sword still strapped to his back) was known as the 'Predator' – on account of his looks. TarmacTired was known as Scarface. It was odd to see images of my old Muter friends as Beans smiling with

families and friends at joyous events and milestones in their lives –
college graduation, travelling, at weddings and in various poses for
the social media machine – only to be followed by photos of them
in action on the streets of London as a Muter. Needless to say it
was a striking change and the commander had done well to present
the starkness of the transformation from human to MDP. When
TarmacTired flashed up as a Bean she was a slim, beguiling,
attractive early twenty-something brunette, there was a murmur of
approval in the darkness. Then the Commander pulled up a picture
of her as a Muter, exclamations of 'Shit, fuck,' punctuated by deep
groans, abounded.

I was pleased with the Commander Bream's presentation – it
was fair and he did his best to present the threat as real. I made a
note to befriend the commander afterwards, he might make a
useful ally. But the presentation wasn't over yet.

As his briefing drew to a close, the commander took a deep
breath.

'Now, I am saving the worst to last,' he said, looking glum.

On the screen flashed two pictures, side by side,....of
ChubbyCheeks. One before she died – almost a studio portrait –
the other, a telephoto image on a street. In both photographs
Chubby looked almost identical – the cherubic image of sweetness.

'We call her Genghis,' the commander hissed, almost scared
to turn and look at the images on the screen behind him.

A gentle, chortling murmur reverberated around the room.

The commander was expecting this. He sighed and managed
to do the impossible – look even more tired and glum.

'If you remember anything from this briefing,' he said,
staring hard at the gathered soldiers, 'remember this: if you come
across this MDP, Genghis, or see her at whatever distance, call for
backup immediately.'

Sitting behind the men, I saw broad, muscled shoulders
bounce as chortles echoed about the room.

'Sir, if we're alone and backup's minutes away?' asked one brave man. 'Can we offer her ice cream in exchange for her surrender?'

The commander didn't bat an eyelid. His face was a stone-cold, sober stare.

'Honestly?' muttered Commander Bream. 'If you see her and are alone. Run. And don't stop.'

'What if we have a clean nappy with us?' asked another Rubber Bean.

Cue more chortles. The commander ignored them.

'Sir, honest question, have we tried using a puppy to throw Genghis off her game?' came a question from the darkness.

'We think this...er, creature, this MDP,' said Commander Bream, 'is the biggest serial killer the British Isles have ever known. We suspect her kills run into the thousands, over four thousand at least.'

The soldiers weren't buying it. You had the sense that they were unsure whether this was a joke. Was the commander ending the session with a little levity? I was probably the only one in the room who believed him. I suspected four thousand was a wild underestimate. I knew forensics labs were running tests on bites, cadavers and were developing DNA profiles of MDPs of interest. Chubby's Z-DNA (along with CCTV and eye witness reports) pointed towards her as being the most productive MDP in death.

I put on my lab coat and gave my own little presentation to the soldiers, but I doubt it was as effective as the commander's. I did end with a little warning, though:

'I've seen these MDPs operate for months now,' I said to the gathered men. They are getting better at what they do and becoming more organised than you can imagine. These MDPs want nothing more for you than death, remember that. I have seen them kill and convert people like you within moments of operational engagement. And at the rate their numbers are rising, there might soon be a time when there are more of them than you. If you are out and about and are attacked, some of your colleagues will reach a point where they will turn and run; but know this, each and every one of these MDPs you have seen today will never, ever stop running at you.'

I don't know if it worked, but it left the room a little silent. I wanted it to be at least a little effective, because I knew that at any moment my 'Special Ops' office might be wound up and my wisdom would be banished to the suburbs.

The following evening I was sitting alone in my office waiting for the axe to fall when there was a knock at the door. I braced myself for another diatribe, but it was a courier with a box. I signed for it and opened it to find a large, brown leather briefcase wrapped in a ribbon. I was confused. Was this a leaving present? Was someone saying pack your bags? Then I saw a London picture postcard on which a small key was taped on the reverse side with a handscawled note.

Hope this works for now. Might need a few trips. Locker 39.
Signed, Your Brother-in-Arms.

It clicked. It was the Whistleblower. A key to a locker? But where in the metropolis was locker 39? I flipped the picture postcard over again. It displayed the British Museum. The briefcase was spacious enough to hold a thick wad of papers. It put me on the spot. I could start dropping off documents to the Whistleblower right away, so why was I feeling reluctant? Fear. I had to dig deep and mine some courage. It felt odd that espionage (if that is what it was), had moved from analogue to digital and now back again to analogue. We were living in a time when leaving an electronic trail was ill-advised, a (literal) paper trail was the way to go.

I felt encouraged. I was being taken seriously by another person. That was twice in twenty four hours – Commander Bream and the Whistleblower. I was not seen as a liability, hurrah. The knowledge I had acquired was felt to be of worth to someone (two people, in fact), but to others (mostly in the policing community) my reputation was legendary, fast becoming folklore, in an unflattering way. It was a shame, because I knew no one would ultimately benefit from my Special Ops office being cut out of the decision-making process. If my contribution, experience were to be ignored, then it would result in yet more death. And so it was proved to be.

A few days later I was advised of an incident in Kensington Gardens. I read the news reports and I also had access to the secret, restricted internal Rubber Bean report that came a week afterwards. Neither made for pretty reading.

Apparently one of the Rubber Bean squads that had been present at the briefing where ChubbyCheeks had been singled out as a particular threat, took it upon themselves to hunt Chubby down. They wanted to be a squad that took down the most feared killer the British Isles had ever known. They had obviously done their research on her activities – including, no doubt, reading my reports on Chubby's hunting grounds being schools, playgrounds and parks. These Rubber Beans made a point of staying alert to reports of potential MDP activities in such places. Therefore, at two o'clock on a warm, sunny Saturday afternoon they responded to reports of concerning behaviour in Kensington Gardens. Now, if you are unfamiliar with the London metropolis, Kensington Gardens is one of the most serene and desirable places in the capital. It has large open spaces with pockets of trees and shrubbery, fountains, statues, avenues and more. It is a favourite of families and sun-bathers. This particular day had been no different. Families were camped out on the grass enjoying the sun. Small children were running, screaming and playing with their siblings and friends while parents lounged about. Young couples also sunbathed across the large, empty grass spaces. Single people

David O. Zeus

soaked up the sun or dozed in the shade of trees reading books. Ice-cream vans were parked around on the perimeter. Metropolis life and traffic seemed miles away. It was as safe as safe could be.

None of the reports that I read quite detailed what triggered the incident largely because those who did have the answers were dead, but the surviving witness accounts suggested that at some point a number of Black Rubber Beans emerged from an unmarked van at the edge of the park and started to advance, weapons drawn, into the park itself. I reviewed the available mobile phone footage; what I saw was half-a-dozen Rubber Beans marching slowly through a group of sunbathers. The Rubber Beans appeared to be focused on something (a target?) deeper in the park.

Suddenly one of the Rubber Beans shouted and pointed into the distance. A shot rang out, then another. Within moments the park was echoing to rapid machine gunfire as children and parents and sunbathers scattered. Apparently, one of the Rubber Beans thought he had identified ChubbyCheeks and opened fire. This created confusion. Many children, who had been playing in the vicinity of the target, started screaming and running back to their parents. The trouble was, the parents were lounging about in the vicinity of the Rubber Beans, so the Rubber Beans suddenly saw dozens of screaming children – their eyes wide in fear (or was it aggression?), their mouths open wide bearing teeth, their faces covered in blood (from the first child victim) – running towards them. Lo and behold, the advancing armed men panicked and, thinking these were possibly Chubby's gang, opened fire on the children. This, understandably, had the effect of incensing the fathers and mothers of the children being mown down by bullets. Leaping to their feet, adopting their own wild, furious, manic expressions, the parents started charging the armed men. The result was predictable. The armed Rubber Beans turned their weapons on to the charging parents and started unloading their magazines into bare-chested fathers and bikini-clad mothers. As the pandemonium

256

erupted, another half-dozen, black-clad (and armed) Rubber Beans emerged from another van and charged towards the fracas firing at will. They were none the wiser and about who was who. All they saw were children either lying in crumpled bloody heaps, or bloodied children charging in all directions while the formerly sunbathing parents (and young couples) were charging their Rubber Bean colleagues or running away.

It was a bloodbath.

All in all, seventy-two were shot to death that day in the park. Forty-one children, twenty-two adult civilians, nine Black Rubber Beans (who had all been overpowered and had their weapons turned on them by irate parents). Not one MDP had been apprehended (or 'destroyed'). Chubby was nowhere to be seen. Or, at least, that was what the reports said. In fact, one of the deceased was a middle-aged man recovered in a small enclosure of trees. He had not been shot, but disembowelled. I arranged a discreet DNA test on the fluids and found that Chubby had in fact been at work that day.

Needless to say, the media had a field day – 'The Somme Comes to Kensington'. The government had a horror day. But I was cleared of any involvement. In fact, I heard rumours that people in Whitehall and the government had been asking 'where was the zombie guy?' Why had the zombie guy been kept out of it? Why wasn't the zombie guy authorising all such activity? It appears the groundwork for my reputation was being restored by the activities of gun-toting Black Rubber Beans and Cloth-Heads.

Little did I know that the gods would smile on me some more. Not too far over the horizon were two other helpful nods in my direction – Nigel's sudden celebrity and, shortly after, an attack on a box of errant Beans

32. Museums and Whistles

'Who *is* this Guy?!' ran the headline in the paper with a large picture of a killer zombie holding, in one hand, an unconscious Bean upside down, head half-submerged in the River Thames (the Black Road) and, in the other hand, another no doubt dead Bean with its head smashed to a bloody pulp. The dead Beans were, of course, Dunky-elect and Smashy-elect, and the killer zombie was Nigel, but only I knew that.

At 9.30 a.m. on the morning the picture appeared in the papers-of-news, I was getting flooded by phone calls from people who had been ignoring me for weeks.

'Is this your guy?' asked Robbie.

'Do you know this guy?' came a call from Downing Street.

'Tap your contacts. Try and find out who this guy is,' came a call from another part of Whitehall.

'Do you have a codename for this guy?'

'What is this guy and what is he doing?'

And more. Many more.

My answers were: Yes; Yes; I know who he is; codename is not needed, his actual name is Nigel (and no, I won't give him his family name); and, yes, he's a killer zombie and he is doing what killer zombies typically do.'

Suddenly, I was in the game again.

You would have thought I would be really excited by all the attention, but I was now older and wiser. Popularity is a fickle bride. I needed to escape for a while, but where could I go? Then it dawned – the British Museum, of course. I put all my calls through to my interns and said I was working on a theory.

I needed time to think.

If I was back in the game, people might start paying attention to me again and I would find it more difficult to slip away. Now I had a small window of opportunity and took it.

I grabbed a handful of documents – printouts of Nigel's blog, police photographs, CCTV screengrabs, medical reports, background reports on the MDPs and a few other simple reports I had drafted and circulated around Whitehall – and stuffed them into the Whistleblower's briefcase gift to me. There was nothing too controversial. I was mindful of two things. Firstly, I wanted to control what the Whistleblower had in his possession. Although I trusted him (based on Bob's recommendation), I needed to test the waters. Whatever I included in the briefcase might end up in a newspaper column, a podcast or circulated on social media. It was sensitive material. Secondly, I was careful to share information that would not lead back to me directly. So, I did not enclose anything exclusively prepared by my unit. I enclosed reports by police, forensics, images from shops CCTV, mobile phones. Maybe I could prepare a USB memory stick with videos and other documents, but I just wanted to see what would happen. There was no way I was going to email a link to download documents and videos. My IT skills were average and it would inevitably be tracked back to me.

I packed the briefcase with a nice selection of material before sitting down in my chair and pausing. Work in the office could become fraught and busy to a point where I was unable to think straight. I needed a few minutes to reflect on what I was about to do – violate all sorts of laws and possibly end any hope of a career, even employment, in the civil service (and the urban design world). Although aware that I had no spy-training I concluded that the documents would not lead back to me. The Whistleblower had only given me the locker key and I had not scheduled a visit, so I was also relatively comfortable that I would not be seen by anyone. I looked at the packed briefcase sitting on the couch across the room and wondered if I should unpack it.

An intern entered the office.

'We're getting lots of calls from everyone. What do you want to do?'

I had two options. The first was to engage and assist the intern with answering the calls, the other option was delivering the briefcase sitting quietly on the couch. My eyes darted between the two and I willed myself for someone or something else to make a decision for me. My instinct and paranoia (the kind of paranoia that keeps you alive when you are dealing with the merchant of death) won the day.

I still could not shake the thought that I might get a visit from the men in suits who would pack up my office without saying a word. And what would the men in suits do with all the work and intelligence I had acquired? Destroy it? Bury it? Ship it off to a government underground archive facility? Even if all my research was stored somewhere, it might not be long before my political masters panicked and wanted my involvement again. By which time it might be too late. The apocalypse doesn't arrive overnight, there is a birthing process, a period of labour. You can't push the apocalypse baby back inside if its mother is already ten centimetres dilated. No, there was no time for delay. I had to get some information out to the Whistleblower.

I let a handful of interns know I was heading out to get a mid-morning cooked breakfast and read some reports.

'It's going to be a long day and night,' I said, walking out the door with the briefcase. 'I need some fuel before I get called into lunch meetings and lose my day altogether.'

'Besides, make them sweat. They've ignored us for weeks. You take your time Josh,' the intern called after me, oblivious to my true intentions.

I waved a 'thanks' as I disappeared down the stairs.

Reaching the street, I realised the Museum was only half an hour walk from Whitehall and that I would avoid all sorts of CCTV if I headed there on foot. After a brisk, nervous walk I entered the British Museum and found the locker in a corner away from security cameras. Opening locker 39 I found an identical briefcase to mine. I slipped my own briefcase into the locker and retrieved the other whose contents were far lighter than mine. On reviewing its contents I saw it held a few newspapers and guides to the Museum itself.

The delivery having been made, I found myself exhausted. Not wanting to blow my cover and aware I still had hours to kill, I spotted a sign as I strolled out of the locker room pointing to the Museum's cafe. Of course, my cooked breakfast! Settling down in the cafe I ordered a breakfast and reflected on my treason. Although I could never succeed as a proper spy, it wasn't so bad. If the Whistleblower delivered the goods (in terms of bringing sensitive information into the public domain), I would have to make further trips. Perhaps occasional cooked breakfasts at the British Museum would be my way to escape the stress. The breakfast itself was fantastic. I had stumbled on the ideal cover. Nobody would question me making time for such a feast.

Thumbing through the museum guides on the exhibits and the newspapers the Whistleblower had provided, I was reminded of Ben's words. The plague of death we were experiencing was not the first time *Homo sapiens* had been threatened. The question was: was it the *final* time? The end of the road? The museum guides showcased galleries on civilisations long disappeared. Peoples, cultures, ways of thinking, all now gone. Looking at the newspapers I read indignant opinion pieces and indignant, inaccurate news pieces. The stories in the paper-of-news would all go the same way as everything else; their fragments wouldn't even make it to a museum.

Ben was right. Hevel was a good word. Vanity is at the core of everything – power, love, ambition, despair, loneliness. And if vanity is at the core of everything, then everything is futile and Death is its master. Beans are but breath in the wind.

But if that were so, what was the point, the meaning of life? I had sometimes reflected on the question and had made peace with the conclusion that at the very least (or at its very core), it was purely and simply the fabulous view or the splendid, fleeting taste; an act of perceiving and appreciating beauty. A flower has no meaning, but its beauty is something to behold, yet it is destined to turn to dust. The view of swirling clouds from the top of the mountain generates a sense of wonder, but it is literally swirling vapour. Finally, the full English cooked breakfast, however fleeting, gives a sense of unrivalled satisfaction, but its destiny is a sewage works.

The 'meaning' is the act of appreciation, of observation, the view, the taste. Does that mean death is the appreciation, the witness to life? I know what Nigel would think: he would think the reverse was true – that life is the witness to death. Without Bean 'existence' there can be no true appreciation of death – Bean existence is simply the witness to the fearsome, profound beauty, majesty and infinity of death.

I returned to the office. I was correct in my prediction. It was a long day indeed. Back at home on my houseboat I realised I had done the right thing. There would be lots of people wanting to leak information to people like the Whistleblower, I was glad the information would find an outlet and I felt comfortable I would not be traced. That feeling lasted all of seven hours.

As a rule I tried to get to the office early so I would pick up any news of an overnight Muter development with my work-hat on. So when my phone rang at six o'clock in the morning, as I was preparing to leave my houseboat, I thought it was odd. My phone displayed 'number withheld', which normally means I would ignore it, but this time I relented. No journalist would phone me so early, surely? I answered.

'Josh Chronides?' said a voice unknown to me.

'Yes,' I replied, hesitatingly.

'You are on your houseboat?' said the voice down the line.

'Who is this?'

'A car will be with you in five minutes,' said the voice.

'I said, who is this?' I muttered, now slightly irritated.

'The Prime Minister wants to meet you. The car will bring you to Downing Street.'

The call ended. I felt some sickness in my throat.

That was quick. They must have been following me or watching someone pick up the briefcase from the locker. Holy crap.

But why was Downing Street involved?

As promised, the car arrived and picked me up a few minutes later and I was whisked to Downing Street. Of course I was not driven down Downing Street itself, but to the rear entrance. Welcomed by an aide, I was guided to a small reception room on the ground floor. A couple of large television screens were playing two different news channels. I knew as soon as I saw the live feed from 'the incident' why I was there. The aide asked about refreshments and I requested tea.

I was left alone to watch the unfolding news. Perhaps I should have checked my phone on the way to Downing Street, but I was in the habit of getting news from my own sources rather than the fear-mongering Press.

Both news channels were reporting on an 'ongoing' incident at HM Prison Wormwood Scrubs in the west of London. It appeared that the prison had been taken over by a gang of MDPs. It was still 'early days' apparently according to the media, but it was reported that the prison authorities had lost control of His Majesty's prison. It was feared that the prisoners might be succumbing to the attacks from the undead.

Shit, I sighed under my breath. This will be a headache.

The news reports fudged facts and the few facts they did have were lost in the delivery of the 'compelling' story.

'There are reports,' said the reporter in fretful disbelief, 'that the invaders almost seemed to be organised and even knew what they were doing.'

You could see the confusion on the reporter's face. He was obviously still of the mind that the undead were lumbering idiots. Feeling my phone buzzing in my pocket, I pulled it out and turned it off. I knew it would not stop ringing, but I was in a place where I felt justified in ignoring it. If anybody complained (I was mostly thinking of Robbie), saying I had been rushed to Downing Street was as good an excuse as any.

The tea arrived, accompanied by some warm pastries. I tucked up and carried on watching the news. I was too restless to take a seat, but my nervousness had found a new home – this meeting might not be about my visit to the British Museum after all.

Suddenly, I heard a door open behind me. I looked over my shoulder and saw the Prime Minister enter alone and walk towards me, hand outstretched.

33. The PM and a Box of Errant Beans

'Sorry, I've been meaning to meet you in person for a while, Josh. Especially after all the recent news stories,' said the Prime Minister, me offering his hand in a warm gesture of greeting. 'I know you have been ostracised recently, but it at least demonstrated to me you were trying to do something when everybody else was procrastinating (myself included, to my shame). What was the sting-thing you tried?'

'I planted two of my team at the end of a street posing as two lovers in the hope of drawing in the lead MDP whereupon we would snatch him.'

'Shame, but, as I said, at least you tried to catch this Nigel chap. You lost a girl, I understand? May she rest in peace.'

'She is actually doing quite well. Now patrolling Clerkenwell, I think.'

'What was her name?'

'It was Fiona. Now known as LoveHurts.'

'Oh dear.'

'Not a great name to have for eternity,' I added.

The Prime Minister nodded. We both took the pause to look back at the television screens.

'Do you think your guy is behind this?' asked the Prime Minister, nodding at the news reports.

I sighed. Took a moment. And thought. Instinctively the answer was 'yes, but', however, this was the Prime Minister I was talking to. I needed to provide a basis for my argument. The answer quickly presented itself.

'There is nothing in Nigel's writing specifically referencing the planning of something like this, but his senior followers (his 'colleagues') are pretty sharp and proactive now. I suspect that two of his early followers who go by the names GlassCutter and Doorstop are behind this. In their previous existences, as John Reuel and Clive Staples, they both spent time in Wormwood Scrubs. They would know the premises and how the building operates. Judging by the reports coming out, the Muters moved quickly through the building and took control. Who knows, it might form part of GlassCutter's and DoorStop's unfinished business.'

'Yes, I have seen you reference such a thing in your reports,' the PM replied.

'It does look as if the dead carry over unfinished business from their lives. Nigel talks about it and we have seen some clear examples with the likes of TarmacTired and, more recently, Peas.'

'Do we know what Nigel's unfinished business is yet?'

I shook my head.

'No, I'm not sure he does either, although my…deceased colleague, Fiona, LoveHurts, was working on some theories. Whichever, his ignorance of his own unfinished business could be a blessing or a worry.'

There was a pause as we both turned towards the television screens again. The reporters gabbled on saying more information 'was coming in' and it appeared the prison had now been completely overrun. Those few guards who had survived the initial attack had now escaped the building.

'Look Josh,' the PM said, turning to me, 'the reason I brought you here is because I don't want your input to be filtered through aides, civil servants, mandarins. I need your thoughts quickly and honestly, so I will be setting up a direct line between you and one of my most trusted aides, Ella.'

'Er, thank you, Prime Minister. I'm flattered.'

'You are also an independent advisor now. You don't need to go through anybody, even your own line manager, er, Mr Robert...'

'Robbie, yes, understood.'

'If you need some leverage, then you'll have a number to call and I can knock heads together. Or arrange for heads to be knocked together.'

'Thank you.'

'I'm not promising that you'll get everything you want, but at least your thoughts and advice will not be filtered through naysayers and advisors.'

'Okay, understood,' I replied.

'So, now that you are here, what would you suggest?' said the Prime Minister, nodding at the events on the television screens.

I didn't feel rushed. It was still just the PM and me in the room and I did not want to blurt out a reply.

'Honestly? Nothing,' I said after a few moments. 'It's a prison, with high walls. Contain them as much as you can. It is possible the MDPs will sit tight for weeks. If you try to go in, it will be a bloodbath. The prison has capacity for 1,200 prisoners, I understand. If they are not dead now, they will be within hours.'

'We'll then have 1,200 MDPs.'

'Yes, if you send in a few hundred armed officers, or even the army, you'll have a few hundred more MDPs on top of that. In this instance, you can't beat death. Besides, I have seen the morale of the Rubber Beans and they are not up to such a daunting task.'

It was clear that I was referencing the debacle in Kensington Gardens. The PM looked pensive. My point had been made. He didn't want another catastrophe on his hands.

'It will take a good few days for the dead to rise,' I continued. 'And when they do there is a period of acclimatisation while they are getting the hang of things. They are pretty ineffective at that time, unless provoked. You have a few weeks, so there is no rush.

Besides, I think this long-term containment might often be the best bet. Once you have lost a place, a space, a large property, let them have it. Don't send in pest control.'

'It might look indecisive,' pondered the Prime Minister. 'That might unsettle people.'

'It doesn't have to be. As you will know from my reports a great many MDPs (including Nigel) are using a deserted factory warehouse south of the river. I've used all my influence to prevent Cloth-Heads and Rubber Beans from raiding the premises. If they went in, it would achieve nothing. We are monitoring the MDP behaviour and I've put in a request for improved perimeter fencing and CCTV. If we can make it clear that this is the strategy, then that should reassure people. It looks as if Nigel and MDPs welcome having a home base of sorts, so it might be mutually beneficial. I suspect there will be other bases cropping up.'

The PM looked worried.

'What's your concern?' I said.

'I fear it might be perceived as a ghetto – that we are controlling them, but, as the numbers grow, what else can we do but control them?'

'Don't think about it as "control", Prime Minister,' I said.

I paused, thought and chose my next words carefully.

'What do you do in politics? What do you do if you want to control a group that does not want to be controlled?'

The PM paused in thought momentarily.

'If you can influence the leader you might be able to guide his followers down a particular path,' he said.

'Exactly. But it is more subtle than that. You can't control Nigel, but you could follow his lead and the effect will be similar,' I replied.

'What do you mean?'

'Muters are nomadic, but they sometimes gravitate to working from bases. Nigel operated from the flat of a woman he acquired and they were based there for a few weeks until they outgrew the premises. The flat belongs to CatNaps...' I paused. I was lost in thought...before continuing. 'Muters can't be controlled. They are like cats in that respect. You cannot herd or marshal them like sheep. But, yes, what you could do is follow their lead, let them find and identify a home, then lock them in.'

'And set the house on fire?' said the PM with a wry look.

'It'll take more than a house and more than a fire, but you could set up perimeter fences and hold them in a square mile, perhaps,' I said. 'Think of it as a quarantine rather than a ghetto.'

The PM nodded.

'That's what I would do,' I said, now glad that I was able to give some advice. 'Forget rounding them up, forget engaging with them and taking them on with conventional weaponry. No noisy gun battles that scare the locals. You'll just have a bloody mess.'

The PM nodded, relaxing.

'A little less noise on the streets would be good for everyone's nerves.'

It was not lost on me that the PM was thinking about the electorate. As if the election in fifteen months was even a possibility.

'It'll buy you time as you sort out the legalities. You'll need a lot of fencing. And, I'm afraid to say, perhaps you could consider throwing some more Green Beans into the mix?'

'Green Beans?'

'The military,' I replied. 'Say it will release the police officers for other duties. I think the police are struggling. It might be an opportunity to introduce the British public to the idea of some soldiers on the street.'

'For a very specific purpose,' said the PM.

'Exactly'.

The PM reflected. Knowing that I might not find myself with such an opportunity to influence thinking, I added:

'Remember, let the MDPs (or rather, Nigel) select the locations. MDPs are targeting larger establishments now as there are more of them. You're aware of the few blocks of flats in Bow that they took over a few weeks ago?'

'Yes, how did they do that? We didn't know.'

'Nigel befriended the property landlord with keys to many properties. But they have moved on now.'

The Prime Minister and I talked some more and I felt comfortable that he was supportive of my ideas, but I could still see he was worried about something. As the conversation was winding up I gave him the opportunity to share.

'Anything else, Prime Minister?'

The PM looked at me nervously.

'Josh. These Muters, MDPs. They catch the virus having been attacked, yes?'

'Yes,' I replied.

'So, they were alive when they caught it, correct?'

'Yes.'

'So, a corpse that *never* came into contact with the virus while it was alive has never been animated-in-death (become an MDP) *after* it died?'

'I'm not sure I understand what you mean…?'

'What I am worried about, Josh, is…. Am I correct in assuming that we won't have the dead – corpses – rising from cemeteries around London in the months ahead?'

I looked at him. I was momentarily thrown. I had been blinkered and hadn't really considered such a possibility.

The PM could, no doubt, see my concern. He continued.

'I've heard of a few cases where MDPs have risen from graveyards.'

'Yeess,' I said slowly, catching his train of thoughts. 'I know a few of them – BroadBean, Plot… – but they were both infected before they died.'

'That is a relief,' he muttered, turning away only to spin around again. 'So there is no possibility of the long-dead rising from the grave?'

I must have still looked confused. I certainly felt as if blood was draining from my features.

'So,' the PM repeated, filling the silence, 'no hundreds (or thousands) of MDPs suddenly rising from cemeteries?'

'No, of course not,' I said, gulping, but my mind immediately turned to what Ben had said – that similar outbreaks had happened before. But what had happened in those previous instances? Had there been instances when the long-dead had risen from graves? I would be unwise to assume anything.

I was also troubled as to the origin of the Prime Minister's concern. It wasn't in any report that I had written. I had assumed those MDPs who had risen had been buried too quickly or buried by the families ignorant of the possible plague infection.

Yet, the PM's words began to haunt me and I shuddered to think of the implications. Nigel had made no reference to being able to raise the dead who *pre-dated* the plague. He had never spoken of spending any significant time in graveyards, but that said, he had made reference to a colleague of his – Plot – whose origin story was, to date, unclear. I made a mental note to insist Ben share everything with me, including that which he had been withholding from me at our first meeting. Gaps in my knowledge were suddenly a source of great unease, especially as I was supposed to be advising the Prime Minister.

'No, no, no,' I repeated, my mouth dry, breaking the silence. 'Nothing like that.'

'Okay, that's good,' sighed the Prime Minister, visibly relieved.

The trouble was that now I was the one who was worried.

One good thing came out of the exchange though – at least I knew not to include a reference to the dead rising from the graves in any upcoming report.

The Prime Minister reiterated to me that he would make clear that I was to operate more independently and we wound up our discussion. I was glad that he was onboard about the containment of the MDPs in the home bases. Not only did it give him time, it gave me time too. I needed to check in with Nigel's blog and see if I could determine a longer-term plan. So, for the time being, it was the wisest thing to do.

The Prime Minister insisted on walking me out of the room to the office of the trusted aide he had referred to earlier.

'Ella, Josh. Josh, Ella. I'll let you two get acquainted,' said the Prime Minister before disappearing.

Ella Ferreira-Burt stuck out a hand and introduced herself. A sharp, no nonsense, attractive, young-looking, early-forty something woman in a business-suited way, she struck me as someone who I could work with straightaway.

'Hello Josh, I haven't been your greatest fan, but you have won me over.'

'I had no idea.'

'Let's just say you have other fans and I have been brought into the fold.'

'Do you know who I am?' she said.

'I might have seen the odd picture of you in the newspaper when journalists are trying to expose the power behind the throne.'

'I have been as cynical as any Brit about all of this, but I have respect for the old ways of thinking about the dead.'

'You sound like…'

'Ben Garfunkel?' Ella said.

'How…?'

Ella explained that Bob Beaumont had been instrumental in introducing Ella (and thereby, the Prime Minister) to Josh's reports and theories. Not only that, Bob had also shared with Ella the concerns and insight of Ben. I concluded that if Bob had confided in Ella, that was as good an indication for me to do the same. It was a relief to have an ally in Downing Street. Perhaps I should give Ben a bit more time. At least it would not fall on deaf ears if I referred to his thinking in my own reports.

'You said you have respect for the "old ways of thinking about the dead", meaning…?' I asked, curious.

'I was born here in the UK, but my parents came over as newlyweds from Sri Lanka fifty years ago. So, I have an additional cultural perspective on all this.'

'So what is the culture in Sri Lanka with regards to the dead?' I asked, thinking I needed as much perspective as possible.

'I'm Catholic, born and raised. There is a strong catholic community in Sri Lanka, but there are other cultural influences from South Asia that find their way to Sri Lanka. Reading your reports about Nigel rising from a crematorium I couldn't shake the image of Riri Yaka from my mind.'

'Riri Yaka?'

'The Blood Demon, a ghoul, a tall, blood-thirsty creature that feasted on the living. It haunted crematoria and graveyards before moving on to stalking living humans and spreading illness and causing blood-related diseases that made the carrier pale, anaemic and confused.'

'The Prime Minister mentioned something about graveyards. He fears the dead will rise?' I asked.

Ella nodded.

'We have been sharing stories and I think he is having a few nightmares.'

'Or visions?' I muttered, with a wry smile.

'But, as I say, I'm Catholic, so no talk of anything other than Jesus in my family.'

'Well, I'm pleased.'

'Well, my parents aren't. I am a pretty-much lapsed Catholic, so I am a bit of a disappointment right now.'

'Oh, right,' I said, not sure whether I should venture into the realm of religion.

' *"You'll meet Jesus one day if you're lucky,"* my mother keeps saying to me,' said Ella, adopting a reflective tone. 'So best make a good impression in life while I can, my mother insists.'

'Mothers can be wise. Even visionary.'

'I might return to Catholicism one day. Just in time. Before death claims me,' Ella laughed.

'Well, me and Death, we're like that,' I said, with my fingers crossed and a wink. 'I'll put a word in.'

34. Talking About World Piece

'You think it will work?' asked Ben, with what I took to be a smirk.

'What?'

'This containment strategy – Area SW51?'

'I don't know.'

'It won't work,' replied Ben without a hint of doubt, which irritated me.

'What does Nigel call it?'

'World Piece.'

Ben's brow furrowed.

'As in a piece of his world in ours,' I continued.

'Holy cow.'

Ben and I were sitting huddled in the same cafe in central London. Private, armed security was standing outside. Not for my sake, it was locally organised. It was the way of the world now. If you fancied nipping out for a skinny double mocha latte, you had to get past the guns. Once upon a time you had to get past signs requesting patrons to wear paper masks, now it was six-foot tall armed guards. With the soon-to-be-mandated wearing of micro-chipped wristbands (or the 'optional-but-encouraged' surgically-inserted microchips) allowing entrance to establishments (and to pay for goods) you would have thought you would feel safe, but no, not always.

'Except there are other 'Pieces' springing up over the capital,' Ben said.

I let the question linger, un-replied.

'Why do that?' he continued. 'Why doesn't the government keep the MDPs all in one place?'

I gave Ben a blank look. I couldn't say anything, but I was willing him to perceive an answer in my blankness.

'Nigel's running the show?' asked Ben, almost incredulous. 'Securing bases from which to operate?'

My blank stare was unmoved.

'Can't you track him?' Ben continued.

I shook my head. Tracking Nigel had been a question asked by all. I was tired of it. We had tried monitoring by CCTV, using mobile phones that he had acquired, using drones, but all came to nothing. Modern technology was designed to monitor and track life, not death. As a result, Nigel was, to all intents and purposes, cloaked in invisibility.

'And when the Pieces eventually make a whole?' Ben whispered. It wasn't a question. It was more a fearful realisation. He paused and looked out the cafe window at the changing world outside. We sat in silence.

Ben turned to me.

'So, that is why you're here?' he answered, suddenly focused. 'For answers? Inspiration?'

I sighed. I didn't know what to think. Or rather I didn't know what to admit.

'So what is it?' Ben asked again.

'Anything, everything,' I said. 'Tell me what you know. What you *think* you know.'

Ben squinted hard as he looked at me. He knew he was the one who now had leverage.

'You first,' he said.

'Me?' I replied. 'You have a direct line to the Whistleblower. You probably know more than me. I've been reading his articles and posts. He is getting information from sources other than me.'

'Okay, so tell me where we are and why you are here,' Ben persisted.

I sighed and took a deep breath.

I spoke honestly. Having lost Tom and Fiona it was good to speak openly. I always had to be careful when talking to Robbie, he always seemed to think about how it would affect him and his workload. With Ben, I had an avid listener, non-judgemental. I described my close encounter with Nigel in Little Clarendon Street and spoke about how the disastrous attitude of the Rubber Beans that had led to the Kensington Gardens massacre. I explained that, as far as I was concerned, most of our problems were not a result of the MDPs, but our reaction to the z-demic. By the end of my confession I had shared pretty much everything.

'Ok, your turn. What can you tell me?' I said to Ben.

'I've been looking less at epidemics, pandemics,' said Ben, 'and more at how cultures and civilizations have viewed the dead. For thousands of years almost all cultures speak of the dead rising, being a threat to the living. The similarities across cultures are uncanny.

'How far back are we talking?' I asked.

'Ancient Mesopotamia myths,' Ben said. 'You know the story of Descent of Ishtar? One of the oldest written stories found on clay tablets – in fact it is just down the road in the British Museum – and these clay tablets, dating to the seventh century BC refer to the existence of the risen dead.'

I raised my eyebrows. Ben took it as a challenge.

'Yes, it's true, the Neo-Assyrian Myth of Ishtar's Descent into the Underworld refers to the dead rising to eat the living and that the dead 'will outnumber the living'. Other clay tablets refer to battles with "ghuilan" – the plural of the ancient word for "ghoul". Additionally, the Ancient Egyptians talk of battling "dead warriors". You've heard of the plague of locusts being unleashed on the people of Egypt in the Book of Exodus? A curse?'

I nodded. 'Of course. A plague of locusts on the people.'

'No. It's a mistranslation, Josh. It was a plague of the 'living dead' on the people for three days. The Hebrew word "locuti" is in fact from the Egyption word "loci" which means 'to be dead'. A plague of the dead.'

Ben rattled on going deeper into details of ancient stories. I could see it was almost therapeutic for him to share too. As he spoke I felt myself becoming drawn into his thinking and storytelling. I couldn't see grounds for dismissing his ideas; not that I was a full convert, but his words were finding a home with me. His reference to the British Museum was interesting. I still had a few deliveries I could make to the Whistleblower's locker in the Museum. Next time, I might hang around and check out a few of the exhibits. With what Ben was saying, I could now legitimately call it research, bizarrely.

'If the ancients were not fighting the dead, they were trying to prevent them from rising,' Ben continued. 'The Ancient Greeks used to weigh the dead down with stones. There are records of a Governor Decimus Fortunis of a Roman province in modern day Algeria in 55 A.D. dealing with an outbreak of exceptionally aggressive creatures that started with plague-infected slaves arriving from sub-Saharan Africa. Records suggest it took two years before the area was brought under control. In Lithuania in the Middle Ages a merchant from Gdansk named Lechter refers to coming across villages of "...death-made folke" that had been cordoned off by the locals. Even Venice suffered at the same time as the Black Death in 1576 when corpses would animate and terrorise the remaining inhabitants of Venice. Eventually the ghouls were transported to an island and eventually disposed of after much soul-searching by the population and bishops.

'British soldiers in Lucknow, India, in the mid-nineteenth century talk about "*wild men...who move like those driven by darkness.*" One soldier wrote "*these creatures are not like us...they seem to come alive when they sense a living man, then their bedevilled urges drive them into frenzy. I feel like I have seen evil and defeated it.".'*

'Blood-sucking demons,' I muttered, thinking of Ella.

'What?'

'The Riri Yaka – a Sri Lankan demon,' I said.

'All cultures had names for them,' said Ben. 'Similar entities – vampires, zombies, they're all the same. "MDPs" might be the last name they'll have.'

'From ancient Sumer to South West London, SW51,' I muttered.

'The definitive origin of the word "zombie" is unclear,' Ben continued, now on a roll, 'but etymologists point to West African sources citing the Kongo words *nzambi* (god) and *zumbi* or *nzumbi* (fetish). Others point to the Kongo word *vumbi* (*mvumbi*) – a ghost, a corpse that still retains the soul or *nvumbi*, a body without a soul. Other dictionaries from the early twentieth century define these words as related to the word *nzumbi* as soul or spirit that is supposed to wander the earth to torment the living. The Haitian and Caribbean origins emphasise the spirit.

'The Philippines have the Tagalog Mandurugo ("blood-sucker"). The Tai Dam ethnic minority of Vietnam were said to be terrorized by the blood-sucking "Ma cà rồng". China has the Jiangshi, sometimes called "Chinese vampires" by Westerners – they are reanimated corpses that go around killing living creatures to absorb life essence (qì) from their victims. There are reports of a regional administrator, Lin Ji Wun, who needed 200 militia to battle an outbreak that devastated several villages in the fourteenth century. The creatures are said to be created when a person's soul fails to leave the deceased's body. What is curious, or unsettling, is that the Jiangshi are usually represented as mindless creatures with no independent thought. To my mind, vampires were in fact MDPs. Written references to vampires have been around in Europe since the eighteenth century and are referenced in cultures around the world before that. They had different names – Shtriga in Albania, Vrykolakas in Greece and Strigoi in Romania.

'Japan. The Caribbean. The Americas. There are numerous records of the living dead and they are often celebrated in traditions and religions. The South Americas have Days of the Dead. The Christian Bible has the Book of Revelation. The book of Isaiah states, *"Thy dead men shall live, together with my dead body shall they arise. Awake and sing, ye that dwell in dust: for thy dew is as the dew of herbs, and the earth shall cast out the dead."*

'I thought you were trying to reassure me that our current problem is just another outbreak of an unfriendly virus and quite typical?'

'No, quite the opposite, Josh. *This* one is serious.'

'And all the others were not serious?'

'This time, I fear, we might reach a tipping point.'

I paused and pulled a face.

'What is happening now has always been destined to happen. This time, however, it might just reach critical mass,' Ben sighed. 'In the distant past and the more recent past, the virus, or whatever it was, could not travel far and those afflicted were disposed of brutally and swiftly by their communities. But in the modern day world, the virus moves quickly, social norms prevent the disposal of the infected in such traditionally brutal ways. Now, with the sheer number of people mixing and the complacency of people around the world engendered by the last pandemic, things might be different.'

I nodded. It was a lot to take in.

'In the reports that I have managed to get my hands on,' Ben coyly admitted, 'you have said that the time between death and an MDP rising is becoming shorter?'

I nodded again in the affirmative.

'Josh, dare I say it, but I believe that it is almost as if the plague of death is fine-tuning itself.'

I sat in silence.

Ben continued.

'Those early MDPs were relatively harmless but, with mentoring by Nigel and as they become more self-aware, it might be different this time.'

I fixed Ben with a stare. He knew he had my attention with the invocation of Nigel – the creature I had nothing but respect for.

'Don't think of what I am saying as supernatural, Josh,' Ben continued. 'It's not. It is…nature at work. Part of the natural world. This was always going to happen. It's…'

'Destiny?' I muttered.

'What?'

'The end?'

'And a beginning, I fear. The end of *Homo sapiens*, very possibly,' sighed Ben.

'So what happens?' I asked.

'What do you mean?' replied Ben.

'Okay, so this MDP phenomenon is not new. The risen dead appear in stories, cultures from around the world for millennia, I get it. But, assuming you are right,' I said, playing along, largely because I realised I spent so much of my time asking others to confront their own complacency, I ought to challenge my own, 'there is still time?'

Ben paused. It was now my turn to press him.

'Ben, you mentioned something about warnings when we last met?'

He nodded.

'That's where my research is headed now,' Ben said slowly. 'I am looking through the myths and ancient stories. Many stories are not about what has happened, but about what is *yet* to happen. There might be clues as to how we might head it off. Perhaps there were visionaries, shamans, who could see where it was going. I think there might be answers in these myths – which ones, I don't know yet.'

'End-of-world myths?'

Ben sighed. 'Maybe. Sort of. Yes.'

We sat in silence, assimilating the words and implications. I suspected Ben had not had an opportunity to talk to anyone else about this.

'I have a question,' I said. 'On a related, more contemporary matter.'

'Sure. Go ahead.'

'In your readings of historical events and your understanding of this whole thing, are the undead, the MDPs, living people who die *then* rise within a specific timeframe?'

Ben squinted in confusion.

'What I am asking is – will the MDPs be drawn from the ranks of those who have been infected and died within these last twelve months?'

Ben still looked a little quizzical. I was not making myself clear.

I continued. 'The virus – it's not, er, retrospective? It cannot infect the *long*-dead?'

My attempts to explain myself weren't improving. I went in for the kill.

'It's something the Prime Minister asked me and it struck me as odd. As if someone had mentioned it. I've checked – there are official estimates of up to one million people buried in and around London over the last eight hundred years, but it could be up to four million or more. My question is: there is no chance that...they too will rise?'

'I see what you mean. That would change things.'

Ben paused and returned to look at the view out the window. It seemed a silly question, but I knew Nigel had been hanging around some cemeteries and had acquired a number of his follower-colleagues from the earth – Plot and BroadBean being just two. There had also been cases of Beans killed by the MDPs being buried by families only for them to rise as MDPs themselves. I had always assumed infection was required *before* or *at* the moment of death. But what if, without our knowledge, the virus was now in the soil or somehow interacting with bodies buried long before the z-demic. It was a horrible thought and I could see in Ben's distracted stare out the window that it had not quite occurred to him.

I needed an answer.

'Because it would change things,' I said. 'We could be vastly outnumbered if the dead did start to rise from their graves.'

Ben turned to face me.

'Who asked the PM?'

'I don't know. Maybe some American General who had seen too many movies?'

'It's not a stupid question,' he said quietly. 'There is a scientific theory that I first came across in a book, *The Science Delusion*, by a chap called Sheldrake.'

'And?'

'It struck me at the time as possibly relevant about how MDPs in other parts of the world seem to be learning at a faster rate than what happened here. Almost as if Nigel's knowledge and behaviour is transferred across oceans.'

'Presumably that's through the virus mutations and variants that are transmitted and allow for faster learning?'

'Not necessarily. It could be morphic resonance,' came Ben's reply.

'What is morphic resonance?'

'It is only a theory. But Sheldrake proposes that organisms and self-organising systems are able to communicate and share habits across space and time. The behaviour of these organisms and systems can be shared locally but also non-locally using vibratory patterns that interact with electromagnetic and quantum fields of the system. A very primitive lay analogy would be: it's like updating the software of your mobile phone by linking to the Cloud (which had been updated by a company a world away in California). To be physically adjacent to one another is not necessary for communicating 'updates' if both subjects are, perhaps unwittingly, connected via the Cloud or electromagnetic and quantum fields. There are many implications if morphic resonance is a real thing. Now if one of those implications means it could transfer to those who died and were buried *before* the z-demic, then we have a problem.'

He looked at me.

'I need to do some more reading,' Ben continued. 'I will email you. But, in summary, yes, you might have to plan for that contingency – the dead rising – all of them.'

35. The Generations Game; More World Piece

The meeting with Ben preoccupied me more than I wanted. I had been looking for answers to the whole MDP-thing for yonks, I felt, and for all these lunar cycles I had assumed the answers would come from within me (in some seismic Einstein or 'Eureka' moment of insight) or from the hard trudge of the work my team was doing. Yet as the lunar cycles had rolled by and the more events had conspired against me, the more the doubt bedded down in my psyche. So, when Ben shared his theories and hinted at answers coming from a different direction entirely (the mythological) I was deeply unsettled. I should have been grateful, but it went against my instinct for 'following the science', the data. Ben's ideas were not empirical. There was no real-world data, it had no epidemiological modelling, it had no description of the protein evolution of virus variants, it had no….nothing. But the one thing it did have, had me worried.

There is no such thing as 'mythological data'. Or 'folklore data'. History was the best attempt at compiling and interpreting data from times gone by, a cousin of archaeology, but Ben's work was purely mythological, folklore – a distant, great, great uncle twice removed from history. Myths and folk stories were just fiction. Surely? Should I forget science and/or start to think that fiction, ancient stories were the answer?

I believed the argument for MDP containment in home bases such as Area SW51 was sound. World Piece was a sort of ghetto, but it worked in harmony with MDP behaviour (the instinct to flock, or gravitate to a home base). I continued to encourage Whitehall to see it as an opportunity rather than fight against it. It bought us time. I explained that if the Muters could be contained either in large, derelict buildings and/or a borough of London, it meant we could avoid the whole metropolis going into hard lockdown and reviving all the horrors, political scandals, frustrations of pandemics past.

That didn't mean everything was confined to the major sites of World Piece. Other instances of World Piece were breaking out across the metropolis, each a bloody mess. I was involved in some of them, visited others, but usually offered advice from a distance; the recommendations being – confine the MDPs and, with regret, their Bean victims to their destiny. There was no point storming the residential building or office block. Just write off the hundred or so Beans to death.

My opinion was partially informed by the passages written up by Nigel. Reading one passage about the interactions between GenerationManager and GenerationMe, I found myself almost embarrassed to be a Bean. In the lunar cycles I had been studying and chasing Muters, never once had I witnessed Muters spit, fight, moan and whinge like Beans did. The relationship between GenerationManager and GenerationMe was an excellent example of the primitive nature of Beans. Is that what modern Beanlife was? Sneering, shouting and fighting between the generations? One generation complaining the other was lucky, the other generation complaining they were not lucky enough. Who was right? Was there an optimum generation? If so, who would measure it?

As the lunar cycle moved through its phases, the media became increasingly hostile. (Not that the media had any answers of its own – god forbid.) Even though I had met the Prime Minister only once, I felt for him. At the end of the light-dark, it was his vision up against Nigel's. Life against death. There was no contest. The PM's assertion that some areas of containment (including 'Area SW51' as coined by the Press) were necessary, was undermined as 'one or two' soon became more. There were now three significantly-sized World Pieces – the derelict factory warehouse (the first and Nigel's headquarters World Piece One), the HM Strangeways prison and the office block headquarters (of GenerationManager and GenerationMe fame). Remarkably all were directly linked to Nigel and his inner-team of Muters.

The limited number of Green Rubber Beans were becoming so stretched that MDPs could largely come-and-go as they pleased from their bases only to cause havoc elsewhere. It had reached a point where some instances of World Piece were supplemented by standard Black Rubber Beans, occasionally even unarmed Cloth-Heads, neither of which were going to stop an MDP from walking through (or around) the security measures.

I had thought that we were reaching a time when people might listen to me – all proposals to address the z-demic would go through me for approval, or at least for consultation. The more fool me. Various government departments announced bizarre and contradictory initiatives. Restrictions and mini-lockdowns were introduced in some parts of London and at certain times in the week, only for mini-holidays from the restrictions to be announced. It was all in the hope of managing the frustrations of people's limits on freedoms. One such contradiction in lockdown policy was the opening up of certain family-friendly (but well-guarded) attractions around the metropolis such as zoos, art galleries and fairs.

I rang Ella in Downing Street.

'Bad idea,' I said. 'This isn't going to work. Everything is unpredictable.'

'Josh, thanks. We did think of contacting you, but the PM has to go along with it. Too much pressure. We have to show that life can operate normally.'

'Ella, I appreciate the tight corner you are in, but trust me, it's a bad idea. World Piece will work until it doesn't (better half-a-dozen large ghettos than a thousand small ones), but the MDPs do venture out and will find their way to these family-friendly places and, dare I say, throw a party.'

'We are getting it in the ear from the Europeans and the Americans,' Ella replied. I could hear the lack of conviction in her tired voice. 'We have to show we are managing this.'

Within a week there had been an attack at an aquarium.

Not long after that there was, as Nigel described it, the 'Attack of the Merry Beans' on World Piece One.

Our brilliant plan to 'contain the threat' of the Muters had failed, spectacularly. We had not planned for the Americans. Or American teenagers to be exact. Teenagers, in fact students, can be dumb. Across the world teenagers are the same. But then there is the American teenager. Everything with America is just bigger and more spectacular. In the circumstances in which we had found ourselves, what could be the worst thing for a living sentient Bean to do? Answer: Run at death.

At any one time there are, in London, four thousand American teenagers – either on gap years or on student exchanges. Like any expat group, they tended to form groups, mix and share. With the minimum age for drinking in the USA being 21, these young people threw themselves into the (legal) pub culture of the UK. Fair enough. The trouble was that Nigel and his team found these Americans easy pickings and perhaps fifty of those four thousand had found themselves hanging upside down on meathooks as resting Has-Beans in World Piece One. As a result of teenagers never wanting to be separated from their smartphones, a great many of those phones were to be found in Nigel's possession (in World Piece One).

Numerous petitions from American teenagers to authorities to recover their Has-Beans friends from Nigel's homebase fell on deaf ears. So it was that on an evening in late summer, a group of American teenagers used their own mobile phone technology to track down the location of their friends and stage their own raid on World Piece One. In a valiant attempt to rescue their Has-Bean buddies, the teenagers literally ran headlong at death.

Now perhaps I should have anticipated it. I had recently seen Nigel's passages on his understanding of the 'telephonic communication devices' and how they proved a useful tool. Discussions with government departments were ongoing about issuing public alerts discouraging people to follow up on the locations of disappeared loved ones, but I had not accounted for teenage Americans.

Perhaps I am being disingenuous and perhaps I should respect their passion and commitment to their friendships. But I could not have foreseen *two hundred* of their ilk staging a raid on Nigel's throne room.

This is where irony comes in. I had a plan that was sort of working – death was being managed, contained, albeit with some hiccups. Then life rushed in.

With almost all the American teenagers deceased after the failed attack, I knew it was a matter of time before it became an international incident. The massacre was all over the Press in the United States. It was the largest loss of American life for decades – and they weren't even servicemen or women, no, there were teenagers. There were moves in American political circles and the American media to label the MDPs as 'terrorists' thereby allowing all sorts of other emergency measures designed to 'preserve life' to be enacted.

'We don't negotiate with terrorists,' was repeated by Congressmen and women. I was almost waiting for memes to appear on the Internet exclaiming 'Ban death', 'Zombies don't deserve to live – kill them all.' 'Death to zombies now!'

We had reached a place where we could not identify irony, sarcasm, parody, humour from actual events. Reality could not be distinguished from fiction. In recent times it would take a few years between the publication of a headline parodying a news item to the same headline reporting a real event or political initiative. In recent months this gap between parody and reality had fallen to a month. Now it was a week or a few days. We were reaching a point where you could not distinguish the wildest fictional parody from the earnest reporting of everyday reality. Perhaps that is what Nigel meant when he said everything was fiction. And that was the moment of death for civilisation – when fiction and reality became indistinguishable from one another.

Wherever you are, whatever you do – irony will find and impale you in the end.

And so I waited. It was now a matter of time before the Americans got involved. But we would have to wait a little while longer – first there was another event (or individual) waiting in the wings to jump onto the stage and spend a few hours in the spotlight. A European, no less.

36. Moving Political Pieces

For the times they are a-challengin'. What could complicate my work and spoil my day any more, you ask? The answer: a politician entering from stage right. And not a British politician, not an American politician, but an European politician no less, presumably operating on the understanding that a good crisis should never go to waste. Politicians attract and repel each other. They exert a force upon one another like magnetism. The trouble is, like iron filings dotted about on nearby surfaces, we (those in public service and even the public at large) are pushed and pulled and spun about by the forces the politicians exert upon one another. In this particular instance, it was one of those distilled, super politicians of the unelected variety – the politico-bureaucrat. The type whose existence was not dependent on the will of the masses, but on a political treaty written by, you guessed it, politico-bureaucrats.

So when the President of the European Council suddenly announced he was visiting London to visit World Piece One to assess the threat (to the Continent) and reflect on containment strategies, I knew it was going to be pickled breakfast. I received an urgent message from Whitehall that neither I nor any of my team should cooperate with the entourage. I must not respond to any requests to assist or brief the bureaucrats from Brussels. I was informed that they were not interested in our containment strategies, but only in embarrassing Downing Street and gaining a little bit of leverage in the UK and abroad. To be honest, I was glad the decision had been taken out of my hands. I did not want to brief any more politicians.

The request from Brussels to assist indeed came through – I was asked to accompany the entourage (including security and media) to the World Piece One containment area, but I declined saying I was on another operation and needed more notice. However, almost as an afterthought, I added that they should not visit World Piece One because nobody could guarantee their safety. I assumed MI5 or some other security agency was listening in on the call, but I couldn't, with a clear conscience, not give the Brussels entourage a sincere warning. Any politician is a fool to think of Nigel as a pawn in some political chess game. I had looked into Nigel's sockets. I had seen the fruits of his labours and every single time he had made his bloody presence felt, much to the regret of any Bean standing nearby.

It went like this:

[Phone rings.]

It is Downing Street. Shit. I've seen the news.

'Ella, why on earth did you approve this?'

'We didn't. Brussels surprise visit. Completely unauthorised. What do you recommend?'

'Avoid it like, er, the plague. Stop them.'

'No can do. It's what they would want – to be stopped by the UK government. They have international Press travelling with them and have tipped off the UK newspapers.'

'So what do you want to achieve, Ella?'

Silence.

I pushed.

'Josh,' said Ella, sounding a little frazzled. 'The Prime Minister has asked me personally to call you. What's your advice?'

'What do you want to achieve?' I said again.

'What does any politician want to achieve?' came the murmured answer.

'Well then. Steer well clear of it.'

'The MDPs are behind the fences. They won't attack will they? They've been quite docile when actually in the World Piece home base? It is only when they venture out that things get messy. We've learnt that from you, Josh, thank you.'

I said nothing.

'So, will there be trouble? Might there be an attack?' she asked.

'You want to walk into the lion's den, to see how a lion reacts when it is woken from its slumber? What do you fear, Ella? More bad publicity?'

Now it was Ella's turn to be quiet.

I relented, but stayed true to my view.

'As Death often does, it will find a way,' I sighed. 'By Death, I mean Nigel.'

I heard Ella breathing at the other end of the line.

I continued. 'If, or rather *when*, it goes south, you can claim it was not authorised.'

The breathing sound became a sigh (of relief).

'That might be the way for you to spin it, Ella.'

'Thanks, Josh. Oh and by the way, the Europeans might call you. They want you to join them.'

No effing way, I thought. If Nigel can indeed detect a whiff of me, it might be curtains.

'Understood.'

'Don't answer the phone then.'

'Thanks for the heads up, Ella.'

'Let's hope it does not get messy.'

'Oh, I don't know,' I murmured. 'Some messes can clean up pretty well afterwards.'

I put down the phone. It immediately rang again. I ignored it, then an intern came running into the office.

'Don't answer it, I'm not here,' I said, snapping at her a little too harshly.

'It's Commander Bream, he wants to speak to you.'

I picked up the phone.

'Commander?'

'Look Josh, we've just had a request to accompany some European bureaucrats to your World Piece One.'

'Yep, so I've heard. Sounds like politics. Downing Street has been in touch, I've told them to stay away from it.'

'Oh, I've asked Downing Street about what I should do and they told me to ask you.'

'Well, stay away from it, Commander, that's my advice'

'I'd like to, but I want to keep my opposite numbers in Paris and Berlin happy. They are also part of the delegation. I might need their assistance further down the road.'

I found myself sighing now.

Silence.

'Josh, are you there?'

'Yes, I'm thinking.'

I could not recommend that the Commander take a team of (Black or Green) Rubber Beans to World Piece One, but I understood his desire to keep his opposite numbers happy. No harm in making unnecessary enemies.

'Okay, tell your opposite numbers that the military should not be near the delegation, it might provoke an attack, but you can take up positions on the surrounding rooftops, with snipers. Muters often move around on the rooftops, so you need to be careful, but you can monitor what is going on by the perimeter fences down below.'

'Thanks. That's helpful.'

'The best place is by the main entrance in the fence on Aldritch Street with all the photos and messages from the public attached to the fencing. You'll find some good spots from which to watch. The delegation is probably headed to that location, anyway. Best for their photo ops – by a fence with hundreds of pictures and messages to missing persons.'

'Thanks.'

'Oh, be careful about opening fire. You don't want to start blowing the brains out of bureaucrats, much as you would like too. Apparently there will be a heavy media presence.'

With that, we signed off. I jumped up and headed out the building. There was no way I was going to be caught on the phone or have a car pull up, or even the whole delegation convoy appear at the entrance to pick me up.

So I headed to the pub.

I sat in a Nag's Head at 11.00 o'clock in the morning and ordered a pint. I had chosen The Nag's Head because I knew it had a couple of televisions running 24 hour news. I sat at the bar, asked the barman to put on the news and sat and watched. I knew it was going to be awful. As I had said to Ella, you don't walk into the lion's den thinking you want to sneak a peak when in fact it is not a lion's den at all, but a dragon's. Smaug was waiting patiently.

Fortunately, the news was covering the arrival of the President of the Council at World Piece One. The reporters asked dumb questions – the sort of dumb questions a President of a Bureaucracy loves when cameras are switched on:

'Why are you here? What can you achieve by visiting? Do you think the British Government should be doing more?'

President nodded slowly, sighed slowly and replied slowly with a look of thoughtful concern on his face.

'Frankly, we have concerns in Brussels that the rights of these people – and they are still people – are being infringed. We are a continent that has seen, in the last one hundred years, ghettos where people were contained because the government of the day had taken a dislike to them...even to the point of wanting to exterminate them.'

'*You're saying you don't want to exterminate the MDPs, Mr President?*'

'These are difficult times for everyone. I understand my colleagues in Downing Street and Whitehall are under a great deal of strain. We are here to help. At times like these we must do what makes us human. We must keep our humanity front and centre in our dealings with these poor, lost souls.'

The President paused and waved his hand at the fence adorned with images of the dead and the handful of docile MDPs now gazing at him from beyond the fence.

'*Will you be meeting with the Prime Minister, Mr President?*'

'I would most certainly welcome a visit with the Prime Minister to discuss this with him and, dare I say, remind him of our common humanity.'

The entourage moved on and approached the perimeter fence. I wondered what kind of perfume the throng of a hundred excited, sweaty bodies (comprised of diplomats, assistants, photographers, security officials) all jostling for position would be generating, because Nigel, no doubt, would be nearby, watching their arrival from high up in the World Piece One structure itself.

I was the only one in the metropolis who knew, with absolute certainty, that this was going to end badly. The Brussels politico-bureaucrats thought they were onto a winner – embarrassing the British government. Their security teams no doubt thought they were a match for the MDPs, the media teams were no doubt thrilled to have their work streaming live on all the networks. On the other side of the political fence, I speculated that the Prime Minister and his teams were grumpily watching the screens thinking they had lost control of the narrative and it was all falling apart in front of their eyes. They were all working on the assumption that the visit would go smoothly. That it would be a media triumph for Brussels. But, as I said, only I knew it would be a bloodbath. Because only I knew Nigel.

The President approached the fences and started reading all the attached messages and photos of missing persons. Then a few cameras swung to activity beyond the fence. I watched as a small group of Muterlings slowly approached the entourage from the other side of the fence. No Muterling was older than ten years old, I suspected. They looked baby-faced and scared, but I knew better. I searched the crowds for known Muterlings – killers all – and swear I saw the KittenFluff-Fluffykins twins. I thought I saw FatLegs and a few other three-and-a-half foot tall known killers. They were mostly Lite-Bites, so looked cherubic and cuddly; the perfect photo opportunity for politicians. The thought of the President picking up a Muterling and kissing it flashed across my mind.

This wasn't an election campaign – I almost shouted at the television – 'it is your f*king funeral!'

My eyes were searching the crowds and I was cursing when the news cameras swung away from the Muterlings to the European delegation. I was looking for one face in particular, of course – the most cherubic of all. You know and fear her name – ChubbyCheeks.

That said, I knew Chubby was a marked Muterling. Rubber Beans had been briefed on her and she had been hunted for a while, but the horrors of the Kensington Gardens killing fields had probably put a dampener on any Rubber Bean's ambitions to annihilate the three-foot-eight-inch-tall killer of killers. This was compounded by the fact that the media presence was huge. I guessed that the media videographers and photographers would love to capture drama on camera. A debacle to be replayed for decades on documentaries about the z-demic. Maybe actual footage would work its way into a Hollywood movie and the licensing royalties for the footage would come flooding in.

Of course, the media didn't know that the Kensington Gardens massacre had been triggered by a suspected sighting of Chubby, nor did they understand the threat Chubby posed to them all. As long as she was photogenic, that was all that mattered to them.

The question was, were there any UK-trained security present in the Brussels protection team? Or had all the security personnel landed at the airport that morning and were unaware of the threat she posed? The advance party might have had a briefing paper on her identity and dangers, but I doubt they would have appreciated her talent. Commander Bream's team did, of course, but they were probably now stationed as snipers on the rooftops, probably with an order not to shoot unless it was absolutely necessary.

Then I saw her – ChubbyCheeks – she was right in the middle of the group of Muterlings. Holy shit. This was going to be brutal and quick. The Muterlings approached the fence and started holding out their hands to the delegation and the President himself. Laughter and chatter could be heard rising from the crowd. The President approached the Muterlings. The Brussels delegation was only separated from death by flimsy wire fencing. I was almost struggling to breathe as I sipped my beer and nibbled my crisps. Normally I would be thrilled to have a ringside seat on these kinds of occasions (in a purely professional capacity, of course), but I had learned by attending sports events that when you are present right next to the action, you don't get the full picture as the television broadcast switches between different camera angles and indulges itself with replays, slow motion shots and analysis. I would much prefer to be in the pub watching it. Besides, I would live to see another day.

Then, as if it couldn't get any worse, the Muterlings moved a dozen yards to their left to a small gate-like opening in the fence and opened the fence further. This was normally heavily guarded, but the Muterlings just moved the fence to the side and walked slowly through to the President and his entourage.

You've probably seen what happened next. The attack was played on news items and was clipped for sharing on social media for weeks to come. Nobody anywhere on planet earth could have missed it. It was brutal. Brutal power. Brutality meets power. The power of brutality. The adult 'powerful' Bean becomes a Muterling's plaything. If anything was to bring home to the Bean masses what they were up against, it was the work of ChubbyCheeks and her crowd at that moment. At last, it was for all to see – if Death can operate with a child-like grin and giggle, it can operate anywhere and against anything.

The President and others in his entourage were dragged into the compound and disappeared into a sea of writhing hungry bodies. The media panicked and the crowd collapsed into a whirlpool of confusion. I heard no shots ring out. It was not entirely surprising. Either the snipers were panicking themselves or bleeding out at the hands of Diesel, GlassCutter and others.

As Nigel later noted, this was the beginning of the end. It was an incident (followed by a series of others, but all flowing from this one) that brought about the Great Change in Bean behaviour and so, in turn, led to the Great Handover itself.

37. Paper-of-News: Baby-Food Splash!

Just when you thought it couldn't get any worse (or more bizarre) the Press had a 'break' of their own. Dunky and Smashy's work wasn't the only show in town. During the European's politician's abduction at World Piece One, a number of other press personnel in attendance had also been snatched and dragged inside. Like everyone else, I assumed they would be feasted upon, however, one crew of three (reporter, cameraman, sound engineer) had been held hostage. They appeared not to be touched by the MDPs and were even 'allowed' (as Beans) to report to the outside world from within World Piece One itself.

I could only watch so much of it because it was so bizarre. On one occasion I was called into a side office by an intern to watch a live news report. (I say 'called', no words were spoken, it was all done by ashen faces, beckoning gestures and pointing.) Standing and watching the television, my arms were hanging down by my side, but I felt as if I was watching through my fingers.

To the credit of the news anchor in the studio, it looked as if she could hardly believe what she was doing herself – conducting an interview with a reporter stationed inside World Piece One.

'So, in a *NewsTime* exclusive,' the television news anchor solemnly announced, 'we can actually go to our reporter on the ground, Jenny Allen, who is reporting live from *inside* the MDP base where the European Council President was snatched not seventy-two hours ago. Jenny, what can you tell us?'

Standing on a floor a hundred or so feet up in World Piece One (a floor still open to the elements), Jenny stood nervously facing the camera with a microphone held to her chest. The view of the outside surroundings, including the perimeter fence, could be seen below and behind her.

'Yes, you heard it right, I am reporting live and 'a-live' from inside the MDP Base, the so-called Area SW51,' Jenny said quietly, nodding, trying to be calm and professional.

'Do you feel under threat? In any danger? Are there any MDPs who have shown a particular interest in you?' asked the anchor, genuinely concerned, but also trying desperately to remain professional.

'Ummm, good question, Sara,' replied Jenny, fiddling with her earpiece. 'So far, you know, so good....but let's talk quietly. They can hear me.'

It was true. Although Jenny was reporting directly to camera, there were a handful of MDPs of varying shapes, sizes and states of decay, loitering around her.

'Of course, we'll keep this brief. And any news on the President himself?' asked Sara in the studio. 'The footage we have seen of the attack shows that he was savagely attacked and dragged back into the structure, almost certainly deceased.'

'Yes, well, in fact, I believe I have indeed seen the President on his feet and moving slowly about the building.'

'But is he dead, Jenny?'

'Yes, he is dead, but mobile – up and about and...networking with other MDPs.'

'Remarkable. Does that suggest that he is still, um, how can I say, politically active?' asked the studio anchor.

'It is too early to say, but early indications are that his political ambitions are not thwarted in death.'

And so it continued. It was becoming a sort of circus. I didn't know whether to laugh or cry. I feared that it might lessen the sense of threat felt by the public at large if this all continued – reporters reporting on Armageddon. It was like cable news reporting from outside the Black Gate of Mordor with Mount Doom visible in the background while, yards away, Orcs loitered waiting for orders to march on the Shire.

However, I wasn't disappointed. The government's media spin-team desperately saw this development as an opportunity to 'humanise' the MDPs and a way to lessen the fear in the general public. Junior government ministers were even caught on camera in interviews saying perhaps the Living and the Dead could live in peace together. Find a way to 'co-exist'. The fact that each existed in direct contradiction to the other was lost on the politicians and the media.

What scared me most in the following days as more reports came from World Piece One, was this media narrative was not only becoming more complacent, but was also beginning to gain some traction. The media presumably had a sense of duty to calm fears and it had now become easier (and more necessary) because a number of their own were either operating from within the belly of the beast as Beans (i.e. Jenny) or MDPs themselves (Dunky and Smashy). If newspaper reporters and other media folk can be MDPs, then they can't be all bad, right? The trouble was, I knew Nigel was aware of what he was doing. He was playing a game. The Jenny-reporter Bean was being used. Nigel would use her for as long as he needed to. Meanwhile the media would lull the population into a sense of false security that would make my life harder (and ultimately everybody else's, one day).

I needn't have worried.

Because everything changed. In just a few short hours a week later.

A newspaper landed on my table.

Splashed across the front page was the image to end all images. It was a long telephoto image of the (late) European Council President (Nigel's 'Van Plumpy') as an MDP himself. If that was not enough, the image showed Van Plumpy in action. The deceased President of the European Council had snatched a baby from a pram in Notting Hill and was pictured devouring it as enthusiastically as an ADHD puppy devours a new toy. The baby, pale and limp, had its intestines half hanging out of its abdomen and half hanging out of the President's mouth. (The newspaper had pixelated certain parts of the image, but helpfully referred readers to its website where the image could be viewed in all its original glory behind a paywall.)

There were many times when I wondered what the political implications would be of Chubby attacking a school or children in the playground. Or Nigel and Pearl paying a bloody visit to self-help groups. Or coordinated MDP attacks on London's Underground train network. Or attacks at wedding receptions. But all paled in comparison to the image of a cherubic baby being eaten by the Prime Minister's political rival. I was not surprised to learn that the PM himself had jumped on a plane and had headed to Brussels at first light and was, by all accounts, berating the Europeans for interfering in the UK's domestic affairs and eating its wholly innocent infants. From now on, the Prime Minister had announced, the British Government would impose its own restrictions on travel to the UK by European bureaucrats.

The European thing was a debacle. The Prime Minister's dash to Brussels had complicated things yet further. Within a few days the Europeans had closed the border themselves. The UK was now in total quarantine. The Brits had lost control and lost the plot. This did one of a number of things.

It was now out of the bag. There was no way to put things back into the box or bag. In fact, the body bag had dissolved. The public could not be shielded from this. It didn't help that shortly after the paper-of-news splash, the World Piece One reporter, Jenny Allen, went dark, only to reappear briefly, pale and confused, on the television screens in a live report from World

Piece One. The studio news anchor noted Jenny's listlessness and enquired after her well-being:

'Jenny are you okay? Are you safe?'

Jenny didn't reply, looked straight into the camera and popped a gobstopper into her mouth and bit. The thing is, it wasn't a gobstopper, it was an eyeball. The live-feed from World Piece One was cut, but not before millions of viewers saw the eyeball-gobstopper explode in the mouth of the fresh MDP and its juice splash the camera lens.

So it was that the argument was lost.

The country had to go into total lockdown. Martial law was imminent.

Furthermore, I heard rumours that the Americans were now putting the pressure on the government and that the pressure was not altogether unwelcome. Rumours were circulating that American soldiers might soon be on the streets of London. I knew much of this from the reaction I had from chasing for decisions on even minor things. I was told decisions were on hold until a new organisational structure was agreed with the 'relevant' parties.

Over the next week, the presence of British Green Beans was becoming more obvious. The Government almost stopped making excuses. It was the norm. It was further complicated by reports of an accelerating rise in the number of MDPs (and MDP-related incidents) in other parts of the country.

Every other day there was another lockdown measure introduced. As a result of dramatically less traffic on the road, the speed limit for delivery drivers and riders (i.e. van and moped) delivering food and necessities was relaxed. As a result, mopeds and vans were screeching around the capital. You were unsure if the drivers and riders were loving the freedom of it or were just downright terrified as they went about their business. Not that there were too many MDPs found loitering in the streets, but it was also later announced that drivers and raiders who hit persons (dead or alive) would not be investigated, let alone prosecuted. The streets of London were slowly becoming the Wild West.

Soon people were beginning to get the measure of the situation. Those that could were moving out of London. As a result, the Government started to limit people's movements beyond the M25 – the London mega-ring road.

As each week passed, I felt I was becoming more and more irrelevant. I understood. After all, what could we learn now? Besides, would anybody listen to me?

I continued to monitor Nigel's blog. He uploaded reflections on the Third Bean Paradox (Ethics) and, to tell you the truth, I began to agree with many of his conclusions. Ethics was completely pliable and did go in circles, which sort of defeated the object of them. As Nigel said, "ethics is largely based around the Bean to influence behaviour or to justify actions already taken or yet to be undertaken". Everybody – the media, the civil servants, the politicians – used ethics as a way to justify whatever they wanted to do. Everything they did had an ethical basis – live in peace in harmony with the MDPs, that's noble; race around the capital knocking people over without any legal ramifications, that's the right thing to do in the circumstances.

Nigel had no time for ethics; he was operating under no illusions. There were no ethics in eternity. We were not in eternity yet, but it felt as if we were getting awfully close.

About three weeks after the debacle at World Piece One, I was called to Downing Street. I had a military escort through the metropolis by the Royal Marines. Arriving at Number Ten, I was rushed by an aide down a corridor. I was asked to wait outside a meeting room. I saw a photographer loitering in the corridor. He looked very anxious – if he had had laughter lines, they had now been lost in frowns and worry lines. I suppose once upon a time he would have jumped at the chance to be at the centre of power photographing history, but he regretted it now, I was sure. I didn't say it, but I wondered what type of world would be left that would be interested in looking at such images.

The aide slipped into the room and I heard the immortal words, 'The zombie guy is here,' whispered to those hidden inside.

38. The PM and the Merry Green Beans

On hearing those words, my heart skipped a beat. I dropped my head in a moment of self-reflection. My life had come to this....being "the zombie guy" at Downing Street on the verge of the apocalypse. After a moment the door opened. I stepped aside to allow the Prime Minister's biographer to rush hurriedly from the room. I caught sight of his notes under his arm with what I took to be the title of the PM's memoirs – 'Leadership'.

'Thanks for coming Josh,' said the Prime Minister, grabbing me by the hand and pulling me into the room. He didn't motion me to sit, not so much because he was intending to keep the meeting short, but because he was too jumpy. I was happy standing.

'I hope I didn't want to pull you away from anything?'

'No, I was just heading out to a long weekend at a spa hotel.'

The PM looked blank.

'I'm just kidding.'

The PM relaxed, nodded and smiled.

'Truth is, Josh, you do look a little worse for wear.'

'Yes, apologies, I need a haircut and I haven't shaved in a while.'

'The beard suits you.'

'Anyway. The reason I wanted to speak to you is that, as you might imagine, matters are escalating. The American military is coming in. It's been agreed. They are going to establish a military base at the Royal Naval College at Greenwich, on the river, but they are also going to establish monitoring outposts at Area SW51 and a few other spots around the capital. Things are going to get busy and political pretty fast.'

'There is a four-star general – General McAllister-Pike – running the show; he will have operational command in London. You will be embedded in his team, advising and briefing. I want you to be right in the middle of things. Make a nuisance of yourself. You have guaranteed place right next to the General. It's part of the deal.'

'Why me?'

'The last thing we need is a politician there or one of our own army commanders there. They will just butt heads. Nor do I want to be a civil servant anyway near them. Decisions will be made about operational matters relating to MDPs on the streets and your man, er....'

'Nigel?'

'Yes, Nigel. He's still with us?' asked the Prime Minister.

I nodded. (Of course, I thought, is Death ever *not* with us?)

'Well, he is going up against General McAllister-Pike and the American military machine, so I think, I hope, he will have met his match.'

I said nothing. I certainly didn't share the image that had popped into my head of Nigel standing in front of the General hung from a meat-hook in World Piece One with the General's rib cage broken wide and Nigel sampling the military man's intestines. As if there could be any competition between a shouty American General and the, er, 'living' personification of Death. In a righteous world, the General should be on one knee with head bowed in the presence of the almighty one. After all, Nigel personified everything an army General aspired to be.

'No,' the PM continued, 'you know more about MDPs, the threat they pose, their behaviour, the way they move about the city. All discussions need to be informed by what you have learned and not by a politician who is thinking of the legal, historical and, dare I say, political implications.'

I nodded.

'Understood,' I replied, albeit a little disappointed. I changed the subject. 'You need to think about evacuating, Prime Minister.'

The PM nodded and sighed. (We must have looked like two spring-loaded toys standing next to each other, sighing and nodding in unison.) 'There are plans to escape to the river, avoiding all street level routes. But it is not something I want to do. Or, at least until the very last minute.'

'Are the Americans going to bomb?'

'No, no. That is not part of the plan. Aerial bombardment, missile strikes are off the table. In part, we have argued, because we don't want a cloud of virus particles – vapourised body parts – being dispersed by the winds. Besides, I do not want to see the finest city on earth in ruins.'

'What about our own military?' I asked, coyly.

'As you know, they are stretched in counties and other cities. Manchester, Liverpool, Bristol, York, Leeds, Birmingham are all under a form of lockdown. We do not have the means to cover the whole country, let alone London. The Americans aren't interested in patrolling Peterborough, Swansea, Portsmouth. And, to be honest, I am grateful. If we can get a handle on the capital, we might just pull ourselves out of this. The Americans are pouring in the numbers….. What is it, Josh?'

I hadn't been aware that my face had fallen. I had been looking for a moment to mention it. Now seemed as good a time as any.'

'About the numbers, sir,' I muttered.

'Yes?'

'We may have a problem.'

'Go on.'

'You asked me about the dead rising from their graves. The long-dead. Those who died and were buried before, even long-before, the end-demic?'

'End-demic?'

'Yes, sorry, it comes after a z-demic,' I said, trying to make light of my gaffe.

The Prime Minister nodded, disguising his panic in his short breaths.

I continued.

'I've been doing some research – consulting with colleagues and exploring some scientific theories. It is not unreasonable to assume that the virus might react with people who died *before* the plague appeared…. They might well rise too. There would be no harm in making contingency plans.'

'What kind of numbers are we talking about?'

'Well, there are approximately forty thousand people buried in cemetery plots every year in and around the capital.'

The PM nodded.

'But there are estimates that there are perhaps four million or more buried in cemeteries and unmarked graves in and around London.'

'Four million?'

'Over the last eight hundred years. But I think that is on the low side.'

I let it sink in.

'How large is the American deployment in the capital?' I asked, on a note of hopefulness.

'Working up to seventy thousand over the next month,' muttered the PM, his gaze falling away to the floor.

'It's only a theory at this stage.' I said trying to be as reassuring as possible.

The Prime Minister's gaze remained directed at the floor between us. He looked on the brink of utter dejection.

'I would say that stranger things have happened,' he said, shaking his head. 'The dead walking our streets would have been laughable to me twelve months ago. And now we're making defensive plans for four-plus million rising from their graves.'

That was the last time I saw or heard from the Prime Minister.

As I was being escorted out of the back of Downing Street I bumped into Ella. We greeted each other with warm smiles. After pleasantries, she got to the point.

'Has Nigel said anything else?' she said. 'Do we have any idea what he is going to do?'

'No,' I replied, shaking my head.

'Will he know what is happening with all this military build-up?'

Before I could answer her first question, she asked another.

'How will he react?'

I sighed.

'Never underestimate Death,' I said quietly. 'It's going to get you in the end, it is a certainty, so, when thinking of Nigel, remember, doubt is not a concept familiar to him and he has all the time in the world. These last four, six months, I have never seen us come out in a better place than the day before.'

Ella nodded. Perhaps it was harsh to be so clear, but what else could I do?

'I also wanted to apologise, Josh.'

'For what?' I replied, genuinely bemused.

'We should have listened to you. I read all your reports coming through and I filed them away in those early days. I'm sorry.'

'No matter. Seems like a long time ago.'

'But you won me over, Josh. Just so you know. In fact, I slipped a few of your insights to your Whistleblower myself.'

'Whistleblower?' I replied with my brow suitably furrowed in confusion and feeling mild alarm that I might have been found out.

'Yes, I knew it was Bob Beaumont feeding the Whistleblower,' Ella said, nodding. 'There are circles and circles within circles.'

'Sounds either incestuous or deeply corrupt, I'm unsure,' I said.

'You'd be right. At times I am surprised that a civilised society can tolerate such machinations in government.'

With the conversation concluded and nothing more to be added we both raised our eyebrows in unison and uttered the failsafe conversation-ender 'Anyway'.

'So, that is what I wanted to say, Josh. Sorry and thank you.'

With that, we parted. Alive, I never saw her again, but even in the last days of the Great Handover, I thought of her and wondered if she and her Downing Street colleagues (including the Prime Minister) ever made it out of the capital.

The next few days were sad days. It seemed odd that, as we were heading to the end of times, that they should be so sad. Why couldn't such times be happier?

The Prime Minister had finished his briefing with me outlining a few confidential details on what would be happening. With the American military coming in, there was no need for my team. It was to be disbanded. The presence of the American military on the streets could not, of course, be disguised as anything else than an extreme measure and underscore the threat to the Bean metropolis. The Prime would announce a total, utter lockdown. London was to be sealed using the motorway ring-road, the M25, as an impassable border. The British military would patrol the M25 – all 120 miles of it. Nobody was to enter or leave unless on official business. The British military would impose martial law in some of the other hotpoints around the country that were about a month behind the capital, but fast catching up. There was no intention to let the other cities and towns reach the state that London had.

Of course, there would be panic, but perhaps people would feel safer now locked in their homes. Of course, they could go out for supplies, but at their own risk.

The morning of the Prime Minister's Press conference (planned for eleven o'clock), I planned to sit down with my interns. I still had to explain the situation. It was now a military operation. The time for monitoring and research was over. It was all about containment. It is not as if they would be seeking other jobs. I suspect many would be relieved. An hour before the solemn announcement I was called downstairs to the street. A car was waiting for me with two American soldiers waiting.

'Josh Chronides?'

I nodded.

'General McAllister-Pike is waiting for you.'

With that I was swiftly driven across London to Greenwich. The streets were pretty empty much like the previous pandemic, but that panic had eased over the course of twelve, eighteen months. This end-demic had been slowly building for six or eight months. There had been no hard start then a tail off. It had been a slow build.

Arriving at Greenwich's famous and historic Naval College right on the River Thames, I was shocked at the amount of military equipment now stationed on the site. This certainly had not been apparent on the news bulletins. Tanks, armoured personnel carriers, Apache helicopters, camouflage tents took up every inch of land. Looking up at the large Greenwich Park on the hill behind the naval college, I was gobsmacked to see it too had been completely taken over by the American military.

Wow, this really is a war, I thought.

For all the military hardware on display, none of it prompted me to think it would do any good. I just instinctively thought it would make the apocalypse all the more spectacular.

I was marched into the grand building, guided down corridors passing dozens of American military personnel each with a serious expression on their face. None exhibited fear, just professional focus. I pitied them. Fear would come. It will burn into your souls, I thought, but there was no harm in thinking that there was a mission to accomplish.

I finally found myself in an office opposite a tall, hard, no-nonsense American General. After the briefest of introductions and pleasantries, he got straight to the point.

'Where do you want to be based?' he asked. 'Here at Greenwich?'

Holy cow, no, I thought. 'Um, I'm unsure,' I said. 'Perhaps I should base myself at World Piece One? I can monitor their leader.'

'Neil?'

'Nigel.'

If the General had been paying attention he would have seen that I was shaking my head in mild despair. I found his failure to know Nigel's name almost insulting. How could anyone not know the birth name of the Lord of Death?

'I've read some of your reports. Is this Nigel really as good as you say?'

I nodded and shrugged in the affirmative. 'I can't do him justice on paper.'

'I have asked my team to come up with a plan to snatch him,' the General said. 'It might disrupt their effectiveness.'

I nodded. I didn't really know what to say. My thoughts inevitably turned to my own pitiful attempt to snatch Nigel that only resulted in the loss of my two greatest allies, Tom and Fiona.

Whether the General was impatient or indifferent, I didn't know. He changed the subject.

'Do you have family?' the General said.

I squinted and furrowed my brow.

'We need you to focus for the next six weeks. No distractions. If you have family, a partner, you are worried about, I can authorise them to be moved to a safe location. Even out of the country.'

There was one person that slipped into my mind. Maria-Amphi.

'Yes and no,' I mumbled, unsure of a plan. 'There is a person that has been on my mind recently and I….'

'Talk to Captain Burns here,' said the General, nodding to a soldier beside him. 'He will make all the necessary arrangements, no questions asked.'

'Er, thank you,' I said.

'Don't thank me. You want to see them again, don't you?'

'Of course,' I said, my brow furrowing again in confusion.

'Well, think of it as motivation. A prize if you don't fuck up.'

I nodded. I could see the soldier-logic in it somehow, but motivating speeches sounded different in the civilian world. I suppose we were now living in different times now.

39. The Great Change

I had one last thing to do with my old life. A few days later I headed back to the office in Whitehall to wrap up the MDP Special Ops office. Time was tight but there were two specific things that I needed to do. I asked my military driver to swing by the grand edifice. Pulling up in front of the building it was funny to think it had been the home of the only unit studying the development of the plague and its effects on the human body and mind. It was a fine building built by master architects, engineers, stonemasons and builders built in the 1800s. It was a physical 700,000 ton testimony to government administration. And in this vast three hundred thousand square metre space monolith to achievement, knowledge and superiority, my civil service colleagues allocated the smallest space possible to the one thing that would ultimately dissolve all memory of them.

A note to self: you can always judge an institution's future by the amount of space it allocates to its activities. The grander the space allocated to the 'leaders' (who often just inherited their roles and the building rather than being responsible for their construction) the shorter the institution's lifespan will be. The institution's failure and the building's abandonment is in direct inverse proportion to the space allocated to dealing with the next threat to its existence (be it man-made – technology, an ideology, a weapon, a virus – or natural – climate, terrestrial, extra-terrestrial, a virus).

This building's Achilles heel started off as a three-hundred nanometre-wide virus particle weighing a million-billionth of a gram. That particle morphed into something that weighed even less – an idea. It gave breath to death. Beankind allocated the smallest attic office space possible to me and a small team, each of whom were single-figure summers beyond their teens.

'Sir?' said my driver, snapping me out of my reverie.

'Yes, of course,' I replied. 'Give me thirty minutes.'

I jumped out of the armoured personnel carrier and jumped up the steps. The building's entrance was flanked by four giant, armed US Marines who were in turn dwarfed by towers of sandbags on either side of the entrance. Someone was expecting the next few weeks to get fiery.

I flashed various new IDs (I had so many cards, the "I'm Classified" ID card seemed like an infant's membership to a breakfast cereal club). The latest ID was the microchipped wristband that I had resisted acquiring as long as I could, but the world marches to modernity's drumbeat. I was waved in. The interiors of the building looked like it had been taken over by an occupying army, because, well, it had. Military personnel were buzzing about and former waiting areas were overtaken with temporary tables on which computer screens were displaying graphs, maps, CCTV from across London to dozens of non-Londoners – Merry Green Beans.

Times had indeed changed.

I raced up the stairs to the attic passing similar scenes, but with more civilians. Many looked familiar but for the terrified looks on their faces as they packed boxes of files presumably for storage in a basement to be retrieved once the assault and the reclaiming of London had been completed. I didn't stop and made every effort not to catch anyone's eye. I didn't know if they would recognise me. Did they know me as "the zombie guy" too? How famous was I? Did they hate me? Resent me? Even blame me? I didn't want to find out.

I had visions of a number of them recognising me, accosting me and then being held back by US Marines as they tried to tear me limb from limb (how ironic).

'You're responsible for all this, you motherfucker!' I imagined them shouting and crying.

'Well, you should have given me a bigger office, shouldn't you,' I imagined shouting in reply.

I reached my attic office. It looked so small and empty. My core team of twelve interns had all departed.

I collected CatNaps' laptop from the safe. I had set up another laptop with links to the Cloud-based memoir, but I wanted to have the original laptop – the one Nigel had used himself to start his blog – while I was based at World Piece One. There was little else for me to collect. I had already sent everything to various cloud storages and also a copy of almost everything to the Whistleblower via a handful of further visits to the British Museum's locker. I didn't know where he was now, but I hoped he would have the sense to survive or at least ensure all the documentation survived somewhere, somehow. Perhaps he would compile and edit all of Nigel's (and even my) notes into a readable format for anybody who survived.

I did grab my white lab-coat and stuffed it in my bag. I knew that I would be in the company of men and women in military uniforms and suspected that my usual civilian dress sense would make me invisible in my new surroundings. I might need the lab coat to remind others I was more than just a civilian.

The office had been tidied by the interns now long-departed. I had dropped the practice of email; all correspondence was now through secure military and government messaging apps. It was ironic that one of the last emails I reviewed was from the Boy Who Saw. Citing changing times, he was withdrawing the offer of his services. (He said he was too busy trying to console his forever-crying mother). The interns had left me a box of miscellaneous papers that they felt they could not throw out. I was happy to ignore it, but I took a cursory glance. My heart sank when I saw what was at the top of the box. It was Fiona's draft report – her personal copy – on the possible origins of Nigel. Handwritten annotations, I recognised immediately as made in Fiona's hand, adorned the margins. I had thought I had passed everything to the Whistleblower, but this document had been overlooked and destined to remain on the premises almost as if to haunt me.

The sight of the numerous little comments and doodles in and around the text punched me in the gut. If it had been a clean report maybe I could have handled it, but exclamation marks abounded reminding me of Fiona's enthusiasm. Her underlining reminded me of her curiosity. The question marks signified her quest. Sadly, for all the thought, care and deliberation put into the report, it had all come to nothing – me standing alone in the deserted office testified to that. I flicked through a handful of pages then saw a comment that incorporated all three annotations – underlining, exclamation mark and question mark. It said.....

Unfinished business. We have been chasing what Nigel knows. Not what he <u>doesn't</u> know. What if we found out what the unfinished business is <u>before</u> he learns it? That is the key! Does it relate to his family?

I felt sick and turned the page. It didn't help. My eye fell upon another note:

Nigel is his Bean name. Nigel doesn't have a name in Death. Who will give him his name in death? Or can we? Is it really Shade?! Or something similar? Does a member of his new family have to give it to him?

Too much curiosity, passion and quest. I thought I was now a hardened and cynical individual, but no, memories of brighter times in that office with Fiona and Tom (and the original office, before our move) hit me hard. They were both gone. Answers wouldn't help now. I felt sick reading it and closed the papers. It was someone else's problem now. I was not hunting Nigel any more. I was now an advisor in the end-game.

I had one other task I had to complete.

I headed down a few floors and made a few familiar turns past the open plan office and smaller offices all being packed up. Again, the worry haunted the faces of yesteryear. I knocked on Robbie's office door and stepped inside.

He was bent over a few cardboard boxes on his desk looking through files and adjusting its contents. He looked up, pushed the papers aside and stood up straight.

A smile was not forthcoming, but I did detect a warmth that he tried to conceal.

'So, I suppose I call you "sir" now?' he said, in his soft Irish lilt.

I smiled.

'Did I give you permission to speak?' I replied, raising an eyebrow.

Now Robbie smiled.

We stepped towards each other and shook hands warmly. But it felt awkward, contrived. So, in an unspoken moment we resolved it – we took another step forward and hugged.

We broke our grips.

'I've been thinking these last few weeks about how to frame an apology,' he said. 'It's not something I've done before when I genuinely meant it.'

'These last few months I have been dealing with hundreds of civil servants in all branches of Whitehall, the police and security services, and all because of you,' I replied. 'There is not one person in this city who has done more to facilitate the work. You accepted the proposal all those months ago, supported us while we got going and protected us every step of the way from the vultures and politics. We couldn't have done what we did upstairs without you here downstairs. London owes you.'

Robbie nodded. He needed to hear it from someone. I could understand he might have been doubting himself. But the synopsis was true and my thanks were heartfelt.

'You think we can rescue this?' he asked.

I sighed. It had been months since I had lied to Robbie. I wouldn't now.

'No,' I replied, my eyes falling away from him. 'London is lost, but maybe we can secure other parts of the country. We could lock London behind the M25 and leave it to another generation to reclaim.'

'You don't have faith in the Americans?'

'The American military and Nigel are both in the same business, who would you back in the circumstances?'

Robbie nodded.

'So what are you going to do, Robbie?' I added.

'Well, I am ashamed to say I have been authorised to be evacuated. I have been issued with an evacuation phone app now along with all the codes. They want me back home in Ireland. To bring all my expertise. Apparently they couldn't afford you, so they settled for me.'

'Good. I'm glad.'

'I feel bad, but who knows what is going to happen. But it is not over yet. I hope I get out before the fireworks.'

I left the Whitehall building knowing I would never lay eyes on it again. Sentimentality serves no purpose in an apocalypse, but I hadn't appreciated that the building stored not only data, committee minutes, handbooks, reports and notes, but also memories. It was a giant memory box. I had met people in it, laughed with them, endured shocking moments and eureka moments. Although the second workplace in twelve months, the

Whitehall edifice represented a workspace in which I had met and interviewed Tom and Fiona and the places where we had shared secrets and discoveries over a handful of lunar cycles. I had lost them both. I knew I would never see Robbie again. He would exist only in my memory for as long as my mind and body remained intact. But for how many days would that be, exactly? Possibly less than thirty. Certainly less than sixty light-darks, surely? As we drove through the emptying streets I wondered if Robbie would remember me. Would he talk about me in some Dublin pub in decades to come about 'the zombie guy' who spotted how the world was changing and averted the zombie apocalypse?

No, I heard less than two weeks later that Robbie had been attacked and lost to death while trying to board a plane at RAF Northolt.

Over the next week I settled into my new digs – what can only be described as a three-storey Portakabin mini-complex built by the military and in sight of World Piece One. The 'military complex' was protected by razor-wire and had floodlights on stilts. It was more suited to a desert in a hostile country, but on reflection, perhaps that was what it was. The military outpost certainly looked the part and I was thankful I had packed my lab coat as a reminder to myself more than anything else.

The ground floor cabin had a rest area with refreshments, a conference room for meetings and an armoury. The cabin above it was the operational command centre – banks of computers and computer monitors and television screens showing all angles of World Piece One and footage streamed from CCTV and military cameras positioned across the metropolis. I met dozens of Merry Green Beans who were staffing the command centre. They all looked smart, focused and operated in an incredibly professional and polite manner. And another thing – they looked so young. I wasn't a decade older than some of them, but I felt at least two decades older. The last eight months must have aged me. It made me sad. They thought they knew what they had signed up for. They didn't. I hoped they would reach the age that I felt. Turns out, they wouldn't. When you have Nigel standing in front of you, the world changes.

The third storey cabin comprised a few offices, a handful of camp beds and wash areas. Life would be simple. I decided I would stay on the houseboat for as long as possible. In some ways it was safer because I now had a military bodyguard. When the tensions ratcheted up (and certainly before the military operation started) I might move to the military compound and survive on a camp bed. For the time being, I was going to appreciate my own houseboat's privacy as much as possible.

The next few weeks were about the Americans gathering intelligence, planning and placing military hardware at specific points about the metropolis. The Americans were planning a shock and awe operation – to hit the Muter population hard (namely the World Pieces – all dozen of them), wiping them out whilst limiting the destruction to property. After all, the MDPs were not a formidable enemy – they did not carry weapons, did not use armoured vehicles to move about the battlefield and, the Americans believed, were unable to coordinate attacks or defensive operations. It would be a cakewalk. Just city-wide pest control. Those Muters not destroyed in the raid on the World Pieces would be driven, street by street, down to (and into) the River Thames.

I did voice my concerns to anybody who would listen, including Ella in Downing Street. I was surprised that I was needed at all. The military plan had already been written and my polite protests were ignored. However, I was advised that I was a valued resource of information. I was invited to monitor the progress of the Muter population while the military plans took shape. And so I did.

My own team of interns had long been disbanded, of course, so I was reliant on making friends with a few of the soldiers in the control room at the military compound. They were helpful and polite. I gradually steered them to incidents or the occasional skirmishes of interest. Nigel was erratic at updating his blog, suggesting he was busy. I monitored Nigel's movements as best I could, but it was difficult. With human movement limited on the streets and no Underground rail network in operation, he was elusive. There was an attack on London zoo and the odd skirmish with Merry Green Beans, but otherwise it was relatively quiet. I thought the Merry Beans might become complacent. I certainly wasn't.

About four days before the start of the planned military operation, I received an email from Ben. He wanted to meet. Although I enjoyed our chats, I always left our meetings feeling a little perturbed. Not that I expect meetings to be reassuring, but what he would be sharing with me at this late stage would probably not influence events. We were beyond that. On reflection I realised that he would be saying things that no one else was saying. Maybe something he said would trigger an idea in me that could prove useful, so, with my options limited and nobody really paying attention to me, I picked up the phone and called him.

'I think I know what it is,' he said, with breathless nervousness. He knew he had little of my time.

'What?'

'Nigel. And it's not just about him. I think there are other players.'

'What are you talking about?'

'Josh, as you know I've said, these events have been foretold.'

I took a breath. I liked Ben. I respected his learning and I took his earnestness as sincere.

'What good would it do?'

'I don't know. But if you see the signs in other activities or incidents around the city, you might be ahead of the game. Albeit briefly.'

There was a pause on the line. The long pause turned into a silence reminiscent of a break-up after an intense romantic affair. I smiled to myself as I realised that I was never going to break up with someone again, let alone date someone. I couldn't recall when I had such a prolonged, awkward silence on the phone with a lady-friend. On occasions like this it was a matter of who would cave first.

'Look Josh,' Ben said, breaking the silence, 'we both know it is going to be the last time we meet. I don't want to explain on the phone. You'll just cut me off. Besides, I need to show you something.'

'What?'

'I'll bring my laptop and talk you through some images and...'

'...and some mythology?'

I heard Ben sigh deeply at the other end of the telephone line.

'Yes.'

Cue the awkward silence again, but the thought of getting out of the Portakabin appealed. I also had a nagging memory of my last conversation with Ella in Downing Street. She had thanked me and apologised to me for not listening earlier in the z-demic. Now here I was on the receiving end of a request to listen to a theory that might help our predicament. Ben's previous conversations had not been insulting, or overly sensational. His comments had been thoughtful and had come from a place about which I had no knowledge. If I didn't owe it to Ben, I owed it to Ella to listen.

'The same coffee place?' Ben asked.

'Everything's closed. Private establishments are locked down. You can't come here – it's a military operation. It'll scare the

living daylights out of you. Have you had the luciferase injection?'
I asked.

The government had been trialing an injection that included
the bioluminescence-generating enzyme, luciferase. It was a
rushed attempt at a part-vaccine (or rather, therapeutic), part-
marker (or tracker) exploiting the bioluminescence quality of the
enzyme. It was being pushed (even mandated in some quarters)
and would replace the microchipped wristband for a quick reading
of the subject's health status and other data.

'No,' replied Ben, dryly.

'Yeah. Well, your microchipped wristband won't have the
necessary security clearance anyway.'

'You could come to my flat?' said Ben, with a hint of hope.

'I'm not going that far north. The only options are secure
government buildings that have a military guard.'

'Does the National Gallery have a military guard?' he asked.

'The National Gallery on Trafalgar Square?' I asked, almost
irritated. This was not supposed to be a cultural day out, looking at
some old paintings.

'Yes,' replied Ben.

'The Americans are camped out on Trafalgar Square itself.
Why?'

'Well, if it is, then I won't have to bring my laptop.'

By this stage of the conversation, my mind was made up.
Getting out of the Portakabin and talking to someone who was not
dressed in green fatigues, (or green rubber suits) would be a
welcome change. My conversation with Ella was still haunting me.
And Ben was right – this was probably the last time we would ever
meet. Furthermore, whenever we did meet, his contributions had
always given me food for thought. Being the important person I
was, I quickly arranged for a military escort to pick up Ben from
his flat and I arranged for the National Gallery to be opened. I
agreed to meet him there two hours later. I justified it by thinking

that taking a little time out to wander around picture galleries would be good for my spirits before the metropolis disappeared behind smoke and fire. It was the least I could expect for all the work I was putting in.

40. The National Gallery

Our meeting at the National Gallery concluded, I left Ben alone in the gallery looking at the grand pictures – priceless artefacts representing the pinnacle of human artistic achievement. I had thought I was already at 'anxiety-capacity' working with the American military, but Ben's nervousness rubbed off on me pushing me to new heights (or depths) of angst. At least I had a permanent army escort. I knew that I wouldn't see Ben again, but if any further thoughts came to me I said I would call him.

'They'll take you home,' I said to Ben as I left the gallery, nodding towards the two U.S. marines who had brought him to the meeting. 'I suggest you use the back entrance again.'

Ben's face was drained of hope yet his brow, his eyes, were full of a fierce conviction muted by a savage desperation. He was sure he was right. Maybe he was, in some way, but what use was it to me? I took some comfort that his military escort would see him home safely. He saw the story in the paintings and I…didn't, quite. Or rather wouldn't. The observations cut deep – they were too incredible to take seriously. His words 'look for the beast' seemed to echo about my head as I walked back through the galleries to the building's main entrance passing the finest works of art and depictions of centuries-old civilisational struggles. Would any of it survive? Would it be devoured in fire and brimstone once the final battle started? The thought of all this treasure, this pinnacle of human endeavour, being lost within the next dozen light-darks made me sick to the stomach. Of course, the politicians and the military scoffed at the idea that the military operation would get out of hand and catastrophic destruction would ensue. The worst any building like the National Gallery would suffer would be a little soot on its exterior walls, they all announced confidently.

I wasn't going to slip away via a back door, I wanted to stand on the steps of the Gallery and look down over Trafalgar Square one last time. This might be my last moment to soak in the grandeur of a capital city. Like the paintings contained within its walls – of Rome, Ancient Greece and other European cities and battlefields – the view from Gallery's steps evoked in me both a pride and a profound sadness.

I nodded thanks to the young National Gallery assistant who had opened up the building for me and Ben. The young man looked tired, scared, even a little wet in the eye. I was only a few years older than him, but once again, I felt so much older. I'm not one to mentor people, provide advice, I'm too young for that, yet I felt obliged to say a few words.

'Thank you for this,' I said, nodding.

'You're the zombie guy?' he asked, his mouth obviously dry.

'I am.'

'What were you doing here?'

I sighed.

'I don't know,' I murmured in reply. 'Learning about the past. Learning about the future.'

'Are the Americans going to launch an attack on their MDP bases? Wipe the fuckers out?'

It was classified, but what difference did it make. I nodded.

'I tried to get out of London, but they're not letting anybody out,' the assistant replied as he closed the building's huge door with a thunderous boom that seemed to echo deep inside the building.

'A lockdown is for the best.'

'What am I supposed to do?' he said, desperately trying to suppress his panic.

'Sit tight.'

'It'll all be over soon?'

I nodded. What he thought would be 'over' was probably different to what I thought would be 'over'. With my own interpretation in mind, my nod must have appeared convincing. He smiled and then dashed off to his own army guard who escorted him down the steps to an armoured military personnel carrier parked on the Square. Within moments they had rumbled off.

On the macro scale I was still longing for insight that would give us an advantage; on the micro scale I longed to provide reassuring answers to questions about their life prospects from young citizens and soldiers. I had hoped Ben could provide something that would help me with either endeavour, but he had spoken of the past, myth and prophecies. What could history tell us about today? What place had myth in the modern world? Ben's perspective was challenging and I committed to writing it up. It would be useful for the Whistleblower. Perhaps he (or others) could make use of Ben's ideas. When the time came to report on these dark days, historians would draw lines, join the dots, see the patterns. But that time was yet to come – when you are in the middle of the apocalypse, nothing makes any sense.

Alone, I took in the view. Trafalgar Square itself was littered with military vehicles – personnel carriers, humvees, machine gun posts and the odd tank. There was no civilian foot traffic. Occasionally you would see a young man sprint down the street clutching a bag – food supplies, no doubt. I pitied him. He thought he would have enough supplies to last a week or until the Americans regained control. I wished I could be that confident.

A column of military vehicles thundered around the perimeter of the Square. The American military was bedding in. The attacks on the main Muter bases would no doubt scatter Muters around the capital. There were pockets of the military at strategic points to mop up any escaping MDPs. I slowly shuffled down the steps leading to my own humvee and jumped in.

'Back to base,' I said to the driver. 'Let's take the scenic route.'

It is odd to see a city prepare for war. London had seen its fair share of ills over the centuries. For all the attempts by invaders to conquer the British Isles, it had not happened for a thousand years. It had been threatened a century before, but despite the bombs falling from the sky, the shores had been protected. Now, the enemy was already here, walking the streets and battle would commence within a handful of light-darks, after which what (and more importantly 'who') would remain standing, was anyone's guess. The opponent was known but unknown. Dead but undead.

The scenic route took us along Pall Mall, Constitution Hill, through Westminster, along the Embankment past St Paul's Cathedral then south of the Black Road. Everything was boarded up. Machine gun posts or tanks were positioned on most corners. Every single window at ground level (and the two floors above that) were boarded up – signs of a classic wartime military occupation. I had heard that when the time came, the soldiers would be firing at anything and everything on sight. No stop-and-search, no deliberation. Just fire at will.

As if the sight of a civilisation preparing for a battle for survival was not enough to trouble me, the conversation with Ben continued to preoccupy me. I had thought a nice drive would be distracting, but no. He was in my head.

Surely Ben was wrong? His was a theory and interpretation that was too preposterous? Yet driving through the capital, I could see that nothing could be deemed preposterous now. The last twelve months had upended the whole world. Beankind had been so naive. A civilisation that did not question itself, that considered the ancient past to be but a novelty, was surely doomed?

'*Those ancient people were simple folk. Their thoughts and achievements are not relevant to us, but we will be graceful and offer them some space in our museums and galleries. Our achievements – helicopters, rockets, electric light, nuclear power, computing technology – run the world. What does the past have to offer us? Quaint stories, that's all.*'

No, soon we were going to learn, their stories were warnings. Being the dumb animals that we had become, the warnings had gone unheeded.

The Great Change in Bean Behaviour ended, I like to think, with me leaving my houseboat. The special military operation was days away and I had just moved into the Portakabin compound for the duration of the military operation. Up until the very last moment I had been staying on my houseboat, but I was having trouble sleeping. Too restless to just lie in bed, I would go up on the deck and watch nighttime London slumber peacefully before the storm.

It was an odd sight. There were no night revellers passing by on the promenade above me. No sounds of laughing, joking and singing. No cruise boats were chugging down the Thames with thumping music echoing across the water. But there was one movement, a silhouette that caught my eye. I saw a paddleboarder on a few successive nights loitering a hundred yards out on the water. I knew who it was – Stiks; she was purposefully keeping an eye on me? I denied it for the first few days, but then denying it became too exhausting. Why was she here? Was I some sort of unfinished business for her? I realised it was not safe and, aware that I couldn't commute to work through a warzone, I decamped to the Portakabin at World Piece One a few days before Operation Reclaim was scheduled to begin.

I was glad to leave to be honest. My floating home had taken a battering in recent weeks. The weather had gone funny, weird – more sudden and violent electrical storms, bizarre cloud formations, the lights in the sky. The rolling thunder was not violent enough to break the glass of the windows, but the hail storms had smashed a few and cracked most of the others. Ella had shared with me the confidential meteorological reports sent to Downing Street and asked if the weather events might be impacting the behaviour of the MDPs. I saw no connection, the unusual weather incidents were freaking out the living more than the dead. (The 'living' included Ben who, as you can imagine, referenced them in his theories.)

When I left the houseboat I closed and double-locked the doors. I even used my spare padlocks to secure all entrances and covered the windows in protective chipboard panels. As I did so I wondered if I would ever return. For a moment I thought of handing the keys to Ron Cha, the river taxi man. He would never leave this river and, of all people I knew, he would be the one most likely to still be here if I returned. He was committed to his role and would be ferrying people to their destinations for eternity. The trouble was, I had not seen him for weeks and had heard he too might have already been claimed by the plague. By whom? Who knows, perhaps by his old buddy, Stiks herself. It was strange times indeed on the Black Road.

The two possible outcomes existed in stark contrast to one another. In the more favoured scenario, the drama of the previous dozen lunar cycles would come to an end and Nigel would be forgotten, his goals left unaccomplished – the metropolis would have been reclaimed thanks to the Americans and I would turn the key to my favourite-ever home feeling a sense of peace I had not felt for months. *Or.* Or, was this the last time I would close and lock up this door to the houseboat?

I turned the key in the lock slowly savouring the resistance, listening for the familiar clicks that had become part of my daily life for the last few years. I realised that there comes a time when everyone closes a door for the final time and that, when they do, they rarely know it is for the last time. We spend decades opening and walking through doors to get to the next room, the next place. But there was always going to be a last doorframe through which we pass – the final door, after which we find ourselves in our final place. It is an important moment yet almost everyone is ignorant of its significance. Is it the door to a home? The entrance to a pub? The entrance to a hospital corridor? The exit of an airport lounge? A train carriage door? Or the door to a bedroom? We rarely know.

I thought about this for the rest of the day in the Portakabin Command Centre as I loitered behind the Corporal Jacks and Sergeant Jones monitoring computer screens feeding live images from cameras around the capital. A few screens were devoted to the images of drones patrolling the skies, but the increasing number of fires popping up around the capital was pushing up too much smoke into the atmosphere and observations of Muter movement were becoming difficult. The infra-red options on the cameras were redundant, for obvious reasons. It was as if Nigel's cloak of invisibility had been wrapped around his whole community.

As the hours to the start of Operation Reclaim ticked down I noticed a slight change in the behaviour of the American soldiers stationed in the Portakabin. In previous weeks there had been simmering bravado and excitement, but as the weeks passed and they saw more of what was going on in the metropolis and witnessed the occasional skirmish or heard about the loss of soldier colleagues, the command centre staff became more nervous. That was when I would catch glimpses of soldiers touching, even kissing, crucifixes that hung around their necks. I even saw bibles being surreptitiously read and, when I approached, stuffed hastily into drawers.

Perhaps their nervousness was a result of a perceived change in the environment. After all, the air itself seemed to change. Perhaps it was less pollution from the lockdowned metropolis, but, whatever the reason, the air had become uncannily still. There was no breeze, no wind. It was almost as if the world itself was holding its breath. Even the sound of vehicles seemed muffled. Perhaps the empty streets were playing tricks on our minds. Nor was there any birdsong. I even overheard hushed conversations referring to flocks of birds that had been seen leaving the capital. The few birds that did stay were, I'm sure, brooding, mute, probably deceased. They perched on rooftops or were high up in trees, always staring down to street level, as if monitoring us. I say 'mute', there were odd creature sounds, a form of squawking, heard on occasions coming from the low cloud, but they did not emanate from anything living. My excursions from the Portabkin became shorter and more unsettling.

Before long, an eeriness poured into one's being through all the senses – nose, mouth, ears, touch and eyes. On a few last nights before the military operation started, parts of the sky took on a peculiar red glow. People tried to explain it away as the sun's rays refracting around the planet, or the lights from the drones flying high above low-level clouds as they monitored the world below. But, in truth, it looked as if blood had been spilt in the heavens. It was an omen.

The time was upon us.

41. The Great Handover

When did the Great Handover actually start? Well, you could hear it actually. It had a sound (or two sounds, I suppose, spread over three days). It was a prolonged starting gun of sorts, but not the one you would expect. It wasn't artillery fire at the various World Pieces as you might expect, nor the drone of helicopter gunships flying over London hovering over Nigel's home bases. No, it started with an unholy, deathly silence. For days the air had held still, but then the stillness condensed into something else entirely – the world was now holding its hands over its ears. Everything was muffled. Sound did not travel. I suppose it was a type of calm before the apocalyptic storm.

For many days the Government had broadcast that the American military were to begin operations and that no one should leave their homes for any reason. The policy was formally announced across the airwaves and on speakers placed around the capital – all persons seen walking the streets would be assumed to be deceased and would be fired upon until destruction; there would be no stop-and-search, no warning. All MDPs were to be obliterated by bullet, tank shell, rocket-propelled grenade. Anything that walked or crawled would be torn to shreds by hot lead.

It was reported that the operation would last ninety-six hours in the first instance. So it was that everybody was waiting for the firing to start. Except it didn't. For three days there was nothing. Yet more complete stillness in the metropolis. The population was advised to keep all sounds to a minimum to avoid the possibility of attracting MDPs to their premises. Like distant thunder, only the muffled echo of armoured vehicles and tanks thundering down Regent Street, Pall Mall, Embankment could be heard. The delays were military, not political panic. General McAllister-Pike was waiting on final intelligence and waiting for all assets to be in place. He thought that the empty streets might draw out the Muters. Once the shooting started, it wouldn't stop.

But the second sound of the starter-gun of the apocalypse wasn't gunfire. It was human.

In the blackness of night it started. Crying. Wailing. Screaming. It started at random places across the city and built slowly until it was uniform across the city. At first I thought it might be Muters breaking into residences and apartment blocks and attacking terrified individuals, but I soon realised that was impossible. Then it dawned on me. It was the cry of the despairing. The wail of the forgotten. The screams of the demented. People had been confined to their homes more and more over the previous months, then in the previous weeks the lockdowns had become stricter. Then in the last ten days it had become absolute. The start of the military operation had been delayed and not properly communicated to the masses. Food had been scarce in the weeks before, but now people had run out of food altogether; some had run out of water as water pumps failed. Repair and maintenance engineers were not to be seen. Sanity was draining from the bodies of the populace.

It was odd. It was almost like a death call. A death rattle of a city, of a civilisation. The cries, wailing and screams bounced off the hard concrete and glass surfaces and never seemed to fade. A sound so ominous, you thought the gates of hell were opening.

Then, of course, five hours later, the gunfire started. It started at random places around the capital. Before you knew it helicopters were overhead and a so-called 'scouting assault' had started on World Piece One. It was slightly earlier than expected. I had been told it would start at seven o'clock in the morning, but it started in the darkness of three o'clock. Not that I was being kept in the loop about final adjustments to plans, but as I headed into the control room it was clear the command centre was surprised. The reason soon became clear as the shouts and screams came over the radio. Greenwich was seeing a sudden rise in the numbers of MDPs in the area. There was panic in the control room as it was assumed the MDPs, Nigel's soldiers, had pre-empted the start of the war and were about to attack the Greenwich military base at the naval college.

I should have known. We were not operating to General McAllister-Pike's timetable. We never would. It was Nigel's timetable all along. Many of the soldiers were coming face-to-face with Muters for the first time. The command centre's screens were relaying scenes from around the metropolis. But to me, nothing seemed quite right. The skirmishes were random and disorganised. Hardly typical of Nigel's work. I scoured the screens for images of MDPs I knew. Nothing.

The US military at Greenwich was adamant they were about to be attacked, but if we were about to be attacked we either wouldn't know it or Nigel would have already overrun this command centre and we'd all be dead already. Yet, as far as I could see, there was no threat. I walked over to the window and peeked out. There was no sign of an MDP attack coming our way. I could see and hear helicopters over the World Piece One structure, but that was part of General McAllister-Pike's scouting assault that had been planned ahead of the full assault twenty-four hours later. The scouting assault had a primary objective and a secondary objective.

The primary objective involved a team of Navy SEALs both dropping onto the roof and approaching the site's ground-level entrances to get a lay of the land, place cameras and listening devices around the structure ahead of a full onslaught. On the face of it it seemed a sensible course of action as the 'intelligence' of the building layout and threat from the MDPs within was unknown. Nobody 'alive' had been inside the structure for months. It was a space from which no traveller returned, so it seemed sensible to do a small scouting expedition first to establish the nature and extent of the threat within. It was not as if the Americans were giving up the element of surprise to an enemy that had weapons and defensive capabilities.

The secondary objective was more dubious and, at my insistence, should be aborted as an objective, if necessary, at the earliest opportunity. This second objective was trying to snatch Nigel himself and/or some of his leadership team. The General had argued it would cut off the head of the snake allowing a more successful main assault hours later. I argued that success would be unlikely, therefore it was best not to waste too many soldiers' lives trying.

My insistence was of course coloured by the debacle in Little Clarendon Street. I still felt the loss of Tom and Fiona keenly and would have dearly given anything to have had them with me in the Portakabin compound.

I returned to the screens and asked Corporal Jones to decipher the reports coming from their counterparts across the city. The radio chatter (with accompanying helmet video and CCTV footage) was confusing. Some of the soldiers were saying normal living people seemed to be pouring in the streets from their residences. The soldiers were asking if they could shoot if the trespassers were clearly not MDPs? People obviously had had enough of the lockdowns. Cabin-craziness, hunger, fear, desperation had driven many to the streets. Being cooped up in a small flat while the zombie apocalypse rages outside seems sensible to some, but not to all. Many regular citizens thought they would take their chances and get out of the metropolis while they still could. At least if you are moving there is a chance you can move away from death; if you sit still, death will find you.

And then there were reports of genuine MDPs attacking machine gun posts, tanks and armoured vehicles. But again, it appeared random, often as a result of being shot at. If Nigel had been responsible, then there would have been an awful lot more coordination and effectiveness. The desperate fear could be heard in the voices of soldiers over the radios as MDPs began to make themselves known. You could never find a soldier battle-hardened enough to face a physical manifestation of death. I imagined a twenty-four year old marine coming up against Diesel or DoorStop. I thought of a twenty-eight year old Navy SEAL meeting TarmacTired coming around the corner. I smiled at the thought of a battalion of Army Rangers opening the doors to half-a-dozen Muterlings led by Chubby. There was no contest. In a battle of life and death, death would always win. 'Twas ever thus.

I knew that I was now just at a point where I was sitting it out. Waiting. My job was done. Over video conference I asked why I couldn't be evacuated before all the shooting started, but the wild and wide-eyed look of 'what the fuck are your talking about?' from the General killed that idea. They were intent on trying to snatch Nigel. I despaired.

As the hours ticked by, more reports kept coming in from around the capital and the scouting assault seemed to have stalled. My mind turned to Nigel's account of the 'Attack of the Merry Beans' – the teenagers who had attacked World Piece One looking for their friends. On that occasion, Nigel and his team had let the two hundred teenagers enter and explore deep into the building without meeting any resistance. In fact, they had welcomed them. I suspected the twenty or thirty or so Navy SEALS were having a similar experience and were getting sucked deep into the building. There was no guarantee they would meet Nigel and be successful in their secondary objective, so it might just end up being a messy, expensive exercise.

Nevertheless, the confusion engendered by the activities in World Piece One and in the streets of the metropolis began to panic the soldiers in the command centre in the Portakabin. The young soldiers now didn't care who saw them touching or kissing crucifixes before placing them back under their khaki uniforms. I noted that they didn't pull out and kiss their dog tags. It was understandable, I suppose. A country is a temporary host to the body, which is itself a temporary host to the spirit. When you are living in an age of biblical events, reality soon dawns.

As I stood behind the soldiers sitting at their computer stations as they witnessed the unfolding anarchy I realised that many didn't really know what was happening. But I did. It was odd and profoundly sad. Nigel wasn't even at World Piece One. It was the mid-morning – not that you would not know it, the sky was ominously dark as menacing clouds of smoke rolled down the streets – when I saw Nigel in action just north of the Black Road in Westminster and Whitehall. I guessed he was just becoming aware of the action being undertaken by the Merry Green Beans and it had brought him to the battle. Much like the Merry Beans who had run headlong to death in their attack on his home base, he was welcoming them with open arms. The sad thing was the soldiers, both on location on the streets and watching in the command centre, didn't recognise him. He was just another MDP wandering the streets.

Then yet more panicked calls came from the Greenwich Base. Apparently there were reports of now 'massive numbers' of MDPs appearing at the fringes of the American base at Greenwich's Royal Naval College. The soldiers at Greenwich had set up cameras and monitored the perimeter of his base at the Royal Naval College and the adjacent Greenwich Park and had suddenly been surprised to see MDPs headed their way.

'Ask them how many?'

'Loads. Many hundreds. Maybe a few thousand?'

'Where are they coming from?' asked Corporal Denvers, turning to me, his desperation beginning to creep into his eyes and voice. 'Have they been hiding somewhere?'

'Resting,' I sighed, in resignation. 'In fields of rest.'

I stepped aside to a computer, pulled up online maps and searched online for cemeteries in the area. There was indeed a handful: Shooters Hill Cemetery, Charlton Cemetery and Greenwich Cemetery itself.

It made sense now. It was beginning, but hundreds or 'thousands' was surely just an appetiser. I knew Nigel had had plans for exploiting Plot's talents. Soon, she and her own colleagues would be soon spreading out across a metropolis that had been burying its dead for a thousand years. The time had come for them to rise. According to estimates I had come across, there were four-plus million buried around this ancient settlement. Morphic resonance had done its thing. The soldiers had no understanding what was about to hit them. The Greenwich base had probably been spooked about this sudden appearance of MDPs and assumed they were under attack. But these fresh-risers were not effective fighters.

The suggestion that morphic resonance was a reality was not what sealed the deal. The deal was sealed by the sighting, on Birdcage Walk, of a physical signifier that the prophecy, about which Ben had spoken, was true.

Corporal Denvers had been monitoring a wall of computer screens showing CCTV, drone footage and military observer footage from around the capital, when his face fell in disbelief.

'What the hell is that?' Denvers gasped.

I joined him at the monitors and watched. The screens showed shaky drone footage from a number of angles of a street scene and also footage from soldiers' helmet-mounted cameras.

Through the billowing smoke and the heat distortion I saw the unmistakable profile of Nigel standing on a heap of rocky debris – perhaps the facade of a building destroyed by tank fire. Fire raged about him, smoke engulfed him. So far, so apocalyptic. It wasn't the image of Nigel that had triggered the response from the young soldier, it was the sight of what was standing next to Nigel – something that shook me to the core. It was a huge, unholy, monstrous four-legged beast. It was something that had *never* been seen on earth. But why would it? It was not of this fair and pleasant land. The only place its form could be conceived was in the deepest, darkest, most dreadful nightmarish of visions….of hell.

'Is that a…lion?' muttered another soldier.

'What's with the heads?' muttered a third.

It might have been a lion, once. A large one. A very large one. But now it was entirely unnatural, other worldly. It was dead. Its skin and fur had taken on a different texture not known in the animal kingdom. You forget how skin, fur and hair softens the stark truth of the skeletal form. Its skull and teeth were on partial display amidst its rotting skin and matted singed hair. Its eyes were blackness searching for your soul. On top of that, the manner of its gait removed it from this world. As for the other heads – it looked like large snakes were curled *through* and about its body. The creature's body had decayed or been eaten and the large snakes were moving through and around it at will. But the snakes were not parasites clinging to the body, no, they were now at one with the creature. It was one being, one ungodly entity. Even in life you sense that lions and snakes are intelligent, sharp and to be feared by Beankind, imagine what they look like in death, relieved of all weakness. The beast exuded an intelligence beyond that of men.

On sight of the creature, I knew. It was done. There was no doubt. I knew.

I retired to my office and closed the door. I picked up a satellite phone and dialled Ben's number. I didn't know if he would answer. There were rumours the power might soon be lost to the capital as either the military operation severed power lines or coordinated MDPs attacks on power stations would result in total metropolis-wide power failure.

Ben answered. He was holed up in his flat.

I explained what I had seen. The beast. He was not surprised. He did not say 'I told you so'. He was just quiet. Almost calm.

I apologised to Ben for my reticence at the National Gallery. I was wrong and he was right.

He asked how long the creature had been with Nigel. I did not know, I replied. With my laptop, I quickly logged on to Nigel's blog. Surely he had been too busy to update anything in the last week, but he might have tapped out something in the quiet dark cycles. My eyes were tired and I hardly had the will to search again the jumble of passages. I searched for words like 'lion, zoo, animal, creature' and eventually found a passage. And a name. CurserBe.

I reported the find to Ben. He said nothing.

I then asked about what we were both thinking – the prophecy.

I asked him if there was anything that could be done, if there was another story or prediction that suggested there might be a way of forestalling the fulfilment of the prophecy. Was there something that would throw it off course? Failing that, was there anything that could be done knowing the prophecy *would* come to pass?

He was silent. We both knew the answer.

For dozens of centuries, perhaps tens of thousands of years, mankind had dodged its destiny and the fulfilment of the prophecy had not come to pass. But the folly, arrogance, and current technological age had brought all the variables together and I had to acknowledge that I was living in a time when this age-old prophecy would be fulfilled. But by whom? Who were the two other players, the brothers? Did even Nigel know?

'No, he probably doesn't,' Ben said before falling silent for a few moments.

'Do *you* know? Suspect anyone?' he continued. 'Any ideas?'

'No,' I whispered, despairingly.

I could offer a guess. Could it be Diesel? GlassCutter? Was it somebody Nigel had enlightened a few lunar cycles earlier? Maybe someone Nigel had not met? Was it a Merry Bean soldier who was being enlightened that very day? Who the hell knew. I felt desperately sad just considering the options. For all the science, the CCTV, DNA, the drones and contact-tracing, it had come to this – attempting to solve an ancient riddle through guesswork.

With nothing more to be said, we bid each other goodbye and I was left alone again to sounds of gunfire and explosions happening fifty yards away, two hundred yards away, two miles away. But that was not what I was afraid of. Out there I knew someone was watching me. Chain-and-Stiks, for a start. Perhaps even TrainTracks. Would Stiks be the one who claimed me? A final kiss from my houseboat neighbour? There was a certain poignancy to it – Mia started me on this journey and Stiks would end it.

Had Nigel instructed Chain-and-Stiks to watch me? He was aware of me, certainly; scrolling through his blog I saw that he had mentioned me, 'Call-Me-Josh', a few times – my name in 'life, no name in death had been assigned. Maybe Stiks was guarding me, protecting me. Perhaps Nigel wanted to keep me intact and as a Bean item of interest, needing further research? He had let me live once before in Little Clarendon Street. Maybe he maintained an interest in keeping my status as a Bean for some reason? I was hopeful. He might overlook me in all the current busyness, but, lest you forget, he had all the time in the world.

I refreshed some of Nigel's blog in the vain hope there was a clue, a reference, a ray of hope for something. There were a few draft notes of events referring to…. the 'Great Handover', otherwise, nothing.

I felt a bit edgy in my own office so I returned to the main command centre to find it half-empty with the remaining soldiers packing up.

'Err, what's going on?' I asked. 'Is it all over?'

Corporal Denvers looked up with a confused, pained expression on his face. He probably hadn't quite appreciated the dark British humour.

'No, we're evacuating,' he replied. 'Or rather, we're being reassigned.'

'What?'

In his rushed manner Denvers explained that the World Piece One scouting assault group had run into some trouble, so some soldiers manning a couple of mobile communication vehicles on the World Piece One site itself had been ordered into the structure to secure an escape route for the trapped navy seals. Some of the command centre team had therefore been assigned to the mobile communications unit for the next six hours; the other half were being redeployed back to Greenwich while there was still a clear route to the Naval College headquarters.

'Helicopters can't land anywhere west of London Bridge at the moment,' said Denvers, as he breathlessly packed up laptops and hard drives. 'Apparently, HMS Bulwark is sailing up the Thames. Once the full assault starts we think it will be too dangerous to move around the streets for anyone. We'll have no air cover.'

The Corporal explained that the Royal Navy frigate HMS Bulwark was intending to collect the Prime Minister, the rest of the

Downing Street team and other Government figures as part of an evacuation. I thought of Ella and was pleased for her.

I also thought of Maria-Amphi. If General McAllister-Pike was true to his word, she might be less than fifty nautical miles from me. When the General had offered to provide a loved one with safe passage I had selected her. But where would I send her? Brazil was succumbing to the plague. All commercial international flights had been abandoned weeks ago. I would struggle to meet up with her and start a new life, so I asked that she be brought to a secure military vessel off the coast – the ship to which I would be eventually evacuated if the military operation failed. From there Maria-Amphi and I could start afresh in some safe corner of the world.

My face said it all.

'Stay put here. We're going to get help,' the soldiers said. 'We'll come back and get you evacuated. Right now, you don't want to go where we are going.'

And then they were gone.

42. The Meaning of Me

So it was that I was left alone in the command centre. Maybe it was my lab coat – I didn't look like someone who was useful and could be redeployed anywhere with any success. There was possibly an upside, however. Now that the military portakabin compound was deserted, perhaps any nearby Muters wouldn't give it a second thought and I would be left alone.

It didn't help my heart rate or breathing. I could very well soon meet my Maker. How had I never anticipated things would end this way? If I had known Death would come knocking, I would have done so many things differently. Is that what everybody feels at this moment of their existence? I'd never know, I thought, because at this rate I'll never see another living human being and be given the chance to ask them....Unless, fate (if that is different to death) had different plans and someone did come to save me.

I barricaded myself into my office, but set up a handful of screens to stream any footage from World Piece One and other sites around the metropolis. If you thought what the end of the world looked and sounded like, it has no surprises. It is resoundingly unoriginal – darkness from smoke and cloud, fires above and below and all around, the growl of fire, the screams of men, the rattle of gunfire and explosions and the howling of creatures previously unknown to the earth. I swear I even heard bagpipes and drums echo in all the madness; a final lament from falling lands. Tom would have liked it. Now was not a time for the living, it was the time for the dead. No doubt it was a busy time for

Nigel – bringing an end to the old world order, introducing the planet to a new eon.

I was almost bored of feeling like this – how many 'beginnings to the End' can there be? How many times had I said it? Well, this one really was the beginning of the end. I felt it in my bones.

Communications had broken down – either there was radio silence from units or radio hell – screams of help and horror from other units. The assault on World Piece One failed, or was failing. We were not at the end of the beginning (of the end) yet, but I couldn't see how I would survive to see the end. It was a shame, I had a ringside seat of World Piece One and it looked as if I would miss the climax. At the last, I wasn't a player, no, I was only an observer.

It's getting late now…. I am writing these notes in the present tense. I don't have time to edit….

So, here I wait. Perhaps if I remain tucked away, no dead person will see me.

It is also a shame I cannot finish this memoir. I have a jumble of writings that could be knitted together into something coherent, I think. I have sent it all to the Whistleblower. Hopefully he'll add it to the other stuff and he'll archive it in a secure basement at the museum. The records of this time ought to survive the fire and brimstone raining down on the city. Maybe it'll be discovered in decades, centuries (or even millennia) to come. Maybe the Whistleblower will survive and can knit it all together himself. If not him, then somebody in ten thousand summers' time will discover these words, learn about these times and the origins of the dust that lies about them.

The last few days have been a nightmare. Now that I am alone, do I really want to spend my final hours, minutes at a keyboard typing up the litany of mistakes, complacency, confusion, disbelief of Beankind? Not really. Would you? Death is fiddling with its keys on the other side of the door and I am rattling off the reasons why I'm miserable and stressed? No. Yet here I am tapping away on a keyboard. It keeps me distracted.

It is odd to think Nigel and I have swapped roles. For months I was the one who was swanning around the capital, sipping lattes, having dinner while hunting the elusive Muter leader down. I would join police patrols, follow leads, recommend militarising the z-squads and visit scenes of devastation, all the while searching for this shady figure in the shadows that would only pop up on pixelated CCTV or shaky mobile phone footage. Now, here we are, a handful of lunar cycles later. I am now the one holed up in the shadows, ready to dive under a desk. Now it is he, Nigel, who is moving about the capital with ease, fearless, unimpeded, unhindered and feasting at will. Maybe he is hunting me now. It is indeed humbling when you know death has your number and has turned onto your street.

With CurserBe now in the picture I realise chances of survival are slim to none. Like Tom said in his farewell letter, we just live out a life in our heads. Hope is not reality. Reality is death. How has Beankind become so complacent? Science and 'learning' – just another strain of fiction, pushing society's agreed narrative.

In a strange way a peace is coming over me.

It would all be over in a few days, I thought. I would not see out the week. Once Greenwich military base has fallen and the other operational commands centres at the other World Pieces are overrun, it will be another two, maybe three days before the metropolis, in its entirety, will fall. The Great Handover would be complete.

That's the funny thing about the apocalypse, it does provide some clarity. There have been moments of mini-clarity before in my life – often when I was ill. I would lie in bed for a few days as my stomach lurched and I stumbled to and from the bathroom and collapsed back in bed in a physical state of near-death. It was the body crying out for peace that brought insight. Sickness tosses and sweeps all confusion away. If death carries a sickle, his brother should carry a broom or a pitchfork.

But in those moments of sickness, my mind would clear. I knew what I wanted and it came down to simple things: Maria-Amphi, the water, peace.

In one's existence there are only a few moments, portals if you like, through which one can pass and reach a life worth living. They exist momentarily before evaporating. If the opportunity is not taken, then you are alone on the dusty road to the final portal. Maybe I am an example of the First Bean Paradox. I moved away from the blue waters of Brazil to the Black Road of the metropolis. There were portals, doors, to other lives, but I sidestepped them. Why? The destiny impulse took me on a quest to discover the fate of my houseboat neighbour. And then the paradox willed me to understand more about the MDPs only to lead me to the Muter responsible for all the horrors. The First Bean Paradox was always leading to Nigel, my deathstiny.

So, what do I feel? What do I think?

I think I feel a bit of regret. Sadness. If I had planned my life, I would not have planned for me to be here at this moment – fretting in the corner of a Portakabin while the world is consumed by fire and drowned in screams. Am I important enough to be evacuated? I am the zombie guy after all. I know more about the MDPs than anyone. I do add value (to the living). So, maybe, just maybe, there is the slightest glimmer of hope that someone (or something) other than death will come for me in this light cycle.

But if death comes? Is regret the cousin of unfinished business? What will be my unfinished business? I can only think of Maria-Amphi. If my body survives the attack, will I rise and go looking for her? How will I find her?

I think I have come up with my own Bean Paradox – my own nod to Nigel's contemplations. I hereby do offer the Fourth Bean Paradox for your consideration. Beans have a lifetime in which to assign value – to people, places, ideas, thoughts and all manner of things. It is our one superpower – 'assigning value'. It is a daily choice, a lunar-cycle choice. Over dozens of summers it accumulates to form the blessing or the curse that is our existence. Did I use my power wisely in my thirty-plus summers? If I could go back in time I would rise every light-dark and ask myself: to what am I assigning value to this day? Alas, to our shame, we tend to assign value only to that which has no value. Yet, during all the summers our bodies heaved with breath, our bodies knew deep down to what we *should* assign value. But Beans choose unwisely: fame, ambition, glory, material goods and wealth, attention, status and even 'the pursuit of happiness'. In fact, modern society is determined to encourage the Bean to choose unwisely. That is the Fourth Bean Paradox – the assigning of worth to that which has no value. We are gifted summers and one superpower, yet we fail.

But what is the evidence of this Fourth Bean Paradox, you ask? Regret, of course. And that is why most Beans fear death – they fear 'the great reveal' – during their lives they have incorrectly assigned value for all the summers they have walked upon the earth. Modern society is the embodiment of the Fourth Bean Paradox. Perhaps that is why the prophecy worked this time. The Fourth Bean Paradox reached a critical mass. Don't get me wrong, I cannot bask in superior knowledge; for all my insight and education, I still succumbed. Regret – the mark of failure to assign value correctly; an awareness of a path not taken.

And so here we are. I am staring at a door. It is odd to think of deathstiny's door as actually physical. It's not a stone block that might protect me, but a chipboard door far too flimsy to stop even the most docile MDP. I've cut the power to the Portakabin, in the hope the Muters will not see me. But the dancing light of the fires outside illuminates the ceilings and walls. I now know fire is a living thing. It keeps moving. You could never catch its nature in a still portrait.

My only thought now is: do I wait it out? Wait until the main assault starts and is concluded? Perhaps in the morning an answer will become clear, but the air is still so black and heavy with smoke, I think it unlikely. I haven't washed, I've hardly shaved, I could almost pass as an MDP. No sooner does the thought occur to me, I dismiss it. I daren't move. If the military is trying to evacuate the Prime Minister, then they are not going to think of me. Nobody will send a naval vessel for me. It is far too difficult to use a vehicle. Too dangerous to land a helicopter; the smoke from the fires engulfing the capital make flying impossible. How many moments or opportunities were there in the last twelve months that I could have walked away? Now I am stuck.

I am hunched over a keyboard in a cabin while the metropolis burns outside. These last words are not to a loved one. A family member. A soldier before he or I go off to battle. No, it is to whomever is reading this. A nameless nobody. Trust me, however important you are or think you will be, you are a balanced bag of flesh imbued with hope but decaying faster than you know. You're nothing.

Before my Merry Green Bean colleagues deserted me, I heard rumours that if the Americans didn't get a hold of the situation in the first forty-eight hours of the main assault they would withdraw altogether and leave the metropolis (and the rest of the UK) to its fate. Apparently the outbreak in the United States has rapidly accelerated with a record exponential growth in Muter risings. I suspect that the States are about six or eight weeks behind the UK. They think they can contain the threat? No chance.

With all the drama blasting away yards from me, it feels like I am a child hiding behind the pillar in the balcony of a theatre. I am a stone's throw away from the lavish, interactive stage production of the apocalypse. Though hidden, I am consumed with fear; fear that I am not in fact beyond the sight of the players on the stage and will get sucked into the production to play a role of my own.

It is all just stories. The narrative and the destiny remain the same, but the names change. Names given to us, the names we exist with for three score years and ten, are not our proper names. Our names are out there and revealed only at death. Our eternal names may be hinted at during our lifetimes, but the characters only settle in the correct order at the end. The existence that we tell ourselves is our own, is nothing. It is like vapour in the wind.

In this last lunar cycle I had been reflecting on Ben's idea that morphic resonance would play a part in this end-of-world production. Reading some of Sheldrake I learned that he challenged the reader to consider whether minds were truly confined to brains. Why were the ephemeral's limits of the mind defined by the physical limits of the brain? Why should anything ephemeral be confined to the physical? Maybe Nigel's mind was in touch with things beyond the confines of his skull and that was where he drew his understanding of deathstiny. Perhaps in death there really is a form of enlightenment. Perhaps that had been the understanding for tens of thousands of years, but it was only in recent times that such an understanding of our world, our existence, had been lost. And with its loss, the stories of old re-emerge. The modern mind is not strong enough to handle eternal truths, it has been weakened by complacency, indulgence, narcissism. And in that weakness, that sickness, came again the story of death. And so the wheel has turned. In sickness, clarity; in clarity, death.

In infirmitas, claritas; in morte, vita.

These are my last words. I apologise, they are a jumble. I wish I could have put them in some coherent form. I am sure I am down to my last hours. Then it will be the last minutes. And then the few last seconds. Then a final second coming....

What was that...?

Was that a noise outside?

Could that be someone trying to get in the Portakabin?

Has someone come to evacuate me?

Is that a child giggling?

O Brother, who is that?

I need to go and check that noise....coming back in a second....

END

[Concluded in Part III]

Cast of Colleagues-elect
(in order of appearance)

Chapter	***Colleague-elect first reference (and [Colleague])***
01.	Josh; Mia [Hoodie; Chain-and-Stiks]; Detective Baker; Ron Cha; Michael Muick [BeanPole]; Jonny Sandy [BroadBean]
03.	Robbie Andrews (supervisor)
05.	Tom; Fiona (interns)
06.	Felicity Goodban [CatNaps]
08.	John Reuel [GlassCutter]; Clive Staples [DoorStop]; Ashli Eco [TrainTracks]; Unknown Target A/Shade [Nigel]
10.	Juggler/Fireman [Diesel]; Arthur
12.	[ChubbyCheeks]
15.	[ColourSplash]; [RooftopSuicide]; [DogSmells]
17.	Erika [TarmacTired]; Chief Superintendent Ian Davie; DCI Luciana Vaccarelli
18.	Deputy Chief Constable Corbould
19.	The Boy Who Saw
20.	Dr Caroline Godall [PlumpCalf]; Dr John Godall [ChimneyBlack]
22.	Bob Beaumont; Maria-Amphi
23.	Whistleblower
24.	Emily [PearlLavaliere]
25.	LycraStew
27.	Prof. Ben Garfunkel
28.	Commander Bathgate
31.	Commander Bream
32.	[Dunky & Smashy]

33.   The Prime Minister; [Peas]; Ella

35.   [GenerationManager; GenerationMe];

36.   President of the European Council [VanPlumpy]
        KittenFluff; Fluffykins

37.   Jenny Allen (news-reporter)

38.   General McAllister-Pike; Captain Burns

41.   Corporal Denvers; [CurserBe]

David O. Zeus

Acknowledgements

Many people, including DMAG, AFG and family. Thanks to Paul Burns and Tiffany Ko for reading. Thanks also to Michael Hensley for allowing me to reproduce the cover illustration here; the illustration itself has been a source of inspiration for Nigel over the solar cycles as this book took shape.

Cover illustration (and on inside page) by Michael Hensley, reproduced here with his kind permission. Illustration Copyright © Michael Hensley. See Michael's websites for details and his other work:
www.michaelhensley.art
www.artistanatomy.com
www.michaelmhensley.com

Cover design by Liliana Resende:
http://lilianaresendesign.com

About the Author

Born in the UK, David O. Zeus was tutored at the Old Granville House School before having a short spell at university, after which he joined the army (11th Hussars) where he saw action at the Battle of the Hornburg. While recuperating from his injuries on the remote island of Nomanisan he began writing. He is married to Donna Mullenger and lives for most of the year in the place of his birth, Little Hintock.

<u>www.davidozeus.uk</u>

Found on Twitter, Facebook & YouTube Channel as 'DavidOZeus'

Available Titles

Collected Stories – Volume I
Collected Stories – Volume II
My Name Was Nigel: Memoirs of a Killer Zombie

Upcoming Titles

Collected Stories – Volume III
Collected Stories – Volume IV
Nigel (Part III)

Collected Stories: Volume One

The seven stories enclosed in this first volume are:

The Legend of Muam Tam Say: An encounter with an ancient wonder of the natural world in the shadows of the Himalayas; a short extract from the diaries of a young soldier on the eve of the First World War describes the impact of the 'natural wonder' on the young soldier.

The Dot Matrix: A young man re-evaluates his office-bound existence when he comes across the printout musings of an old dot matrix printer.

Scary Afternoon in the Garden: An eleven year old boy describes his encounter with the 'creatures from the woods' when they visit his garden one really, really, scary afternoon.

The Florin Smile: A meteor shower brings a new chemical compound to earth resulting in a change to some people's smile and changes the way people assess (and assign) value in modern society.

Parked in a Ditch: 'The course of true love ne'er did run smooth for a middle-aged, middle manager stuck in the mire of administration.' The planning (and execution) of Plans 'A' through to 'G' of a office-bound, wannabe romantic.

Fear of Lions: A doting uncle offers advice to his niece on how to confront her fears...and deals with the unhappy aftermath.

The Totty Boat: A grumpy uncle writes a letter to his young nephew offering advice on the stuff that matters.

Collected Stories: Volume Two

The seven stories enclosed in this second volume are:

Foggy Love Bottom – a story of love and loss set in a little village with a peculiar name and history.

In ***Scary Morning in the Woods***, the garden attack (as described in *Scary Afternoon in the Garden)* leads the townsfolk to nervously take the fight to the creatures in the woods.

In ***I'm Not Matt Damon*** a lone human being, Duncan Sheldrake, is recreated by aliens (after the destruction of planet earth) in their mistaken belief that he was once the great leader of humanity and finest representative of life on earth – Matt Damon.

The Elephant of Marrakech – a man retraces his steps to Marrakech to 'find the elephant' and make the decision he should have done seven years earlier.

Book of Giants: Journal 9 – a survivor's journal written eighteen months after an apocalyptic solar flare led to the disintegration of society and the re-emergence of ancient giants.

Sack Truck – a man loses his job as a result of the perfect storm of a confused memory (of a *Viz* comic character) and the fast-changing social mores of the modern world, all prompted by an innocent reference to a 'sack truck'.

A Life's Work – a 100 year old New York mob-boss is released from prison after 50 years and is given the opportunity to reflect on his life as a gangster.

Printed in Great Britain
by Amazon

24347268R00211